YESTERDAY'S GONE

Season Three

SEAN PLATT

DAVID W. WRIGHT

STERLING & STONE

To YOU, the reader.
Thank you for taking a chance on us.
Thank you for your support.
Thank you for the emails.
Thank you for the reviews.
Thank you for reading and joining us on this road.

YESTERDAY'S GONE

Episode 13

(FIRST EPISODE OF SEASON THREE)

"Paths Not Taken"

ONE

Other Will Bishop

Other Earth
June 14, 2011
Black Island Research Facility
Black Island, New York
FOUR MONTHS BEFORE THE OCT. 15 EVENT …

ONE MONTH HAD PASSED since the boy last opened his eyes.

When Will got the call from Boricio, his heart nearly burst from his chest. "Your brother? He's okay?"

"Yes, Dad, he's fine."

"I'll be right there," Will said, almost falling as he jumped from his seat and raced down the hall, to the elevator, and slipped inside just as the doors were closing.

Will smiled at the researcher already standing in the elevator — a man whose name Will didn't know, even though he'd seen him several times. The keycard/badge hanging from the man's lanyard read, *Eric Rodgers: Aerospace Division.*

Though Will had occasionally consulted for the aerospace division of Black Island, most of his work was now with the psychic warfare and genetic engineering branches. He rarely spoke with anyone outside of his division, except for the all too regular but unavoidably awkward moments in the elevators and dining hall.

Will closed his eyes, trying not to pick up any of the man's thoughts. Too late.

Oh shit, it's the freaky guy. Is he reading my mind now? Oh shit. Stop thinking. Think about anything other than last night . . . cocaine . . . Shit! Did he hear that? Oh God . . . Come on, elevator, come the fuck on!

Will kept his eyes closed to shield his vision from the man's nervous face.

The elevator stopped on the third floor, and the man rushed off, saying, "Good day, sir," only when he was three steps away.

Will couldn't think of anything to say before the elevator doors closed and he was on his way to Level 7. Alone, his mind returned to his son who had somehow miraculously, recovered. The doctors said he might never surface from the coma. The operation to remove the tumor in his brain was enough of a risk to be considered a death sentence.

And yet, four weeks later, he had opened his eyes.

Can he really be fine?

Will tried to pick up his son's thoughts, but couldn't feel him "online." At first, Will was nervous, wondering if the child's thoughts were somehow dead, but given the drugs in his system, he was likely still in a fog. Some drugs had a way of interfering with Will's abilities.

The elevator stopped. Will squeezed through the still-opening doors, then practically ran to the recovery room. He passed a few nurses, then opened the room's door to his two adopted sons, separated by more than two decades and different parents.

Luca's eyes lit as Will stepped through the door, "Dad!"

Will's heart practically melted. "Oh God, you're awake!" he cried, falling to Luca's bedside and hugging him through the tangle of wires running to an IV drip, then over to the bank of machines monitoring his vitals. "Thank you, God."

"Why are you crying?" Luca asked, his voice brittle and full of scratches.

"I'm just so happy," Will said.

Will stood, then turned to Boricio, pulling him into a bear of a hug. That's when he sensed it — the secret Boricio had been hiding. The doctors had done something radical to revive Luca, even though they were supposed to wait for him to come out of the coma.

How the hell did they keep this from me?

Then Will saw that, too.

Boricio hadn't told anyone outside of a small circle, at least not until the last minute, and somehow managed to shield his thoughts enough to prevent leaking the information himself. Boricio could do this better than anyone, especially when Will was busy, which he had been for the majority of the past several weeks.

Will pulled away, and met Boricio's eyes.

Boricio knew he knew. "I'll explain later," Boricio whispered.

Will swallowed his knot, furious, wanting *later* to fuck itself so Boricio could explain immediately.

"I'm thirsty," Luca said.

"Hold on, I'll get you some water." Will smiled at Luca, rubbing the top of his son's head before leaving the room. He nodded at Boricio with a silent instruction to follow him out into the hallway.

The door slid closed behind him; Will narrowed his eyes, stealing a glance around them to see who, if anyone, was within earshot. The coast clear, he said, "How could you?"

"He was inches from dead," Boricio said. "How could I *not?*"

"The serum hasn't been tested on humans," Will said. "You had no right to use Luca as an experiment."

"Oh please," Boricio said. "He wasn't an experiment. Haven't you been reading the research notes? You've seen what the serum can do! Apes, mice, monkeys, pigs, and anything else Old McDonald can throw in the lab. It's worked everywhere they've used it. And it worked on Luca."

Will swallowed again, trying to control his rising anger. He had never wanted to hit anyone in all his life so much as he wanted to smash his fist into Boricio's arrogant face right at that moment.

He exhaled from his nose and drew a deep breath. "What if something went wrong?"

"The doc said he's in perfect health," Boricio said, standing straighter. "And you've known me long enough to know I'm not wired to sit around and swing a sack of nothing while my baby brother is beating on his final breath." He shook his head. "Not a chance. Those vials were a gift! You know it's just a matter of time before we're using the serum as a chemo-cocktail to cure everything from cancer to carpal tunnel." He took a step toward Will and bored into his eyes. "Shit, Dad, isn't that the ditch you said we're supposed to be digging?"

"Not like this." Will shook his head. "How can you not see how foolish this is?"

Boricio pointed at the door and the brother on the other side. "How can you not see how *right* this is? You taught me to take risks. You taught me to believe in myself. It's about damned time you listen to your own advice. If this had been some random test subject, cleared through the proper channels, you'd be the first one popping the cork! So, stop looking at the red tape and start walking on the red carpet, Dad. This is *our time*. Three surgeons made a miracle in there today! A miracle that would have never happened if you and your buddies hadn't found those vials. At some point you've gotta start being able to see destiny dancing, Dad, especially when it's twisting in a tango in front of you!" He shook his head again. "You've gotta stop turning your head from what's supposed to happen."

Will took a step back and stared through the door's window at Luca, lying in bed, smiling and waving. It was a smile Will had been afraid he'd never see again. Boricio was right. Will hadn't allowed himself to believe in miracles for far too long, even though he had always believed in fate.

Maybe this was an even blend of both.

~

TWO

Boricio Wolfe

Kingsland, Alabama
  The Sanctuary
  March 28
  Sometime after midnight …
  FIVE MONTHS AFTER THE EVENT …

WELL, *this is some beer-battered bullshit.*

The second the old fucker pulled the trigger, Luca's memories started spinning through Boricio's brain — how Luca and Will had met, how Will had comforted him after his dog died, plus dozens of others — like a bad acid trip, blended with anger, betrayal, and confusion.

Boricio shook his head, trying to flush the memories so he could deal with the immediacy of the old man with the gun.

"What the fuck?" Boricio said, raising the shotgun he looted from one of The Sanctu-fairy fucksticks, and drawing aim at Will, pointing the barrel right between his eyes.

Will acted as if Boricio wasn't even there, dropping his pistol to the snow and staring down at Luca. "I'm so sorry," he said, falling to Luca and cradling the man-kid's head in his hands as blood pooled beneath him, spreading like an angry, dark stain in the snow.

"How do you get off swinging a sack of sorry, you Santa Claus-looking pile of shit? You're the motherfucker who shot him!" Boricio stepped forward to hit the old man, but stopped when he nearly lost his balance.

His head was still dizzy from Luca being inside, and odd as a smiling bitch who wasn't asking for crap, Boricio still felt a lingering need to protect the kid. He wasn't sure what sorta voodoo bullshit Luca had done in his head, but he'd definitely done something.

Luca had said he'd "fix" Boricio, but what in the fuck-all did that even mean? What was there to fix? Ain't no one ever had any complaints about the way Boricio worked before. At least no one still breathing.

Boricio took a step closer to Will. "He said he *fixed* me. You wanna tell me what in the hell that means? I'm guessing by the way you tore in here like Steve McQueen, you have a pretty good goddamned idea."

Will looked up at Boricio, eyes watering, as if he were going to break down and cry. "I don't know. But you're a killer, aren't you?"

Boricio showed Will all his teeth. "I'm a heartbeat adjuster. What in the fuck does that have to do with the price of tea in China?"

"You haven't killed me yet," Will said, an odd smile crossing his face, like one of those fuckers who thinks his IQ has another digit to keep his shit from stinking.

Boricio stepped forward, craving a pull of the trigger, and barely resisting the urge.

See how he smiles with half a face.

"No, not *yet*," Boricio growled.

Will said nothing, staring down at Luca's closed eyes. Then he looked up to Boricio and said about the dumbest fucking thing that could've come from his mouth, "He's dying."

"No fucking shit!" Boricio said, and this time he couldn't resist. He swung the barrel of the shotgun and hit Will hard in the forehead, knocking him back to the snow.

Boricio looked down at Luca, confused as an odd, new feeling flooded his body, filling him with something he couldn't remember feeling before: sympathy.

Fixed me? More like he took out my batteries!

Fuck.

Boricio felt tears welling in his eyes.

What the fuck is this shit?

He turned away, wiping his eyes. The anger returned, and he shoved the barrel of his shotgun at Will's head.

"Why the hell did you shoot him, you Sasquatch-looking pile of shit? He trusted you!"

"I had to. The dreams told me."

"Dreams? If I did everything my dreams told me to, Brad Pitt's head would've been an ashtray on my coffee table watching me bang Angelina sunrise to sunset. The fuck you talking about? Start speaking English, or I'm gonna shut you up permanently."

"Tell me. Did he try to heal the others?" Will asked.

"Yeah, a couple. But he said it's not working now."

"Yes," Will nodded, "that's what I saw in the dreams."

"You wanna stop speaking in ancient Chinese secret and tell me what the fuck you're goin' on about, old man?"

"You can save him," Will said. "In fact, you *will* save him."

Boricio laughed.

"*Me?* Save him? Clearly you're new to this program, hombre. I ain't the fucking hero. I don't save the day."

Will shook his head, pointing back at Luca. Blood was spilling from Luca's mouth.

"Hurry!" Will said.

"What the hell am I supposed to do?!" Boricio asked,

annoyed, and suddenly feeling a need to try and save the man-kid. "Tell me what to do!"

"Put your hands on him," Will said, his voice rising in anger or urgency. "Like you saw him do with the others."

Boricio was going to argue, but something in his head, maybe instinct, or remnants of Luca playing puppet master, pushed Boricio to kneel beside Luca. He saw in his mind what to do next, like a memory.

How do you have a memory of shit that ain't happened?

Boricio felt like he was on another trip like when he drank that shit back in the rich fuck's house.

He leaned down and put his hands on either side of Luca's face, feeling warmth like liquid fire spreading through his limbs and into his fingers. And then from his fingers and into the man-kid.

Boricio stared at his hands, as if they were being moved by another. He wondered again what in hell's sweet honey pot Luca had done. He had *fixed* him, but he'd sure as shit done something else, too.

Luca's eyes shot open like someone had flipped a switch inside him, and he started coughing up blood then sucking at air and gasping for breath.

Boricio started to pull away, but couldn't. His hands were locked onto Luca, as some sorta whatinthefuck kept flowing from Boricio and into Luca — as if the boy were sucking his life from him. Warmth turned to pain and started shooting like a scattergun through all of Boricio's body, as he clenched his teeth and tried to work up the strength to break the connection.

Let go!

Boricio pulled, but felt as if someone had glued his hands to Luca and if he pulled too hard he might rip the kid's face off. The pain, however, gave him no choice but to keep trying to break free.

Finally, Boricio was able to wrench himself away. He fell back into the snow, writhing in pain.

Luca rose from the dirt, staring at Will, who was still sitting on the ground from when Boricio knocked him down. He looked at Boricio, then back at Will, his face twisted in confusion.

"Why?" Luca asked, his voice caught between confusion and anger.

"I'm sorry," Will said, wiping a tear. "It was the only way."

"Only way for *what?*" Luca asked.

"For that," Will said, pointing at Boricio, rising to his feet, body feeling like it was on fire.

"Why you all looking at me like that?" Boricio asked.

Luca's eyes were wide, as if he were staring at a two-headed demon sucking on a dick made of fire. Luca opened his mouth, but said nothing.

"What the fuck you looking at?" Boricio growled.

"I'm so sorry," Luca said.

"Sorry? For what?" Boricio asked, confused, and feeling another new feeling: fear. They were clearly looking at his face.

What the hell happened to me?

He reached up to touch his face, but his hands were buzzing, too numbed to know what he was touching. He looked around, then saw the headlights of Will's car shining on them. He stepped past Will and Luca, moving toward the car as fast as he could despite the 15 bags of fuck-all that had slapped him in the face and now seemed to rest on his shoulders.

Boricio reached the car, driver's side door still open, then bent to see his reflection in the mirror.

Oh Fuck.

He looked like he'd aged a decade, maybe more.

"What the hell did you do to me?!" Boricio roared, spinning around.

"I don't know," Luca said, surprising Boricio by not stepping back. "I swear."

I should shoot this pair of fucks right here, right now, and get the hell out of Dodge.

But Boricio couldn't leave.

Something was holding him here.

The need to stay with the man-kid sang in the same, sweet tune of instinct that had fueled the engine of Boricio's entire life. He screamed in frustration, grabbed his shotgun off the ground, and pointed it at Will.

"Talk! Now!"

Will shook his head, "I don't know any more than you do. Only what I saw in the . . . "

"Yeah, yeah, the fucking dream!" Boricio curled his lip and gritted his teeth. "Then tell me what you saw."

Will looked at the ground and swallowed, "Whatever's in Luca. Whatever makes him special. He transferred that to you. I had to make sure you gave it back."

Boricio wanted to shoot the old bastard right there on the spot, just to satisfy the itch. But, again, something inside him kept his finger from squeezing the trigger.

"Why?" Luca asked. "Wait. Does this mean I can heal people again? Can I ... " Luca looked back toward the barn where Linc and Rebecca's bodies lay in a heap, slaughtered by monsters. Then he looked toward the dungeon where Mary and Paola's bodies lay on their way to forgotten. Finally, Luca looked past the barn where Desmond's corpse lay, along with the dozens of others, man and creature alike, littering The Sanctuary like a battlefield.

Luca swallowed, then whispered. "I can bring them back?"

Will looked up from the ground after a quarter of eternity spent chewing the question.

"Yes, you can bring them back. But not all of them. Only three. After that, you'll have aged to near dying."

"Just three?" Luca whispered, eyes on Will.

"Three," Will repeated, as he struggled to stand.

Something looked off about the old man. Then, as Will flinched and fell back a step, Boricio saw the crimson bleeding between his fingers and realized the old fucker had been hiding an injury to his gut.

Will fell to the ground, gasping for air, about to add one more body to the battlefield.

~

THREE

Charlie Wilkens

Charlie was in a room he didn't recognize, and without any memory of how he got there, or where he'd been before he woke handcuffed to a table. Three of the walls were gray concrete, just like the floor. The fourth mirrored, like he'd seen in interrogation rooms on TV and in the movies. The room was empty, except for the chair he was sitting in and the table his right hand was cuffed to: a metal bar on top of the table which seemed built expressly for the purpose.

A bare light bulb hung limp from a chain, flickering on and off above him with an intermittent buzzing sound.

Where the hell am I?

Charlie stared at his reflection. He looked like he'd aged five years or more in the last five months. He looked down at the cuffs, so sturdy, shiny silver, and official-looking. He wondered if they belonged to a cop and whether he'd been arrested for something.

For what, though? And are cops really on duty at the end of the world?

It wasn't as if any law was left in the land, let alone officers to enforce the rules. Arrest seemed unlikely. Yet, here he was.

But who else could've done this? And what the hell do they want from me?

"Hey!" he called. "Show your face, pussy!"

Charlie got only an echo as a response. And his scared reflection, which betrayed the bravery of his taunt.

"Hey!" he screamed, loud enough to put a scratch in his throat, shaking his hand, the cuff biting into his wrist.

Behind him, a door opened. Charlie looked up in the mirror and saw Boricio enter the room, wearing a dress shirt and pants, his hair neatly trimmed and styled.

"Boricio?"

"Well, I ain't the goddamned Easter Bunny," Boricio said, closing the door and circling behind Charlie before settling himself on the other side of the table.

"Where the hell are we? Why am I in handcuffs?"

Boricio looked up and held his finger to his lips, "Shhh, keep it down, Charlie Brown. You don't want to wake the others."

"Others?" Charlie asked, looking around the room. "What others?"

The light bulb lightly swayed above them, as if someone had tipped it. Charlie looked up, then watched as Boricio's shadow bounced back and forth alongside the light's movement.

Boricio looked around, rotating his finger in a small circle before he said, "You don't see them?"

Charlie stared at Boricio, waiting for him to break into a laugh. But Boricio was playing it straight.

"Come on, this is some kinda joke, right? You're fucking with me. You, Adam, and Callie, you're all fucking with me. Ha-ha, real funny. Now let me out," Charlie said, shaking the handcuffs.

Boricio stared him in the eyes. "Nobody's joking," he said. You need to wake the fuck up right now, Chuck E. Cheese-

Dick, because shit's about to get thick as a handful of jism hair gel out there."

"Out where?"

Boricio pointed again, "You really can't see them?"

Charlie looked around again as the light continued to dance with the shadows. Charlie thought he saw something move past him, quickly flying by on the left.

He turned to find the shadow just as the light above him died, casting the room into pitch black.

"You need to wake up, man," Boricio said in the darkness, his voice sounding muffled, as though underwater. Only it was no longer Boricio's voice, and it was coming from someone beside him.

CHARLIE WOKE up to Adam shaking him on the left shoulder and whispering, "Wake up, man. Something happened."

Charlie's head was throbbing behind a tangled web of confusion. He shook his head, wondering where in the hell they were and how they got there. They might have been in the back of a cargo truck or something; he couldn't tell. Wherever it was, it was a winter of black and cold. And he heard no sounds of movement, so if they were in the back of a truck, the wheels weren't rolling.

"What's happening?" Charlie asked.

"Shhh," Adam said, "I don't think the others are awake yet."

"Others?" Charlie said, thinking of the dream.

Adam moved a bit in the darkness and then a moment later, Charlie heard the unmistakable sound of the a lighter top flipping open, immediately followed by a couple of flicks and then a flickering flame that nearly died in the gust of Adam's excited breath.

"See," he said, his face seemingly red in the glow of the

flame, then pulled the lighter away and waved it back and forth.

They were indeed in a truck. A dozen or so other men, women, and children were lying — either unconscious or dead — on the floor surrounding them.

"What's happening?" Charlie repeated in a whisper as Adam flipped the lid to smother the flame.

"I dunno," Adam said, keeping his voice low. "I woke up about a half hour ago. We were driving then, but the truck stopped a few minutes after I woke up. Then I heard someone scream, and what I'm pretty sure there were assault rifles firing."

Adam fell silent, and the darkness seemed to wrap around them like a huddle of angry arms.

"Then what?" Charlie asked, surprised he'd slept through gunfire.

"Nothing. It's been 20 minutes or so. I heard something out there, but I'm not sure who, or *what*, it was."

"Think it might be those things?"

"I dunno. What else would they be shooting at?"

Someone moved in the dark.

"Hello?" a voice called. It sounded like a child, though Charlie couldn't tell if it was a boy or girl.

"Shh," Adam whispered as he flicked on his lighter, then held it to his face to display his friendly smile. "It's okay, we're only stopped for a minute."

Adam held out the lighter to see who they were speaking to. It was a boy, 9 years old or so. His eyes went suddenly wide as Adam made the error of moving the lighter back and forth across the cargo hold, showing the boy all the bodies around them.

The boy screamed.

"Shh!" Adam said, flicking the lighter shut and casting the truck into darkness again.

The boy screamed louder, and Charlie heard him scramble back and hit the side of the truck's inner wall.

"Put the lighter on," Charlie whispered. "You scared the kid!"

Adam fumbled in the darkness, and the lighter hit the ground. "Shit," he said. "I dropped it."

The boy continued to scream as Charlie rushed to his side, fumbling in the dark and cursing himself for his clumsiness, hoping he didn't wake anyone else, or worse — alert whatever enemy might be lying in wait outside the truck. He had to calm the kid down before he drew attention to them.

"Shh," Charlie said, inching toward the boy. "Everything is okay."

He stumbled in the dark, then fell face first onto one of the sleeping people. "Sorry," he said, carefully reaching around the woman beneath him as he tried to stand. The woman squirmed beneath him and cried out, as if she'd just woken to Charlie's jabs.

"Sorry," he repeated, pushing himself up and toward the crying boy, who had stopped screaming, but seemed on the verge of hyperventilating.

"It's okay, it's okay," Charlie said. "Did you find the lighter, Adam?"

"Not yet!"

Idiot!

Charlie's hands found the wall, then he slid down and pressed his back against it as he listened for the kid, still inching toward him. Finally beside him, Charlie put a hand awkwardly on his shoulder. Charlie felt the kid flinch.

"It's okay, we're gonna be okay. The people are just sleeping."

"Where are we?" the boy said.

Charlie was about to answer when he heard a shriek outside. One of the creatures.

Shit.

"What was that?!" the kid screamed far too loudly, grabbing Charlie's arm, and curling his fingers into Charlie's flesh.

The monster, or monsters, slammed on the outside walls of the truck, creating an echo chamber that rang through Charlie's ears as they continued their shrieking. Must have been two of them, one on either side, judging by the sounds.

The kid cried out, "Please, I don't wanna die!"

"Find that fucking lighter!" Charlie growled at Adam as more people in the truck began to wake up, some murmuring to themselves and some asking what happened. A few started to cry louder to match the increasing volume of the creatures trying to get inside the truck.

"I'm lookin'! I'm lookin'!" Adam whined. Then finally, "I found it!"

Adam tried to get the lighter to light, but his fingers had apparently stopped working.

"Just bring it here!" Charlie snapped.

Adam stumbled forward in the dark, making his way toward them as the truck started to shake. The pounding continued to echo inside the truck like thunder rolling through a tunnel. The boy screamed so loud that Charlie couldn't hear what the people were saying. All hell was about to break loose if Adam didn't get that fucking lighter to him.

"Sorry, sorry," Adam said, stumbling his way over to Charlie until he practically fell into his lap.

The inside of the truck was a chaotic mix of people screaming, crying, combining with the pounding and shrieking coming from outside.

This is what death sounds like. Confusion. Chaos.

Adam thrust his hands forward, and Charlie found his arms in the darkness. He followed them down to the wrists, then snatched the lighter from Adam, flicked it open and spun the wheel.

Darkness persisted, and Charlie heard someone vomit, and splash of putrid mess instantly wafted to his nostrils.

"Oh God!" someone screamed, already panicked and at the edge of hysteria, and someone else, or maybe the same person, puked again.

Charlie's hands shook as he feverishly fought to make a flame.

Come on, come on, come on!

Someone in the truck cried out, a scream that instantly registered above all others for its sheer intensity. Then Charlie heard the unmistakable sound of wet flesh being torn.

What the fuck?!

More screaming as everyone started pushing and shoving, moving toward the closed doors of the truck, as if trying to escape.

Charlie finally got the lighter on and cast the truck and its occupants in an orange glow. Given the gift of sight in the dark, fresh screams erupted in the hold as Charlie scanned the flickering movement of bodies and shadows in search of a sign to tell him what was spooking the natives.

The lighter went out.

"Fuck!" Charlie said as someone slammed into his body.

Charlie fell back against the wall, dropping the lighter as the truck turned into a bedlam of screams, punching fists, clawing hands, and kicking feet. Charlie fell on top of the boy, instinctively trying to protect him as Adam tumbled over them both.

"Get the fuck off of me!" Adam screamed. Charlie could feel Adam's weight shift over him as he shoved someone back.

Outside, the shrieks grew louder.

The truck rocked harder as Charlie's hands scrambled for the fallen lighter. Someone stepped on his fingers, and Charlie screamed, yanking his arm back and cradling his injured fingers.

"I got it," Adam yelled, then moments later the orange light flickered across Adam's face. He smiled as he held the lighter in front of him, basking in the glow of his awkward accomplishment.

Charlie laughed at Adam's simplicity, to find joy in such madness. Then Charlie saw what had drawn the screams.

Behind Adam, a woman stood, her head hanging limp, barely hanging by bloody flesh and bone from her neck, replaced by a bulbous, shiny black head of one of the creatures, its mouth open wide and bloody teeth glistening in the flames.

"Oh fuck!" Charlie said.

"What?" Adam said, turning around.

The creature lunged at Adam, its fingers fused in a fleshy blade, clawing across Adam's face and then through his neck. The creature's other hand found the opposite side of Adam's face then wrenched Adam's head free from his neck in an eruption of hot blood and sudden black as the lighter fell to the floor of the truck.

"Adam!" Charlie screamed.

FOUR

Luca Harding

Luca dropped to Will's side, ready to heal him.

"No," Will said, slowly shaking his head as his eyelids fought gravity. "Not me. You can only save three. Don't waste it on me."

"I can't let you die!" Luca cried.

"I'm only injured. I'll be okay," Will said, covering his stomach wound with his left hand, and raising his head to meet Luca's eyes. "I can be fixed. But only you can bring back the dead. Go. Now."

"Who do I save?" Luca said, turning around to the sea of bodies. Most were well beyond help, with missing limbs, many sitting in sloppy piles of guts, feasted on by the army of monsters. Saving any of them would be impossible, Luca figured.

Luca thought of his fallen friends — Paola, Mary, Desmond, Linc, and . . . Rebecca — — whom he lost in the barn when the creatures overran it. Everyone was fighting for their lives, with whatever they could get their hands on — axes, bats, and pitchforks — as the fire spread into the barn. The smoke and flames were blinding. Somehow, Luca lost sight of Rebecca.

He found her a few moments later, at least a couple two late. She was sprawled across the ground with her throat slit, one of the monsters standing above her, blood dripping from its clawed hand.

Luca lost it, swinging his axe with blind rage into the creature's head with a thunk. The creature fell to the dirt, but Luca yanked the axe out and kept hacking, screaming, until Boricio pulled him back.

"We've gotta get outta here," Boricio said, as flames licked wood and planks began to fall. "They're gone."

Everyone was dead, except for him and Boricio, until Will showed up with the gun one minute later, shooting Luca, only God knowing why.

Now Luca had to decide who lived and who stayed dead — assuming he was really able to bring anyone back. How could he choose? His heart immediately chose Rebecca, Paola, and Mary. But he felt a high wave of guilt for not choosing Desmond. Then a smaller wave for not saving Linc. He didn't know Linc as well, but the man had risked his life to save them on more than one occasion. If not for Linc, they wouldn't have even made it to The Sanctuary.

How am I supposed to choose?

Luca looked to Will, but his eyes were barely open.

"I need to rest," Will exhaled, allowing his lids to close fully.

"Help me move him to the car," Luca turned to Boricio.

Boricio looked about a decade older, and still seemed half in shock.

They lifted Will's sleeping body, then carried him to the car. Snow started to fall faster as the wind began to howl around them, whipping his hair into his eyes. Once they set Will in the back seat, Luca hopped into the driver's seat and started the car. The gauge showed nearly full, so he turned on the heat and closed the doors, leaving the driver's window open enough to reach inside, in case the doors locked.

Luca and Boricio stood three feet apart in awkward silence, staring at one another.

Something happened between them, something Luca couldn't fully understand. He had fixed something inside Boricio. He knew that much. Yet at the same time there was something else happening — something Luca didn't understand at all.

Boricio had seen inside him, just like he had seen inside Boricio. Had Boricio "fixed" him in some way, too? Or was Luca now broken? Is that why he hadn't been able to heal earlier? Had Boricio taken his power, giving it back only after bringing Luca back from the brink?

"I don't know what to do," Luca shook his head, looking down at his boots.

"He said you can save three, right?" Boricio asked.

Luca nodded, then looked up at Boricio. "Yes."

"I'd say save that girl you like so she can play with your acorn. Then save Black Godzilla. And even though I don't trust the beady-eyed fucker a bit, I'd say Desmond's as good a bet as any. He looked like he could handle himself and smarter than the average bear."

Luca shook his head. "I can't just let Mary and Paola die! They're my new family."

"Yeah, that may be truer than the titties on your girlfriend, but right now family might as well be the fucking flu," Boricio said. "Right now, it's survival of the fittest, and saving either Mary or her little lamb will be a smear of fuck-butter on your bread. You weren't fast forwarding through the commercials when that shit went down, right? You saw them creature features fuck this shit up, right?" Boricio swiveled his hand up in the air, indicating the charred lot that used to be The Sanctuary.

"Yeah," Luca said, trying not to cry. At times like this he still felt like a child, which made him hate his adult body even more. At least he could cry when he was a kid, and no one would ridicule him or tell him to act like a man.

"When shit went down, who was left? You, me, and Black Godzilla."

"His name was Linc," Luca interrupted.

"What?" Boricio said. "It's not like I called him Niggerzilla. Truth, when shit went down, *we* were the ones standing. You, me, and him! You think that's by accident? Fuck no, that shit is by design. Strongest plus youngest plus smartest equals Fuck Yeah! That's the only math you need to get through this shit."

Luca flashed back on Paola dying, and how he'd been unable to stop Brother Rei from pulling the trigger. He had to undo that.

Luca turned from Boricio and walked toward The Hole. The door leading to the basement was still intact, not burned like most of the rest of the attached house.

"What the hell are you doing?" Boricio said, following close.

"I'm saving Paola first."

"Paola?! Dude. That wasn't even the girl you liked! Was she letting your bald butler get away with the crime and I don't know about it? Because if not, leave her in the dirt."

Luca kept walking, ignoring Boricio's lewd comments.

"Listen, man," Boricio tried to reason, "you save her, and you're gonna have to save her momma, too. And unfortunately, I left my *Men are From Mars and Women are From The Crack of Uranus* book at home, so I don't quite know how to put up with these bitches."

Luca continued to ignore him.

"You're *really* gonna save three broads? With two of 'em bitchy?"

Luca spun around and glared at Boricio. "Shut up! You don't even know them! I'll save whoever I want." Then under his breath he said, "You're not the boss of me."

Luca regretted getting in Boricio's face before he was even in it. The glimmer in Boricio's eyes reminded Luca who he was dealing with.

Boricio's right arm thrust out like lightning, his fingers instantly curling around Luca's throat. A smile spread across Boricio's smile — the smile of his namesake, a wolf.

"Surprised the puppy's gone pouncing from his leash?" Boricio cackled, as if he'd picked up on Luca's thought of wolfish smiles. "You managed to get in my head for a bit, kid. And I'm not sure why, but I can't quite hate you enough to hammer you with the sort of fuck-all that makes my itchy stop itching, but don't make the mistake of thinking you can talk to me like that and keep all your teeth. Now, do I sound like I'm speaking some ching chong ramma lamma ding dong language, or are my words American as a chocolate milkshake and a titty fuck to you?"

Luca tried to speak, but could only choke as Boricio's fingers dug into his throat.

Boricio relaxed his grip, then released it completely. Luca fell to the ground, clutching his throat.

"I'm sorry," Luca said, not apologizing because he was afraid of Boricio. He actually felt bad for getting in Boricio's face. Luca wasn't sure why, but he didn't want to upset Boricio. It was as if Boricio were an older brother or something. He didn't understand why he would want the approval of something that was more monster than human, but it didn't change the fact that he did.

Boricio stared at Luca. "Sorry, man. *Maybe* I overreacted. I keep forgetting that you're missing the hair on your balls inside that noggin of yours." Boricio knocked his knuckles on his own head. Luca nodded, trying to keep his emotions flat as he worked up the courage to say what was inside his head.

Luca hoped his calculations were right — that Boricio wouldn't, or couldn't, hurt him. Because what he was going to say might bring out the beast.

"I'm going to save the girls," Luca said. "So, please don't try to stop me."

"Don't I have any say in this?" Boricio asked. "I gave a decade of my sweet life to keep you breathing! I get at least one vote, right? And I vote for Godzilla."

Luca thought for a moment, then said, "Okay, you can have a vote. But I'm bringing back Paola and Mary, first. And they get a vote, too."

"You might wanna think twice on that, kid. If you think there's any way in hell they're gonna pick to save your girl-friend over ole Quiet Eyes, then you're not the sharpest Crayola in the box."

"So, what am I supposed to do?" Luca said, his voice rising an octave higher than he wanted, and cracking along the way. "If I bring Paola back, she's going to want her mother."

"And if you bring back the mother, *she's* gonna want her boyfriend. All the more reason to listen to ye ole Boricio. Hell, I've got an even better idea: Bring back your girlfriend and Godzilla, then save the rest of that juice for yourself. The old fucker said that tic-tac-toe, it was three in a row that would fuck you up so bad you couldn't save anyone else. So, why not stop at two?" Boricio nodded with a smile as if the idea had just occurred to him. "I'm telling you, it's a bad time to be an old fucker. There ain't one goddamned Perkins left out there."

Luca hadn't thought about it, but Boricio had a point. How old would he be if he saved three people? Would he be old like his great grandpa, Sal, who died two years earlier at 99? Who would take care of Luca if he aged that far? It wasn't like doctors were around. Or medicine, or any of the things you needed when you got old. He wouldn't be able to move fast, making him an easy meal the next time they ran into monsters.

"Ah, well, at least I can see you're thinking about it,"

Boricio said. "About damned time you started giving a shit about yourself! I imagine you've not yet had the chance to make a boneless beef burrito with a bitch tortilla yet, but I'm guessing you haven't. And I've gotta be honest," Boricio cackled, "ain't nothing better in this wide, blue world than blowing a load of cock snot and having a pair of lady lips to catch it. And it don't matter if those lips are camping up north or down south. Believe you me, Rip Van Freakshow, you bring Mary and her little lamb back, and you'll be too droopy dicked to take the skin boat to tuna town. And seriously, fuck that shit with a crowbar, kid. Save one lucky fucker, my money's still on Godzilla, and consider yourself Santa Claus."

"I don't know what to do," Luca turned from Boricio sighing, his stomach twisted from all the gross words that he didn't quite understand.

He finally said, "I have to do what feels right."

Boricio looked at Luca, eyebrow arched, shaking his head in resignation. "I don't think I like where this is going," he said

"No, you won't," Luca said, marching past Boricio, then down into the basement where they'd been held — the basement where Mary and Paola died. He was going to do what he couldn't before, save them both — whether Boricio liked it or not.

"Damn it, kid!" Boricio said, though he didn't put up a fight.

Luca stepped inside the darkness, past the corpses littering the ground, until he found Mary and Paola's bodies, lying just as they'd left them.

They looked so pale. So dead.

No way are they coming back.

Luca wondered how much damage he could repair. Could he heal a gunshot to the head? What if a big chunk of the girl's brain had been damaged?

What if I bring her back and she can't think right anymore?

Maybe I should find someone without brain damage?

Stop stalling — you don't have much time.

The evil is coming.

Luca wasn't sure if the voices in his head were made from truth or fear, or if it even mattered.

He dropped to his knees and laid his hands on Paola's face, feeling the familiar warmth flow like a current, spreading through his body and into Paola's.

Luca glanced at Boricio, who was shaking his head as he watched. Luca closed his eyes, avoiding distraction.

Please, wake up, Paola.

Please.

Luca wasn't sure what to expect — whether he'd take a trip inside the girl's head as he had before, or if she'd simply wake up as though she'd been sleeping.

Neither was happening. After a full minute, Paola was still nothing but dead.

"Come on!" Luca cried, opening his eyes, and looking at Paola. He shook her shoulders. "Please, wake up, Paola! Please!"

Luca squeezed his eyes shut tighter, both hearing and feeling Boricio pace by his side, probably ready to tell him to stop trying, with more words that would make Luca sick.

No, I have to do this. I have to bring her back.

Luca thought again of how Paola had died, until he could feel the anger coursing through him. Anger at Brother Rei. Anger at his inability to save Paola or Mary. Or Rebecca, Desmond, Linc, or any of the others he could have saved. Anger at whatever the hell took his family from him last October.

The warm current flashed brighter, then flowed faster inside him, like someone lit a fuse. It burned hotter than it had before; the heat was suddenly everywhere inside him, flowing from his body and into Paola. Luca could feel her skin warming at his touch. He opened his eyes as Paola's eyes opened, too.

Her eyes met his, and her mouth parted, but her ragged voice couldn't crack into words. Paola could only cough instead.

"Shh," Luca said, tears of joy streaming from his eyes. "You're alive." He smiled. "You're going to be okay."

~

FIVE

Edward Keenan

Somewhere in Georgia
   March 28
   FIVE MONTHS AFTER THE EVENT …

THREE DAYS HAD PASSED since their capture.

Ed and Brent were shackled beside one another, hand-cuffed to giant metal shelving in the grocery store's stockroom as four Black Mountain Guardsmen took turns, along with the kid, Billy, keeping watch. The power was out, but enough daylight was spilling through the skylights to see by.

Lisa, the woman from the parking lot who had lured them inside the store, was standing guard. Ed wished he'd followed his instincts and simply shot her and the kid when he first saw them. But that would have freaked Brent out, big time, just as it had with Teagan when he took out those men in the gas station.

One more reason I should've fucking gone alone.

Ed glared at Lisa, lounging in a reclining leather office chair — the kind where executives sat, not the hourly workers — while thumbing through a stack of magazines left behind on the crate by either the guards, or maybe some of the vanished employees before the world went adios.

Lisa hadn't sent more than a few words in their direction since their capture, at least anything beyond the occasional order to, "Shut the fuck up!" or the vague promise that she'd tell them the shit they needed to know, when they needed to know it.

Ed had overheard enough from the others last night while pretending to sleep, and he figured he knew enough to know what was going on.

Ed said, "They're not coming back for you."

"Excuse me?" she said, looking up from her magazine. Her response sent Ed from suspicion to certainty – Lisa would love for Ed to give her an excuse to use the Remington 870 propped against the wall beside her.

"I said they're not coming back. The rest of your squad." Ed grinned. "How long since you last heard anything?"

Lisa ignored Ed and turned to Brent. "You wanna tell your friend to shut his face?"

Brent turned to Ed and smiled, "She said to shut your face."

Brent was in remarkably better spirits than Ed would've imagined. Perhaps, he figured, it was because Lisa, and the others, had been far nicer to Brent than they had to Ed. They were treating Ed like he was some sort of treasonous spy, while practically apologizing to Brent for the inconvenience of holding him hostage. Ed figured they were working Brent in preparation for splitting the two of them up — to help turn Brent against Ed, in hopes that he'd surrender intel on Black Island.

"You know that isn't protocol, right?" Ed said. "I don't know how different Black Mountain is from the Island, but way I figure, protocols can't be that different. Little things, sure. But not something like, don't ever fucking contact your squad. Something happened. So, the only question is, how long are we gonna sit here and wait for more of them aliens to come at us?"

"Until I fucking say so, all right?" Lisa yelled, voice cracking right in the middle where it mattered the most.

Ed nodded, "Oh, I see," his eyes widened in mock surprise, "You're not the one in charge, are you? Your commander is out there, eh? And you're afraid of leaving and getting reamed."

He watched her eyes as they pretended not to see him.

He continued, his confidence growing muscles. "And I'm guessing you're not moving because you've either dropped the ball a few times already and are worried that you'll make the wrong decision. Or . . . you're scared."

"I'm not scared," she said, no hint of emotion.

"You'd be stupid *not* to be scared, Lisa," Ed said, using her name to worm inside her head. "I've seen these things do some scary shit. They nearly killed my daughter."

She looked up, "You're with your daughter?"

It worked. Maybe.

"Well, I was. And I'm gonna level with you right now. God's honest truth, because way I see it, there's no point in lying. The people on Black Island are holding onto her until I do this job for them."

"What's the job?" she asked.

Ed wasn't sure if he should continue with his honesty, but if they got a hold of Brent before he and Brent were able to get their stories straight, they'd find out, anyway. Besides, they'd already taken the picture of Boricio from his wallet. And if they were in fact already seeking him, then the jig was already up. May as well consider changing teams, even if only long enough to just get away.

"They want me to find someone and bring him back to the island."

"Who?" Lisa asked.

"A man named Boricio. The guy in the picture you lifted from me."

"Ah, *Boricio*," Lisa said. "Interesting."

"You looking for him, too?" Ed asked.

"Not exactly."

"What's that mean?"

The door in the front of the stockroom crashed open, killing their conversation and drawing their attention. A pint-sized steroid case named Rojas ran inside the warehouse, holding his M16. He looked — for the first time since Ed had met him — nervous.

"We've got a problem, Sergeant," Rojas said.

"What?"

"The parking lot. There's a shit-ton of them out there."

"A shit-ton?"

"Hundreds!"

Ed's eyes widened. No way he heard Rojas right. He'd never seen more than two dozen together.

"Hundreds?" she asked, "Are you fucking with me?"

"No, Sergeant. They're out there, like they're waiting for us to come outside."

Lisa swallowed, visibly shaken.

A gunshot suddenly echoed from somewhere inside the store.

"What the hell?!" Lisa shouted, grabbing her shotgun and running out the door behind Rojas, leaving Ed and Brent handcuffed to the shelving.

"Hey!" Ed screamed to no one.

Shit!

More gunshots echoed inside the store, followed by the sound of crashing glass.

Ed looked down at his cuffed right hand, and pulled as if he'd somehow get loose, despite hours of trying already. Brent frantically tugged at his own cuffs, also without luck. Ed scanned the area, searching for anything he could reach with his left hand or feet, but there wasn't anything that hadn't been there 10 minutes earlier.

More automatic gunfire, followed by more shattering glass, then more gunshots again. A man screamed — a quickly fading scream, thick with death and torment, followed by more blasts, rapid fire — the M16.

"Shit, they're inside the store," Ed said, now looking up at the shelves above him to see if anything was there he could maybe shake down. The only thing he could see above him was more of the same — wrapped pallets of cardboard boxes and neatly stacked cases of soft drinks.

More gunshots, then another scream. Another Guardsman. Or maybe the same man in even more pain. The scream was chased by the deafening thunder of what sounded like someone throwing cars across the store. Ed could only imagine the hellish chaos on the other side of the warehouse door.

Soon, he realized with a terrible clarity, he wouldn't have to imagine it at all.

As if fate was reading his mind, the door at the front of the stockroom banged open and two of the loping dark aliens crashed through, immediately spotting Ed and Brent — snacks held captive.

"Fuck!" Brent screamed as he began to pull harder, the cuffs digging deep into his wrists.

Ed wondered if Brent might pull his own wrist off to get away. Ed began to pull at his own cuffed hand as the aliens stood fully upright, towering in triumph as they approached, as if enjoying the conquest as much as the coming kill.

Ed met the black, glassy eyes of the creature closest to him.

"Fuck, you things are ugly," he said as he stopped pulling on his cuff, and instead braced for whatever defensive measure he might be able to make. He had one hand and two feet, and would be damned if he allowed the first, or first five of the fuckers, to kill him.

Brent was tugging hard and screaming, "Oh God! Oh God! I don't want to die!"

Ed would have tried to talk him down, but Brent was in a fat panic, and Ed couldn't afford to pay attention to anything but the approaching threat as it stepped forward, stopping six feet in front of him.

He thought of Jade back on the island, and hoped like hell that Sullivan would keep her safe. That his counterpart — the other Ed — wouldn't, or couldn't, be so cruel as to kill his doppelgänger's daughter.

The two creatures stood side by side. The one on the left opened its mouth and screamed its unholy shriek, digging into Ed's skull like razors scraping over his nerves.

"Come on, you fucker!" Ed growled through gritted teeth, as he squatted, rolling from foot to foot, preparing to move — as much as possible — and kick the fucker as hard as he could.

The one on the left ran toward him, clawed hand raised, ready to swing down and tear Ed's face to Big League Chew.

Ed fell on his side, pushed himself forward as far as he could, then swept his feet out, knocking the alien down, on top of him.

Ed screamed as he brought his knees up and into the alien's chest, then head butted the creature as hard as he could in its face. The alien screamed, then slid back as Ed kicked out, hooking the alien by the neck, and yanked it back into the metal shelving beside him.

The creature screamed as Ed twisted his body and kicked it square in the face, his boot pushing through its soft head, and pushing whatever bones it had back into its skull as its body fell into death spasms.

Brent screamed as the second alien ran toward them.

Ed's boot was stuck in the first alien's face.

Fuck!

Ed struggled to pull his foot free, but the creature was charging too fast. He hoped like hell Brent could do something to protect them.

A gunshot thundered through the warehouse, causing instant pain, and whistling, inside Ed's eardrums. The alien fell to the floor in front of him, its head caved in, and black goo oozing out onto the gray concrete.

Ed looked up to see Lisa standing with her shotgun, and Billy with his Glock 22.

She raced toward Ed, then slid to a stop just inches from him, holding the keys to his handcuffs.

"Hold them off!" she yelled at Billy, who took aim at the aliens spilling through the door and into the warehouse.

Lisa slid the key into the keyhole, but it slipped and fell to the ground.

"Fuck!" she said, glancing back as the aliens barreled down on Billy. He opened fire. She grabbed the key and put it into Ed's other hand, "You do it!"

She grabbed her shotgun, then fired at the aliens pouring inside. Lisa would run out of shells soon. She needed Ed's help.

Ed slid the key into the hole, clicked the handcuffs open, then handed Brent the key. He ran to Billy, who had a second Glock in his waistband. Ed grabbed it, not even bothering to see if the clip was full, as an alien soared toward them on all fours, shrieking.

Billy's gun was out of ammo but he kept pulling the trigger, either not realizing, or not knowing what else to do as the alien came toward him, ready to bite.

Ed stepped in front of Billy at the last possible second, and the alien's open mouth came up to bite Ed instead. Ed shoved his hand, with the gun, into the alien's mouth and pulled the trigger twice.

The alien's body went slack as the back of its head exploded in black goo and bits of fatty meat and fleshy bone.

Ed flung the alien from his body, then brought the pistol back up to fire at another charging alien.

Lisa blasted it down before Ed had a chance.

Ahead of them, one of the men, Rojas, entered backward, firing his M16 at aliens following him.

All the aliens that had made their way inside the stockroom were lying in piles. "Come on!" Ed screamed, above the whistling in his eardrums. "We've gotta block the door!"

They raced toward the door as Rojas dispatched the last of the approaching aliens, then slammed the door shut. Ed slid the lock shut. It looked strong, but he didn't want to take any chances. Ed and Brent pushed four wooden pallets between the door and the immediate wall, stacking one on top of the other to keep the bottom of the door secure.

Aliens began to bash against the door from the other side, as if to test the lock's integrity. Ed wasn't sure how long the lock, or makeshift braces, would hold up to dozens of aliens battering their bodies against the door.

Ed looked toward the back of the stockroom. It was shaped in a giant L, and he would have bet his left nut, and maybe even his right, there was at least one other entrance into the room from the back of the store. That meant aliens could be storming in to flank them. They had to find safety now. He looked up and saw that the top shelf was close enough to one of the skylights that they might be able to stack some stuff to climb out and onto the roof.

"Let's climb the shelves!" he yelled, pointing up. "I don't think they can climb!"

"Better idea!" Lisa shouted. "There's a ladder around the corner, leading to the roof!"

Ed gave her a thumbs-up, and they raced toward the back of the store, climbing the ladder as the sound of destruction echoed from the store and into the stockroom.

Rojas went up the ladder first, pushing the hatch open, then peeking out to make sure no aliens were on the roof.

"All clear!" Rojas shouted from above.

They followed him onto the roof one at a time, with Billy going second, Lisa third, and Brent next. As Brent began to climb, two aliens made their way in through one of the other doors in the rear of the store. He raced up the ladder behind Brent, his face practically in Brent's ass.

Ed heard shrieking beneath him, but didn't dare look down. He hoped to be up and out of their line of sight before the aliens could see where they'd gone. He'd hate to find out this way that they could climb. If the aliens got onto the roof, it was only a matter of time before Ed and the group were overrun, even if they were able to pick the fuckers off one by one as they crawled through the hatch.

Once Brent was standing up top, he reached down and pulled Ed the rest of the way. Then they quietly closed the hatch.

Ed stood on the gravel, and let out a gasp, "Holy shit!"

Ed leaned over, sucking wind, his legs in pain from being forced into action after three days of inertia. He caught his breath while staring at the hatch, hoping like hell it wouldn't pop open.

"Oh my God!" Brent said, looking out at the parking lot.

Ed stood, went to where Brent was standing, then stared out at the sea of creatures. The lot was packed with more aliens than Ed had seen during his entire time patrolling New York.

He saw hundreds. Maybe a thousand.

All of them waiting for something.

~

SIX

Boricio Wolfe

Mary's little lamb took 10 minutes to start batting her eyes. She was probably getting the man-kid's kibbles 'n' bits to do a little batting, too. Weird how Boricio didn't see the aging happen, it just was, like when you look down and see the blood but wonder when in the fuck you were cut. He looked over at Luca, poor fucker looked older than he did, maybe over 40 and not even half as handsome.

Boricio wondered if maybe he should just get the flying fuck-all out of Dodge while the gettin' was good. It wasn't like he'd never been the only one howling at the moon before. Maybe he'd find out where those fuckers Charlie and Adam got off to.

Mary's little lamb may have been able to bat her eyes in 10 minutes, but she took a year and a goddamned half to open her mouth, and when she did, it was to give the man-kid a bullshit "thank you."

Luca petted the side of her cheek and said, "I need you to help me."

Her response wasn't much more than a whisper. "What do you need?"

Luca smiled, fucker looked like he was half crying, then said, "I want to save your mom."

A tear fell from the lamb's cheek, and she said, "Thank you, Luca," her voice about cracked in half, like she was choking on a chicken bone before she managed to squeak another. "Thanks so much."

"But," Luca got ready to thicken the plot. Boricio smiled. "I can't save Desmond."

The girl's eyes went glassy. "I just can't." Luca shook his head. "I love Rebecca. I have to save her."

"Why can't you save them both?"

"I'll be too old. I can only save three people. You, your mom, and Rebecca."

He looked down.

Paola said, "Oh," as though she just realized how old Luca really looked, even older than he did before the monsters stopped her breathing. Shouldn't have been too hard to see, since Luca's hair had a bunch of salt where there'd only been pepper before.

"Mary's going to be mad at me," he said, eyes getting watery as a bucket. "And I need you to help me make her not mad."

Boricio was getting bored of the live action Disney Channel movie scene. Mary's little lamb finally said, "Okay."

After a pause, Little Lamb added, "Are you sure? About Desmond?"

Boricio said, "And circle gets the fucking square!"

The man-kid didn't even look, like Boricio wasn't talking at all.

Boricio paced in a circle, waiting for their scene to finish while wondering what sort of shit Luca had actually "fixed" inside him. Shit seemed broken, like the wrong feelings were assigned to the wrong shit. Like he knew what he wanted to fucking order but the goddamned waitress kept screwing the pooch with the wrong dishes in each of her hands. You could kill a waitress for not getting shit right, but what were you supposed to do when the shit that was wrong was coming from inside you?

Boricio still felt a driving need to follow his favorite set of Darwinian directives — fuck and kill — but the passion almost seemed gone. He still thought tearing the head from a fucker's neck, then using it to knock down enough pins to celebrate a strike, would be funny, but for the first time since Tom taught him how to make everything black, he felt bad for having the feeling. Maybe not bad, exactly. But almost like he felt bad for not feeling bad. That meant shit was *broken*, not fixed.

Fuck!

Boricio wasn't the sitcom dad on some laugh factory fuck-all. He needed his instincts, had to know he could do what needed to be done without some mystic shit slapping the pause button and making him hesitate.

Luca and his little lamb were trading mumbles until Paola finally stopped sobbing long enough to say, "Okay, Luca. I understand."

BORICIO WALKED UP TO LUCA, put a hand on his arm, pulled him to his feet, then led him out of the basement, into the courtyard to a car that had died, along with the driver's hope, a hundred or so feet from the front gate.

Boricio turned him to the window and his reflection against the dying orange flames behind them. "See yourself?"

Luca nodded.

"You probably look older than your old man, am I right?"

Luca swallowed, then slowly nodded.

"Think about it, man. Do you really want to be any older than that? One more time with you raining sunlight, or whatever the fuck it is you do, and you're gonna be old enough to cash all the Social Security checks you ain't never gonna get.

One after that, and you're a bad cough from lining a coffin ain't no one gonna lay you in. If you're gonna save the girl no matter what, and I can see by staring at that too-stupid-to-know-what-the-fuck-you're-doing face of yours that you're going to, then fine, save your girl, and let's get the fuck outta' here. But do not save Mary."

Luca shook his head. "I can't do that, Mr. Boricio. I have to save Rebecca, and Mary."

Boricio shook his head, though he wanted to shake Luca, at least long enough to rattle a lick of sense to the center of his insides. Not enough beatings in his life had clearly turned the Tiny Tim half stupid.

"Listen, man, I'm serious." Boricio held his hands in the air. "No ulterior motives. Honest Injun and all that shit." He made the peace sign. "I think you should put yourself first for a second. It isn't like you're going around chopping fuckers up. They're already dead. You're not making them any deader than they'd be without you."

"Sorry, Mr. Boricio," Luca said again, still shaking his head, like he didn't know how to do anything else. He turned from the car, went to Mary's body, then knelt on the ground beside her. Luca ran his hands along Mary's face, then over her hair as he stared at her. After what seemed like a surprisingly long time, Luca finally closed his eyes and started rocking slowly back and forth.

Probably in the woman's head. Like he was in mine. And now I'm fucking broken. Boricio don't like to be broken.

Her eyes fluttered, and her lip twitched. Then her right hand spasmed, followed almost immediately by her left. She started to murmur.

Luca stood up, his head down, and walked toward the stairs leading down to the basement, his head in his hands. Boricio couldn't see his face, but he looked to be crying. Boricio looked away from Luca and back to Mary and Paola, who were hugging one another.

"Oh my God," Mary cried. "Is everything okay?" She lifted her head and looked around. "What happened?"

She was pinching her eyes as though that made remembering shit faster.

Paola said, "We're going to be okay. Luca saved us!"

Mary turned to Luca, who was still turned away from the group. "Thank you," she said. She swallowed, then said, "You've helped us more times than I can count."

Luca nodded, though he was turned away from them still.

"Are you okay?" she asked.

Luca nodded. "Yeah, I guess," he said, turning to them.

Mary and Paola both gasped. Boricio stared in disbelief. Luca had aged a hell of a lot more than he should have. The pepper was all gone. Luca's whiskers were pure white, everywhere on his face, and long. His hair wasn't quite as white, more of a dirty-silver gray, hanging slightly past the tips of his shoulders, and spilling toward his chest along both the front and back.

He looked close to 90.

"What?" Luca asked, his voice creaking.

Boricio went over to Luca and helped him up the steps and back to the car to see his reflection.

Luca's eyes widened in disbelief.

Boricio stayed silent, letting Luca go toe-to-toe with the truth. Finally, Luca couldn't take it anymore. His bottom lip started to tremble, and both of his eyelids started to twitch. His shoulders rose, then fell, then rose higher. For a second, the old kid looked as if he would manage to gather his strength and force the moment to pass. But he didn't, or couldn't, and collapsed into tears instead.

It was a heaving heap of horrible shit, watching the man-kid cry. Part of Boricio wanted to slap the crying right out of him, maybe even kill him to shut him the fuck up. But those impulses were faded, barely there, and far from doing a titty dance like they'd done for Boricio's entire goddamned life.

It was the weirdest fucking thing in the world, but Boricio couldn't deny it — he was tuned into the pain. Like when some asshole's stomach growls and you feel hungry, or how when a bitch yawns in line it would make you yawn, too.

That's what Boricio felt as he stared at the old man in front of him crying, staring at the mirror like it showed anything more than a Santa without any toys.

Boricio had to take a step back and look away.

No, he shook his head. *This can't be happening.*

He was actually feeling sympathy for the child turned old man. Feeling pain for what Luca was going through, and how he'd selflessly sacrificed his youth to save the others. He'd always been able to recognize emotions, sure as the smell of shit on a toddler. But this was the first time he'd ever felt a response to anyone's pain.

As Boricio fought the tears welling up in his eyes, he cursed Luca for "fixing" him.

~

SEVEN

Will Bishop

This wasn't an ordinary dream, Will realized as he drifted above the balcony, floating like a disembodied ghost, watching Mary and John in discussion below.

Mary was frantically yelling at John, telling him something was wrong. Brother Rei was planning something big. But John didn't seem too concerned.

This is how the end began.

Though Will hadn't been there, he'd seen enough in his visions to know that this was the spark that lit the fuse that ended in the wholesale destruction of nearly everyone at The Sanctuary.

Will watched as Brother Rei stepped forward from the house and onto the balcony, put the gun to John's head, and fired. The shot was thunder, cracking the night into two ugly halves. John remained standing, half his face missing, before his body finally fell to the ground.

Mary screamed before being rushed from the balcony and into the house by Rei's men as the courtyard below erupted in chaos.

Will tried to follow them inside, but his body didn't move. He was meant to stay — to see something else. He floated in the moment's confusion, looking around as people ran below, screaming.

What am I supposed to be seeing?

Then he saw it — the dark shape flowing from John's corpse. The darkness, the thing he'd been seeing in his dreams ever since the day his Air Force unit had found the *thing* they shouldn't have found.

The darkness oozed from John's body, rising like twisting vines of liquid smoke as it floated into the house. Will followed, also floating, watching as the darkness flowed above one of the Brothers, who took a shot but did no damage, then entered the mouth of the man standing outside a doorway, its entire mass flowing through the man's throat until it vanished entirely into him.

The man then turned, opened the door, entered the bedroom, and looked down at The Prophet, lying in his bed. The man's mouth opened. The darkness slipped out and then into The Prophet, taking command of his brain, along with his breath.

Will woke with a start, lying in the back seat of the car alone, cold and shaking. The orange glow from the burning buildings bled through the snow-covered windows in spattered speckles and dancing dots, painting the car's interior with a lightly smeared tangerine hue. He looked down to see that his wound had grown worse, blood now staining the entire front of his shirt in soaking-wet crimson.

A gallon of blood must have fled his body. The pain in his gut had receded to a dull ache, and he could feel the Grim Reaper creeping as sure as he'd felt him in the hospital room a decade back when he came to claim Sam.

No loopholes.

And fuck you, Reaper.

A shadow draped the car as someone approached from the front.

Will had hoped to die before Luca's return. Will couldn't

stand to see him as a man older than himself. Nor could he stand to see the boy come to the realization that Will had lied, and would indeed die. That would shatter what was left of Will's heart.

But the shadow carried only one body behind it.

The Prophet. The darkness. It has returned.

I have to warn them.

Will swallowed the phlegm in his throat as the shadow drew closer, then he leaned over and into the front seat, desperately trying to reach the horn on the steering wheel.

The seat bit into his gut, and the dull pain turned as sharp and sudden as the flat of a cold blade.

Will screamed, then fell back against his seat, unable to reach the horn. The pain was overpowering. He struggled to gain enough strength to try a second time as the figure outside the car drew closer and its shadow grew large on the windshield.

The footsteps outside were a few feet away.

Oh God.

Will leaned forward again, and the pain stabbed harder into him.

The shadow grew smaller as the person on the other side approached the door. Shadow met form on the other side of the window, as a figure reached for the door handle.

Will cried out, bracing for a violent end. He hoped that the darkness wouldn't go into his body next.

Oh God, it could enter me, and use me to get to Luca.

No, no, no.

The shadow on the other end tugged at the door.

Will reached for the lock, though he'd only be able to reach the door closest to him. If another door was unlocked, the darkness would enter.

Must reach the lock.

Will's fingers were centimeters from the lock when his door swung open. He was too late.

It wasn't The Prophet, or the dark thing, or anyone he expected to see on the other side. It was Luca, as a child.

"What?"

Will blinked his eyes. He must be dreaming, or already dead.

Luca was 8 again, looking almost exactly as he had when Will first met him, and how he had appeared to Will for years in his dreams, except he was wearing pajamas.

"Daddy?" Luca said.

Daddy?

"No, it's Will."

Luca nodded, as if he knew he wasn't his dad all along, then looked down at Will's wound. "You can see me?"

"Yes," Will said, wincing as a sharp pain stabbed him fresh in the gut.

"Oh God," Luca said, "What happened?"

"One of the monsters got me," Will said. "How are you young again?"

"I'm not your Luca," he said, looking around. "I tried to talk to him, but he can't see or hear me. Then I keep going back."

"What are you talking about?" Will asked, every word an effort to cling to consciousness.

"You and Luca aren't from here. You were . . . . brought over here. This isn't your world."

"What are you talking about?" Will said, confused.

"You have to find the other Will. You have to go to Black Island. It's in New York. Tell them that Luca sent you. They will let you in."

"What are you talking about?" Will asked again.

"Find the other Will and tell him I said to look in the moon. I think he can bring you home."

"The moon?"

Luca was about to say something when an anguished scream tore through the dream, vision, or whatever it was, and shoved Will back into the harsh reality of the burned-out compound.

Though his voice was different, the scream belonged to the same soul he'd been connected to, deeper than anyone since Sam: Luca.

~

EIGHT

Edward Keenan

Ed blinked a half dozen times, but he still didn't believe his eyes, even though the acrid scent of the monsters' sweat, or whatever it was, should have made it easier.

Ed stared over the edge of the roof, shaking his head at the sea of aliens below. With his nerves frayed and attention divided, Ed was half tuned to the hatch that might pop open at any moment, while the other half was focused on the certain death below.

The aliens didn't necessarily look like they were making a formation to attack, but they did look like they were waiting for something. They were milling about the entrance, with some of them heading into the store, but they weren't charging inside like Rojas said they had been earlier. They seemed almost orderly, as though waiting their turns.

The gun felt right in Ed's hand. He wrapped his fingers around the handle tighter, finger kissing the trigger, itchy to squeeze it and knowing the math was impossible. Aliens to bullets were at least 10 to one.

Ed turned from the aliens, then glanced at the hatch before his eyes landed on Lisa. "There's no way I'm letting you cuff me again. You realize that, right?"

Lisa said nothing.

Ed continued, "We're gonna get through this, and when we do, you'll know you couldn't have done it without me, and I'll know I couldn't have done it without you. That will be enough. We'll say our thank yous, and then our goodbyes. Once this is over, so are we. Hasta la bye-bye, and no coming back."

Lisa added empty silence to her pile of verbal nothing, while Ed said the same thing with different words. "You never saw us, and we never saw you. You got it?"

Lisa finally nodded, then said, "Let's just wait until this shit is over. Then we'll talk."

"No talking," Ed said. "I'm taking off when this shit is over, and you're going to let me and Brent head into the sunset with a smile on your face. I want your word, Lisa, or I'm going to find it awfully hard to pay attention to what's happening all around me when shit starts flying from the fan." He raised his eyebrows. "And believe me, I'm exactly the man you want ahead, around, and behind you, from right this minute until whenever we get the hell outta here."

A horrible chorus of shrieks rolled through the parking lot to punctuate the thought.

After a long pause, Lisa said, "Fine," then walked to the far side of the roof and looked over the edge, in case something had changed in the two minutes since Ed last looked.

Ed wondered if his training was what kept him from fully trusting Lisa, or whether Lisa was simply that kind of a bitch. He looked out at the sea of aliens and shook his head. The odds of them seeing the next sunrise with an enemy who wore night during the day and invisibility at night was slim to none.

The clouds grew dark overhead, and night wasn't far off.

"We need flares," Lisa said, as if realizing his thought and opening her mouth to the first lick of sense all day. "Maybe if we light a few flares, we can get some help. Black Mountain must be looking for us by now."

No one said anything, so she finished the thought. "I have some downstairs in my pack."

"I'll help," Ed said, with no room for no in his voice.

Lisa nodded, then turned and headed toward the hatch. Ed stood a foot behind Rojas, while he, Brent, and Billy all circled the hatch, aiming their weapons at its closed mouth.

Lisa swung the lid open, and half of them gasped. She looked up at Ed, the relief on her face delivered along with a half of a smile. Ed couldn't help but smile back. Lisa climbed inside the hatch, and Ed followed.

Smile or no, Lisa couldn't be trusted. As they descended the ladder, then crept through the stockroom, Ed divided his attention between the eerie silence and the woman walking one yard in front of him.

Ed wasn't too concerned about Lisa trying anything down here to harm him. For one, she'd attract the aliens, which was probably why she didn't mind turning her back on him, either. And second, they needed one another — for now. But once they'd dealt with the problem at hand, things were gonna get tricky, and there was a strong chance that blood would be shed.

Lisa walked along the back of the stockroom, and through a long, narrow hallway that opened to the left into a deli, and beyond that was the store and the aliens. Lisa held a finger to her lips, and Ed nodded to show that he'd seen them. So far, they'd been undetected.

Lisa was three feet from her field pack when something moved in the deli. Ed twisted his body to aim at a shadow that raced by, banging against something, before vanishing into the darkness.

Lisa turned, startled. "What was that?" she whispered.

Ed shook his head.

Then he heard the familiar clicking sound coming from the deli they'd just passed. And would have to pass again to get back to the ladder.

"Follow me," he said. He held his gun in front of him as he inched toward the opening to the deli. Behind him, Lisa held her shotgun, ready.

He peered into the deli, and saw nothing out of the ordinary. Beyond the deli, he spotted two aliens wandering the aisles of the store, oblivious to him, and seemingly walking without purpose.

What the hell are they doing in here, browsing?

Lisa screamed behind him. Ed spun around and watched as Lisa was knocked to the ground by an alien behind her. The gun slipped from her hand and slid on the floor, and Ed took aim at the creature, but it was too tangled with Lisa to get a decent shot.

Lisa kicked up at something that looked like it might have been a stomach, and the alien fell back. Lisa scrambled to get up and run toward Ed. The alien reached out and grabbed at her. It wasn't able to catch her, but its claws lacerated her arm in one violent sweep and sent her bouncing off the wall.

A jet of blood shot from Lisa's arm, and she screamed. Then Ed could swear the creature sniffed the air before it charged back at her.

Ed ran toward the creature, pushing Lisa to the ground as he passed her and thrust himself between her and the alien. Ed opened fire. His first and second shots both landed somewhere in the middle of the alien's face, but the creature didn't slow and was on him before he could squeeze off a third shot.

Ed's momentum met a brick wall as the creature hit him full force and sent him back hard into the ground. Ed's head smacked the concrete with a loud, sickening thwack, which felt like thunder cracking his skull. The alien was on top of him, mouth gnashing, dark, putrid saliva dripping from its jagged rows of teeth and onto Ed's face.

Ed's hand, trapped between himself and the alien's slippery body, still held the pistol. He twisted the gun into the thing's guts and fired three more times until the alien's hot guts bled onto him and it began to go into its death spasms.

Ed pushed the alien off of him and sat up, his head throbbing and woozy.

There was movement in the store, not far away, accompanied by shrieking. They had to get back to the ladder. Now.

He looked up at Lisa, who was aiming at the deli with her shotgun. "Do you have the flares?"

She nodded, holding the bag in the air and stealing a glance at her gushing wound.

Ed said, "Come on, we'll get that cleaned upstairs." He grabbed Lisa by the wrist, then led her toward the ladder. Beneath the hatch, Ed stepped to the side and motioned for Lisa to climb first.

Behind them, a cluster of the aliens poured through the deli and into the stockroom, shrieking and knocking into boxes as they came.

"Go!" Ed yelled.

Lisa scrambled up the ladder, the field pack on her back and shotgun wedged like a sword. The first two aliens dropped to all fours and ran toward them like some kind of demon hell hounds.

Ed fired, but only had one bullet left, which missed its mark.

"Fuck!" he screamed as the aliens raced toward them. They were 40 feet away and closing.

"Go! Go!" Ed screamed as Lisa was only about 10 feet up the ladder. They had to get out of range of the aliens' long limbs.

It sounded like an army behind them. She scrambled faster. Ed raced up the ladder closely behind her as the shrieks and clicks multiplied beneath them. He was about six feet from the ground, and didn't dare to look down. He raced up blindly, praying a large claw wouldn't swipe at his feet and bring him down to his death.

Something clanged on the ladder just beneath his feet, and Ed had to look down. He saw an alien reaching up, swiping at him, missing him by just inches.

Lisa sped up and crawled through the top of the hatch. Just as Ed was within reach of the hatch something sharp stung his left calf. He looked down to see a razor-thin wire with a curved hook on its end fall from his leg. He looked down to see the alien beneath him to which the wire was attached. It had shot the wire from its palms, as if it had extended part of its body out to attack him. The alien raised both of its palms up, taking aim at Ed again as it let out a clicking sound that sounded a hell of a lot like laughter.

Ed screamed, looked back up at the hatch as Lisa looked down at him.

As their eyes met, an image flashed through his mind of her slamming the hatch shut just as the alien's razor wire flesh lassoed him and yanked him down.

Don't you fucking dare!

Lisa leaned down, and Ed wondered what the hell she was doing as he was just inches from the hatch.

No!

Lisa reached down with both hands and yanked him up the rest of the way, surprising him with her strength.

Ed rolled off of her, and got to his feet, offering her a hand up.

She took it, and their eyes met. And for the first time, her eyes softened a bit. "Thank you," she said, "for saving my ass down there."

"Thank you," Ed said, "for saving mine just now. One of them shot some kinda hook and wire out of its palm and cut my leg."

Ed pulled up his pants and examined the injury. It was minor, just a scratch, but stung like hell. He looked up at the others and said, "I don't know if they can all do that, but don't think you're safe just because you're outta reach."

Rojas asked, "Did you get the flares?"

"Sure did," she said, pointing to the field pack on her back.

Ed said, "So, what are we hoping for with these flares?"

"That one of the helicopters on patrol might see it, or maybe one of the vans. If they spot the flare, Base will send out units to investigate. That part's certain. It's just a matter of them seeing the flares."

Ed said, "How many people are at Black Mountain?"

Lisa looked thoughtful for a moment, then said, "Enough."

Ed wondered if they had as many as Black Island.

"And we've got a lot of Guardsmen."

"What are they guarding?" Brent asked.

The question seemed to surprise her. She broke eye contact and looked away, nervously Ed thought, then said, "The world."

"Hey, guys," Billy called from the edge of the roof. "Take a look at this."

They all ran over to Billy and looked down into the empty parking lot. "Where did they all go?" Ed asked.

Billy shrugged. "I dunno." He pointed to the far side of the lot, bordering the gas station on the other side. "There's some over there, but not nearly as many as there were before."

"Are they all inside the store?" Ed asked.

"Some," Billy said. "But then a few minutes ago, they started walking toward the gas station and then out into the woods." Billy pointed out into the darkness.

Ed swallowed. Whatever this was, it wasn't good.

Ed looked down at the headlight beams pulling into the parking lot — not a van or a jeep, or something that Black Mountain Guardsmen might be driving. It was a station wagon, maybe 30 years old.

Everyone on the roof was staring as the wagon came to a full stop and the driver's side door swung open. An old, heavyset man stepped onto the asphalt and cast his eyes across the lot, looking around as if expecting to find someone.

He raised his head and spotted them on the roof. "You okay?" he called, waving.

Lisa cupped her hands around her mouth and yelled, "Get help!"

"What?"

"Get help!" Lisa repeated. "Get to Black Mountain and tell them to come here." She pointed toward the highway. "It's right there, just up Highway 14!"

The man opened his mouth, probably for a question, but a scream fell out instead. The first alien charged toward him as another six came running at him from behind.

Rojas was the first to fire, but a second later, Billy, and Brent joined. Lisa didn't fire her shotgun, and Ed was out of ammo. Ed hoped none of them missed and hit the old man, given how far he was out of ideal range. The creature closest to the old man stopped like a broken toy, then spilled to the asphalt. The old man started running toward the grocery store at the speed of fright as bullets buried themselves in the half dozen aliens behind him.

The crew on the roof made a fresh pile of six, but then hell opened its doors and sent a thin line of aliens into the world. A sea of black spilled from the woods and toward the parking lot.

The old man then did the impossible — stopped running toward the grocery store, and turned back toward the station wagon, quickly closing the distance. He jumped inside the station wagon and slammed the door.

"What the fuck is he doing?" Lisa said.

Rojas said, "The aliens have the perimeter. No way he's getting out of the lot. They're gonna tear that station wagon to shit."

The old man then surprised Ed again as he stepped out of his car and into certain death, slamming the car door behind him. He grinned toward the roof and then held an air horn triumphantly in the air.

The air horn's blast bellowed in the air.

The monsters started shrieking, screaming, and clicking, a few of them falling to the asphalt before scrambling up and running into the woods. To Ed's open mouthed surprise, the remainder of the aliens in the parking lot joined their brothers, fleeing into the dark woods as if their very survival was buried in the leaves.

The old man blasted his air horn again, and the aliens ran faster. Swarms of aliens flooded from the store, running around and past the old man as if terrified of the mighty air horn, as he blasted it on repeat.

The scene was almost comical. Their weapons did nothing to scare the aliens, but this old man and a horn was like some kinda Pied Piper herding them away.

"What the fuck?" Ed said, shaking his head as Lisa whispered the exact thing behind him.

"You've gotta be kidding," Brent said.

Lisa said, "A fucking air horn? They're doing shit all wrong at Mountain."

Rojas laughed, but no funny was inside it.

Ed was still shaking his head as the old man smiled in triumph, standing in the empty parking lot waving his air horn in the air.

"We're coming down!" Ed called. The group went downstairs, one by one, Ed in the middle, Lisa in front and Rojas and Billy pulling rear. The stockroom and store looked as if they'd been hit by a tornado. The only thing left of the other two Guardsmen were chunks of flesh and pools of blood.

Ten feet from the doors screeched a wounded alien stuck underneath a fallen shelf. Rojas fired his rifle into the alien's head, gritting his teeth and squeezing the trigger like he was waiting for a ding and the prize to follow.

They crossed the parking lot, approaching the old man.

They stopped at their black van. The doors had been torn off and the tires punctured by the aliens.

The old man said, "You'll never be driving that thing again," shaking his head. "I'm awfully grateful for you saving me from the demons the first time around, before I got 'round to using the sense the Good Lord gave me." He laughed. "I'd be thrilled to give you a lift, anywhere you need to go."

Lisa, Rojas, and Ed all exchanged glances.

The old man mopped his brow. "That was Black Mountain, you said, right? Just up Highway 14?"

Ed said, "Yeah," looking at the old man, up and down, trying to decide whether he was sharp as a bayonet or wacky as a dime bag.

Lisa stepped in front of Ed and said, "Thanks for the ride, sir. That would be great. And yes, we're headed to Black Mountain."

The old man bowed his head. "Of course, miss. It's my pleasure." He smiled again, beamed actually, then turned and led the group back to his station wagon.

At the car, Lisa turned around, shotgun aimed at Ed. "Everyone in the car. Except Ed."

Lisa pulled the handcuffs from her back pocket as Ed stood, nostrils flaring. "Sorry, but you've gotta come with us."

"I thought we were gonna talk."

"And we will. Back at Black Mountain. I swear, I'll make sure nothing happens to you or Brent. You've got my word."

"Yeah, because your word means so much."

Lisa slid the cuffs on, at least giving him the courtesy of binding his hands in front of him and not behind his back.

Everyone piled inside the wagon, and the old man pulled from the lot, pulling a left onto the first road they hit. He was two blocks out when Brent broke the silence.

"Thanks for the ride, sir," he said. "We're all really grateful." Then, like a good reporter, "What's your name?"

The old man said, "You can call me The Prophet."

NINE

Luca Harding

Luca stepped into what was left of the barn and stared down at Rebecca's dead body.

Her throat was slit, and her eyes stared up at him in a death gaze that would never close unless he fixed her.

He had to try and save Rebecca. And he didn't care what Boricio said.

And Boricio was saying a lot as he followed Luca, stuff about how Luca had to stop already. He'd done what he could. If he tried to save the girl, he would age to death. Luca didn't know why Boricio cared so much what happened to him. It wasn't as if Luca served much of a purpose to their group now other than slowing them down. If saving Rebecca meant death for him, it was worth it.

Luca didn't want to go on like this.

It wasn't just that he was old. He'd seen people older than he looked who seemed to do alright. But Luca was also in pain. Physical and mental.

So, let Boricio run on and on about how he was making a huge mistake. Luca tuned him out. Boricio would get over it. Just like Mary would get over him not bringing Desmond back.

Boricio was pacing three feet behind him as Luca carefully dropped to one knee and put his hands on either side of Rebecca's face. Luca was about to do the thing he didn't quite know how to do, the thing that just sorta happened, when he heard Will speak inside his mind.

"You can't save her," he said. "It will kill you if you try."

Luca tried not to be angry. "I thought you said I could save three people. I only saved two."

"You *did* save three," Will said. "You saved an entire family, Luca. Paola, her Mother, and her unborn sister. That makes three."

Luca gasped. "Why didn't you tell me?" He wanted to cry.

"I didn't know," Will said. "I didn't see it ahead of time, and was out cold when you were on your way to rescue Paola. I couldn't have stopped you."

Will's mind went suddenly silent, and made no noise for a minute, almost like he was dead, but then he came back, almost louder than before.

"I'm sorry," Will said. "I'm sorry about Rebecca. But I have an answer."

"To what?" Luca said.

Will's laugh was too broken to call anything but a bark. When he was finished, he said, "An answer to a question I didn't know we were asking."

Luca was quiet, waiting for Will to continue. When he finally did, his voice was so weak it was barely there. "You can go home, Luca. You can all go back home."

Luca swallowed. "How?"

Could he and Paola and Mary, and the new baby inside Mary, really all be safe together?

"How?" Luca asked. "How do we get back home?"

"There is another you and another me," Will said. "Like us but different. We're on their world. Not our own."

Will's signal was barely there and his color almost gone. "You have to get to Black Island. It's just off New York. And find the other Will. And tell him . . . tell him to look in the moon."

"Look in the moon?" Luca asked.

The silence was so long after Will said the word moon that Luca couldn't keep himself from asking any longer. "Will?"

He called and called with all his mind, but Luca couldn't find Will anywhere.

"Will!" He called again, this time out loud.

Boricio was suddenly in front of him, looking down at Luca cross-eyed.

"Will!" Luca screamed, again in his mind, but with everything he had.

Luca heard the cry of silence.

The man with the lobster tacos was dead.

~

TEN

Charlie Wilkens

Charlie had no time to grieve as his friend's corpse threatened to crush him.

Instead, he pulled the boy toward him, then Adam's body on top of them both, shielding their huddle from the erupting chaos and bloodshed. The truck continued to rock back and forth.

It had to be a terrible nightmare Charlie would wake up from any second.

Nothing in reality ever gets this bad.

Wake up. Wake up. Wake up!

But he wasn't waking up.

The boy cried under Charlie. Charlie put his hand over the boy's mouth and whispered in his ear, "Shh, it's gonna be okay. It's gonna be okay."

Charlie kept repeating his promise, over and over, as if repetition bred truth.

More screams amid the echoes of tearing flesh and deathly gurgles that flooded the death chamber. Charlie squeezed his eyes tight and continued to repeat the phrase over and over.

"It's gonna be okay. It's gonna be okay . . . "

Gunfire erupted outside, and Charlie felt warmth from a thin ray of hope as the truck finally stopped rocking.

The kid squirmed his mouth from Charlie's hand and cried out.

Charlie said, "Shh, wait."

Bodies continued to shuffle, kick, scrape, and scream everywhere around him as Charlie held tight to Adam's body, praying like hell that the monster wouldn't smell his attempt to play dead, then head back over to feast on his flesh.

The shrieking outside stopped, though the screaming, and now shrieking and clicking inside the truck, continued. It seemed as if at least two creatures were inside with them.

Two monsters among a dozen people. It wouldn't be long before the creatures had killed everyone and turned their attention to searching for survivors, and finishing their jobs. Charlie hoped like hell that whoever was outside would open the truck before then. He would take the boy and run, as fast as they could, and never look back.

After what felt like minutes, the gunfire stopped, but the truck stayed sealed. The screaming inside the truck had ceased, replaced by the sound of clicking, shrieking, and dying.

Oh fuck, they killed everyone.

We have to keep quiet.

Charlie's grip on Adam's body slipped, and he let go of the kid's mouth to grab Adam's body to use as a shield. The child's cry brayed loudly over the swiftly fading final seconds of death all around them. One of the creatures shrieked, then advanced toward them in the darkness.

Fuck!

Charlie was torn, not sure if he should stay put, push the kid out to let him die, or scream for help. He was tempted to let the kid die, but shame kept his arms wrapped around the child. He screamed instead, "Help! There's a kid in here alive! Help! Help! Help! Help!"

Charlie started to pound on the wall as both creatures shrieked, and continued toward them.

He had seconds until they were on him.

Something clicked, just inches behind him.

Charlie turned to face the black surrounding him, clenching his hands like claws and bracing for impact.

The door to the truck suddenly rolled toward the sky, slapping the top of the truck with a clank of metal as twilight illuminated the carnage inside the truck, with two creatures looking like some twisted and mutated monstrous set of Siamese twins.

Fresh gunfire erupted into the truck, and the creatures' bodies danced under a hailstorm of bullets. The few bullets that didn't sink into their flesh whizzed by and into the back of the truck, plinking off or sinking into the metal with a series of hollow but nerve-rattling thuds. Charlie pushed himself against the boy as close to the wall and as low as he could get as the boy continued to cry.

When the creatures both finally fell, and the bullets stopped blasting, Charlie called out, "There's two survivors in here. We're human."

"Show yourselves — *slowly*," a man's voice commanded.

Charlie pushed Adam's headless body out of the way and onto the slaughterhouse floor of the truck, swallowing his need to vomit, distinctly aware that puking might make him a target of the three men in black uniforms holding their guns steady on his crawl.

The men were also wearing masks with air breathers on them, like he'd seen in post-apocalyptic movies. Charlie held his hands to the roof and stood, coated in blood which was not his own. The boy stood, too, shaking, looking up at Charlie's face, and then over to the gunmen. His face was streaked red with tears and blood.

Charlie immediately wondered if these were the men who had taken Callie. Then, in a second disgusted moment, wondered if Callie was among the bodies in the truck. He wanted to look, but didn't dare turn his eyes from the men. He still couldn't believe Adam was dead, and the reality made his heart heavy in his throat. He couldn't stand to consider the possibility that Callie was also dead.

"What happened?" one of the men asked.

"I dunno," Charlie shook his head. "We were all asleep inside, and the truck was stopped. Next thing I knew, I heard these things outside, and then all hell broke loose in here. I think one of them got inside the truck somehow."

Charlie didn't dare say the monster he'd seen wasn't just a monster, but half human. It was becoming clear that these things could somehow take over people's bodies, like in those *Aliens* movies. Or maybe they were killing real people and replacing them with pod people like in some *Invasion of the Body Snatchers* bullshit. Either way, Charlie didn't want the men in black having any reason to suspect him, or the boy, of being one of the creatures.

"Did you see what happened to the Guardsmen transporting you?" the man to the far right asked.

"No," Charlie said, looking down at the boy. He was blond, freckle-faced, and wearing a dirty, blue New York Mets T-shirt and jeans, all covered in blood, most of it probably Adam's. He looked terrified, but was staying still and mute.

"Step down," the same man instructed. "Slowly."

"Thank you for saving us," the kid said, his voice hoarse from screaming. He looked up to Charlie, "And thank you, mister."

Charlie smiled, both at the kid's thankfulness and for calling Charlie 'mister.'

Nothing ages you quite like the end of the world.

They stepped out of the truck and onto the road where Charlie saw two matching black vans parked about 100 yards away. He remembered Adam saying that Callie had been thrown into the back of a black van.

How many black vans were rolling around nowadays? The odds were too slim for coincidence. The people had also taken him, Adam, and presumably all the people in the truck. But why?

One of the Guardsmen, as they called themselves, climbed inside the truck and surveyed the damage. He then climbed back outside and turned to the man who'd been doing most of the speaking, "They're all dead, sir, including the two infected."

Infected. So, they know.

"Shit," the man on the right shook his head.

Charlie could now see a small, silver tag on the man's vest which read, *Foster*.

"Test these two," Foster instructed the man who'd been looking in the truck.

That man, whose badge read, *Lennox*, pointed his assault rifle at Charlie and the boy, "Walk."

The boy immediately started walking, while Charlie was inclined to go a bit slower, annoyed that Lennox felt the need to give instruction with the end of a gun. Charlie was getting a bad feeling about whatever was about to happen next.

They walked to the closest of the two vans while the other men, Foster, and the one whose name Charlie had yet to see, followed. Foster opened the back doors, and Charlie felt hope swelling in his chest that he might see Callie sitting in the back. But the van was empty, except for some molded plastic storage units built along the left wall, which also had space for a small desk and a computer built into a console, along with a black stool attached to the floor.

Lennox grabbed a long flashlight, or at least something which looked like a flashlight, with a long, blue bulb running along the side. He instructed the boy to stand with his arms outstretched, "like an eagle." Lennox waved the bulb over the boy like he was checking for hidden weapons beneath the kid's clothes. The light made a slight beep as it went over the kid's left knee, and the other two men, now standing behind them and watching, immediately put their hands to their guns as if they might need them at any second.

What the hell is happening?

Charlie winced, bracing for the worst as the man ran the light over the kid's knee again. This time it didn't beep, which seemed to relax the other Guardsmen.

"OK, he's clean," Lennox said, then pointed to Foster. "You go stand with him."

Clean? This must be some kinda test to see if we're infected with that monster shit.

The boy walked over to Foster and stood beside him, watching as Charlie assumed the position, standing in front of Lennox and spreading his arms.

Lennox began to run the light over Charlie's body, stopping when it began to glow bright, beeping while hovering over his chest.

The Guardsmen grabbed their rifles again, and Charlie swallowed.

Oh God, don't say I'm infected.

Charlie felt a roll in his stomach as Lennox brought the light back up to Charlie's chest. Again it beeped.

Oh shit.

Charlie swallowed.

Infected? I'm gonna become one of those?

"He's infected," Lennox said.

"Put him in the van," Foster said.

The kid cried, "No, he saved me. Please don't hurt him."

Lennox turned his attention from Charlie and onto the kid to see how the scene played out, as if Foster might change his mind if the kid gave a compelling argument to spare Charlie any harm.

"We're not going to hurt him," Foster reassured, "We're gonna help him. We're going to save him. How would you like to join him in the van?"

The kid stared at Foster, nervous, and probably thinking that maybe Charlie would go *Incredible Hulk* while in the van.

"Can't I ride with you guys?"

"We're all going to ride together," Foster said. "Go ahead."

The boy seemed uncertain, but then started toward the van.

He'd gotten maybe six steps when Foster raised his gun and shot the kid in the head.

The child fell face first onto the road, and Charlie screamed, "No!"

How can they shoot the kid? He wasn't even infected. What the hell?!

"You fuckers!" Charlie screamed, wanting to run at Foster, and smash his face in.

Lennox put a gun to Charlie's head, stopped him in his tracks, and shoved him toward the second black van.

"Time to take a ride," the man said, marching Charlie forward.

"Where are we going?" Charlie asked.

"Black Mountain," the man said. "And don't give me an excuse to shoot you in the head."

∽

ELEVEN

Other Luca

Black Island Research Facility
    Level 7
    July 2011
    THREE MONTHS BEFORE THE EVENT …

LUCA LOOKED DOWN at his hands on the table, not wanting to meet the mirrors.

They made him uncomfortable. It was like a funhouse without the fun. Mirrors surrounded the room, except for the metal door in the middle. No matter where he turned his head, his eyes stared back. Luca could feel the people behind the mirrors staring back. He could hear some of their thoughts, too.

Today was the big day, the day everyone had been waiting for. Today was the day of the test. Luca knew it was important, but he didn't know why. His dad never really said, even when Luca asked. He was sure the test was why they were back in the underground room on Black Island, where he'd come for the surgery to remove his tumor.

Of all the people on the other side of the mirror, Luca felt his dad most, along with his dad's colors. His dad was usually the color blue. Sometimes his blue was so light it was almost white. That was because his dad never really seemed like he was afraid of anything. That was probably why he was never mad. Not like Luca's brother, Boricio.

Boricio was always nice to Luca. Actually, Boricio was always nice to everyone, but he still wore the color red, almost always and no matter what. At least as long as Luca had been seeing the colors, since he woke up from his surgery.

Today, his dad's blue was gone, and he was somewhere in between yellow and green. Yellow and green were nervous, and that made Luca a little scared.

Luca didn't fear many things, but disappointing his dad was definitely one of them. His adopted father had done so much for him, the thought that Luca might let him down was terrible. *Scary.*

Luca could feel everyone breathing faster as the steel door opened and the man named Mr. Sullivan came into the room.

He smiled at Luca, and Luca smiled back. Mr. Sullivan sat in the chair opposite Luca at the table and said, "Good morning, Luca. How are you today?"

Mr. Sullivan was wearing sky-blue. He didn't seem nervous at all. "I'm great," Luca said.

"Are you scared?"

Luca shook his head. "Nope. I'm not scared."

"Are you nervous?"

Luca nodded. "A little."

Mr. Sullivan smiled, then laughed. "Have you been seeing any sad spiders?"

Luca laughed, too. His dad made up a game when Luca was first adopted. Whenever Luca was sad, his dad would tell him not to let the sad spiders start crawling on his body, then he would reach down and scoop the invisible creatures from Luca's skin and throw them on the floor and stomp on them with a giant, angry smile. Lately, Luca had been having bad dreams. His dad, and some of the other men in white coats, had asked Luca to draw pictures of his dreams. Luca drew only two kinds of pictures: sad spiders or Terrible Scary — the place that held all the bad stuff that had ever happened to Luca, like when his first family died.

Mr. Sullivan said the tests were supposed to help make the "sad spiders" and "Terrible Scary" go away forever.

They had done practice versions of the test before, but this one was more serious. The real thing, his dad said.

Mr. Sullivan held a card in the air, blank side facing Luca, then asked him what was on the other side. Luca guessed correctly each time.

A spaceship.

A carton of milk.

Two girls skipping rope.

Two boys playing video games.

A happy family having a picnic.

"Great job, Luca. Keep going," Mr. Sullivan said.

Luca smiled, feeling proud as his dad's color softened from green and yellow to a baby-blue on the other side of the mirror. His dad was happy, and that color was closer to proud.

His dad was the first person to notice how Luca could sometimes read feelings, and sometimes even thoughts. He had always been good at it, since before he even realized it was something special, and not a thing most people could do. Before the operation, Luca could only do it sometimes, and not necessarily when he wanted. Now he was great at it, and could figure out feelings and see stuff on the other side of cards whenever he tried.

It was like learning to ride his bike. At first, it had been super-hard and Luca kept falling. One time when he was first learning, Luca fell off the bike and onto the sharp side of a rock. It tore his knee open, and so much blood spilled out, his dad had a hard time calming him. His colors went from blue to almost red, while Boricio's went from red to almost blue as he tried to make jokes to keep Luca laughing.

Boricio had said, "Don't let fear inside your house, Luca." He tapped the side of his head. "That's valuable real estate, and fear will try to squat without paying." He shook his head. "Don't let him." Boricio dropped his voice to a whisper. "Fear's a real bad guy, you know. A total jerk. And manipulative. The second he moves in, he's gonna try to get you to live a boring life. So, you never wanna let him in. You with me so far?" He winked at Luca.

Luca winked back and nodded. He was always with Boricio.

"He'll keep knocking on your door, hoping you're home, so you'll want to be extra quiet and wait until he leaves. Fortunately for us brave guys," Boricio pointed at his chest, "fear's not patient, and he'll leave after a while. Once he's gone, there's nothing to worry about." Boricio slapped Luca on the back. "Now get back on that bike and kick his ass out!"

Boricio always had a way of making Luca feel safe. Luca climbed on his bike and rode it to the corner without falling. He hadn't fallen since.

Now Luca was great at riding his bike, just like he was great at doing all the stuff inside his mind.

Luca wasn't sure what they did to him, but it had something to do with his blood. He'd picked up enough on the thoughts of his dad and Boricio to know that the doctors had used some kind of special serum on him. Something super-special, and secret. He'd also figured out that his dad was mad at Boricio for telling the doctors to do it. But he didn't seem so mad — or scared — these days as he had been at first.

Whatever they did, it made Luca feel better than ever before. Stronger. Smarter. Well, not smarter, but his thoughts seemed more together, and he could remember lots more stuff easily. Things that hadn't made sense to Luca before finally had their colors right. Things and people. Suddenly, and with ease, he could see the patterns in the world around him, and all the many things no one else could.

Since the surgery, people seemed incapable of hiding their thoughts from Luca. Even when he didn't want to hear them. His dad was able to do the same thing, had been able to for a long time, but not quite like Luca was able to, his dad had said.

Now, Luca was learning to do other stuff. Stuff Luca didn't understand. That's what the tests and the room were for, and what all the people behind the mirror were waiting to see.

Mr. Sullivan finished with the card part of the test and smiled. Luca could see the man's colors start to change as his heartbeat gathered speed.

This was the part of the test he really wanted to see, the part everyone behind the mirror cared about.

Everyone already knew Luca could guess the spaceship and the carton of milk and the two girls skipping rope. Now they wanted to see the new stuff.

Mr. Sullivan moved the stack of cards to the right, then traded them for a small, metal box, which he set in the palm of his hand. Mr. Sullivan looked up at Luca as he lifted the lid of the box, smiled, and drew a small, silver ball from the inside.

Mr. Sullivan held the ball in the palm of his hand, then closed the lid of the box, moved it to the corner of the table just beside the cards, and turned his full attention to Luca. "Do you know what to do with this?" he asked.

Luca looked at Mr. Sullivan, then down at the ball. He said, "You want me to see if I can move it by using my mind."

Dr. Sullivan smiled. "That's right, Luca," he said. "Do you think you can do that?"

Luca smiled because he knew he could. He'd already figured that out on his own a week ago.

He narrowed his eyes in concentration, staring at the ball

for several seconds before it lifted into the air and hovered three inches above Mr. Sullivan's open palm.

Mr. Sullivan beamed. Luca couldn't feel his dad behind the mirror at the moment, but he knew he must be proud of him, just like Mr. Sullivan.

"Can you lift it higher?"

Luca smiled because he knew he could.

He narrowed his eyes in concentration again. Two seconds later, the ball was floating nearly a foot above Mr. Sullivan's palm.

The man smiled wider, still holding his palm steady beneath the hovering ball. "Is that all?"

Luca shook his head, smiling so wide his face nearly split into a laugh. He narrowed his eyes further, focusing. The ball stopped floating, then suddenly shot across the room in a zig zag, across the room and back, up and down from ceiling to floor, then across the room in several wide circles before returning to its soft and silent spin above the man's palm.

Luca then let the ball drop into Mr. Sullivan's hand.

Mr. Sullivan kept his face straight, but Luca could see his colors and he was very, very happy. Probably like his dad was on the other side of the mirror, even though Luca still couldn't feel him.

Luca laughed and clapped. His giddy "YAY!" screaming on repeat was enough to push the serious Mr. Sullivan into a bottomless laugh.

"That's enough for now, Luca," he finally said, catching his breath. "Thank you."

"Did I pass?" Luca said.

Mr. Sullivan smiled again, then said, "Your dad will tell you how you did."

Mr. Sullivan left Luca's room and closed the door behind him. Ten minutes later, Luca's dad came in.

"We're going home?" Luca said, grinning.

His dad nodded, but looked upset. Luca couldn't read him, and felt suddenly confused.

"Is everything okay?" Luca asked.

His smile was thin. Luca's dad said, "Let's go home and get you something to eat. We'll talk then, okay, Captain?"

Luca said okay, even though his dad only called him Captain when he was trying to get him to do something he didn't want to do, or had to tell him something Luca didn't want to hear.

THEY QUIETLY WALKED to their house on the island. Luca spent most of the walk hoping Boricio would be there when they got home, though Luca knew he probably wouldn't be. The walk took 10 minutes. One minute after that and Luca knew Boricio wasn't home. Luca went to the bathroom, then washed his hands, and went into the kitchen, where he sat on his side of the bar and watched his dad chop tomatoes and garlic.

Luca sat in silence until the sizzle of garlic in olive oil filled the kitchen and made his tummy growl loud enough for his dad to hear. His dad turned to him, almost laughing. "Hungry?" he said, smiling.

Luca nodded. He wished Boricio was home, but was happy to see his dad almost laugh.

"Dad," Luca said. "Why are you mad at me?"

His father was facing the stove, back to Luca. He flicked off the burner, then turned to his son. He walked to the bar and put his hands around Luca's waist, then lifted him from the barstool, set his bare feet on the hardwood floor, and dropped to one knee to look him in the eye.

Both of his dad's eyes were welling with tears when he said, "I'm not mad, son. I'm scared."

"Why?"

"I don't know exactly," he shook his head, his colors agreeing that the words from his mouth were true. "I just want to make sure you're okay. You did great today, and I don't want you to think for a second that I'm not proud of you, because I am." His dad took a moment to think, then said, "Sometimes, people are so awesome that everyone in the world wants to share them. You might be that awesome. And if that's true, I'm not ready to share you."

The colors weren't all the way true, but they were mostly there. Luca figured his dad was trying to explain one of those grownup things where he could only use most of the color. Luca tried to see beyond the words his dad was saying, and see the ones he was thinking. However, his dad was good at keeping Luca out of his head when he wanted to.

His dad pulled him into a giant hug, the kind Luca liked best, then said, "How are you, Luca? That's the most important thing to me. How are you feeling right now?"

Luca thought about it, then told the truth. "I've never felt better in my life."

Will broke into a laugh, some of it funny and some of it sad, but almost all of it white like relief.

~

NIGHTTIME ...

LUCA THRASHED IN HIS BED, trying to wake up, prisoner of the Terrible Scary like he sometimes was in his sleep.

Luca could see the scary man, the Man in the Middle, the man who used to be there before Mom and Dad and Anna died in the car accident. He had disappeared for a bit, not long enough to make Luca forget, but enough to let him believe he might not come back.

The Man in the Middle was after Luca, laughing and

cursing and growling like a dog, saying all the bad words he liked to say, the words that made Luca's stomach sick, pulling him by his hair and dragging Luca kicking and screaming into the depths of the Terrible Scary.

Luca screamed, trying to wake up, wanting to force himself back into the bright light and true colors of his bedroom.

The scream died in his throat as he opened his eyes.

Luca wanted Boricio. Boricio, even more than his dad, would be able to help him feel safe from the Man in the Middle. Would teach him how to kick the Man in the Middle out of his dreams.

When Luca opened his eyes, he realized he wasn't in bed, but standing on carpet in his bedroom, lit by the blue nightlight on his dresser.

But he didn't have any carpet in his bedroom, only hardwood floor. And the dresser wasn't his dresser. At least not anymore. It was his old dresser — the one he had in California, before the accident that killed his family.

He also didn't have any Ninjago Legos even though he had been wanting them forever. The Lego table that wasn't his had them in piles. Luca walked to the table, dropped to both knees, and started picking up the Ninjagos one by one, examining each before setting each back down, trying to figure out whether his memories of putting them together were actually his.

No, they weren't.

Except they sort of were.

Like everything in the room. This was his old room, and he was somehow standing in it.

This must be another weird dream.

Luca stood from the table and looked around the rest of the bedroom, his heart freezing in his chest at the sight of the lumped covers on the bed, rising and falling under the breath of the sleeping child.

Luca crept toward the sleeping boy, then peeled the blanket from his face, knowing what he'd see before he did: himself.

No. This is impossible. It has to be a dream.

Luca wanted to shake the other Luca awake and start asking him questions, but then he spotted something on the nightstand next to the bed. A blue, wood-framed photo that had the word *Family* written in white, cartoonish letters.

He picked up the picture, tears welling inside him.

Luca was in the picture, looking the same age as he did in this year's school picture, but Mom and Dad and Anna were standing behind him, instead of being dead. Luca started to cry, remembering the accident.

Mom told him to buckle his safety belt, but he didn't want to. He kept taking it on and off and on and off. It was off when the car swerved off the road and rolled over and over. Luca was thrown from the car, through the front window, screaming. He might have been out for a minute, maybe more. But when he went back for his mom and dad and Anna, the whole car got swallowed by fire.

Luca looked at his sister, smiling in the photo. It had been forever since he remembered her smiling. And suddenly he missed Anna the most. He left the sleeping Luca alone, then went into Anna's bedroom, crying because she was actually there.

Luca crept to her bedside, then reached out to touch her hair. Her eyes shot open, and a surprised half smile appeared on her face.

"Luca?"

Before he could answer, Luca was gone.

A second later, Luca found himself standing in the middle of his dad's bedroom. His dad had been reading his iPad, the soft-blue light illuminating his face in the otherwise dark room.

The iPad fell from his dad's hands as his father leapt from

the bed. "Oh my God, Luca!" he yelled. "How in the world did you do that?"

That's when Luca realized it hadn't been a dream. He'd gone to another world.

TO BE CONTINUED ...

Episode 14

(SECOND EPISODE OF SEASON THREE)

"We Are Accidents Waiting To Happen"

TWELVE

Boricio Bishop

Other Earth
  Paddock Island, New York
  Sunday July 10, 2011
  Morning
  FOUR MONTHS BEFORE THE EVENT ...

BORICIO WOKE from the dark emptiness relieved to hear the sound of the ferry's horn braying in the distance. It was either the ferry that shuttled people between Paddock Island and the mainland, or between Paddock and Black Islands. Which one didn't matter, as either of them served as a sweet beacon, letting him know that the death and destruction he'd emerged from had only been yet another nightmare.

He was back in the real world, lying in the warm layers of blankets and comforters of Rose's bed, unable to wipe the stupid smile from his face. Today was gonna be the day.

It was finally here, the day Boricio had been anticipating for more than a month, though in a way, he had been waiting since around six seconds after he first saw Rose, as she was wiping cheese from the side of her cheek before shoving another fork full of dripping omelet into her mouth.

She had been eating alone, just like Boricio, sitting two small tables away, overlooking the C-shaped harbor where all the Richie Riches docked their fancy pants yachts.

The yachts matched the menu, and while Boricio thought the prices at Schooner or Later were big-ticket ridiculous, the army of taste buds in his mouth was ready to declare war on his brain if he dared to claim the meal wasn't worthy.

The mystery woman must have thought the same thing since Boricio had seen her sitting and wiping cheese from her face three Sundays in a row, always two tables away.

Something about her spoke to Boricio in a whisper. Her whisper was soothing, worming its way not into his head, but his heart, making Boricio long for more of what he'd never really had.

Boricio had been with more than his fair share of women, yet those encounters were a result of the sum of his good looks and natural charm; thin and brittle connections that left him disconnected and cold. While he never doubted the existence of true love, Boricio had never felt the warmth of its fire. Something about the woman wiping cheese from her cheek, two tables away each Sunday, made Boricio believe true love could happen to him, and that he, too, could find the happy ending beneath true love's clear, blue sky.

In the three or four months before Boricio first saw her sitting just two tables away, he had been living with an edge of discomfort coating his sanity like a layer of rust. This perfect stranger somehow, and quite suddenly, stirred a longing inside him, a longing that promised to soothe the growing shadows inside within.

Boricio had no idea how which feelings were in his head, and which were the result of reality. He didn't even believe in love at first sight — a product of romance novels and people yearning for something more than their boring, stale relationships — yet he couldn't ignore how from the moment he saw her, the rest of the world seemed to have vanished like the wispy plumes of a dying fire. The vague promise of the amazing unknown was enough to push Boricio to his feet and move him to her table.

"Acapulco?" Boricio asked, pointing at a chunk of avocado laying beside a thin wedge of tomato and a quickly disappearing pile of egg; the gravesite of an omelet the waitress had set on her table around four or five minutes prior.

She looked up at Boricio, smiling. "It's the best omelet on the menu."

The music of her reply made him long to hear more of her song.

Boricio sat. "You're right," he said. "The Acapulco is the best omelet on the menu, no argument." He shook his head, almost playfully. "But I never order from the menu."

Boricio volleyed a smile; she batted it back. He said, "The kitchen will make anything you ask; you just have to know what you want."

The girl chewed on her lip, looking up at Boricio with interested eyes. He wanted more, maybe everything she had. For a moment, she looked as though she wanted him, too. "And what do you ask for?"

Boricio laughed, thrilled she was asking. "Are you sure you're ready?"

She smiled. "Why wouldn't I be? It's not nuclear is it?"

Boricio smiled as if looking right into the center of a secret, then surprised himself by saying, "Boricio always knows what he loves." He leaned across the table. "And the omelet I'm about to describe is enough to teach your tongue at least 10 new ways to savor."

"Boricio?" she laughed, almost as if she couldn't help it. "Is that your name?"

Boricio nodded. "Nice to meet you," he said, extending his hand.

"I'm Rose." She took his hand. It felt warm and sun kissed in his. "Tell me, Boricio, do you always talk about yourself in the third person?" she asked with a laugh.

Boricio returned the laugh. "Actually, I've never done that before in my life. I'm not even sure where it came from, but it came out before my mouth could stop moving." He should have been nervous, but something about Rose made Boricio bold. He said, "Have I ruined my chances?"

"Well, I guess that depends on what you're hoping to get!" She laughed, bringing a fresh sip of coffee to her lips. "You do realize that '10 new ways to savor' might be overselling it a bit?"

Boricio shook his head. "Well, that sounds like the testimony of someone who's never had the pleasure of tasting the Boricio Breakfast Bomb."

"Ha, is that what it's called?"

"Yup," he nodded, "and it's had the name for a good five and a half seconds. Seven now," he added.

"Okay, let's hear it. The suspense is killing me." Rose leaned back in her chair and smiled, then brought more coffee to her open mouth.

"Well," Boricio said, eyebrows raised in display. "I've gotta warn you: This recipe is as definite as the details on any designer gown. And," he added with a conspiratorial smile, "Schooner or Later is the *only* place you can get it, at least on all of Paddock Island. I'm only saying that to warn you that I might be setting you up for a *Matrix Revolutions* level of disappointment."

Rose spit coffee through her laughter, passing the first page of Boricio's geek test. She said, "As long as it's better than *Sucker Punch*, I think we're good."

Boricio wanted more.

"So," he said. "Does that mean you're prepared to accept the risk?"

"I am," she nodded, "as long as you realize that reality is the enemy of expectation."

"Okay then," he nodded, laughing, four minutes into their conversation and already feeling four feet from a fireplace. "Making the perfect Boricio Breakfast Bomb means starting with the right herbs, and when I say herbs I don't mean the stuff they sprinkle on the white bread at Applebee's." He smiled. "I mean the genuine stuff: tarragon, chervil, coriander, etc. And that last one right there is the secret, the one that makes this Boricio Breakfast Bomb go nuclear," he smiled wider. "Now, no one thinks of coriander as a fine herb, but that's their mistake. I'm telling you, it's coriander that gives the bees their wiry, little knees." He narrowed his eyes at Rose. "Please tell me you know what coriander is?"

"Of course," she said. "Life without curry is like watching *Sucker Punch* on repeat."

"Well, in that case, I think you're gonna dig what I'm about to deliver." He laughed.

"I'm waiting for you to prove it."

Boricio continued. "You'll also need butter — real butter not that fake sh . . . crap — and you'll have to ask your waiter because they're gonna want to use oil in the kitchen. And while there's nothing wrong with oil, oil isn't butter. Now you don't need a lot." He paused, then said, "It's like a kiss, start right, and everything that follows is infinitely better."

Boricio luxuriated in the blush of Rose's cheeks as she shifted in her seat.

"Besides," he said, "how can you not love the sound and smell of butter in the pan?"

"It's impossible," she said. "But I can't hear or smell it all the way out here, so the omelet has to be damned good. So far, it sounds like an herb omelet with butter. So, what makes it so bombtastic?"

"Well," Boricio said, "that's because we've not yet discussed the dairy. There's no water allowed near a perfect omelet, which is why the Boricio Breakfast Bomb needs milk or cream. Fortunately, Schooner or Later makes their omelets with milk anyway, so you don't have to ask." Boricio leaned across the table. "Now here's the part that's gonna blow your mind, and why Schooner is the only place on Paddock where you can order this omelet."

"I'm ready," she said. "Blow my mind."

Boricio laughed. "You've gotta use mizithra cheese."

"Mizithra?" she cried. "That's too salty. And it would taste horrible with coriander. Blech!"

Boricio shook his head. "Nope," he said. "It's a perfect blend. It's what the gods would eat if they ever ate breakfast."

Rose laughed, shaking her head furiously back and forth. "Sorry, but that sounds terrible. I feel like *I've been* sucker punched."

"Have I ever lied to you before?"

"No," she said. "Not that I know of. But I've only had five minutes to catch you red-handed."

Boricio wanted more of her, maybe more than he'd ever wanted anything else. He wanted to give her a lifetime to catch him red-handed in all the lies he would never dare tell her. Boricio's desire made him bold. "Promise you'll try it," he said.

She wrinkled her nose and said, "Okay, I promise I'll try the *Boricio Breakfast Bomb*. Someday."

Boricio waited through three seconds where he almost didn't unleash his heart, but swallowed and said, "How about I make it for you? I make it even better than Schooner."

"If you make it better than they do," she said, "then why come here?"

"Because otherwise I'd never have had the chance to meet you."

Boricio was as surprised to hear himself say *Because otherwise I'd never have had the chance to meet you* as he had been to hear himself speak in the third person.

Boricio ate at Schooner or Later because he liked to leave the house on Sunday morning, and get away from Black Island, where he stayed rent-free in one of the small furnished houses provided by the Guardsmen who paid his salary. Paddock was a short ferry ride, the place was nice, and he loved to chew his food while staring out at the water.

Rose knew the truth by the following Sunday, and had lived it with Boricio each Sunday since. Now, several months later, the day Boricio was waiting for had finally arrived.

He had been planning the morning for a month. Boricio was taking a short vacation, and wasn't scheduled to be back at Black Island for the next five days. Rose had delivered the final pages of her manuscript the week before and had little on her plate until she started her next novel in November. They would spend five days together, uninterrupted, and after breakfast, they could spend them celebrating their engagement.

Boricio rolled to Rose's side of the bed, empty but warm. She was probably making coffee. He was about to yell for her to stop, because Boricio had wanted to wake up nice and slow and sleepy with her, lying in the coziness of freshly laundered sheets for a while. They could caffeinate themselves later.

Boricio knew things wouldn't go quite according to plan when he heard what had to be the sound of Rose weeping in the bathroom. He tore off the sheets, leapt from the bed, and then sprinted down the hallway and burst into the bathroom.

"You okay, baby?"

Rose nodded, shook her head, then nodded again. Boricio looked down at the thin strip of white plastic in her hand, then at the blue line dividing the middle.

Oh. . . Wow.

He had to hide his surprise, lest it come off wrong, and said, "It's okay, baby," as he pulled her body against his.

She mashed her face against his chest as her soft cry fell into a full sob. Boricio swallowed on repeat to keep his tongue in his mouth. His words had to be perfect. Rose was too fragile, shuddering against him as her swirling emotions were licked by uncertainty's fire.

They had barely grazed through the one or two conversations they'd had about having children. Their relationship was still young, even though they both considered their union inevitable. Boricio was certain Rose felt the same as he did — they would spend the rest of their lives together. But she'd also feared having kids and how it would change things, as it had for so many people she knew.

For the first time in her life she was truly happy. Everything had lined up — her career, her finances, and her relationship — in perfect harmony. Having a child would disrupt that harmony. The only question was, to what extent?

As Rose held the piece of plastic in her hands, Boricio imagined all the thoughts racing through her mind that they'd made a horrible mistake — that they'd done something wrong, something to jeopardize their perfect future by accelerating their present.

Life was hard enough without having someone kick you from the inside, but there was something remarkable about creating something from nothing. Becoming a parent turned humans to gods. Though Boricio had harbored fears, they melted away seeing Rose holding the strip. Maybe he wouldn't be perfect, but he wouldn't be the monster his father had been.

This was a blessing.

And there was no better time to propose, than the day when you found out you were about to spend the rest of your life being a father.

Rose was scared. Maybe terrified. Boricio had to be careful, especially since a big part of her fear was likely his fault. He had always been evasive when their conversation drifted toward his childhood, the vicious years before Will. He had never said anything specific, but Rose was sharp, smart enough to see that Boricio's early life had bled far outside the lines of a healthy childhood, and she had likely hypothesized at the many marred hues that colored Boricio's personal history.

His life with Will had been mostly blue skies, but life before that was dark — spilled ink that still blotted his dreams with repellent memories of monsters that no amount of therapy, pills, or hugs could ever hope to erase.

Boricio owed it to Rose to open the drapes on his past, if for no other reason than to give her the truth of who he was. True love deserved nothing less, just not today. Today was about their future, not his past.

Boricio continued to stroke her hair as Rose cried herself to a sputtering shudder. He pulled her deeper into his arms, then pushed her slightly away, crouching a third of the way to the floor so their eyes aligned.

"Baby," he said. "I've never lied to you, right?"

She nodded her head.

"Do dogs have three eyelids?"

Rose nodded.

"Does the human brain generate enough power to light a light bulb?"

She nodded again.

"Does mizithra with coriander kick unholy ass?"

She laughed then cracked out a half broken, "Yes."

Boricio squeezed her hands inside of his. "This is the best news ever. Especially this morning. So, thank you." He smiled. "This is great for us, I promise. Right now, I'm the happiest I've ever been in my life. And I'll stay that way until this afternoon, and then I'll be even happier."

Boricio took Rose by the hand, then led her to the bedroom. He stopped in front of the bed, turned back toward her, then lifted her hands over her head.

Boricio pulled her T-shirt from her body, and while he was always especially attentive to her breasts — he called them her rosebuds — he quickly passed them after a light kiss, dropping to his knees and burying his face in her belly. His lips lingered at her button, then he finally stood, pushed her back to the bed, and peeled her pink panties down her legs and past her ankles.

Boricio showed Rose how happy he was until they both fell asleep.

THEY WOKE up nearly two hours later, closer to lunch than breakfast. Boricio's arms were still wrapped around Rose. He lightly squeezed her to see if she was awake.

"How was your rest?" she said, turning toward him.

"Amazing, you?"

"I never really fell asleep. I was thinking instead."

Boricio brushed the side of her cheek. "Me, too," he said. "I was just keeping my thoughts in the middle of my snores."

"You mean your thunder," she laughed.

Boricio lightly slapped her cheek, a tickle really, then climbed over her body, hopped from the bed, held out his hand, and pulled her from bed. They kissed again before heading into the hall, then into the bathroom for a quick shower together.

Boricio dried off, then threw on a pair of jeans and a black tee. He grabbed the step-stool from the kitchen while Rose finished applying her makeup, then, as quietly as he could, he crept back into the bedroom, over to the closet, then up on the ladder. Boricio reached for the small, black box shoved all the way at the back of the top shelf.

He lifted the lid, smiled at the ring, then slipped the box inside his pocket.

Boricio returned the stool to the kitchen, then poured a tall glass of orange juice for them to share. She was suddenly in the kitchen, smiling. "You seem so mysterious this morning," she said.

"No mystery," Boricio said. "That's just change you're sniffing. And I think you're the one who started the morning getting all Darwinian on me." He opened the door, waited for her to step out, then followed and closed the door behind him. "I always figured that if you don't like something, it's your job to change it," he said. "And if you can't change it, well then you have to at least change the way you think about it. But since the day I met you, Rose, I haven't wanted to change a thing about my life, or any of the ways I think about it. But this change is good. This change is great."

Boricio opened the door to her Mini Cooper and kissed her softly. Rose kissed him back hard, like she wanted to pull Boricio back into the bedroom. He wanted that, too, but he wanted breakfast and all that would come after even more.

The drive was mostly silent — a sky of sunshine fine with Boricio. The flat of his foot kept slapping the pedal, coasting through the empty four-way stops, and quickly closing the short distance to Schooner or Later, where he would ask Rose if he could watch her wipe cheese from her lips every Sunday for the rest of their forevers.

Quiet was best — it gave Boricio time to reflect, and perhaps even perfect his proposal. He thought about how grateful he was to have someone like Rose calming the grizzly that had been waking inside him, the same bear who had been sleeping at the mouth of Boricio's cave as long as he could remember. Just when Boricio thought the old monster was finally ready to open its eyes, stretch its arms in a yawn, then amble outside the cave, Rose came along to wave it back inside.

Boricio had spent the last month obsessed with the idea of marrying Rose. She would probably want a wedding, maybe invite her sister, Mary, from Missouri. Boricio would be happy to go to the courthouse on Tuesday, since he still wanted to spend Monday in bed.

Boricio had even started looking for a house. They were comfortable in Rose's place, where Boricio had been staying recently — though he still kept the place on Black Island for nights he worked late — but if they were going to raise a family, they'd need a bigger place, something Boricio had considered a few weeks before he had seen the blue line neatly dividing the center of the white plastic.

Boricio found a pair of houses that would be perfect for the two, and now three, of them. Both lay in Paddock Island's interior, where houses were much cheaper, though Boricio thought buying a house somewhere else, off the island, would be better. Boricio's work at Black Island wouldn't last forever, and Rose could write anywhere in the world, though she preferred to live near the water. But the US of A was a mighty big place, with several long coastlines to choose from. Besides, who said they had to stay in America? Boricio would live anywhere with Rose, wet or dry; red, white, and blue, or any color of the rainbow.

Only one dark cloud sat in the middle of Boricio's otherwise perfect blue sky. But it was ink-black, and held every memory of his monster father, the demon who murdered his childhood, then flooded it with ghosts who never stopped haunting.

The ghosts were still there; they lived in the cave with the bear. But they were afraid of the air around Rose, which was one of the million reasons Boricio wanted to draw his breath beside her. On the short drive to Schooner, those wretched memories were only a flutter, flickering through his mind like the final shot in a fading reel.

He would be a great father. All Boricio had to do was be the opposite from the heap of unspeakable who had been his father. Boricio wouldn't tell his son to be a man; he would show him how to do it. And if he had a girl, well then, he'd spend the rest of his life loving his junior Rosebud more than any other girl in the world, except for her mommy.

Schooner or Later was one block away, nestled between calm water and the rest of Boricio's life. He looked over at Rose and wondered what she was thinking and if she had any idea what was going to happen, any clue about what he'd been planning.

"We're going to Schooner or Later?" She said as she realized where their route was taking them, then shook her head. "I thought we were doing something different this morning. A surprise? I'm not even sure I'm hungry."

"That's okay," Boricio said. "Order something sweet to pick at, while I mow on the mizithra missiles in my breakfast bomb."

Rose took off her seat belt, then turned to Boricio.

Boricio turned to meet her gaze and caught the widest smile he had ever seen.

She *knew*, and something was so beautiful in her knowing, Boricio couldn't break her stare. She held his gaze and wouldn't release. Boricio surrendered inside it.

By the time Boricio realized he was driving off the road, Rose's Mini Cooper was crashing through the first table, flying half way across Schooner's relatively small Patio. The first table was empty, but the second wasn't.

Boricio swung the steering wheel hard to the right, narrowly missing a pair of brunchers sharing a waffle before crashing through the wood and lattice separating Schooner from the water.

The Mini Cooper landed on a boat, then tore into the cabin's interior. Boricio looked to his right as Rose was thrown hard from her seat. Her head smacked the dashboard, which launched a fat chunk of blood from her throat onto the windshield.

Another jolt lurched the car back then forward and sent a piece of the boat crashing through the glass. Boricio felt a sharp pain stab his left eye and hot blood gushing down his cheek.

He turned to look at Rose — to see if she was okay — but the crunch of metal, shatter of glass, and water rushing into the cabin around him sent the world to black before he could see her.

~

THIRTEEN

Charlie Wilkens

Black Mountain, Georgia
  March 2012
  FIVE MONTHS AFTER THE EVENT …

CHARLIE WOKE naked in a glass cell, without any memory of falling asleep. He was lying on a mattress, with no blanket or sheets. One pillow, no case.

The cold floor was gray concrete, just like the ceiling and the one wall without windows. The ceiling wore a blanket of ominous-looking holes, and a metal toilet sat in the far corner of the 20 by 20 cell, though it offered no walls for privacy. A metal band separated the longest width of glass at a door with no knob. Above the door, a speaker.

The other side of the glass offered nothing but darkness. Bright lights burned in a ring around his ceiling, turning the three windowed walls into mirrors reflecting the truth — Charlie was a caged animal on full display for his unseen watchers.

Charlie sat on the bed, placing the pillow over his crotch. He'd never felt particularly comfortable about the size of his penis, particularly when flaccid, where it seemed more like a turtle head peeking from a shell than any sort of useable cock. He wanted to get up and run, but his birthday suit made him vulnerable enough to feel almost grateful for waiting.

How did I get here? Where am I?

He remembered what the men in black had said after waving the blue light over him.

Infected.

He looked down at his arms and chest, pale beneath the harsh lights above. He wasn't sure what the signs of infection were, but he felt no different. And his skin was its normal pasty shade of pale.

They must have it wrong. Besides, when would he have been infected? *How* would he have been infected?

Charlie thought back to the monstrosity in the back of the truck. Then to the bald fucker who had tracked him and Adam to Boricio's compound, the one who had turned monster. Charlie didn't want to become one of those things. He would rather die.

They had to be making a mistake.

Yes, that's it. They made an error. Like when the light beeped on the kid, then it didn't. I need another test.

I feel perfectly fine.

Thinking of the kid, and how they'd shot him even though he wasn't infected, sent a chill through Charlie's already icy body.

What kind of fuckers do that? What do they want? Are they looking for infected people, and fuck the rest? And if so, why? They starting a zoo? Or some kinda freak show carnival?

And if these are the same people who took Callie, is she infected, too? Is she in a cell just like me?

As Charlie sat on the bed with the pillow still covering his lap, certainty spread through his body. He was being watched.

Though he couldn't see anything beyond his reflection, Charlie was suddenly certain that someone was standing on the other side of the glass; he could feel them as sure as he felt the flow of cold air creating goose bumps across his naked flesh.

He looked down, feeling even more exposed, shifted on the bed, then stared up at the holes in the ceiling again, wondering at their purpose.

Is that where the air is flowing from? No, that's the black grid above the toilet. So, what are the holes for? Gas, like the Nazis used to gas the Jews in World War II?

Movement pulled Charlie's eyes to the other side of the glass and straightened his back. He pinched his eyes, but saw only his reflection staring back.

"Well, ain't this some beer-battered bullshit?" a voice said, surprising Charlie.

He nearly leapt off the mattress before realizing the voice had come from Boricio who was sitting beside him, also naked, though no pillow covered what looked more like an anaconda than a cock. Unlike the dream he'd had in the truck, this Boricio wasn't neatly dressed. His hair was long and his face unshaven. Boricio's appearance, along with the mirrored walls, made Charlie hopeful that this was just another dream. If so, perhaps the truck, Adam's death, and all of that had been a dream as well. Maybe he'd wake up on the road next to the van they stopped to investigate.

"Is this a dream?" Charlie asked.

"Sorry, Charlie Brown," Boricio said. "This shit's as real as it gets."

Charlie wasn't sure he trusted Boricio's assessment. Dreaming up a lie was easy to do. So was dreaming of Boricio to substantiate the lie.

"Are you really here?" Charlie asked.

"Nope," Boricio shook his head. "I'm in your noggin, though that don't make me a molecule less real."

"What the hell does that mean? You're either here or you're not."

Boricio turned and smiled, "Open your mind and think outside the box, Chuckie FuckStick. Your head has room for a little hippie bullshit. This is some *to be or not to be* shit here. Do you think you're going insane in the membrane, insane in the brain?"

Oh fuck, I'm losing my mind!

"And Bingo was his name-O," Boricio sang.

"Wait, you heard me thinking?"

"Yeah, and you might wanna stop talking out loud, because they're listening, and nothing makes you look crazy quite like a fucker talking to himself."

Charlie moved his eyes across the walls of glass, trying to see through to the dark on the other side. He saw nothing but Charlie, Charlie, and more Charlie. It was The Charlie Show everywhere he looked, without even a hint of his co-star, Boricio.

So, what? I just think and you can hear me?

"Yup," Boricio said, still talking with his mouth, though Charlie figured they couldn't hear him if he was only an imaginary version of Boricio.

Where am I?

"A place called Black Mountain," Boricio said.

How do you know what this place is called if you're not real?

"You must've heard it, but don't remember. I'm just telling you what you already know."

So, what good are you?

"Fuck you, Charlie Chum Water. I'm here to keep your ass from crackling in the heat of the fire. You ain't even gonna get by, let alone outta here, without me. And you can believe the fuck outta that."

I can get by just fine on my own. I don't need you.

"Yeah? How's that whole going-it-alone thing working so far? Let's take a minute to tally all that's happened since we last saw one another, mkay? You got eaten by some giant fucking tornado, then spit into a snowstorm. You lost Callie.

You almost froze to death until Adam saved your ass. Then you both got caught. Adam lost his fucking head, and you let a boy get shot to death. Now you're infected and trapped in a cell. So yeah, America voted, and we're gonna have to be sending you home."

Shut up!

Charlie closed his eyes so he wouldn't have to look at Boricio.

Boricio whistled, then said, "I'm still here," singing like he was Tweety Bird.

Go away. I don't need you.

"Okay," Boricio said.

CHARLIE LOOKED around the room to see where Boricio had gone, as if he were real and confined to the same laws of physics as Charlie. But the figment was nowhere. Charlie felt alone again, wishing he'd not banished his only companion, even if that companion was only a man inside his mind.

Sudden movement from behind the window grabbed at Charlie's attention. He sat straighter, perking as he heard a crash, like something dropping just outside the window. A light flickered in the distance, then brightened into life, washing a second cell in white. And then another, and another, and another, until a row of cells identical to Charlie's were all screaming with light. Every cell held a prisoner — some lying on mattresses and others standing, while many were curled into balls in the corners.

He saw two rows of 10 cells, lining either side of a long hallway. Charlie counted 12 others, with no more than one prisoner in any of the cells. At the far end of the hallway separating two rows was a thin beam of light bleeding through the bottom of a door.

The door whooshed open, like in *Star Trek*, then two men wheeled a gurney down the hallway toward him. Both men were wearing yellow hazmat suits with enclosed masks and air tanks concealed beneath the yellow suits on their backs.

A second chill ran through Charlie as he stared, open mouthed and waiting, hungry to see which of the prisoners the two men would wheel out. But the men had come for a deposit, not a withdrawal, so said the long lump beneath the white sheet.

One of the men leaned toward the cell door across from Charlie, then tapped a black glass pad in the chrome frame of the door, probably entering a code on the panel to open the door.

The men wheeled the gurney inside the room, then hoisted the body from the gurney and onto the bare mattress, where a pillow lay waiting. The men blocked Charlie's view of the new prisoner.

Charlie was already wearing a chill, but it seeped into his every pore with the realization of what he was seeing. Lying naked on the mattress, either unconscious or maybe even dead, was Charlie's best friend and unrequited love, Callie.

~

FOURTEEN

Brent Foster

Somewhere in Georgia
   March 28, 2012
   FIVE MONTHS AFTER THE EVENT...

"THE PROPHET?" Brent said, his weirdo alarm buzzing like crazy as the old man's station wagon quickly closed the distance between the grocery store and Black Mountain.

"Yes, sir," the old man said. "I ran a little church round here for years; The New Unity Church parishioners were a humble bunch, and all of them blessed with visions of the Lord's Wrath on the 15th of last October, before He gathered so many of his loved ones to Heaven and cast others into Hell."

Brent tried to bury what he feared was an obvious bristle. He'd had little patience for charlatans and their shams before 2:15 a.m. a half year earlier. Less now.

Brent met the man's eyes in the rearview and felt sickened by his self-righteous smile.

I wonder how much he'd be smiling if he knew that God had nothing to do with any of this. We were the ones pulled away, and delivered to another world. Our world isn't empty.

"You don't believe me, do you, son?" The Prophet asked, meeting Brent's eyes and deepening his chill.

"I don't know what I believe," Brent said, "but I imagine I'm a ways away from saying God had anything to do with it."

"I'm sorry to hear … "

"Well, why are *we* here, then?" Rojas asked. "I'm not saying I was any kinda Saint, but I was good, and I went to church every Sunday, and prayed every night before I went to bed. Why didn't He take me?"

"Well now, son, can you really tell me you're free of sins?" The Prophet smiled kindly at Rojas, his eyes twinkling as if reflecting the sins counted in Rojas' personal book of life.

"Are you free of sins, *Prophet?*" Lisa finally cut in. "I mean, He left *you* here. What sins did you commit?"

Brent didn't pick fights, and hadn't planned to get confrontational with the old man, especially since the guy was giving them a ride to Black Mountain, but Lisa didn't seem to have the same reservations. She almost seems to be looking for a fight, like she hadn't flushed it from her system during the battle at the store.

"We're all sinners, my dear. Just some of us are more honest than others. In answer to Mr. Rojas' question, I can only say that God works in mysterious ways. Perhaps He is testing you as He is testing me."

Brent wondered how in the hell The Prophet had picked up on Rojas' name. He didn't recall any proper introductions. Maybe he'd gathered it like Brent had, from the man's name tag on his tactical vest.

Still, something's weird.

Brent caught Ed, sitting beside him and wearing the same set of black handcuffs, nodding subtly, as if in silent agreement that the old man was definitely suspicious. If Ed felt suspicious, too, then Brent felt a hundred times better about his hunch.

"I know it's hard to have faith, especially in the End Days," The Prophet said, speaking to everyone. "Believe me, I've grappled with my own faith from time to time over the years." He laughed as though delight were in his secrets before raising the sad in his voice. "I grappled again after He took my family. Then again after I lost my congregation, followed most recently by The Good Lord setting demons upon my church." He shook his head. "Though, I was wrong on that last one. He did not set the demons upon me. That was Satan. The Lord is the one who told me about the air horn. Told me in a dream the night before my church was plagued. Do any of you ever have weird dreams?"

Although Brent thought The Prophet learning of the air horn's use as a weapon against the aliens in his dream was interesting, it was hardly divine intervention. If anything, it was dumb luck. But he wouldn't argue with the man, so long as The Prophet didn't try to sway Brent's beliefs.

Whatever gets you through the night.

"I think we've all had weird dreams," Lisa said. "Most people call 'em nightmares."

Brent flinched at her briskness, wondering why she was being so prickly. Though he shouldn't have been surprised, she'd been the same way with Ed. Still, he didn't want to see religious debate erupt in the car. He wanted to get to Black Mountain so that whatever was gonna happen could finally be over and done with.

Brent had been wondering what was next for some time. Ed seemed anxious about Black Mountain, but Brent figured that with all the chaos in the streets, he'd happily take his chances with another government entity, even if it were at odds with Black Island's Guardsmen. Differences like these were usually political, and if Brent had one area where he was most confident, it was in his ability to navigate tricky political currents.

He despised politics, but Brent had plenty of experience playing the game as a reporter. Even though he worked features, politics had a way of invading nearly every section of the paper, from the front page to the sports page. People were political animals by nature. Brent hoped his skills would still be useful when the bullets from Ed's one-gun-fits-all solution thudded into a brick wall.

Brent was easing tensions when The Prophet slowed the car to a crawl, and stared into the darkness ahead.

"What's going on?" Rojas asked.

Brent looked up to see why they had stopped, his jaw nearly dropping at the shadows barely illuminated by the wagon's high beams.

The highway was blocked with tall dark towers of stacked cars, trucks, and debris, soaring 10 stories and higher, vaguely visible in the moonlight.

"Holy shit!" Lisa said, leaning forward and shaking her head. Then, "What in the hell? This wasn't here the other day."

The Prophet stared for an eternity, as if he were trying to wrap his head around who or what might have made the impossible possible. Something in his expression seemed to indicate that he didn't think it was divine work.

"I saw the same thing in New York," Brent said. "Except with bodies."

"Bodies?" Rojas asked.

"Yes, thousands, maybe tens of thousands, all stacked in Times Square."

"I wonder if those were the sinners or the saints," Lisa said, glaring at The Prophet.

"Where do we go now?" The Prophet asked, still preoccupied with the stacks of cars, still visibly shaken, maybe all the way to his core.

"Turn the car around," Lisa said. "We'll get off at the last exit and find another way."

The Prophet put the car in reverse just as the engine died. The car began to roll backward, and he slammed his foot down on the brake pedal, jerking the car to a halt.

"What the hell?" Lisa said, leaning over. "Out of gas?!"

The Prophet leaned forward and stared at the gas gauge, seemingly as surprised by the red as he was by the stacks in the road. "Sorry. It's been a while since I've had to drive myself anywhere."

"Great!" Lisa said, opening the door and stepping from the car. Everyone followed, Brent growing more certain that Ed would make a break for it soon. Rojas was tasked with keeping an eye on him, but the Black Mountain Guardsman was distracted, if not outright spooked, with everything else happening. Brent watched Ed for any brewing signs for action. If he were going to make a move, it seemed like the right time.

But Ed was quiet, perhaps biding his time.

"Shit," Lisa said, looking down from the overpass railing to the road below, or the crumbles that were left of it. Though dark, they could see enough detail to know that the landscape below was littered with jagged crags of debris as far as the eye could see, as if an earthquake had split the road into thousands of chunks of asphalt and earth.

"I think there's aliens down there," Billy said, his first words since they'd left the shopping center.

Brent didn't see any signs of life, however.

"We have two options," Lisa said. "We can go down there and try not to break our asses. Or we go through this pile and hope that the towers don't fall on us. Anyone have an opinion?"

Brent was surprised she was asking anyone for input, but the question seemed mostly directed at Ed. Perhaps Ed had earned a bit more respect back at the grocery store than she was verbally willing to acknowledge. Brent stared at the road ahead of them. His eyes had adjusted a bit to the darkness, so he could see that the towers of cars sprawled for a few hundred yards or so, with just enough room to walk, or maybe drive, a motorcycle through. It reminded him of the vehicle piles they'd found as he and Luis were trying to make their way to Times Square, except those cars were only jammed side by side, not *on top* of one another, too.

What the hell could have done this? Not the aliens?

They can't even climb; surely they're not stacking cars like toys.

Ed's eyes narrowed as he looked down from the overpass and then back toward Lisa. "I don't like the looks of anything down there." He shook his head, then turned to the stacks. "I say we head straight through the maze and hope there's a working vehicle on the other side of this maze."

Lisa stared at him as if trying to read what else he may have been thinking. Maybe she was wondering if he were looking for an exit, too. Hell, maybe she didn't even have it in her anymore to care. Perhaps with everything else going on, a prisoner was the last thing she had the time, or the ability, to look after. Brent thought about Mr. Ebers, his 11th-grade shop teacher who would often turn the other cheek, pretending not to notice as several of his students fled his classroom when his back was turned. Mr. Ebers didn't seem to have the energy to care anymore, figuring his life was easier if he just let the people who didn't want to be there leave. Lisa's life would be far easier if she didn't have to deal with Ed.

But perhaps Ed had proven himself so valuable an ally against the aliens that Lisa couldn't stand to lose him, and therefore wasn't about to look the other way — for even a moment.

"Alright," Rojas said, gesturing with his rifle. "Let's move forward."

As they headed into the maze, The Prophet stood beside the stalled station wagon, unmoving.

"You coming?" Lisa asked.

"I don't know," he said after a long moment spent slowly shaking his head.

"We'll be fine," Lisa said. "Bring your air horn."

Something flashed inside The Prophet's eyes, and for a moment, Brent could have sworn the man's face went blurry for a split second. Brent blinked and rubbed his eyes. The Prophet was looking at him. "You okay?" he asked as he reached into the car and grabbed the air horn.

"Yeah," Brent said, not wanting to meet the man's eyes.

They headed into the maze together, with the old man walking in the middle, and Brent feeling more uneasy than he had since their excursion into the city.

~

FIFTEEN

Other Will Bishop

Other Earth
Paddock Island, New York
Saturday, July 9, 2011
Night
THREE MONTHS BEFORE THE EVENT ...

WILL WAITED in a chair next to Luca's bed, waiting for his son to return from the bathroom down the hall.

Will had decided to test Luca at home from now on. Will tried his best to mask his emotions — both the excitement of discovery and the fear of the unknown — never wanting the boy to be afraid, or get too deep inside a mind where getting lost was too easy to do.

At least they weren't in the lab. Level 7 put Luca on edge, a feeling that Will could understand given the sheer number of people who were following Luca's progress. Luca was the first human subject of an alien technology that their best scientists barely understood. Yes, the boy had healed completely, but he'd come out of his coma enhanced, a possibility easily predicted from the animal testing. But Luca's abilities had grown beyond simple enhancement of latent human abilities.

Luca was already doing things that Will, whose proximity and early exposure to the vials had changed him, had never done, but now he was doing stuff Will didn't even think was possible.

Luca told Will that he had been going to another world, like theirs but different. A world where his mom and dad and sister were all still sleeping in their own beds and living the life fate had stolen from Luca.

Of course, that was a scenario any child in Luca's position would want to create. So, while Will believed Luca was seeing what he said he saw, he had a rather large question about whether Luca was the architect of that world.

Teleporting to another dimension — if that was in fact was what Luca had done — was beyond the scope of anything they were prepared for. Will was torn between his commitment to science — he couldn't allow future testing on others without divulging this information — and protecting his son. Once Black Island Research found out about Luca's new side effect, he would go from child to lab rat. And even though Will was valuable to Black Island Research, particularly in dealing with the vials he'd discovered so many decades ago, not even he could protect Luca from that fate once the truth was out.

Could Luca really be visiting a parallel world?

If true, the possibilities were enough to cripple his mind. Not counting a parallel world, two possibilities existed: Either Luca was imagining the other world entirely, or he was somehow traveling back in time.

Will didn't want to consider time travel. That rabbit hole was just too goddamned deep, worse than string theory and the infinite worlds that went with it.

Believing Luca was manufacturing it all was easier for Will, especially since Luca's mind was able to bleed color onto empty canvas. More than he, or anyone at the island, had ever seen. But things that had happened over the last several weeks made Will wonder if the impossible could be true.

He was slowly starting to believe that it probably was.

It started with the subtle but obvious changes in Luca. Level 7 was pulling too much from him, drawing on too much of his power. Luca's mind seemed stressed, yet when he returned from what he said was the other world, he seemed refreshed, almost like a new boy. Will wondered where he was getting his energy, and if he were somehow pulling from the mind of his doppelgänger to make himself stronger.

Will theorized that if Luca could truly establish tangible interaction on another world, maybe he could return with evidence. It was a crazy long shot and utterly ridiculous, but wasn't that always the way — today's science was yesterday's magic? Luca certainly seemed to be waving a wand.

"Are you ready?"

Luca nodded as he returned to his bed, wiping water from his lips with the back of his hand. He sat on the edge of his bed, legs folded.

"And I can bring back anything I want?"

Will said, "Whatever you want, Luca. I think the more special it is to you, the more likely you'll be able to bring it back with you. But don't tell me. Let it be a surprise."

Will didn't really believe that it mattered *what* Luca brought back — the idea was to keep Luca from planting any thoughts in Will's mind to taint the results.

Luca said, "Okay, Dad. Should I go now?"

Will swallowed. Luca had vanished twice in his sleep, including the first time a few weeks ago, when Will saw him appear before him on his return trip. Both times had been during the boy's sleep, and Luca had been unable to stop himself from leaving.

Last week, Will was able to get Luca to do it again, that time in a controlled setting while the boy was awake.

An uneasy knot returned to his throat, and he hoped he wasn't putting Luca in harm's way. At the same time, he had to figure out what was happening and help Luca learn to control it — if that were even possible. The last thing they needed was for Luca to teleport in the middle of a crowded room and draw attention to himself. He'd be in a room on Level 7 within an hour, and there would be nothing Will could do to keep it from his bosses.

They would learn to control it together. But for now Will had to know where Luca was going. A parallel world? Back in time? Or was he even *really* going somewhere else? Perhaps, Will speculated, Luca was removing himself temporarily from their dimension but not really *going* anywhere, outside of a mental trip.

Will told himself that this test was best for Luca and said, "Yes. Go now. I'll be waiting right here."

"Okay," Luca said, squeezing his eyes shut. He went blurry for a moment, as if two images of Luca's had merged into one and were trying to separate from one another before both of them vanished.

Will stared, stunned, and put his hand on the bed where Luca had been.

Will waited through 20 minutes of silence until Luca finally appeared, standing in the bedroom, cradling a framed photograph of his family. As Luca held it out, Will could clearly see this boy in the photo was the same age as Luca now — an impossibility if he'd time traveled. *That* Luca would have been 6 years old or younger, not 8.

Will gasped. "Oh my," he said, nearly leaping from his chair. "This can't be."

Luca looked down at the photo, and a tear splashed onto the glass. Will dropped to his knees beside the boy. "It's okay, buddy," he said. "You don't have to be sad." Will ignored the impossible to focus on the reality of Luca's obvious pain.

"But they're all still alive," he said. "All of them, even Anna."

"I know," Will said, patting Luca's head.

"I miss them so much." He started to sob.

"I know," Will repeated, now rocking Luca back and forth.

"I don't want to go back there," he sobbed into Will's shirt. "Ever again. It hurts too much."

"Okay, you don't have to go back," Will said, scooping Luca up in his arms and carrying him to the living room where they plopped down on the long L-shaped black sofa. Will wanted to ask him questions about the trip, what he'd seen, but Will had the only answer he needed at the moment — the framed photo that Will sat on the floor, just out of Luca's sight.

"Goodness," Will said, rubbing his aching lower back. "We're both getting too old, too fast." He smiled. "Difference is, you're getting bigger, and I'm getting smaller, or at least a whole lot weaker." He laughed. "I'm not sure how much longer I'm going to be able to keep that up! So, you better enjoy it while it lasts."

The maybe of a smile flickered on Luca's face, the first chink in the armor of his sorrow.

Will said, "Wanna watch TV? We can watch whatever you want — something you've never seen before, or something saved on the DVR."

"Something I've never seen before!"

"Okay," Will said, heading to the DVD cabinet, where he opened his extensive selection and moved his finger along the bottom row of flicks that Luca had never seen before. The bottom row was the most often studied and requested. Will chose from the row wisely, a masterpiece at a time.

"*Indiana Jones, Indiana Jones!*" Luca said, a smile threatening to take over his face.

"I'm not sure." Will frowned and shook his head. "It's kind of violent."

"I'm old enough."

Will said, "Oh, all right, I'm easy to convince tonight. Let's start with the first one. The second is too dark to watch without Boricio on the other side of the safety sandwich. Maybe he'll come over for movie night, and we'll watch it then."

"Yay!" Luca said.

Will smiled, then slipped the disc into the player and pressed play.

Will went to the kitchen to make popcorn, dumped the bag into a bowl for the two of them to share, and was digging in beside Luca before the boulder was rolling toward Indy.

Luca loved *Raiders of the Lost Ark*, just as he loved *The Temple of Doom*, which they watched even though Boricio wasn't there to be the other side of the safety sandwich. He also seemed to love what he saw of *The Last Crusade*, but that wasn't much, since Luca was asleep before Indiana even got to Vienna.

Will brushed the hair from his son's face, petting his head as Harrison Ford outsmarted the Nazis, Will smiling through every one of Sean Connery's one-liners and Luca's long bouts of snoring. He wondered what Luca was dreaming almost the entire time, but wasn't willing to step inside his mind as an intruder. Finally, Indy chose life over immortality and the credits started to roll. Will pulled Luca into his arms, then stood from the couch and carried him to his room and tucked him into bed.

It was almost morning outside, and Will was pretty sure he'd regret his decision to stay up so late.

Ah, what the hell, it's Sunday. I'll take a nap.

Will was halfway to the door when Luca turned from the wall, clutched his pillow tightly to his chest, and mumbled, "I love you, Daddy."

"I love you, too," Will said, closing the door quietly behind him, feeling bad for hoping that Luca was speaking to him instead the father still alive in his dreams.

Will pissed, brushed his teeth, and then went to his room and climbed into bed with his iPad, figuring he'd run through his e-mail until his eyes were too tired to stay awake any longer.

Fourteen e-mails, and two were from Barry, a guy he had met at The Red Herring, an indie bookstore in New York, two months earlier. They'd gone out just once, but the spark wasn't there. Will had tried to let him down easy, but Barry wasn't getting the hint, or figured he'd go with the persistent approach.

Will had liked Barry well enough, but even if Will wanted a relationship — which he wasn't even sure he did — he didn't have the time. Will's responsibilities lay firmly with his research, and with Luca. Reading Barry's first e-mail made Will wonder if he'd made a mistake in shutting others out. Staring at Barry's second e-mail, and all the kind things he'd said, made Will feel lonely, like he was missing out on a life he should've had.

There was a time — decades ago — when Will thought he would find the right guy and settle down. But that time had passed. He had never met the right guy, then life and circumstance conspired to keep him on life's treadmill, from his time in the Air Force and the Alaskan discovery, which changed everything, to Boricio, to his work at Black Island with the Remedy Project, and now Luca.

Will wasn't incapable of a relationship. He'd had several, with men and women, though ironically his best relationship had been with a woman, back when he dated women to douse his internal doubt.

Sissy Braddock was a social worker, as haunted by her work as Will was by his. They dated for nine months, and nearly moved in together. Sissy introduced Will to Boricio, a 9-year-old boy who had sat front row for more suffering than any child Will had ever known. Of course, Will hadn't known too many, but Sissy agreed.

Will had just left the Air Force the year he met Boricio, and hadn't been looking to raise a family. But something about the lost boy in himself connected with the broken kid inside Boricio.

The boy's mother had died, and his stepfather, Joe, had been thrown in jail for 14 counts of being a monster. Boricio was sent to live with his aunt in New York. He stayed with her for a short while, but ended up being nothing but trouble. He was suspended from school twice before finally getting expelled for creating a cardboard gambling shack in the park across the street from the school. Boricio's fledgling, but already thriving, business catered to anyone K-5 willing to pay for a play, but also to any passerby in the park. Authorities confiscated $211 from Boricio when they broke up the game and took him into custody.

Boricio was passed from home to broken home, until he became a file on Sissy's desk. She said that Boricio was the scariest and most fascinating kid she had ever seen. Will thought she was grossly understating both.

Boricio was highly verbal with off-the-charts intelligence. But he needed roots and stability, someone to encourage him, tell him how good he was so that he would learn to slay the demons that would otherwise eat him alive.

Boricio was placed with a family, and Will was content to let the boy fade from his thoughts. Then, on a lark, Will did a background check on Tom Chambers, the patriarch of Boricio's new family. Will didn't like what he saw, so he dug deeper. The next layer of dirt had Will tailing Chambers for two weeks straight until the monster killed again. Or almost killed until Will caught him in the act.

Boricio lived with Will from then forward, even though Sissy never did.

Will managed to pull Boricio from the depths of darkness,

and spared no expense in finding him the finest therapists, teachers, and support systems. Will was there for Boricio every day, teaching him to channel his anger, or at least bury it in a safe place.

Then, a couple of years ago, Boricio and Will were kicking back some beers watching a baseball game when a news story flashed on the TV: A family visiting New York died in a freak car accident, killing everyone, including the cabbie, except for 6-year-old Luca Harding.

The boy had miraculously survived the crash, though he shouldn't have, and no one could explain why he had. He was found 50 feet from the crash site, without a bruise on his body. Just one paper cut, barely visible on his pinky.

Boricio felt drawn to the boy in the hospital, like sun to morning.

Luca lay in the hospital for two weeks, comatose, off the front page for 11 days and under the fold for 13, before Boricio finally decided to have Will call someone at the hospital to get him permission. He wanted to sit a spell inside the child's room, though he didn't know why. When Will insisted he needed a reason before he could make the call, Boricio said, "Instinct is the nose of the mind, Dad," then added, "Just make something up. Please!"

Will did, then the two of them went to the hospital together. Boricio sat in the boy's room for 15 minutes of nothing, then stood to leave, not quite sure how he should be feeling. He was one step toward the door when the monitor beside Luca switched rhythm and the boy slowly opened his eyes.

Boricio had wanted a son forever, to help him heal from the thousand lashes across the broken body of his childhood. Will had never considered adopting another child, but Boricio wasn't ready to be a custodian on his own, not without a wife, and Will couldn't bear to refuse Boricio when he had the chance to finally close the painful loop. So he adopted Luca, though it was as much to help Boricio as it was to help Luca recover.

Will shook his head, staring at Barry's e-mail, wondering what life would have been like if he had met someone when he was younger, or maybe taken a chance on love. Perhaps, Will figured, fate hadn't meant for him to fall in love. Fortunately, fate had allowed him to find the love of family, and not a day went by that Will regretted adopting either Boricio or Luca.

Will leaned back, then lightly shifted left to right in bed before leaning forward to read Barry's e-mail again.

HEY THERE, *Will. Would love to get to know you better. Had a great time at dinner, but I feel like there's so much more Will to see. And I'd love to see it! So take a chance. Call me. Or hit reply. :)*

WILL DELETED THE E-MAIL.

~

WILL FELL asleep and was woken just a few hours later by the shrill sound of his house phone.

What in the hell?

The sound was especially startling since Will couldn't even remember the last time he'd heard it. When someone called Will, they called his cell. He usually thought about his landline once a month, each time he was stupid enough to sign another check to the phone company.

The phone rang three times before he managed to grab the phone from his nightstand.

"Hello?"

"Good morning, sir. Is this William Bishop?"

"Yes."

"Are you the father of a Mr. Boricio Bishop?"

The lump in Will's throat was as big as a golf ball. "Yes."

"We're sorry to inform you, sir, but there's been an accident."

~

SIXTEEN

Boricio Bishop

Other Earth
  Paddock Island, New York
  Sunday, July 10, 2011
  Night

BORICIO WOKE up feeling like he was trudging through the desert, knee deep in sand, pulling a fat bag of hammers by the thin of his neck.

It took him a moment to realize where he was — a hospital in the city.

How did I get here?

His throat was raw, and his head was pounding. His earlobes felt like they were on fire. Even his teeth hurt. The coppery taste of blood coated his tongue and the roof of his mouth. Below the neck Boricio was nothing but numb. Whatever was working to kill his pain from the shoulders down wasn't working on the top floor, though.

Boricio scooted himself up on the bed, then wiggled his toes just to make sure they could still dance. Sure as a sack of sugar they did, so Boricio wasn't paralyzed. Just temporarily frozen from the pain.

He blinked again, then swallowed, wincing through the pain.

Boricio ran his fingers across his bandaged head as he looked around the hospital room, his eyes starting at the far right and the partition with all the silence behind it, then slowly grazing to the left, stopping at Will, sitting in a chair beside him with his arms crossed, waiting for Boricio to see him.

"Hey," Will said with a smile. "Good to see you blinking."

Boricio tried, but couldn't smile back. Finding two pieces of what happened so he could put them together was hard enough. His memory was a blur. The naked recall, along with the ache and the pain, made the idea of a smile almost absurd.

Boricio forced a question from his raw throat. "What happened?"

"You were in a crash this morning. Do you remember the accident?"

Boricio narrowed his eyes, then rocked his head slowly back and forth, and ever so slightly left to right. He went completely still, looked down, then finally shook his head.

"What's the last thing you remember?"

Boricio tried to think back, but the only memory he could come up with had him back at Black Island, saying goodbye to Will, then stopping by the house to give Luca a high-five and tell him he'd see him after the weekend.

Boricio was trying to blink himself into the next memory when he realized he was only blinking from his right eye, and that his left was showing nothing but black. Boricio felt suddenly trapped in a vacuum of horror, gasping for breath as his fingers ran over the bandage covering much of the left side of his face, including his left eye.

Will was at his bedside a second before Boricio started to scream. "It's okay," he said. "It's okay."

"What happened to my face?"

"You were in a car accident," Will put his hand on Boricio's shoulder.

Boricio felt a flicker of rage toward Will, seeing his face twitch the way it did as he hesitated to deliver the news to Boricio as if he were a child. He wanted to snap at Will to just fucking tell him what was going on, because Boricio was imagining the worst-case scenario lurking beneath the bandages.

Boricio breathed himself into calm, then said, "How bad is it?"

"You lost your left eye in the accident." Will paused, rubbing his hand on Boricio's shoulder, then said, "And your face and back of your head were badly lacerated, requiring lots of stitches, including one from your forehead to your left cheek which is gonna be pretty scary looking for some time. It's too soon to say, but I believe the scarring can be minimized with cosmetic surgery, but not right away. Fortunately, your other injuries were minor."

Boricio tried to swallow again, this time managing to push the lump all the way to the bottom of his chest. He wondered if he would ever be able to grow hair around the gash again. He couldn't care less. Boricio would be perfectly fine being bald as a baby. But Rose loved Boricio's hair. "You realize most women would kill to have hair this thick," she often said while running her fingers through it. He loved when she stroked his hair. It was second only to sex in the pleasure department.

He gasped, suddenly remembering everything: the drive, the look, the accident. Boricio shivered through the icy chill that chased the memory.

"Rose," Boricio said. "How is she?"

Boricio didn't like the hesitation on Will's face a bit, even gave him a good goddamned three seconds to wipe it from his nose holder before he started yelling. "I said where is she, Will?!"

The word "Will" came out in a roar. He watched his dad swallow and take a step back, then Boricio breathed himself back into another calm. "Sorry," he said. "You didn't deserve that."

Will said, "It's okay, son. I understand." Then he swallowed again and said, "We're not sure how Rose is doing yet."

"I want to see her."

Will shook his head. "You know that's not possible, Boricio. Not yet. You were both injured, badly. Rose worse than you. Right now the doctors need time and space to do what's best for her. To do what's best for you both. And we have to give it to them. Do you understand?"

"I want to see her," Boricio said, nostrils flaring at the memory of their final seconds, exchanging one last look before he tore through the Schooner or Later patio and murdered his chance for the Happily Ever After, which seemed an almost certainty when the day started.

"Soon," Will said, returning his calming hand to Boricio's shoulder.

Boricio shrugged the hand from his shoulder then started yanking wires and tubes from his body. He'd see for himself what Will was hiding in his eyes.

"Stop, son; it's okay." Will's hand moved from his shoulder to press down on his chest, firm and urgent. "I'll tell you everything I know, I promise. But you have to relax."

Boricio's nostrils still flared, but he managed to calm himself long enough to lie back on his bed. He kept his mouth closed, afraid of what would come out if he left it open.

"I don't know of any other way to do this then to simply tear the Band-Aid." Will pulled his chair closer to Boricio's bed, then sat and leaned in, holding his son's hands as he whispered, "Rose suffered significant damage to her spinal column. The surgeons were able to repair much of that damage, but there's a good chance that Rose will never walk again."

Will held Boricio's stare.

Boricio asked, "Is that it?"

Will shook his head.

"What else, Dad?"

"Rose suffered significant swelling in the brain. And they're not sure how bad it is."

Almost too hoarse to hear, Boricio said, "What about my baby?"

He didn't have to wait for Will to respond. The answer was written all over his face.

Boricio's roar tore through the hospital.

~

SEVENTEEN

Brent Foster

They moved cautiously through the dark maze, listening intently as the towers of cars creaked and swayed with every intermittent gust of howling wind blowing over the highway. In the moments of silence, every step was echoed and every breath exaggerated, every inch forward a blend of exertion and relief.

"What did this?" Billy whispered to Brent, who was walking beside him. Ed was to the right, while Rojas followed in the rear, ordered to make sure the "prisoners" didn't escape — not that Brent had any desire to do so. Brent had his eye on Ed, waiting for a sign. But Ed kept his plans close to the vest, sewing his lips as his eyes scanned the towers.

"I dunno," Brent said, wondering if The Prophet would say God, or maybe the Devil. But The Prophet, who was walking behind Lisa in the front of their formation, was also keeping his lips sewn shut. His eyes were wide as he held his air horn like some sort of magical battle axe which would ward off any evil.

They'd gone no more than a tenth of the way through the pile when a thick fog rolled in on a cool breeze, so fast it seemed almost sentient.

"We should be careful," Brent said. "The aliens use the fog to attack from above."

Lisa looked back, but said nothing.

"Maybe you should take off our handcuffs and give us guns," Ed suggested.

"You'd like that, wouldn't you?" Lisa said.

"Do I need to remind you that I could've easily left you in the store if I wanted? But I didn't, did I?"

Lisa didn't say anything, too stubborn, or too suspicious, to cede Ed's valid point. Maybe she was right not to trust him, Brent figured, but Ed was the best prepared of all of them to handle the threats. The guy was like Rambo by way of Jason Bourne or something.

The fog grew thicker, and obscured the top halves of the towering cars, which did nothing to lessen the sense that they might topple on them at any moment. If anything, it added to Brent's claustrophobic fear. The car's creaking seemed to grow louder in the fog, as if the mist were reaching around with its wispy tendrils to purposely rattle the towers.

Everyone seemed to step up their pace, but no one said a word.

Suddenly, a loud thump thundered above, like something had flown down and landed on one of the crooked steel piles.

"What was that?" Billy shouted, his voice five octaves higher than normal.

Rojas aimed his rifle up and rolled the barrel back and forth, scanning the fog for a sign of whatever made the noise. A sudden, second thump came from above, closer. Then another. And then something dark fell in front of Billy, who screamed as he fell back on his ass and hands.

Brent stumbled backward as Ed thrust himself in between Billy and the fallen thing, twitching on the ground and gushing blood — a giant crow in the spasms of death.

Another thump from above, and then another, until the horrible scream from thousands of wings flapping tore through the air. Swarms of cawing birds careened through the maze assaulting the group with bruising force that could easily kill them.

"Get on the ground!" Ed screamed, pulling Billy — who had gotten up — back to the asphalt.

Brent fell to the ground and curled to a fetal position, covering his face with his handcuffed arms as seemingly hundreds of birds pelted his back on their way by. Brent cringed through the battery. Some hit his body so hard they were injured and fell to twitching lumps all around him.

Billy screamed, though his scream was barely audible over the swarming caws and flapping wings.

Another sound grew suddenly louder above the chaos, though — something that sounded like a train barreling toward them.

The assault on Brent's body eased as the sound of birds began to fade. But the sound of the train grew louder. Brent raised his head and peered past his bruised and bloody arms in time to see a swirling vortex of dirt and debris that looked as wide as a city block churning toward them. The towers of cars started to buckle around them in the monstrous tornado's wake. Lightning pulsed from its middle, and struck out from its center. And then the towers began to tumble — cars raining down upon them.

Lisa screamed, "Run!"

They scrambled and ran, slipping on and crushing the corpses of hundreds of birds as they raced their way back through the maze toward the opening of the car maze. Streaks of lightning arced out, crackling loudly in the air, above the sound of the swirling mass. Chunks of dirt and rocks swirled through the corridor, assaulting them with the same ferocity the birds had brought just a moment before — stinging Brent's eyes and clogging his throat as he spit and then closed his mouth and tucked his chin against his chest. He kept running.

Brent, Ed, and Billy were close to catching up with Rojas, who was in front of them by 20 feet. Brent didn't dare slow long enough to look back and see if either The Prophet or Lisa was keeping up.

Lightning flashed above, close enough for Brent to feel its heat. The flash that followed was so bright, Brent felt as if it tore something in his mind. In that flash, Brent saw Rojas disintegrate into debris, slightly larger than the dirt swirling en masse around them.

Brent gasped, thinking he'd never see anything so terrifying again. He was right . . . for two seconds.

A car soared overhead, faster than a jet, and slammed into the highway a hundred yards ahead, then bounced and rolled. Brent heard another vehicle slam into one of the towers. He glanced back to see the dark shape tumbling down into another tower. As Brent braced for the dominoes to fall, Lisa pushed past him. Brent screamed and followed, as Ed and Billy raced toward the railing, barely visible through the storm of debris.

Something exploded behind them as Brent reached the railing and hurled himself from the overpass, hard onto the grassy incline, and rolled down to the street below. His body was stunned and his breath ragged as he spit dirt from his mouth. Rain and debris continued to pour down on them all.

Brent, paralyzed by fear, could do nothing but stare into the dark, swirling heavens.

Above him, arcs of bright white spilled like spider webs into the darkness, shooting out for what seemed to be miles of pulsating strobes of light like a dance club in hell.

Brent sat, transfixed by the beauty of light fighting black and by the seething hues of the battle. Time slowed to nothing as Brent felt wrapped in serenity. Peace, awe, and a weird feeling of enlightenment spread through his body. Even though he had no idea why, Brent felt — for a moment — as though he were staring into the eyes of God. His awe was so deep, he almost felt like dying would be fine.

Ben would be fine.

So would Gina.

They would move on.

And he would simply cease to be.

Just close your eyes.

Before he could close his eyes, however, a dark, solid shape filled his vision — a truck being lifted high into the sky, dangling above him, as though taunting him with the inevitable.

Oh God.

Someone suddenly pulled Brent hard, then dragged him under the overpass seconds before the truck plummeted to the ground in an eruption of metal and glass, raining fresh pain all over his body.

Brent closed his eyes and welcomed surrender.

WHEN HE CAME TO, the darkness had ceded to the light.

It was morning. Or maybe afternoon, and Brent was lying in the back of a van, feeling as if he'd been beaten to hell. Ed lay beside him, eyes closed and face battered. Billy was sitting, leaning against the wall of the van, his face bruised and scratched, clothes covered in dirt and blood. Brent had no idea how much was his and how much was from the birds.

Brent's head was pounding, his throat was dry, and his tongue was coated in blood and dirt. He craned his neck to see up to the van's front. Lisa was driving with The Prophet beside her, somehow wearing hardly a scratch, though Brent was certain the old man had been behind him.

How did he survive all that?

Brent noticed that Billy was looking at Brent oddly. Billy

looked down at Ed's hands, and then Brent's, and then back again and managed a smile.

What's he trying to tell me?

He looked down, then over at Ed. Both of their handcuffs had been removed. Brent went to return Billy's smile, but Billy's eyes were then on the front of the van. Brent followed his gaze just in time to see they were entering a wide, dark tunnel.

"We're here," Billy whispered. "Black Mountain."

EIGHTEEN

Luca Bishop

Other Earth
Paddock Island, New York
Sunday, July 10, 2011
THREE MONTHS BEFORE THE EVENT …

THIS WASN'T FAIR.

Luca's dad was visiting Boricio, making sure he was safe, while Luca was stuck at home with his sometimes babysitter, Sarah.

Sarah was pretty, in her early 20s, and had always been nice to him. Even made him two bags of popcorn when she knew Will only wanted her to give him one.

But it still wasn't fair.

His dad said he had to go see Boricio in the city alone. He also said Luca wasn't allowed to "travel" while he wasn't in the house. He even made Luca cross his heart.

Luca crossed it like his dad told him to, but that didn't make it fair.

His dad said he would be back later tonight, maybe tomorrow. Luca wasn't supposed to wait up. That wasn't fair either. He wanted to know if Boricio was okay, and shouldn't have to wait until morning to find out. His dad said he'd call with news, but sometimes his dad got busy and forgot to call, and Luca worried that this might be one of those times.

"Thanks, Sarah," Luca said, taking the bowl filled with his second bag of popcorn.

"You're welcome," Sarah plopped beside him, hugging her own bowl.

"Do you want to watch TV?" She looked at Luca. "You're just staring at the screen. It's okay to watch it, you know. Your dad wouldn't mind."

"Okay," Luca said. "But I don't care what we watch. Whatever you want is fine with me."

Sarah picked up the remote and started flipping channels, pausing on some show with people yelling at each other on MTV for a minute before moving to the Cartoon Network.

Luca leaned back on the couch and shoved a handful of popcorn into his mouth, then started to chew. That's when he heard Sarah say something that wasn't so nice inside her head.

I dunno what happened, but this kid got weird enough to be the top of a totem pole. Fucking. Creepy. Like a kid from a King book.

"I want to go to bed," Luca suddenly said, setting his bowl on the end table and pushing it away. He stood from the couch, gathered crumbs from his pajamas, then swept them into a pile on his hand and poured them into the bowl.

"Goodnight," he said. "Maybe I'll see you tomorrow."

"It's not even 8 o'clock!"

Good, now I can call Brad, she thought.

"Sometimes I like going to bed early," he said just wanting to get out of the room before he heard her think something else.

"Um … okay." Sarah kept her eyes on Luca for another half minute or so, said, "Goodnight!" then picked up the remote and turned it from the Cartoon Network back to MTV.

Luca went to his bedroom and paused at his door, half in and half out, knowing he was probably about to do something he'd crossed his heart not to do.

Luca swallowed, then stepped through the door and shut it behind him. His dad would be mad, but he wouldn't be too mad since Luca was doing the thing that was smart. Smart meant going to the place that would make him less lonely, while giving his dad more of the answers he was looking for.

Luca still wasn't sure how he crossed over to the world where everything was how it was supposed to be. He'd been able to do it a few times while awake, but that had been with Will standing by. To do it awake without Will around felt scary for some reason. Better to just go to sleep, where it would just happen on its own — that way Will couldn't get mad.

So, Luca curled on his bed and counted backwards from 100 like he always did when he was trying to fall asleep.

Luca hit 47, then started to think about stuff that didn't make sense. The more he tried to make the stuff make sense, the less sense it made. He was spinning around and around, the circles swirling faster in his mind, like a merry-go-round of confusion until it finally spun Luca into a clarity where everything made sense.

Luca felt himself coming to color somewhere between the black and white. When he opened his eyes, Luca saw himself standing in the middle of his bedroom, except it wasn't *his* bedroom at all. This bedroom belonged to the other Luca. The one who was happy because he lived with his mommy and his daddy, and his sister, Anna. The one who never had to see the car when it burned. The one who had new pictures taken in new places with his family still alive.

Luca was sleeping in his bed on the other side of the room, the covers rising and falling along with his breath. On the other side of the door lay the faint echo of a fading memory: the sound of Luca's father working in his office.

Luca swallowed, filled with a sudden, desperate need to

see his father. He took one last look at the other Luca, then left the room and walked down the hallway to his father's office.

Luca's first dad was surprised to see his son open the door. "Oh my goodness, Luca," he said, spinning his chair toward the door. "I thought you were asleep."

Luca said, "I was."

His dad laughed. "Okay," he said, "so you've changed your pajamas." Luca looked down at his *Iron Man* PJ's, then back at his dad. His dad said, "So, why did you fire *Captain America?*"

Luca said, "*Iron Man* is better."

His father raised his eyebrows. "Since when? I didn't even *know* you had *Iron Man* pajamas. Your life was all about *Captain America* last week." He leaned in to Luca and whispered, "You know, you really should do a better job of keeping me updated on your super hero preferences. There are always birthdays and random trips to the Galleria, and I don't want to be caught buying a present ill-informed."

"Okay, Dad," Luca said, not knowing what else to say. He felt almost guilty because the joke was for a him who wasn't really him.

Luca stared at his father, like he was the ghost that he kinda sorta was. Staring at his dad's face was weird because Luca had forgotten exactly what his dad looked like. He had memories, lots of them, but there were little things that had faded in the past two years, like the cleft in his dad's chin, and a small faded scar over his dad's left eye that Luca had almost forgotten about.

"Are you okay?" his father stared back, left eyebrow raised. "Luca?"

Luca hated nothing more than crying in front of his real dad, especially now that he wasn't even really there. His bottom lip started to quiver, but he managed to tuck it in before his dad said, "You okay?"

"I'm just feeling sad spiders."

"Sad spiders? What are those?"

Luca felt like maybe he shouldn't say anything. His second dad might get mad.

Luca spent a long time saying nothing, the entire time wanting to leave this world that belonged to the other Luca and return to his home on Black Island. After too long without an answer, his first dad said, "Should I be worried about anything, Luca? Anything at all?" He tugged on his right earlobe like Luca remembered he used to do. Another memory that he'd almost forgotten.

Luca looked up at his father and felt a sudden flare of jealousy toward the other Luca. The Luca who wasn't adopted, the one who was still living with his first family.

Luca didn't really hate anybody; he didn't even hate Tommy Wilcox when he made Luca eat a cricket, but right then as he stood close enough to his dad to smell what he could never have again, hating him was easy. For a moment, Luca did, no different than if the small boy had been the drunk driver who murdered his parents.

Luca turned to his first dad. "I'm tired," he said. "I'm going to bed now. Will you ask me about the sad spiders in the morning?"

"What do you want me to ask?" his dad said, still puzzled.

"Just ask me about the sad spiders."

"Okay ... "

Something about Luca was scaring something inside his first daddy. Maybe it was because Luca didn't even know why he was telling his dad about the sad spiders. He thought maybe it might get the other Luca in trouble.

He could hear his dad wanting him to go back to his bedroom so he could finish his work. Luca felt bad for being scared, guilty for his unkind thoughts, and curious why he was suddenly trying to get the other Luca into trouble.

"Goodnight, Daddy," Luca said, giving his father a giant

hug. Luca did his best to hold in the cry he wanted to release in that long hug.

It had been so long since he'd hugged his real dad, and he didn't want to ever forget this feeling: the warmth, the love, and . . . the safety of his old life.

Luca wanted to stay and never leave.

Never.

His father held the hug, then said, "Goodnight, Luca."

Luca reluctantly went down the hallway, then back into the other Luca's room, where he stared at the sleeping boy under the covers.

At first, Luca thought how easily he could hurt the other him. He was lying there, helpless. Then he realized how dumb that would be. And how mean. He hadn't done anything, after all.

But then Luca had another idea. One that brought a thin smile to his lips.

Maybe I can bring this Luca back to Black Island and I can stay here?

Then Luca could return to this room and live the rest of his life with his mom, dad, and Anna.

As the idea took root in his mind, Luca wanted to, but he couldn't bring himself to do it.

First, he wasn't even sure if he could bring a person back with him. A person was a lot bigger than a photograph. Second, his new dad would be too mad. And his real parents would be mad if the other Luca did that to him. He would be mad, too.

Though the idea made him happy for a moment, it was wrong no matter how he looked at it.

Luca shook his head. These were wrong thoughts, and Luca only wanted to do what he knew was right. So, he went home, sad, waking back up to his lonely world.

A world without his family.

A world without his real dad's hugs.

NINETEEN

Charlie Wilkens

Charlie lay on his mattress, blinking in his cell, draped in the same darkness he had been in most hours since he arrived. He wasn't sure how long he'd been there. It felt like at least a day, and the lights had only come on once since Callie arrived.

The lights went on as a man in a yellow hazmat suit came down the row and slipped a small, black tray of food and two water bottles through a slot in the bottom of each occupied cell's door. Charlie was starving, and scarfed down his peanut butter sandwich and bag of pretzels in seconds. Callie looked just as dead as when they'd left her on the mattress. He watched her cell as he ate, staring and praying she was only sedated, rather than dead.

Charlie was curled up with his pillow, staring at Callie's cell even though he saw nothing through the darkness. He wondered if she was infected, too. Maybe all the people on the block were infected. If so, why were they being held in cells?

Are they keeping us quarantined? Or something worse?

A few hours later, the lights went bright again. Callie was standing at her window, naked, screaming, though Charlie couldn't hear her anguished cries from his cell.

He ran to the glass wall and put his hands across the cold surface, sobbing with relief. *She's alive!* Charlie had considered covering his body, but it felt somewhat wrong to do with her standing there so raw and vulnerable. She wasn't just naked, she was scratched and bruised, with her hair in a storm. Dark circles ringed beneath her hollow, red eyes. She looked as if she'd been through hell since he'd seen her, and Charlie felt sick to his stomach that he could do nothing to help. Sick to his stomach that these fuckers had kept her naked in a cage like an animal.

Charlie vowed to kill every fucker responsible.

Callie put her hands on her glass wall and wept, her red eyes meeting Charlie's.

"I'm going to get us out," he mouthed slowly, hoping she could read his lips.

She mouthed something back, but Charlie couldn't make out the words. He shook his head and shrugged, then mouthed the word, "What?"

She said something again, but to his frustration, he still couldn't make it out. Then she stopped talking, her attention turned down the hall, where two men in yellow hazmat suits stepped onto the cell block. A Guardsman in black gear, wearing a black mask and respirator and carrying an assault rifle, followed as the pair of men headed toward them.

Callie covered her breasts and crotch, and Charlie covered his flaccid penis. The men stopped in front of a cell, two down from Callie's, where a heavyset, nude, redheaded woman stood shaking her head.

The man in black pressed the code on her door, then stepped back and raised the gun as the men in yellow entered.

The woman screamed, her mouth visibly repeating, "No!" as she backed her body against the wall. The men in yellow grabbed her arms and thrust her through the door before marching her down the hallway. She fell to the floor then held her hands together, as if praying.

Or maybe she was begging the men not to take her.

The redhead melted into a puddle, crying and screaming.

The man in black lifted his gun and held it to the top of her skull, promising what would come if she didn't obey them.

The woman kept shaking her head, violently back and forth, faster and faster.

Where are they trying to take her?

She must have good reason to fear them. Maybe she's been taken before. Or maybe she's seen others taken who haven't returned.

What the fuck are these people doing?

The man in black thrust the gun at the redhead again as the men in yellow waved their hands, instructing her to get up and walk. The woman refused, her head down and shaking as her long, tangled hair waved back and forth in a violent swirl.

The man in black thrust his gun at the redhead again, but she was no longer looking at him. He fired his rifle. Charlie flinched and closed his eyes. When he opened them, she was on the ground, face first in a spreading pool of blood.

Charlie backed away from the glass, screaming.

One of the men in yellow looked down at his clipboard, flipped to the following page, then looked up and down the long rows of cells. He pointed at another cell on Charlie's row and ordered an old, naked black man to be pulled from the cell. The man didn't resist — *as if anyone would after seeing the woman shot dead* — walking with his shoulders slumped through the door with the three Guardsmen.

They left the redhead on the ground, probably as a warning.

Charlie looked up at Callie, who was staring at the dead woman and crying. The lights dimmed to black again, returning their world to darkness.

I will kill them all.

~

WHEN THE LIGHTS came back on, two men in yellow hazmat suits were dragging the dead woman from the block, then down the hallway to a door at the end. Then a third man in yellow came in to mop up the mess.

Charlie took advantage of the light, and turned his eyes to Callie.

She came to the glass, still not hiding her body. Nor did Charlie as he splayed his fingers on the window. For a long while, they simply stared at one another as Charlie felt a confused current of mixed emotions.

He thought he'd never see her again. Though Callie had rejected him before, and though they might never see freedom again, Charlie wanted to tell her that he loved her. He didn't need her to reciprocate. He just needed her to know because who knew how fleeting life was for them?

Maybe it wasn't love.

Maybe in the real world, they would have never met, and maybe they would both die here in the unfortunate hell where they finally found themselves together again. But as Charlie met her eyes and found nothing inside but sorrow and fear, he felt compelled to conquer the one fear that would make him ready for death.

As the cleanup man finished mopping the last of the redhead's blood, Charlie put his hand on his heart and mouthed the words, "I love you."

Callie's face crumbled, and she brought her hands to her face, crying.

He wasn't sure if he'd made a mistake in thinking that love in a place like this was pointless and that he'd only succeeded in upsetting her further.

The lights dimmed again, and the darkness returned.

Charlie went back to bed and cried into his pillow . . . until the cry turned into a scream.

～

CHARLIE DIDN'T REMEMBER FALLING asleep, but it didn't seem long before he was waking up to bright lights burning in his cell again.

The trio of death began its descent down the hall again, two men in yellow, one holding a clipboard, with the man in black behind, rifle in hand. Charlie and Callie were in the last two cells on the block, and as the trio drew closer, the swirl in his stomach turned especially sour.

"Here they come, Charlie Brown. They're coming to get you," Boricio said from behind him.

This time, Boricio was wearing all black. Pants, shirt, duster, and a black derby to match. Charlie wondered why he'd imagined Boricio dressed like this, or why he was apparently unable to imagine Boricio with a firearm or three to take these fuckers out.

The trio was two cells away. The lead with the yellow clipboard looked up at Charlie. Their eyes met.

"Uh-oh," Boricio shook his head. "This looks about as good as a *Showgirls* sequel."

No one was to Charlie's immediate left, and the trio had already passed the last of the cells except for his and Callie's. They were coming for one of them.

Fuck.

The man in yellow looked at Charlie, down at the clipboard, then over at Callie.

Oh no.

They walked to Callie's cell.

Please, please, turn around. Don't open her door. Don't open her door. Open my fucking door!

Charlie closed his eyes, not wanting to see reality as it spilled before him.

"They're opening her door," Boricio said.

Charlie opened his eyes.

"No!" he screamed.

The soundproof cell swallowed his screams.

Charlie pounded on the glass.

The man in black turned back toward Charlie. He could see the man's icy eyes behind his glass mask. Then he turned from Charlie, ignoring him, as the men in yellow pulled Callie from her cell.

She screamed, trying to crawl back to her cell, her eyes wide, staring at them and then at Charlie.

Charlie pounded harder, "No! Take me! Take me, you fucking cunts!"

He couldn't tell if they could hear what he was saying, but he was sure they heard the pounding and were choosing to ignore him.

Charlie pounded his fists harder. "No!" he screamed as each man in yellow grabbed one of Callie's arms, shoving her forward.

She turned back, her feet kicking, as she looked back at Charlie, screaming something he couldn't hear from her mouth or read from her lips.

He screamed, bashing the glass harder and harder, as it purpled his fists.

"Take me!"

"They can't hear ya, Charlie Cheesedick," Boricio said, as the men pushed Callie past another cell, now halfway to the door. "I think it's time to turn up the volume."

"How?"

"You know," Boricio said, even though Charlie didn't have a clue.

"What am I supposed to do?" Charlie screamed at Boricio.

"Go get her back," Boricio said, his eyes a set of steel marbles, settling on Charlie's. "Go and fucking get her. Now!"

Something sparked in Charlie, and he slammed his hands against the glass again, opening his mouth and screaming an unholy wail, far from human.

Glass shattered to the right of his cell door. Charlie stared in surprise, then turned to Boricio, who was pumping his fist in the air and screaming, "WOO HOO!, Chuckie Cheese-Dick, THAT'S what I'm talkin' about you panty jacking motherfucker! Go get 'em!"

Charlie stormed into the hall, naked, armed with nothing but an exploding fury.

The three Guardsmen stared at Charlie, and the damage he'd done to his cell, their eyes wide in disbelief. Callie's eyes were wide, too, as the men in yellow tightened their grips on her arms.

The man in black raised his rifle, aiming at Charlie.

Charlie ran at him, and as the man fired, Charlie sprang forward, leaping at least 20 yards before slamming into the man in black, sending him sprawling backward into the cell behind him. His rifle fell to the ground.

Charlie looked up at the man to Callie's left, his eyes wide behind the glass helmet. Charlie's arm thrust out — as if driven by instinct — and his fist smashed straight through the glass, and he plunged his fingers into the man's eyes, gouging them.

The man released Callie with a scream.

The other man let go of Callie, then dove for the rifle. She kicked it from reach as Charlie grabbed the man by his helmet, yanked it sideways, then shoved him forward and into the man in black.

Callie grabbed the gun and squeezed off a burst of shots into the men until the clip was empty and all three men were lying dead on the floor.

Charlie stared in disbelief at the carnage beneath them, then down at his arms and bloodied fists, expecting — and terrified — to see that he'd become a monster. But he looked normal, at least every part of his body he could see.

"How did you do that?" Callie asked, staring, eyes wide, and looking around, maybe trying to figure out what they should do next.

"I dunno." Charlie shook his head, not daring tell her the truth — that he was infected with God knows what.

He stared at Callie, feeling the warmth of her body, then reached out and embraced her, crying. "I thought they were gonna kill you," he said.

She held him back, her hands circling around his waist. He felt the warmth of her flesh against him, hardening his cock. He pulled away, embarrassed, then looked to the side, awkwardly.

The other prisoners started pounding on their cells, eyes and mouths wide open in likely pleas to be released.

Callie turned to Charlie, "What do we do?"

Charlie looked at the closed door in front of them, with its black glass hand panel to the right. Then he looked down at the dead men, trying to formulate a plan. Did they have keys, codes, or something he could use to get away? He bent to search, but the lights went black before he was halfway down.

"Fuck!" Charlie screamed.

The door in front of them opened, the light from the hallway beyond illuminating another four men in black coming toward them, armed with infrared goggles and rifles.

The door closed and cast them back into darkness.

Charlie turned to cover Callie with his body, shielding her from their intent.

Arcs of blue light shot from one of their weapons, sending Charlie to the ground, twitching in pain.

He tried to fight, but whatever bit of strength he'd been given was failing him now.

Charlie's world was nothing but pain until it was nothing but black.

~

TWENTY

Boricio Bishop

Other Earth
  Black Island Research Facility
  Level 7
  July 17, 2011
  One week after the accident …

I'M A MONSTER. *A fucking monster.*

Boricio stared at his reflection, unable to turn away from the ugliness.

He was on edge, his body in pain, and he was doing his best not to give into the swelling darkness within. Part of him just wanted to punch the mirror and let the rage out.

He clutched either side of the bathroom sink to keep himself from giving into impulse. As he stared at the ugliness in the mirror, his growl turned to laughter, dancing along the thin fissure between humor and pain, comedy and sorrow. If he didn't laugh, the rage would swallow him.

He looked like a goddamned action figure, with a patch over his right eye like a pirate. With his freshly shaved head, giant scar, and semi-permanent scowl, Boricio was a catch-phrase away from a Saturday morning cartoon.

Boricio snarled into the mirror. When life gave you lemons, it was time to get the salt and tequila.

"Staring all day won't change a thing," Will said, surprising him as he opened the bathroom door. "Don't worry, you make bald work," Will slapped Boricio affectionately on the shoulder.

Boricio was nervous as hell.

It had been three days since he and Rose were transferred to the Facility for rehab and treatment. Today was going to be the first time he saw Rose since the accident. The doctors had made him wait, saying she needed some more time, and that things were still fuzzy for her. Apparently, she was having trouble remembering stuff, though Will said it was a normal thing following head injuries, and that they shouldn't be too concerned yet. Will warned that she might not remember Boricio, but Boricio couldn't believe it.

Boricio had quipped, "Ain't nobody ever forgotten me yet. Even if they wanted to."

Though he'd been confident when he said that to Will, the fear was starting to take seed.

What if she did forget me?

Boricio wasn't sure what to expect, but his stomach was in knots as the moment drew closer. He looked down at the ring box on the sink — the one the cops pulled from the water — and hoped Will hadn't noticed it.

He didn't want Will to talk him out of what he was planning. He knew what Will would say — wait and do it right. Wait until she's out of the hospital and all this is behind you. But Boricio didn't want to wait any longer.

He'd waited too long already.

It was that hesitation that had kept him lonely for so long. Perhaps if he'd asked Rose sooner, they'd never have gotten into the accident. Perhaps they'd already have a child.

"Are you ready to see Rose?" Will asked.

Boricio nodded, but stayed silent as he palmed the ring box and put it in his pants pocket.

"Well, then let's get going," Will said, turning to leave the bathroom.

Boricio said, "I'll be right out," then stared at his reflection for another minute, feeling the anger rise again, his right hand shaking as he again resisted the urge to punch the mirror.

It shouldn't be like this.

When his right fist finally stopped shaking, Boricio left the bathroom, grabbed a sweater, and followed Will from his room.

The walk down the hall was silent as most of his time had been with Will since the accident. Boricio wasn't in the mood for Will's misguided efforts to cheer him up.

Boricio wanted to go somewhere to let off some steam, but didn't know where, or what to do when he got there. Will didn't have any ideas either. He kept telling Boricio that he had to just let it all out, and had to give himself permission to grieve the loss of their child because if he kept everything inside, it would all turn to venom. But Will was full of bullshit. What did he know of Boricio's pain? He didn't have to live in the icy shadows of his past, and had never lost a child.

Boricio didn't want to be angry with Will for not understanding, since it wasn't his fault, but the dark thoughts crawled through his mind like cockroaches anyway.

Will turned to look at Boricio. "You ready?"

What kind of a goddamned question is that?

Boricio tried not to snarl as he stepped past his adopted father and into Rose's room. Will stayed outside.

Boricio gasped, devastated, swallowing his shock as he looked at Rose. She barely looked like the same person.

Her face was puffy and pale, save for the bruised parts. Her hair was clean and brushed, but hanging from her face without any life. And when she looked up at him, there wasn't the slightest spark of recognition.

"Hi," she said, and then turned her attention back to the TV that was showing CNN Headline News. As if he were some kind of stranger.

No, this can't be happening.

She thinks I'm an orderly or something!

Will was right. And Boricio hated him for it.

"Hi, Rose," he said.

She slowly moved her eyes from the TV back to Boricio, giving him the thinnest of smiles but saying nothing. That nothing killed everything inside Boricio, then turned it inside out and black and rancid.

That nothing made him want to give in to the swirling darkness within him.

"Rose?" Boricio tried again, giving the light one more chance before he let the darkness come to claim him.

TWENTY-ONE

Charlie Wilkens

Charlie woke to find himself in another shroud of darkness, lying on another mattress. He thought his body should have been aching, but it wasn't.

He was tired, though. And his brain was foggy. Memories fell in snippets, glimpses of impossible playing out in his head — how he had somehow leapt impossibly far, knocking a Guardsman to the floor before thrusting his hand through another's glass helmet.

Impossible.

Unless I'm infected.

Where's Callie?

Charlie sat, trying to pull shapes from the darkness. When he sat, a bright light whitened the cell, blinding him with its sudden intensity.

"Remain still," a man's voice said through speakers above the door. "Do you understand?"

Charlie said yes, nodding as an uneasy feeling swirled through his gut.

"I'm going to explain something to you, so you need to pay real close attention." The voice paused, then said, "Do you understand?"

"Yes!" Charlie shouted, annoyed, and terrified of what was about to happen.

They'd better not do anything to Callie.

"I don't like a single dingleberry on this shit-laced ass crack," Boricio said, appearing beside Charlie again, still in the black duster and hat.

Boricio paced the room, looking around, "Come on, do some of that voodoo hoodoo that you do so fuckin' well, Charlie Brown."

Something tapped on the cell beside Charlie, and he jumped, surprised.

Callie was now in the cell beside him. They'd not taken her, after all. Or they'd taken her and brought her back. She was still naked, and looking exhausted as she set her hand against the glass. Though the light in her cell was off, it had a faint glow from the light of his cell that allowed him to see her well enough.

Callie said nothing. Charlie smiled, then looked up at the ceiling.

"Good, you see your girlfriend," the voice said. "Now, I'd like to direct your attention to the holes above you. Notice, there are 16 holes per cell. You've probably noticed them already." The voice paused, then added, "Am I correct?"

Charlie nodded, assuming they were watching him from a hidden camera.

"Good," the voice said, confirming his suspicion.

"Now I'd like to direct your attention to the cell directly across from you."

A light went on in the cell across from Charlie. Beside that cell, Charlie saw his old one, glass still shattered. The lit cell led Charlie's attention to a naked man lying on his mattress, looking up at the lights, confused. Though the man appeared around 20, he was gaunt, and extremely tired-looking. Dark circles painted the undersides of his eyes, and his long, dark hair was a rat's nest. The man muttered something toward the ceiling.

"Are you watching?" the voice in Charlie's cell asked.

"Yes," Charlie said.

"Pay close attention. And I suggest you direct your girl-friend's attention to the cell as well." Charlie looked over and saw Callie nervously looking at him, rather than the guy. Charlie pointed at the cell across from them.

"Watch closely," the voice repeated.

The guy began to cough and cover his mouth, as if some sort of gas was getting piped into the room. *They're gassing him!* Charlie wanted to tell the voice to stop, but knew with a cold certainty that the Guardsman in charge wouldn't. Charlie wanted to look away, but morbid curiosity wouldn't let him.

Flames suddenly shot from the ceiling, igniting the entire cell in a single explosive ball of fire. Charlie jumped to his feet and stared, mouth open without any words, screams, or whispers of terror.

"WOO-HOO!!" Boricio cackled. "Let's get us some marshmallows, because THAT right there is a fucking fire!"

Charlie turned to Callie, who was still staring, unable to look away, her eyes wide and brimming with tears.

"What did you think?" the voice said.

Charlie said nothing, just glared at the ceiling.

The voice moved from calm to sinister. "Well," it said, "it doesn't really matter. What does matter is your understanding that if you try another stunt like the one you pulled earlier, I will roast your bitch alive and make you eat her for fucking dinner." The voice still deceptively pleasant, said, "Is that clear?"

Charlie stared at Callie, fear twisting like a serrated blade through his stomach.

The voice waited through a long minute before it said, "I asked you if that was clear. I suggest you answer the second time since I never, ever ask a third."

"Yes!" Charlie roared.

"Good," the voice said, almost hissing.

The lights went black.

Charlie ran to the wall beside Callie's and ran his fingers across it as flames continued to lick the other cell's interior, casting a faint, orange glow inside both of their cells, barely illuminating Callie.

Charlie touched the cold glass opposite her, their hands separated by inches that may as well have been miles. He wanted nothing more than to be anywhere else with Callie and a couch, where he could wrap his arms around her and fall gently to sleep.

Charlie didn't even want to have sex. He just wanted to lie beside her and feel not so alone. So devoid of hope.

The fire died inside the man's cell, and the entire block went dark. Charlie lay on the mattress, his hand on the glass, and cried himself to sleep.

~

"WAKE UP!"

Charlie woke to the voice again.

A few hours probably had passed since the fireworks. He'd fallen asleep with his hand on the glass, meeting Callie's, their mattresses propped against the dividing barrier.

A light went on above him, about a tenth as dim as it was before, just enough for him to see, but far less blinding. Charlie glanced over and saw the shadow of Callie, still asleep on her mattress, her hand against the wall.

"You have a visitor," the voice said. "Someone interested in what you did yesterday. Someone who would like to have a word with you. Remember the rules. One more stunt, and your bitch is dinner. Understand?"

"No, he's fucking retarded," Boricio snarled, suddenly in

the room, wearing the same outfit as before, except now he had on a miner's hat, with a light that wasn't working.

"Yes," Charlie said. "I've got it."

The door at the end of the hall opened to a single set of footsteps owned by another yellow hazmat suit, without any clipboard or weapon.

The footsteps made their way down the row of cells.

"What the fuck does he want?" Boricio asked.

I dunno, Charlie thought, not wanting to speak out loud since they were monitoring him.

"Well, this should be good and goddamned interesting," Boricio said, plopping on the mattress and crossing his legs. "Looks like you've made yourself someone worth talking to, Charlie Boy! Maybe you can ask for a raise!"

Boricio looked at Charlie's dangling dick. "You mind tucking the turtle away, Charlie Brown? I didn't come here to give you a conjugal visit. Though, I'd love to step on over and give ole Callie a bit o' the bone and splatter, if you get my drift."

I'd have to be an idiot not to get your drift. You're as subtle as a forest fire.

"Don't worry, I'm not gonna bang on Callie's precious backdoor. Remember, I'm in your head. And well, let's just say, that makes *me* part of *you,* and you know she ain't gonna have any part of you in any part of her, so I'm sorta screwed, fuck you very much." Boricio shook his head.

Charlie watched Boricio's hat turn back and forth and wondered why he'd imagined Boricio wearing a miner's helmet — a broken one, at that.

The man in yellow reached Charlie's cell, then pressed something on the panel outside his door.

The voice above Charlie crackled to life. "Remember," it said, "be a good boy, or … "

"Yeah, yeah," Charlie shouted as the man in yellow entered his cell.

The man looked Charlie up and down, then spoke, his voice now coming through the speakers above. He wasn't the same man who'd been taunting him over the speakers, but his voice was oddly familiar.

"That was some show you put on out there," the man said from inside his hazmat suit as he continued staring at Charlie like some kind of lab animal.

Something about the man's accent was unsettling in its vague familiarity, as was his appearance, though Charlie couldn't quite place where he might have seen the man before.

Boricio jumped up and down behind Charlie. "Holy shit, Charlie Brown! What the fuck is this?"

What?

"You don't see it?" Boricio said, pointing frantically at the man's mask. "Look closer, you dumb, lanky pile of shit, squeeze those beady fucker eyes of yours together and tell me you don't recognize who in the fuck-all you're looking at!"

Charlie examined the man's face. He was in his early to mid-30s and bald, with an eye patch over his left eye and a long, ugly scar running in a deep ravine from the high above his patch to the low of his cheek below.

Something about him *was* damned familiar, like a word on the tip of Charlie's tongue he simply couldn't remember.

"Dude," Boricio said stepping right beside the man in yellow, pointing manically back at the man and then himself. "Look, Charlie! It's me! It's me!"

Charlie's jaw dropped.

It was beer-battered bullshit, no doubt, but Boricio was right.

TO BE CONTINUED ...

Episode 15

(THIRD EPISODE OF SEASON THREE)

"Team Building Exercise"

TWENTY-TWO

Teagan McLachlan

In the dream, the sun had kissed Teagan's skin. But when she woke, it was darkness that met her. Darkness and the sound of whistling. Above her, a dark cloud engulfed the inside of the car.

But the dark cloud wasn't a cloud; it was something else — pulsating with serpentine motion, shifting form, and hovering its attention toward her as if it were alive.

Her eyes widened in fear, and the cloud seized her terror, using it to multiply its mass into a swiftly spinning billow, melting through the air on its way toward Teagan's trembling body, crackling with a cool current of live electricity that made the tiny hairs on her arm dance.

Teagan was paralyzed, unable to move.

Her father was asleep, slumped over the steering wheel, and her mother an echo beside him. The car slowly rolled forward, the headlights slicing through the inky silence of the highway, flashing on a guardrail quickly growing larger as the car rolled forward.

Teagan panicked. She wanted to scream, but had to move first, needed to reach across the front seat, but couldn't. The cloud started spinning faster and whistling louder — an angry tornado tearing through the tiny interior of the car.

The whistling kept screaming, splitting the sanity inside her head. Teagan reached up to cover her ears and cried out as if that might mute it.

Light suddenly appeared — brighter than anything Teagan had ever seen.

The bright light was then enveloped by something blacker than the darkness outside, and in that instant her parents were gone. The car smashed into the guardrail with a grinding crunch, and then a thundering thud before coming to a jarring stop. The darkness above her had evaporated into wisps with her family.

Something seemed familiar, *too familiar* — flooding Teagan with a sense of déjà vu she couldn't shake.

Trembling and confused, Teagan leaned forward and looked at the clock on the radio: 2:15 a.m.

The odd, familiar current grew stronger inside her.

She'd been here before.

Teagan heard the sound of a baby crying. Her baby, Becca. She frantically searched every seat in the car, but her baby was nowhere. She swallowed hard, realizing the sound was bleeding into the car from outside, somewhere in the dark.

She looked out the window but couldn't see her. Teagan was terrified of the darkness outside, thinking of the black cloud that had crackled to life and taken her parents away.

What if it's out there — waiting?

Teagan couldn't leave her child out there alone, though. Becca was only 1 month old and defenseless against the darkness.

Teagan forced herself into bravery, then threw the rear door open and launched herself into the night, moving with a fluid grace she could only find in her dreams.

Yes, this is a dream.

None of this is happening.

Becca's cries dragged Teagan's attention toward the trunk of the car. Her baby was in the trunk. Milk spotted the front of her shirt as she ran to open the trunk.

Where are the keys?!

She looked up and through the rear window of the car where she was drawn to the keys dangling from the steering wheel. But that wasn't the only thing Teagan saw in the car — the dark cloud was back as well, churning fast, spinning in furious circles as its mass spread throughout the cabin.

The keys were held captive in the icy heart of the darkness. Teagan had no choice but to swallow her fear, then reach inside and grab them.

Hurry. Do it!

Becca's cries echoed louder inside the trunk as Teagan's heart furiously pounded. She forced herself toward the car's front door as her fingers trembled at the handle.

Open the door. Reach in. You'll be in and out before it can do anything to you.

Teagan watched as the mass spun even faster, growing inexplicably darker. Something from the center of the vortex smacked hard against the window, leaving a red, bloody smear before it was pulled back violently into the vortex.

Something else hit the window, a torn chunk of flesh that used to be wearing her father's watch, but now wore only his fat and tarnished silver wedding band.

Every window exploded at once — an eruption of a million shards, spitting a swarm of glass and black from the car, where the cloud instantly gathered into an even larger mass above the car, spinning and growing with intensity.

Teagan screamed and ran from the car — away from her child, still crying in the trunk — slicing her heart into a hundred guilty ribbons.

How can you leave your child to that?

Teagan could leave her child because she was too terrified

to go back, even though she hated herself further with every fresh step she took from the trunk. She stopped for a moment, turned, and looked back at the growing darkness.

Go back. Save her!

What kind of mother leaves her child to die?

She's safer in the trunk. I'll go back to get her.

The darkness began to shake the car as its tendrils reached down and ripped the lid from the trunk and tossed it into its vortex, where it spun with the darkness and then shot out into the woods off the side of the highway.

Teagan screamed as it reached in to claim Becca.

Teagan woke to the sound of her daughter sobbing.

BLACK ISLAND, *New York*
April 2012
SIX MONTHS AFTER THE EVENT …

EVEN WITH BECCA CRYING, she was relieved to be away from the dream, and safe in her bedroom. A soft-blue light beside Becca's crib illuminated her weeping infant. Teagan was at the crib in seconds.

"You need to be changed," she said, lifting Becca to her lips, giving her a kiss, then setting her back in the crib. "I'll be right back, Baby B. Just one sec."

Teagan fumbled in the dim light, and gathered the diapers, cream, and wipes. As she changed Becca, named after her older sister, Teagan couldn't help but feel the stain of guilt left to linger after her dream's decision. What should have passed moments after waking was soaking deeper into something inside her.

Teagan started to cry. "You okay?" Ed asked from bed.

"Yes," Teagan said, nodding even though he probably couldn't see her in the dark, wiping her eyes and feeling like a fool. She had been so hyper-emotional since delivering Becca in February, and hated feeling so raw all the time, always at the edge of every emotion. Having such limited control over her emotions made Teagan feel even younger than sleeping with a 44-year-old man did.

She finished wrapping Becca in warm clothes and swaddling her in a blanket like a baby burrito, then returned to bed and started to nurse. The frail infant's lips sucking away, fingers curled and eyes closed, made Teagan feel even guiltier for leaving her baby in the trunk, regardless of whether it was a dream.

She tried to tell herself that she'd never do that in real life.

I would die to protect her.

"What's wrong?" Ed said, wiping his eyes and sitting up beside her, then wrapping a long arm around her and drawing her and Becca closer.

"Just a nightmare," Teagan said, laughing at how silly she felt. "It's nothing, really."

"Do you want to talk about it?"

Teagan suspected Ed didn't really want to discuss her dream, though. While he was far more communicative than the Ed from her world — the one who had saved her life — this "other Ed" was still rough around the edges with talking about stuff like feelings, dreams, and other things that weren't black and white and made of logic.

She turned to face Ed in the dim light of their bedroom, thinking how much safer she felt with him beside her. Their friendship had only recently blossomed into something more — almost in spite of them each denying the feelings they had both developed over the course of a few months. Teagan wasn't sure if she could call the feelings inside her *love*; they weren't as pure or true as what she felt for Becca — that feeling that she would do anything and kill anyone to protect her child. But still, the feelings were stronger than anything she'd ever felt before, even if they were born from sorrow and a bounty of mental baggage.

"Nah, it's just a silly nightmare," Teagan said, nudging herself closer to Ed.

"Well, you're safe now," he said, kissing her forehead. Ed leaned over and kissed Becca's nearly bald head.

He's so sweet to Becca.

He would never leave her in a trunk!

The new thought pushed Teagan into a fresh batch of tears, which then pulled further concern from Ed.

"You *sure* you're okay?" His brows were now furrowed enough for Teagan to see in the dark.

She was about to answer when sirens outside started to wail, scratching the silence into an agitated scream, as the one screech quickly turned to chaos.

Ed's phone rang, and Becca started to scream.

"What's that?!" Teagan shouted over the loud siren. She had never heard a siren on the island before.

Ed didn't answer. He had the phone in his hand and his lips at the receiver, and his expression had already gone from concerned to something she'd never seen on his face before, or the other Ed's for that matter. His eyes were dilated wide with a horrible fear. He hung up the phone and set it on the nightstand.

"What is it?"

Ed said, "They broke out."

"*Who* broke out?"

He leapt from the bed, threw on his clothes, then turned to Teagan. "The infected."

～

TWENTY-THREE

Boricio Bishop

Black Island Research Facility
Black Island, New York
Other Earth
Aug. 17
TWO MONTHS BEFORE THE EVENT …

BORICIO WASN'T willing to wait another day.

He had waited too long already. Rose could already be a full month into recovery, and *should* have been a month into recovery. Instead, Boricio had allowed Will to warm his hands beneath the fat of his ass.

Boricio was sick of the month-old argument, and angry at the old man for standing so decisively in his way. For a guy with a third eye, Boricio was sometimes shocked at how much shit Will was blind to.

Will kept saying, "We'll talk about it later," but later was a word that couldn't be measured, so fuck it with a meter stick.

Rose wasn't getting any better. If anything, she was getting worse. Her days were often filled with pain, and her memory wasn't coming back. She was also having trouble with her short-term memory. There were a few days during Boricio's visits that a glimpse of the past would come forth, and she'd smile and remember a snippet of their life together. And those moments helped to bridge the distance between them, helped her feel comfortable with him and not treat him like a stranger. But the next day, the memory was gone, and it was if she'd never remembered anything. The coldness had returned.

Some days, he felt as if she were looking at him for the first time.

And each of those stranger's glances was a knife in his heart.

He would take a hundred, hell, a million, such knives if she weren't also in constant pain.

From the waist down, she felt nothing. And likely never would again. But the parts where she could feel anything usually felt only pain. Boricio couldn't stand to see her in such misery.

He had to go over his father's head and see Dr. Williams, the lead scientist overseeing research on the vials.

Williams was instrumental in Luca's success, and would be a fool to ignore the data and deny Rose the same fighting chance. He may have been many things — egotistical, obsessive, unable to relate to humans — as far as Boricio could tell, but he wasn't a fool. Especially not when compared to Will, who was becoming more of a fence-sitting philosopher than a man driven into action by curiosity. Telling the difference between philosopher and fool was increasingly more difficult for Boricio.

Boricio did wonder for a small moment if maybe he was wrong, and he was perhaps overestimating Williams' willingness to bend the rules. Then Boricio thought back to the wide smile slathered all over his face in the aftermath of Luca's tests and felt certain that Williams simply needed the right question asked in precisely the right way to give them both the only answer they wanted.

Boricio reached the middle of the hall and the pair of access elevators and stepped inside, with someone coming in behind him. He pressed 7, then set his hand against the graphite-colored palm reader, fingers evenly splayed.

"Access: Denied. Insufficient Clearance Level," the display read.

What the fuck?

Boricio tried again, pressing harder. The green lines on the display rose, then fell, then turned red.

"Access: Denied. Insufficient Clearance Level."

Boricio started to breathe slowly, exactly as he'd been practicing to steady the rising anger, but a thick wad of air was suddenly trapped in his throat, and his clenched fist was shaking at his side, one bad second away from flying into the hard alloy of the elevator door.

"You okay, Mr. Bishop?"

Boricio slowly turned to face Richard Styley, the dweeby systems designer from Level 3 who had followed Boricio into the elevator.

"Yeah, Richard, I'm doing great. Thanks." Boricio smiled, the need to slam his fist into the door of the elevator making itself too comfortable to leave — a lot like Styley, who stood three feet from Boricio, staring.

"Can I help you with something, Styley?"

It must have been something in the way he said it, because Styley took a dweeby step back from Boricio and started shaking his head furiously back and forth. "No, Mr. Bishop," he said. "You just look upset, so I was seeing if there was something I could help you with. Like maybe you were having trouble with the elevator."

No, I'm not having any trouble with the elevator. I'm having trouble with a know-it-all philosophizing dick tip, fuckyouverymuch.

"No," Boricio shook his head, unclenching his fist and relaxing his fingers. "No trouble at all, Richard. I just forgot what I was here for, and I hate it when that happens."

"I know how that feels." Styley smiled, though Boricio thought the smile looked thinner than a summer sweater.

Boricio nodded, then pressed 5, and set his hand on the scanner. The green line went up and down, then dinged as the elevator began to move. Boricio ignored Styley as the man pressed the 6 and put his hand on the scanner.

The elevator doors dinged closed. Boricio quickly scowled, then scrubbed it from his face before the doors opened to Level 5 a few seconds later. He stepped from the elevator before the doors were even half open, ignoring Styley as he said a meek "Goodbye," and marched down the hallway toward Will's office, trying to keep his calm, despite an inferno of rage burning inside him, licking an inner certainty that Will had revoked his access to Level 7.

Boricio spent the entire hallway breathing in and out and in and out as he tried untangling the pretzeled thoughts and twisted circles threading through his head. Another 15 minutes of Boricio's practiced breathing, or hell, even a long hour of Lamaze wouldn't be enough. He stormed into Will's office, barely able to keep accusation and anger from owning his voice.

"Wanna tell me why the fuck my security clearance has been downgraded?!" Boricio yelled. "I just tried to get to Level 7, like I have every day since you dragged my ass and entire life onto this island."

Will calmly looked up from his desk, sighed, then held Boricio's angry gaze for a half minute or so before turning his attention back to the thin stack of sheets scattered across his desk. He stared down for another second, then shook his head and pushed the papers into a pile toward the corner.

"Boricio," he said, "I don't want to fight, not about this or anything else."

"If you didn't want to fight, then you wouldn't have done sh … *stuff* behind my back." He watched his language, giving

Will nothing to bitch about and only the facts to argue. Boricio swallowed and breathed, waiting for Will to respond.

"I understand how you're feeling, and hear what you're saying," Will said, "And I'm sorry you're angry. But I did what I had to do and stand by my decision. Unfortunately, you weren't around when I made it. If you were standing beside me, I would have told you. *I* certainly have nothing to hide. Can you say the same?"

Boricio's fingers curled back into their fists.

Will shook his head, sighed, and then stood up and walked around his desk to face Boricio.

"I'm not afraid of you, Boricio. I am your father. And I will do what is right, always. I'm sorry about Rose." He cleared his throat. "Truly I am. But there's nothing I can do. What's happened has happened, and the best thing we can do now — the healthiest thing for us to do together — is to accept that reality and do what we can within the realms of proven medicine, not the vials. What I cannot allow to happen," he bored his eyes into Boricio's, "what I *will not* allow to happen, is for you to go over my head again. That isn't good for Level 7, Son, and it's definitely not good for our family."

"I didn't go over your head," Boricio said. "Or behind your back. Unless you've suddenly been named as head of the Remedy Project and didn't take me out for a steak to celebrate, then I beg to fucking differ."

Will had walked around to Boricio's side of the desk, but the words spilled from Boricio's lips without a single breath taken, and nearly every word from the inside of a snarl made him take a surprisingly large step back.

Boricio finished. "You're a *consultant* to the Remedy Project, Will, a *consultant* just like me, not in charge. And what I thought had to be done with Luca didn't require your particular brand of it *ain't gonna work*, so I took it to Williams, who knew I was right, and helped to save *your* son from the death sentence *you* were all too willing to accept."

"It was wrong," Will said. "And *you* were wrong. *Are* wrong. The only reason you're even allowed to step foot inside this facility is because I brought you in and put my name beside yours. You may be too old for me to be your legal guardian out there," Will pointed past the wall of his office, "but in here, that's exactly who I am, like it or not. I gave you full access, and you abused your position."

"Sorry that your memory's only working in bits and pieces, Pops, but the truth is that you brought me into Level 7 to bail you out, and we both know it."

"I never needed you to bail me out, Boricio," Will said. "That's ridiculous."

"Well, you sure as shit needed me to help you 'deal with all the assholes and politics of the job,' or is that not the exact words you used when you asked me to come work here?"

Boricio took another step toward Will. "I'm the only one in here who gets you, and that's why you need me. So, what are you gonna do if you downgrade me, *Dad?* How are you gonna get by?"

"I managed before, and I'll manage again, but *this* is unacceptable. I will not be held hostage by my son, or made to feel as though my instincts are frail. You don't know everything, Boricio. Some things you don't know on purpose because you can't. And there are times when you have to be okay with that. Despite your access, and our relationship, I am privy to classified information that I cannot legally share with you."

For the first time, Will's eyes held a hint of apology. "I'm sorry, Boricio, but that's the way it is. This is one of those times where you just have to trust me. Honestly, after all these years I feel it's the least I deserve." He shook his head. "You have no idea how much acid you give me." He pushed his hand against his stomach, as though the acid was leaking.

For a second, Boricio felt so bad he wanted to vomit, but

the bear inside him knew it was all bullshit. Will was making excuses. If Boricio knew something that Will needed to know, then he wouldn't give a dozen undigested kernels worth of crap whether it was classified or not.

Boricio said, "What am I supposed to do with my day then, Will, huh? If I'm not heading into Level 7, then what in the hell am I doing? Why even be here? I might as well go to New Orleans and be a cook."

"No need to be all dramatic, Son," he shook his head, now standing beside Boricio. Will set his calm hands gently on Boricio's shoulders, and looked him in the eyes. "This isn't a forever decision. It's temporary; difficult to make but the right thing to do. The downgrade is in effect immediately because I felt it was necessary. The second I no longer feel that way it will fade like a hangover. I promise." Will smiled at Boricio. "Okay?"

Boricio didn't say anything because he didn't know what he could say. No, it wasn't fucking okay. He was about to nod anyway when Will said, "There's plenty to do, Boricio. Marshall needs all sorts of help on his lab work and filing. Wilson, too. Most of Level 5 in fact. There's more than enough to keep you busy for now."

Will suddenly brightened, as if only at that moment realizing the true abundance of available work.

Boricio wasn't smiling.

"What in the hell are you saying, Will?"

"I'm not saying anything," Will shook his head, suddenly flustered. "Except that there's plenty of work to be done and that you don't have to worry about having nothing to do."

Boricio said, "Well, then maybe you can clarify. Because what it sounded like you said was that you wanted me to be an administrative assistant for all the Dilberts on Level 5. Did I misunderstand your message?"

Boricio's shoulders felt like they'd grown three feet. Something inside him enjoyed watching Will retreating back to his side of the desk, and the way his pores were practically bleeding fear.

If Boricio couldn't get the respect he deserved, he'd damned well settle for fear.

"Boricio," Will said. "Be reasonable. I'm not asking you to leave. I'm asking you to be patient, and to trust me." He leaned across the desk, either less afraid or swallowing his fear. "I promise, I'm only thinking of you. As much as you think you deserve my faith, and you do, Boricio, I deserve yours, too. And I asked for it first." Will gave him a weak smile then said, "Please believe I know what's best. At least this time."

Boricio shook his head. "I can't do that," he said. "Because you don't. You didn't know what was best for Luca, and you don't know what's best for Rose."

"Boricio … "

"I don't want to hear it," Boricio breathed slowly in and out, barely keeping the snarl from his throat. He tore the badge hanging from the lanyard around his neck, threw it onto Will's desk, then ripped a bright-pink Post-it from the top of a multicolored stack.

Boricio wrote *I QUIT* in black Sharpie, then said, "I've always hated the goddamned lighting in this place anyway. Fucking fluorescents."

Boricio stormed from his father's office, barely containing the swelling rage.

~

TWENTY-FOUR

Charlie Wilkens

Black Mountain, Georgia
March 2012
FIVE MONTHS AFTER THE EVENT …

CHARLIE STARED at the man standing in the yellow hazmat suit. Though he was bald, scarred, and wore an eye patch on his left eye, he looked *exactly* like the Boricio who sprang him and Adam from the weird-ass cult compound not too long ago.

Yet, judging from the lack of recognition in his eyes, he may as well have been a stranger.

Just as Charlie was about to say something about being Boricio, the Imaginary Boricio beside him finally spoke up.

"Wait! Don't say anything, Charlie Brown. There's something weird about this guy. Yeah, he looks like me, but there's something . . . off."

Imaginary Boricio looked closer, then turned to Charlie, "I haven't been gone long enough to have a scar that faded. That isn't me! Maybe he's some long lost twin or somethin'!" He laughed. "My real daddy musta been a bad, bad man."

Charlie looked the hazmat-suited man in the eye, "Who are you?"

"My name is Boricio Bishop," he said. "And you're at Black Mountain Research Facility."

"Whoa," Imaginary Boricio spun on his foot. "Looks like they're slopping up the beer-battered bullshit in piles over here in the *Twilight Zone Inn*! Don't say dick about him not knowing you, Chucky Fuckstick! There's something about this shit that's fishier than Fat Betty's sloppy tuna. I say keep your mouth shut. Just the facts, ma'am, least until we figure this shit out."

Imaginary Boricio paced the glass cell as the hazmat-suit Boricio continued to speak.

"Have you heard of Black Mountain?"

"No," Charlie said.

"We're pretty much all that remains of the United States government. There's a few other facilities throughout the world, but we lost contact after The Event. Our job now is to try and return things to normal."

Charlie wanted to snap, ask the one-eyed asshole if his idea of normal was killing innocent people, but instead he chose to ask a question since this was the first person he met — even if he was Boricio's twin — who seemed to have some insight into whatever in the hell happened to the world on Oct. 15.

"What was *The Event*?"

Boricio looked down for a moment, then back up at Charlie. "That's classified information. What I can tell you is that we're trying to cure the outbreak. Which is what makes you a curious oddity."

"What outbreak?" Charlie asked. "And why am I an *oddity*?"

"The outbreak is alien in nature. The aliens infect humans, like parasites, and eventually take over their hosts. Our tests say that you're infected, and your blood work clearly shows infection. And judging from the way you laid my men out, I'd say you're clearly not *just* human. Yet you show no signs of degeneration like the others. It's as if the infection enhanced you, but has not taken over your system — suggesting a symbiotic relationship, which is either an anomaly or an evolution. We need to understand what's happening with you."

"I'm not infected!" Charlie said. "When did you take my blood?"

"While you were unconscious. It's standard procedure. And yes, you *are* infected. Have you been bitten by an alien or infected human?"

Charlie tried to think back to his run-ins with the creatures. He couldn't recall having been bitten. "No, I don't think so," he shook his head. "Scratched, maybe, but not bitten. Can you be infected through a scratch?"

"Possibly through any exchange of fluid, do you remember how long ago?"

"I dunno. A few days I guess. We were attacked by a guy who'd turned into one of those things. He might've scratched me, I can't remember."

Hazmat-suit Boricio said, "Hmm. Yeah, you should be showing more physical signs by now. Most of the infected begin to visibly mutate within 48 hours or so."

"Is it possible that I'm a carrier and can't catch it?"

"It's not like a virus," Boricio said. "They are parasites. If it's in you, it's in you. It's not a matter of catching something. You are infected. Yet, it hasn't advanced to later stages of the infection as we understand it. My scientists are speculating that perhaps there is something unique about your case or you that would explain this — something they may be able to use to develop a cure to drive out the parasites. Or reverse the mutation to restore an already infected person's humanity. We'd like your help."

Something was calming in this Boricio's voice, which cast

him as day to the other Boricio's night. This Boricio seemed more intelligent and deliberate, calmer in his approach. Imaginary Boricio had momentarily vanished again, leaving Charlie alone to contemplate what he should say or do next.

He wanted to trust this new Boricio, but was still shaken by what the Guardsmen had done.

"Why should I trust you?" Charlie asked. "You have us locked in here like animals. And you burned a man alive in front of me!"

"You're locked up here as a quarantine measure."

"Is everyone here infected?" Charlie interrupted. "Is Callie?" He pointed at Callie, who was still sleeping in the next cell.

"No, she is not infected. Nor is everyone else. Some people are here because they'd volunteered to help us."

"She didn't volunteer!" Charlie said. "Your men in vans came and grabbed her. Just like they did me and my friend, Adam!"

Boricio looked over at Callie, then back at Charlie. "We did bring some people in from the outside, but I assure you, they're better off here than out there. It's dangerous out there. No one will survive long once these things colonize the planet. We need people to help us test. Not only to cure the infected, but to stop the aliens. To kill them."

"So, you're testing people against their will? You're testing Callie against her will? What kinds of tests are these? Are you infecting people?"

Boricio sighed again. He was far more patient than the Boricio whom Charlie knew, who would have long ago smacked Charlie into obedience, saying something like, "You don't like it, Charlie Cocksucker? Tough shit." Then he would've given Charlie the finger and added, "Sit on this and rotate, Chuckie Fuckstick!"

This Boricio chose his words wisely, which made Charlie wonder why he was being so patient.

Wait . . . do I have some leverage to negotiate?

"Ding! Ding! Ding! Tell the boy what he's won," Imaginary Boricio suddenly chimed, appearing beside Charlie again. "These fuckers need what you've got in that body of yours! I'll bet it feels good to finally not get handed a rock, eh, Charlie Brown?"

The real Boricio finally spoke, "Sometimes, our hands are forced to do things we'd rather not do, for the greater good. We must test a few to save the many."

Charlie shook his head. "You're killing people. Turning them into monsters!"

"It's science," Boricio snapped, his patience thinning. "We don't have the luxury of fancy computer models or a supply of lab animals to work with now. These aliens are spreading, and we are this close to understanding the how's and why's and actually helping people. This close," Boricio repeated, holding his yellow-gloved fingers about an inch apart. "Would you have us abandon our research and throw our hands up in defeat until every man, woman, and child left in this world is either infected or food? Because that's what happens when we do nothing."

Charlie shook his head, "No, I guess not."

"We're not the bad guys," Boricio said.

"Then why did you burn that man? What had he done to deserve that?"

Boricio's eye met Charlie's. "We needed something to get you in line. To see that we mean business. That man was no innocent. When we found him, he'd been keeping a child in a cage — as a sex slave. So, I have few compunctions about experimenting on, or killing, a child rapist. How about you?"

"No," Charlie shook his head. "But you guys killed an innocent child, too! One who wasn't even infected!"

Boricio's head tilted ever so slightly, "What are you talking about? We don't have any children as test subjects."

"No, in the truck I was being transported in. There was a

young boy with me. We were the only survivors. The men tested him, and he showed negative, or whatever you call it when someone's not infected. So, they told him to come to the van with me, and when he started walking they shot him in the back of head. Pow! Just like that. Dead! How the fuck is that you being the good guys?!"

Boricio stared at Charlie like his eyes were lie detectors. After a long moment, he asked, "Which of my men did this?"

Charlie remembered the man's name clearly on his badge. "Foster."

Boricio pushed a button on the side of his helmet and instructed someone over the radio to send Foster to Level 9.

Moments later, Foster appeared, in his black uniform, gun holstered at his side. He wasn't wearing a helmet like some of the other Guardsmen on the block.

"Yes, sir, you wanted to see me?" Foster said, looking at Boricio. If he'd noticed Charlie at all, he wasn't showing it.

Boricio turned to Charlie, "Is this the man?"

Foster turned, meeting Charlie's eyes. Charlie swallowed as the man's steely gaze almost dared Charlie to say something. He wondered if Foster knew why he'd been called by Boricio — if he knew that Charlie had ratted him out.

Imaginary Boricio piped up, "Yeah, that's the fucker, right there! Only a dick with no balls would be pussy enough to shoot a kid!"

Charlie nodded. "Yes. That's him."

"What?" Foster said, his facade cracking.

"Did you shoot a child in the back of the head?"

Foster swallowed, saying nothing at first.

"And don't you dare lie to me. You know I can sniff your lies like shit in your crack," hazmat-suit Boricio said.

Foster swallowed again, his eyes wide and unable to break from Boricio's gaze.

"Yes, sir. But . . . "

"No buts!" Boricio shouted, so loud Charlie leapt back involuntarily.

Foster zipped his lips.

"Give me your gun," Boricio said.

"Why?" Foster asked.

"I said, GIVE ME YOUR GUN!" Boricio shouted, spittle flying from his mouth and coating the inside of his helmet.

Foster cowered. If Foster could have shrunk and run away, or melted into a puddle on the floor, Charlie was sure he would have. He handed Boricio his pistol, his hand trembling. Only when Charlie saw the trembling hand did he realize what was happening. Boricio wasn't asking him to turn in his gun like a police chief would ask a cop to turn in his badge and gun.

"Why would you kill a child?" Boricio asked. "Who the fuck do you think you are to go around killing children?"

"I dunno, sir, I was just . . . "

"No!" Boricio said as he pulled one of his bulky, yellow gloves from his hand. Beneath that glove he wore a slimmer, skintight black glove. Boricio took the gun, then checked the chamber.

"You are a Black Mountain Guardsman, not some mercenary thug! Am I clear?"

"Yes, sir," Foster shouted like he was in boot camp.

Boricio stared at the man while Charlie wondered what was going to happen. The tension was a fog in the room, and his heart a machine gun emptying its clip.

Finally, Boricio said, "No, I don't think you do understand, turn around."

Foster cried, "Why?"

"I said, turn around!" Boricio snapped.

Foster turned, slowly, his whole body trembling, waiting, and unable to see what Boricio was going to do next.

"Leave," Boricio said.

Foster's eyes widened, though Charlie wasn't sure if it was a sign of relief or a deepening fear as he began to walk away.

He made it six steps before Boricio took aim at the back of the man's head and pulled the trigger.

The gunshot crackled in the speakers above Charlie as Foster fell face first into the concrete ground, blood splattering on impact.

Charlie jumped, but held his scream inside.

Boricio looked back at Charlie. "There. Problem solved."

"Fuck yeah!" Imaginary Boricio shouted, pumping his fist in the air and prancing around the cell. "I fucking LOVE this guy! Now THAT is how you handle personnel conflicts! That right there is the goddamned Robocop of human resources!"

Boricio leaned closer to Charlie, returning the yellow glove to his hand. "As I said, we're not the bad guys. We're here to help. And I won't condone my men murdering anyone — especially children."

"What do you need from me?" Charlie asked.

"Just work with us. Allow us to take your blood, and don't pull any more stunts like you did. I now understand your fear of the men you attacked, but I assure you that we're not going to hurt you. We need to keep you alive. You might be our only hope."

Charlie glanced at Imaginary Boricio, who was staring at the still-sleeping Callie in the next cell.

"I'll help you under one condition," Charlie said.

"What is it?"

"Nothing happens to her. No tests. No infection. Nothing."

Boricio looked over at Callie, then back at Charlie. "Deal."

"I can trust you?" Charlie asked.

"Yes. But can I trust you?" Boricio asked.

"Yes."

"I'd like to believe you, Charlie. But I am having one problem."

Charlie felt a knot in his gut as if the carpet — or illusion — of safety were about to be pulled from under him.

"What's that?"

"I'm wondering why you didn't tell me about the other Boricio — the one standing beside you."

TWENTY-FIVE

Mary Olson

Dunn, Georgia
  Boricio's Compound
  March 29
  Sometime after midnight …

MIDNIGHT WAS MADE FOR REGRET.

Even before the world had whispered itself to nothing, it was always in the bony middle of midnight when Mary found herself hating every wrong turn she'd ever made. Tonight it seemed especially easy to hate her latest: agreeing to stay at Boricio's compound despite every alarm bell inside her ringing in unison.

It was another mistake, turning her back on her instincts, just like she had ignored them when surrendering to Desmond and Will by agreeing to stay at The Sanctuary.

Staying at The Prophet's compound was the worst decision Mary had ever made, and she paid for that poor decision with her life, and the lives of her children, both Paola and the new life inside her. Luca had somehow brought them both back, but Desmond wasn't so lucky. Desmond, the father of the baby growing inside her, was dead, and he was never coming back.

Now, following Boricio to his compound was another massive mistake, and Mary *knew* it. The man was clearly some sort of monster. Coming with him was like agreeing to load Paola into a Volkswagen Beetle, then drive it at 90 into a tall brick wall.

Boricio was obviously a man who hadn't been truly loved a day in his life. All humans were capable of atrocity. It was simply a matter of falling into a sequence of events that would drive them from timidity to terror. When violent instincts weren't properly channeled they easily erupted. Most violence was the result of a mind fooling itself into believing internal pain came from something, or someone, else — a someone or something that deserved to be punished. And typically, these people were able to cast anyone into the role of that someone who deserved their wrath.

Mary came up with this theory on Boricio while still standing in the ashes of The Sanctuary and deciding what to do and where to go. She should have listened to her whisper. She would have, too, except Luca had just aged what looked like a thousand years to save her and her children; and she couldn't tell him no.

Luca insisted that Boricio was there to protect them, and that he would do what he was supposed to, whenever it was time to do it. Mary was used to the mystical *I know what I know because I saw it in my dreams, science-fiction weirdness* by now, but she didn't buy the balderdash for Boricio, at least not enough to keep herself from sleeping fitfully through the night.

Mary could eventually forgive what Boricio had done to Desmond, and could even forgive that he had helped the crazy cultists holding them prisoner. If that was what Luca wanted, it was the least she could do. But even if she could forgive, Luca couldn't ask her to *forget* what Boricio had done. Forgetting was impossible. Her Desmond was dead. How could she be expected to simply forget someone who had become so much of her light in such a bleak world?

Luca said the boy inside Boricio was broken, at least until Luca had fixed him. But she didn't believe that Luca had "fixed" Boricio at all. Once broken, one could never truly be fixed, Mary believed.

When Mary pulled Luca aside to plead with him privately, and maybe convince him that he'd be better off going with her and Paola alone, the ancient child refused, insisting over and over that Boricio was no longer broken. He said it would take time for his healing to "show up." Even if that were true, and Mary wasn't convinced it was, Luca clearly didn't seem to understand the danger Boricio posed until then.

"Luca, we'll take care of you," Mary said. "Boricio won't." She squeezed his hands. "And you're in no shape to survive out there on your own. That man will leave you the second he thinks you're slowing him down." She held the old child's eyes, begging him to believe her. "That won't take long to happen in your condition, and we would never, ever do that to you. Please," she said. "Come with me and Paola."

Luca shook his head. "I can't, Mary. I'm supposed to go with Boricio." Then he repeated, "He will protect us. I *know* it."

Mary looked into Luca's sad, empty eyes, bleached from their blinking youth. "There's nothing I can say to convince you, is there?"

Luca shook his head.

And that was that.

Mary could never let the 90-year-old boy who had saved her life ride into the sunset with a repugnant creature like Boricio by himself. But just because Mary had managed to avoid making the wrong decision didn't mean she made the right one.

She hated how Boricio looked at her, with what seemed like a sour brew of perversion and hate. He hadn't been much better when dealing with Paola. He wasn't rude, exactly, nor had he ogled her. As foul as Boricio was, he was probably smart enough to understand that the wrong string of words, or perhaps the wrong look, would send Mary into a fury that was sure to end with one of them dead. But Boricio clearly didn't want a kid around, and made no effort to shade his impatience.

Luca knew Mary was upset, and was trying to soothe her in the only way he knew how. On the ride to Boricio's compound, Luca leaned into her ear with a whispered promise that everything would be okay. Mary was doing the right thing. Luca needed Boricio around, and that meant they all did. Something had happened inside The Hole, and whatever that something was, it had altered things between the two men, and led Luca to trust the monster with a line of reasoning that had nothing to do with logic.

Even if Luca weren't anywhere near 8 years old — and Mary had to believe his mind was mostly stunted — he couldn't possibly have the lifetime's worth of experience one earned from decades' worth of navigating the best and worst of humanity.

Mary had known plenty of raging assholes and con men, from the days before she went freelance with her cards, where everyone in the copywriting offices carried a penis and the asshole personality to prove it, to the marketing department, where no one ever spoke without seeming as though they were pulling a long con.

A large part of Mary felt as though Boricio was playing the long con on Luca, getting on his good side so he could somehow screw the ancient child somewhere down the road. She had no idea how or why, or what Luca could possibly offer a monster like that, but then again she had no idea what they had exchanged inside their minds.

Mary was here now, and there was no turning back. She couldn't imagine getting a decent night's sleep until they were finally far away from Boricio and again on their own. Even then, without Desmond, Mary didn't imagine she'd ever find a peaceful night's sleep again.

Resting well with one eye open was impossible, and there was no way in hell Mary trusted the predator not to sneak into her room, or her daughter's, which was why she and Paola were sharing one room, and why Mary slept with a loaded gun under her pillow — just in case.

She glanced over at Paola, as she had every few minutes since she set her cheek to the pillow, and continued to do until finally falling asleep, probably sometime between 2 and 3 in the morning.

~

MARY WOKE up several hours later to an especially bright morning sun beating its way through the blinds. She rubbed her eyes, then looked over to the empty spot in her bed where Paola had been. Her heart instantly sank to the pit of her stomach as a flashback of the Drury Inn and all that happened there flooded her morning with acid.

Gun in hand and no shoes on her feet, Mary bolted outside to find her daughter.

Everyone but Mary was standing in a semicircle in back of the house. Paola and Luca were side by side, with Luca leaning on a cane, while Boricio stood by himself slightly to the side. Paola was holding a pistol and looking toward a row of bottles, lined on a precarious looking shelf that Mary imagined Boricio had set on the top of a wooden fence post, which neatly divided the spacious back yard from the forest beyond.

"Paola!" Mary screamed. "What in the world do you think you're doing?"

The girl's finger pulled the trigger, and thunder crashed through the early morning quiet, sending a flock of birds from distant trees. Mary looked again at the fence. Not a single bottle was broken, and she hadn't woken to the sound of a shot, so Mary figured target practice had only just started.

Paola didn't turn her head toward her mother, just pulled the trigger two more times, then wrinkled her nose at the trio of missed shots. Boricio ignored Mary as well. He turned to Paola and said, "You're giving your shots way too much thought. Don't blink and don't think. Just squeeze that fucker like you were popping a zit."

Boricio cackled. Mary was still walking from the house. "Don't speak to my daughter like that," she said, stopping just three feet from Boricio. "And she's too young to be out here playing with guns."

Boricio laughed again. "Are you kidding, Mary May I?" He looked at her like she was the one who was fat with crazy. "Did you already forget about the early Fourth of July show back at the Sanctu-Fairy Fuck-all? Because if you want your little lamb to go Bo-Peeping into battle seconds from good and dead, well then, by all means keep on batting your pretty, blind eyes." He shrugged and said, "What's one more corpse to me? And we're not playing with guns — I'm *teaching* her, something your Desmond Do-Right might have thought to do before the figurative shit hit the literal fan."

Mary shuddered, remembering the pair of bodies — one a mutated-looking thing that had been a man that Boricio had known and the other an apparent victim of said man they found in the house when they first returned to the compound, and how Boricio dragged them out back like they were soiled laundry waiting for the machine. She still had no idea where they went, or what Boricio had done with them.

Paola looked back at Boricio, her mouth hanging open in shock at Boricio's 'one more corpse' comment. He grinned, then winked and shook his head with a light smile before turning back to her mother. "I prefer that all my compadres learn to be good, little commandoes, and since right now I don't see anything else pressing on our agenda, I'm not really seeing any reason not to hold a little morning session of Blowing Fuckers Heads Off 101."

"She's my daughter," Mary said. "And that means that *I'm* the one who gets to decide whether she's old enough to handle a gun."

Boricio shrugged. "You know what?" he said. "You're right." He walked over to Paola and held out his hand, nodding at her to hand over the gun. She did.

Boricio shoved the gun in his pants, then said with a grin, "Mary, Mary quite contrary, how does your daughter grow? Like all the whores, on all their fours, lined all nice in a row."

He stood a few inches from Mary, while she tried not to cower.

"Your daughter's an awful pretty thing, Miss Mary," Boricio continued. "You really want her out there without a gun? You think monsters are the only thing you've gotta worry about? Hell no," Boricio shook his head, almost snarling, his voice settling somewhere between a growl and a hiss. "You've gotta worry about monsters like *me*, and worse than me, Miss Mary — men who didn't even wait for the proverbial 'grass on the field' to 'play ball,' three weeks before Hallo-Fucking-Ween, and sure as the Great Pumpkin's orange ball sack, ain't gonna start caring now, ya dig?"

Boricio pulled the gun back out of his pants and offered it to Mary, holding it by the barrel. But Mary kept her hands at her side, ignoring the invitation.

Boricio said, "You sure you don't want your baby girl to have this?" He raised his eyebrows. "Seems like you'd at least want to keep her armed against anything like me."

"If you so much as look at my daughter with an impure thought, I won't need a gun to fucking kill you," Mary said, eyes boring into Boricio's.

She grabbed the gun roughly from Boricio, then handed it gently to Paola.

Boricio smiled a big grin, ignoring her threat.

"Much better!" Boricio started clapping. "I need Team Boricio fit and ready for a fight if we expect to get our asses up and over to Mordor. Rip Van Creepy ain't gonna do shit to help us, since unfortunately he's used the last of his voodoo to bring you all back from Zombie Island, instead of Black Godzilla like I suggested, no offense to any of you estrogen carriers. I'm glad we can get started. Now, if you'll excuse me," Boricio said, patting his stomach. "I'm gonna go inside so I can make my morning grunt sculpture."

Luca looked confused and said, "Huh?"

Paola said, "He means he's going inside to take a crap."

Luca smiled, then lightly laughed.

Mary said, "Paola!"

Boricio grinned, then turned his back to the crew and headed inside, slamming the screen behind him.

Once Mary was certain Boricio was inside and halfway to the bathroom, she took Luca gently by the arm and turned him toward her. "Are you still sure about all of this, Luca?"

He nodded. "I already told you," he said. "Going with Boricio is what we're supposed to do. If you don't believe me, you can do whatever you want. I'll understand. But my answer isn't going to change." His voice was ancient, almost stoic. If you'd just met him, you'd never suspect an 8-year-old was speaking. Mary said nothing, as Luca continued. "I saw Boricio as a boy. Before he was like this — before his stepfather broke him."

He turned to her with swollen eyes. Mary couldn't tell if they were sad or tired. "But I fixed him, Mary. I promise."

"Life doesn't work like that, Luca," Mary shook her head. "I understand how you can *think* you fixed Boricio, but trust me, you didn't. People can't be fixed that easily. Believe me, Luca. I've wasted a lot of my years, too many actually, trying to fix broken men. But unless a man wants to be fixed, Luca, there's nothing you can do to change him. And trying is useless."

Mary caught Paola from the corner of her eye, listening in and pretending that she didn't know her mother was talking about her father.

"But that's just it, Mary," Luca said.

"What?"

"He *did* want to be fixed. And I fixed him." Luca used the hand that wasn't holding his cane to point at his head. "From the inside."

Paola said, "Yeah, Mom, Boricio's super-creepy. No doubt. But we're better off with than without him. At least for now. I agree with Luca on that. Besides, I have to learn to defend myself." She paused, then said, "And you."

Mary looked surprised. Paola went on. "You're gonna be like major pregnant soon, Mom. Who's gonna defend you then?" Paola's bottom lip started to tremble. She tried to say something else, but her voice cracked, and she seemed as though she could barely swallow. Finally, she shook her head and said, "I can't stand the thought of not being able to protect you and the baby, Mom. And I shouldn't have to think about it. There are plenty of guns; why can't I learn to use them?"

"Because you're a kid. Kids aren't supposed to be learning how to use guns and defend their mothers. They're supposed to be going to school, having crushes on boys, and fighting with their moms — like it used to be," Mary went from Luca to Paola and pulled her daughter into an embrace.

"That world is gone, Mom. You're being naive. I need to learn, and Boricio said he would teach me to shoot."

"I can teach you to shoot," Mary said

The screen door slammed, and Mary could hear Boricio heading back toward them.

"Well, that was fast," Mary said.

Boricio laughed. "I've read that issue of *Entertainment Weekly* by the crapper 15,000 goddamned times, and I didn't give a nugget of fuck about *Breaking Bad* or *The Vampire Diaries* or any of that other crap that got cancelled forever. Besides," he smiled, "I'm what you might call a prolific shitter. One of the benefits to being full of shit, I guess."

Mary hated herself for laughing, but she couldn't help the small giggle that suddenly escaped from her mouth. Fortunately, surrendering to humor seemed to make everything better.

Boricio sidled up to her side and said, "Look, I'm sorry if I was stepping on those purty, little digits of yours, Miss Mary, but I swear on my fat sack and all the creamy fun inside it, I was just trying to help your little lamb. You and Luca, too."

"You're a pig, you know that?" Mary said.

Boricio grinned. "You've been living high on the hog, sister, but now it's time to get down with the sows. When the apocalypse comes, you gotta be able to get in the mud."

Mary held her hands in the air. "What does that even mean?"

"It means you're lucky as fuck that you've managed to find yourself on Team Boricio."

"Lucky?" Mary snorted. "*Team* Boricio had exactly one player when your last three players were drafted."

Boricio cackled, probably appreciating a woman with balls. "Yeah, but when you're the Michael Fucking Jordan of murder, it ain't like you need a full roster."

"And you're right," Mary said. "Paola *should* learn to shoot. But there's no need to impose target practice on you, especially since you clearly have issues maintaining your patience. So, thank you very much for the offer, but *I'd* rather be the one to teach my daughter to shoot."

Boricio laughed, then kept on laughing for a long minute, sucking for air as his eyes went red, slowly making Mary madder. Finally he said, "*You're* gonna teach her?"

"You think I can't shoot?"

Boricio answered with another round of laughter.

Mary marched up to Paola, gently pulled the gun from her

hand, then aimed at the bottles and fired six shots, evenly spaced, missing the glass every time.

Boricio's laughter roared louder than the gunshots as Mary handed the gun back to her daughter.

Suddenly, the wood beneath the shelf shrieked, then splintered and cracked before collapsing to the ground and spilling shattering glass to the ground.

Boricio stopped laughing, and a new breed of smile settled on his face. "Well, tickle my pickle, Miss Mary, that is some sharp-as-shit shooting."

Mary said, "*Desmond* taught me well."

Boricio said, "Well, well, it looks like old Desmond Do-Right got two things right then." He winked and smiled at Mary.

She wanted to throw up in her mouth for thinking it was almost charming.

TWENTY-SIX

Teagan McLachlan

Teagan didn't want to go back underground.

She had been beneath the earth since October, until a week ago when Ed finally decided it was safe for them to live above ground. She wasn't sure why it hadn't been safe before, and for all that time, but suspected it had something to do with the other Ed, who was now working with the Guardsmen on a secret mission.

Teagan had lived her entire life sheltered beneath her ultra-conservative parents, dreaming of escape from the trailer park. Then she'd spent the past five months so far underground that she thought she might never see sunlight again. For the first time in forever, Teagan finally felt like an adult. She had a relationship, a child, and most importantly, freedom. And for one glorious week, life felt amazing.

Ed rushed her outside into the cold night air and then into the waiting truck, where Sullivan was waiting in the driver's seat. She took one last look back at the garden she'd been watering regularly for exactly one week, and the neat row of plants she nurtured to health beneath the warm sun, and felt it — along with her newfound life — slipping through her fingers.

Her dirt road street, shared by 11 other homes, was lined with black carts and bobbing lights as Guardsmen with face masks, flashlights, and weapons scrambled from house to house making sure everyone had pulled their shutters down and barred their doors.

The sirens' wail was louder outside, turning Becca's cry into a terrified pitch.

"We've got it, sir," one of the Guardsmen said to Ed from behind a speaker's crackle as they passed on their way to the truck.

Teagan climbed into the back seat with Becca, then quickly shut the door to muffle the siren and calm her baby. She rocked Becca in her arms, whispering in her ear, "It's okay, baby. Mommy's got you. It's okay."

"What's the status?" Ed asked, climbing into the front seat and slamming the door as Sullivan tore away from their house.

Teagan looked back to see Guardsmen pulling thick, black, metal shutters down over their windows and doors, sealing the house from God only knew what.

"Subjects 7XY and 17XZ were missing from their cells when the guards checked on the hour. Video screens for both cells went black for a one-minute period about 10 minutes prior, at the same exact time. They were in their cells one minute. But after the screens went black, they were gone. There's no registered activity on the security logs or door logins, until they appeared outside the compound about five minutes after they were reported missing. They were last detected on the north side, but could be anywhere by now."

"How the hell did this happen?"

"We think Dr. Williams has something to do with it. He's not answering his communicator, and people said he was acting weird all day."

"Has anyone told Will Bishop?"

"That's the other thing," Sullivan said. "We can't find him.

No one has seen him all day or night. Not that that's unusual, given the circumstances, but when I phoned him to report what happened, there wasn't any answer. I went to his house, and he was gone."

"And surveillance?"

"You know he disabled his surveillance a while ago."

"Oh yeah," Ed said.

Teagan wanted to lean forward and ask what was happening, but figured it would be better to keep quiet, concentrate on making sure Becca stayed in her silence as she tried piecing the puzzle together from the relative safety of the back seat. Plus, Ed seemed visibly shaken by what Sullivan was saying. Asking him questions he probably wasn't prepared to answer was sure to only make things worse.

They passed another road where a second row of houses was being shuttered. From what Teagan could tell, nobody else was being brought to the Facility, which meant the others were expected to ride out the mystery threat from inside their shuttered houses.

"Where's the sphere?" Ed said.

Sullivan reached into the glove compartment, keeping one hand on the wheel as he navigated the quiet, dark, dirt road, and retrieved a dark, glass orb, about half the size of a tennis ball. The sphere glowed with a red luminescence as it passed from one man's hand to the next, sending an unexplainable shiver down Teagan's spine.

"What's that?" she asked as Ed slipped the sphere inside his jacket pocket, as if to shield it from her view immediately.

"Nothing to worry about," he said, then turned to Sullivan. "I want you to bring them to my room, and station two guards outside until I return. Make sure you're underground in case I have to use this."

"OK," Sullivan said.

"Use what?" Teagan asked again, not liking the finality in

Ed's "in case I have to use this," as though it were the sort of last resort that meant he wouldn't be coming home.

Teagan met Ed's eyes, and was about to insist he tell her what the sphere was, but something in his stare begged her not to ask — she wouldn't like the answer, and he didn't want to lie.

Ed said to Sullivan, "I'm going to go find Will."

"What about the doc? What do we do?"

"Shoot him on sight."

They pulled up to the Facility's hangar and stopped the truck just past two Guardsmen. Sullivan got out first, then opened Teagan's door. She climbed from the truck with Becca, who had stopped crying on the ride.

Ed kissed Becca on the head and Teagan on the mouth.

"Don't worry," he promised, "everything will be fine."

"Are you sure?"

"Yes," Ed nodded, giving them each one more kiss. "I love you both."

He climbed back inside the truck, then left Teagan standing beside Sullivan in the hangar's interior. She couldn't move as tears began to flood her eyes.

"What's wrong?" Sullivan asked, leading Teagan toward the doors and into the Facility.

"He's never told me he loved me before," she said.

Teagan couldn't finish the second half of her thought — the part that was tearing through her heart.

He's never coming back.

❧

TWENTY-SEVEN

Boricio Bishop

Black Island Research Facility
  Black Island, New York
  Other Earth
  Aug. 22
  TWO MONTHS BEFORE THE EVENT …

BORICIO SAT at Rose's bedside, hating the guard standing on the other side of the door. Not that it was the guard's fault for being there; he wasn't the one who had restricted Boricio's access to Level 7. But still, it was a special sort of bullshit that Boricio was only allowed to hear the breath that kept his heart beating with an armed guard on the other side of the door.

Boricio stared at Rose sleeping, her chest rising and falling like a flatline with rhythm. He pulled her hands into his and squeezed, biting his bottom lip hard to keep from crying.

Boricio remembered the time they'd spent an entire rainy Saturday afternoon cozied up on a comfy sofa in a trendy bookstore a month after they started dating.

. . .

ROSE'S FRIEND Annabel had warned her against spending too much time with Boricio, whom Annabel had not yet met. "That man clearly has an agenda," she said.

Boricio laughed. "Of course, I have an agenda!" he had said. "What sort of fool flies through the forest without a map? That's called wandering, Rose. And I don't like to wander. You can't get to your best life when you spend your time wandering. Know what you want, then know what you're willing to give up to get it. That's the recipe for the best possible life. That's my recipe, and an agenda worth having."

Rose smiled, then laughed and said, "I love your agenda, Boricio."

She always smacked her lips when she said his name, like she was tasting it for the first time. After a long second, screaming its silence in his memory's eternity, Rose added, "And I love you." It was the first time she had said it, and Boricio didn't waste a second before he said it right back.

"I love you, too, Rose."

She said, "You've never said that before, have you?"

Boricio wasn't sure how she knew, she just did. Like she always seemed to know stuff about him that he'd not yet given breath.

"Not to a girl." Boricio shook his head. "Just to Will and Luca, and only when they say it first."

She rose from the chair beside him, set the copy of *Twilight* she was reading to "see what the big deal was all about" on the small table in front of them, then sat on Boricio's lap. "Let's stay here the rest of the night," she said.

"Okay, Rose." He leaned into the back of the couch, then pulled her to his chest and lightly stroked her hair. The rest of the night ended up being nearly 20 minutes. Another 20 minutes after that and the pair of them were spending the remainder of their day in bed.

. . .

BORICIO BLINKED his eyes at Rose, now a shadow of her former self; the tender memory fueling his anger, both at life and at Will. He had to speak with Dr. Williams. Williams would see reason, and that reason would lay the first bricks for the road to Rose's eventual full recovery.

But how in the hell was Boricio going to get to Williams?

He considered stealing an access badge to come back later, but that was stupid. Boricio had a working badge before he threw it on Will's desk, but that didn't change the palm problem. It wasn't like Boricio could cut off someone's hand.

He could make up an emergency, perhaps trick Will into getting him onto the floor. Even if that managed to work, it would only show Will the cards he intended to play.

Boricio got an idea that turned his face into a sudden, wide smile. He stood from his chair, kissed Rose on the cheek, then went into the bathroom and hoisted himself onto the toilet, pulling keys from his pocket and unscrewing the four tiny screws in the corners of the air vent.

Boricio removed the grate, set it down gently on the floor, and then hoisted himself up and began crawling through the metal network of air ducts on his way to Dr. Williams' office, four doors down from the bathroom.

When Boricio reached the vent in Williams' office, he pulled back his arm and thrust the flat of his hand flush against the grate, popping it from the wall and launching it onto Williams' office floor.

The doctor leapt from his desk, clearly startled as he stood staring at the wall and Boricio climbing from nowhere. He reached for the phone. Boricio said, "Wait, Doc! Just one second, please. Hear me out before your fingers finish the dialies." He dropped to the carpet. "I know of a way we can change the future together."

A bit dramatic perhaps, but it got the good doc's hands to hover somewhere other than above the receiver.

"What do you want, Boricio?" Dr. Williams said. "You're

not supposed to be here. The fact that you are, and that you came in through the vent," he pointed up at the wall, then down at the busted grate, "is making me uncomfortable."

"Well, Doc," Boricio said, "I'm only not supposed to be here because Will's served up a special sort of bullshit for the both of us. I've done nothing wrong. And the only reason he doesn't want me on Level 7 is because he doesn't want me talking to you. So, this right here," he pointed at the grate on the ground, "is as bad as it's gonna get."

"Make it quick."

Boricio said, "Thanks, Dr. Williams, I will. And I appreciate it." He walked from the wall to the doctor's desk, but didn't sit. He stood, looking Williams right in the eyes instead. "I think we should use the vials on Rose."

"That's what I thought you were going to say." The doctor shook his head. "But that's not possible, Boricio. I simply cannot agree to do that."

"Of course, you can!" Boricio cried. "You're the *only* one who can. He'll listen to you. It's me Will has a problem with. He trusts you, Dr. Williams, and your judgment. Will won't listen to me, because he thinks I'm blinded by my allegiance to Rose, which maybe I am, but that doesn't change the facts, or why you should care. The vials work, Doc. And they'll work on Rose like they worked on Luca. All we have to do is try."

Williams was looking everywhere but at Boricio. When he finally looked at him, he said, "I won't go over Will's head."

"I'm not asking you to," Boricio said, growing impatient. "I'm only asking that you ask Will. If we pitch from your lips instead of mine, we might get the ball over the fence."

Dr. Williams shook his head. "He'll never agree."

"Please," Boricio begged. "Please just *try*. Don't let Rose live like this. She deserves more. Hell man, *I* deserve more. The vials worked with Luca; they'll work with Rose, too." Boricio repeated himself in case he'd been speaking Chinese the first time.

"Rose has been through enough," Dr. Williams said. "Will won't put her in any more jeopardy."

"How much worse can it get? She's in constant pain, and her memory is getting even worse!"

The doctor shrugged. "It's too soon to gauge her recovery, Boricio. Things like this take time, and it's too soon to throw in the towel on her chances. I'm not sure how much you know, or what I'm allowed to say, but I can tell you that *something* is happening with Luca — something we don't understand. Something directly related to the vials. There's no way Will is going to risk us using it on another person."

Boricio's growing anger went to worry. "Luca? Is he okay?" Boricio only gave Williams a second to speak before the anger returned and he growled, "What's happening, and why don't I know?"

"You'll have to ask your father."

"You've gotta give me something," Boricio insisted. "There must be something in Luca's folder that you could tell his older brother."

Dr. Williams sighed, swallowed, paused, then said, "Luca's abilities are rapidly increasing, Boricio. And appear to be growing unstable." He shook his head, though it looked to Boricio like he wanted to say more. But he didn't. Just, "I'm going to have to ask you to leave now."

Boricio scowled, said, "Fine," then turned his back to Dr. Williams and climbed back into the air vent, leaving the grate on the doctor's carpet. He crawled back to Rose's bathroom, dropped onto the floor, replaced the vent, and then returned to her bedside.

"I'll figure this out, baby," Boricio whispered in her ear. His lips lingered on her cheeks in a long farewell before he left the room.

The guard outside turned to Boricio. "I didn't expect you to be in there for half a year."

"Yeah," Boricio said. "Sorry about that. I had to make a

grunt sculpture. Hope you don't need to use the bathroom before we head back." Boricio waved his hand in front of his nose, while the guard soured his face as if he could smell what wasn't really there.

Boricio swallowed, then followed the guard down the long hall, scared for Luca, and terrified that the drop of hope waiting like dew on his Rose had just evaporated under an angry sun of nothing.

TWENTY-EIGHT

Charlie Wilkens

Charlie turned to Imaginary Boricio, who was standing beside him, shrugging his shoulders.

"You can see him?" Charlie asked the yellow hazmat-suited Boricio. "I thought he was in my head!"

"He *is* in your head. But I can see in there."

"What kinda voodoo hoodoo French fried vanilla fuck shake is this?" Imaginary Boricio said. "Can you see this, ya fuck?" Boricio asked, giving hazmat-suit Boricio the only finger that mattered.

If he could see the insult, bald Boricio didn't react.

"How can you read my mind? What are you?" Charlie asked, feeling invaded, and quickly trying to bury his thoughts, though the more he tried to hide things the more his brain wanted to put the sordid images of his memory on full display, like any number of the 2,348 or so times Charlie had jerked off to Internet porn.

Stop it!

Think normal shit!

Imaginary Boricio looked at Charlie with feigned disgust, "Whoa, you are one sick puppy, Downtown Charlie Brown! I thought I was sick, but the red lights in your district are downright nasty!" He laughed.

Fuck you.

"Excuse me?" Hazmat-suit Boricio said.

"No, not you. Fuck, you heard that? Stop! Stay outta my head!"

"I'm sorry. I can't help it. It's a side effect . . . Anyway, um, how do you know me? I see all these memories you have of me. But I've never met . . . Oh. Shit."

Hazmat-suit Boricio was staring off into space, looking like he might have just untangled string theory.

"What?" Imaginary Boricio said. "Spit it out, Fucker!"

"What?" Charlie asked.

"I don't know why I didn't see it before," hazmat-suit Boricio shook his head. You're not from here. You're from the other Earth. The one where Luca went." Then, "Holy shit. . . . *he* did this!"

"The fuck are you talking about, Willis?!" Imaginary Boricio said.

Hazmat-suit Boricio either ignored or didn't hear his imaginary twin. Perhaps he couldn't read Charlie's mind when he was deep in thought himself.

"What are you talking about?" Charlie asked.

"I want you to tell me everything that's happened since Oct. 15."

"What? Everything?"

Hazmat-suit Boricio raised his eyebrows. "You got somewhere else to be?"

CHARLIE FILLED him in on everything from the moment he woke up in the basement of the cult compound to the moment he woke up in the glass cell.

"Where is this other Boricio now?" hazmat-suit Boricio asked.

"Like I said, we haven't seen him since we went back to the compound. But he wasn't there the last time we were."

"You think he might be there now?"

"I dunno," Charlie said. Then, "When are *you* gonna tell me what the hell is going on?"

Imaginary Boricio chimed in, "Yeah, we told you our *Iliad* and our fucking *Odyssey*, so start gettin' chatty, Kathy!"

"On Oct. 15, so far as we know, almost everyone on this planet died or vanished in an instant. A few were spared, for reasons we still don't know. But everyone else, dead. At least, I thought the people still here had been spared, anyway, but now I'm wondering if he didn't pull a bunch of you all over somehow."

Charlie wasn't sure he believed a word this Boricio was saying, though he had no reason to doubt him, not with everything else he'd seen. It made a hell of a lot more sense than any theories he'd come up with on his own.

"How? Why?" were the only words Charlie could think to ask as he continued to process Boricio's words. "Wait a second. Does this mean my mom is still alive? And that everyone else I know is still alive back on *my* Earth?"

"I don't know," Boricio said, seeming to marinate in the thought. "I can't even guess."

"So, can I get home?" Charlie asked.

Boricio said, "No."

"Why not?" Charlie said, almost whining.

"Because you're infected. If you go over there, this could spread. Then it would wipe out your planet like it did mine."

"So, what will it take to cure me?" Charlie asked.

"We're working on that. With your help, perhaps we can figure this out."

Boricio put his hand on the pad outside the door and opened it for Charlie. "You're not going to do anything stupid again, are you?"

"No," Charlie said.

"Good, I would like to show you something so you can understand what we're up against."

Boricio led Charlie down the hallway and out the door. He watched as they passed two Guardsmen. "Have someone mop up that mess in there, eh?" hazmat-suit Boricio said to the two men, referring to Foster's corpse.

Four other doors were on either side of the hall, then another at the end, which looked like an elevator. They turned through the first door to the right, then walked up a steep incline along a narrow but well-lit hallway until they came to another door, to a room that — if Charlie had been charting the course correctly in his head — was directly above, or close to above, his own cell block.

The room was dark until Boricio said, "Lights."

Lights illuminated the cell block. It was smaller than his own, with two glass cells, one of them empty. The other held a mutant, equal parts human and monster — legs were human, one arm a clawed appendage, his torso appeared split almost down the middle between human and black, monstrous flesh. His face, however, was entirely human. He opened his eyes, weary, and dull.

"Hello, Ryan," Boricio said. "How are you today?"

"Today's been a bad one," Ryan said, his voice full of gravel. "Who's this?"

"This is Charlie Wilkens. And he might save your life. Or," Boricio said as he turned to Charlie, "Ryan might be the end of yours."

∾

TWENTY-NINE

Mary Olson

Mary was shocked.

Maybe shocked wasn't enough. Dumfounded might be better.

She held the spaghetti in her mouth, almost scared to chew too fast and miss a detail of flavor.

The pasta in her mouth wasn't just the best she'd had since October; it was the best meal she'd had period. And the aroma reminded her of a small Italian restaurant she used to eat at, which served the best food ever. And seeing how Boricio had "exactly dick and six curly ball hairs to work with," the dish was that much more amazing.

"Where did you learn to cook like this?" she asked Boricio.

He shoveled a full fork, twisted full of pasta, into his mouth, *then* answered. Red-stained spittle slurred his speech. "I went to the Institute of Culinary Education in New York," he said. "Spent six years perfecting my craft."

"Really?" Mary was shocked. Paola and Luca both looked up from their plates, their faces as filled with surprise as she imagined hers was.

Boricio cackled then slapped the table. "Fuck no. Boricio don't need no Rachel Ray to show him how to rip shit the fuck up. I learned how to cook by loving my taste buds like they were a perfect pair of titties, and I learned to cook by working in a million and one restaurants, making everything from grilled cheese to arepas."

"Arepas?" Paola said, before Mary could. "What's that?"

Boricio lit up. "Shit, girl, your tongue is a crap pile until it's tasted an arepa. They're these corn-dough patties. Least that's the canvas. Cheese and tomato and avocado and meats; shredded chicken, carnitas, steak; that's all the paint. The dish is Venezuelan, and the most beautiful thing about the country outside of the bi ... the boobies." He smiled and took another bite of spaghetti and smiled.

"You've never been to Venezuela have you?" Mary asked.

"Do you need to see a pile of shit to know it stinks?"

Mary was as shocked to find herself enjoying the last few verbal spars with Boricio as she was by the quality of his cooking. While she didn't ever expect to lose the edge she felt while around him — or the anger for what he'd done — at the moment Mary thought Boricio seemed more loud than dangerous.

She opened her mouth to challenge him, but was cut off by a sudden roar of motorcycles from outside. Boricio's fork clattered on his plate, and he bolted from the table, his back against the wall and his finger lifting the curtain as he peered outside a second later.

"Get the fuck on the floor," Boricio barked. "All of you!"

They all hit the floor, Paola assisting Luca. Mary said, "What is it?"

"Looks like we have ourselves an intruder alert at Boricio's Clubhouse," he said. "Too bad we can't call in G.I. Fucking Joe." Boricio clucked his tongue. "Ain't no never mind. Looks like there's four of them, and even with two bleeders and a feeb, that seems like an even match for Team Boricio." He looked back out the window and whooped. "Holy shit, one of them thinks he's King Fucking Arthur!"

"What do you mean?" Mary whispered, her heart hammering inside her chest.

Boricio was crazy enough to wear a smile.

"Three of them fuckers are smart enough to come packing, two with sawed offs and another with what looks like a .45, though I'm not sure from here. But the biggest fucker is wearing a sword on his back like he's goddamned He-Man!"

Boricio laughed again.

One of the bikes went quiet, then the other three followed, seconds apart. Boricio pulled his head from the window, dropped to a crouch, then started to whisper. "All right, Team Boricio, it's showtime. I'm gonna need you to hightail it upstairs and stay up there until I deal with the Dreadnoks. Take your guns but stay away from the windows. Keep your backs to the wall and shoot any fucker who comes into the room, in case something happens to me outside — which it won't."

Boricio paused, then added, "They'll be handing Pluto back its planetary status before four dumb bitches on bikes can fuck with ole Boricio."

"We have guns," Mary said. "Why don't we just shoot them from inside?"

"I shouldn't have to explain myself while death is waiting to be dealt outside, so I'll just say this once and hope you've got your listening cap turned to high, Miss Mary." He took another quick look outside, then turned his eyes to the three of them on the floor. "Never mind. They're about to come inside this house. You all need to scoot your asses upstairs — right fucking now. And get your guns ready!"

~

WITHOUT ANOTHER WORD, Boricio kicked open the front door, then went outside and hollered, "Well hello there, weary travelers, welcome to Motel Boricio where roaches check in, but they don't fucking check out!" Mary pictured him spreading his arms like wings and twirling around.

"Come on!" she whispered, crawling toward the stairs while Luca and Paola crawled behind her. She paused at the first step, waiting for Paola and Luca. Paola went up the stairs first, then Luca. Mary followed behind. By the time they were upstairs, peeking out the window like Boricio told them not to, Mary could clearly see that Boricio was even crazier than she thought.

He was surrounded by a semicircle of four men, who all looked like they were from that Mel Gibson movie from the '80s that she couldn't remember the name of — the one from back when Mel Gibson was handsome and not yet crazy. Like Boricio had said, all four men were armed, three with guns, while the tallest, largest, and obvious leader wore a sword in a scabbard at his back.

Boricio said, "I'll admit, since I don't have much company these days, I'm easily flattered. But I also have to confess to all sorts of warm fuzzies seeing as how you could smell Boricio's Famous Sloppy Spaghetti from whatever side of Mad Max Island you've all come riding in from."

Mad Max, *that was it!*

The leader grunted into Boricio's bravado. "How many people are in the house?" he snarled.

Boricio laughed. "Ah, I wish there was more than just me, because I tell you what," Boricio leaned closer to the leader in a growling whisper that was loud enough for Mary to hear, upstairs and behind a window, "man, woman, or something with fur, it'd be nice to give ole Rosy Palms a break. But sadly for me, my many calluses and our bottle of Jergens, it's just us."

"Bullshit," the leader said. "I'm gonna ask you one more time, how many people you have in the house?" He pulled his sword from its scabbard and waved it in front of Boricio.

"Ha," Boricio cried. "Aren't you gonna say, 'I have the power'? That's how He-Man does it, you know."

Mary might have laughed if she wasn't terrified; half certain they were minutes from dead. He may have been scarier than the Boogeyman himself, but Mary had to admire Boricio's unvarnished grit.

The leader growled, and it looked like he was about to start swinging his sword, when Boricio took a giant step back and said, "Wait!"

Boricio held his hands high in the air. "Now, not to alarm you," he said, "but I'm gonna reach behind my back and pull out my Beretta. Then I'm going to set it right here on the driveway. If I point it at you, or make a move that looks like it has a ball hair of danger, I grant you full permission to open fire on my stupid ass. And you can keep pulling the trigger until I finally stop twitching. If not, then let me set my gun on the ground so you can give me a minute of your time."

Boricio didn't wait for anyone to agree, just reached his hands behind his back and pulled out the gun like it wasn't suicide, then set it flat on the ground like he said he would.

"Now," he said. "You strike me as a smart bunch of young men. And since you're smart men with intelligent transportation and a brilliant set of weapons," Boricio grinned and nodded his way from the pistol to the shotguns, then back to the sword in the middle, "I figured you might appreciate a once-in-a-lifetime opportunity to join Team Boricio." He waited for a second then added, "So, what do you say?"

All four looked confused. The leader looked like he was seconds from lobbing Boricio's head off and into the garden.

Mary's heart continued to race. She wanted Boricio to take a step back, so he was at least clear from the sword's orbit, but she knew Boricio well enough even after only a few days to know that in his mind even a small step back was retreat, and retreat was a recipe Boricio would never cook.

"I can see your confusion," he went on. "And I don't want

you to be confused, so I'll explain." Boricio cleared his throat. "Team Boricio is the winning team at the finish line of the world, and I'm the team captain."

Boricio's back was to Mary, but she could picture him beaming, and was pretty sure he was pointing at his chest. Why the three men with guns hadn't opened fire on him already was beyond her. Then again, it was beyond her how they could circle so calmly around Boricio, with none of them seeming to worry whether there might be people at the windows with guns, waiting to shoot. Like they should be doing now.

"So, I'm giving you one chance to join." Boricio turned from the leader to his men on either side and added, "Now, I'm not asking you to overthrow nothing. This isn't a mutiny in motion. I'm just letting you know your options, and seeing if maybe you want to take advantage, and join right now while we're still offering a free membership package."

Mary looked to Paola and Luca, who both looked as amazed as she was. How Boricio could keep the men from killing him, simply by spouting sentence after sentence of uncut nonsense was simply astonishing.

Boricio had no weapon, and all of them were armed. And she had no idea what his plan might be. Short of a miracle, Boricio was seconds from dead, and the three of them were minutes behind, if lucky.

"First thing I'm gonna do is cut your tongue out," the leader said, finally speaking.

Boricio hollered. "Woo-hoo! Now that's what I'm talking about. That's exactly the sort of initiative I'm looking for with new recruits. Now," he shook his head, "don't get me wrong. I do understand why you wouldn't want to surrender your leadership role, and I also get how your 'boys on the side' there might not realize how it's in their best interest to join me, so I propose a little battle between us."

The leader raised his eyebrows. Mary might not have seen

it all the way from the second floor if it wasn't right above the obvious scrunch in his nose.

"You three cowboys can keep your guns all aimed on me, while He-Man and I punch shit out. If I win, all four of you become proud members of Team Boricio." He smiled over at the leader. "You can be the General, or maybe we'll make up a title if you'd prefer, like Cobra Commander or Optimus Prime or some shit. If I lose, then I'll join your team, Team Taco, or whatever the fuck it's called. You can pick my team name, though I rather like Boricio. Destro would be cool. I also like my last name, Wolfe, like the thing that can rip your throat out while growling, but with an E."

Boricio paused, and Mary was certain the next thing she'd hear was his final cry as the leader's sword separated his neck and throat. There was nothing but one bird answering another until Boricio spoke again about 20 seconds later.

"I imagine you're probably thinking that your little four-some is a perfect set, ready for all four corners of the blanket; I can promise Boricio is an asset to any picnic. In this partic-ular instance, I can promise you some nicely gift wrapped, sweet pink meat. And by gift wrap I mean panties, in case it's been so long that you didn't know what I meant by the meat. Now I know I said it was just me and Rosy, but I was lying. I've actually got two peaches in my garden, one that's nice and soft and another that's not quite ripe. Not my taste, but I'll let your tongue be the judge."

Mary felt a sudden flush of fresh hate race through her body. Luca put his hand on her shoulder. "It's okay," he said. "He's just going fast enough to keep them from thinking."

The four bikers all started laughing. The leader dropped his sword to the ground, then took a step toward Boricio and swung. Boricio dodged what Mary thought seemed like a surprisingly slow throw, then took a step back and said, "I suggest we move over yonder so we have ample room to brawl."

Boricio nodded at the gunpowder trio, said, "You guys can keep your guns pointed on me," then turned to the leader and pointed over toward a spot by the garden about 50 feet away. "We'll take this over there."

The leader nodded, then headed toward the clearing. Boricio followed, then turned back, and for one half a second, when nobody else was looking, turned his eyes to Mary's window and winked.

Mary didn't believe she could read Boricio's mind, but her usual *knowing* was spoken in Boricio's voice.

It's just like shooting bottles from the fucking fence. Even your sweet, little lamb can do it. But not Rip Van Creepy. The kick'll be too much. The two of you will do fine.

Paola knew what they were about to do before Mary said a word. "I'm ready, Mom," she said.

"You make your momma wait this long before you fuck her?" Boricio said, dancing from side to side around the leader.

The leader roared, then charged at Boricio, landing an easy blow to the side of his head that Mary was positive he could have avoided. Boricio moved like a cat even when he was going slowly.

The leader tackled Boricio, and they tumbled to the ground in a ballet of fists as they rolled across the grass.

"Ready?" Mary said. Paola nodded as Luca crawled toward the corner. Mary stood, opened the windows. There were no screens to get out of the way — just nice open space to fire.

Distracted by the brawl, the three bikers never saw the shots coming as Mary and Paola fired at them.

All three painted the ground in crimson before managing to fire a single shot. Boricio started to cackle, taking control of the scuffle by climbing on top of the leader's body and launching both of his fists repeatedly into the man's pasty face.

Boricio climbed from the leader's crumpled body, then turned his face to the window. "Woo-hoo!!!" he screamed. "Too bad every fire department in creation is on permanent retirement, because Team Boricio is on fucking fire!"

He looked down at the leader's face, then pointed and laughed, turning back to the window. "Looks like Boricio's Famous Sloppy Spaghetti!"

The leader started squirming on the ground. To Mary's horror, she found herself hoping Boricio would do exactly what he did a moment later.

Boricio walked over to the leader's sword, picked it up from the concrete while wearing a giant smile, then walked back to the body and thrust the blade deep into the leader's chest.

"One hundred thousand sperm in your daddy's shot, and you were the fastest?" Boricio howled as a fountain of blood erupted from the leader's twitching body.

Boricio turned back to the house and took a bow for his audience.

~

THIRTY

Other Ed Keenan

Ed raced along the dirt road leading to the north side of the island. The moment Sullivan said the infected had been seen in the north end, Ed knew where he had to go: the old monastery tucked inside the woods. He doubted the infected would have gone there — not on their own, anyway — but Williams would have. It was the oldest structure on the island and a historic destination back when the island was public.

It was the only other place on the island not monitored by Guardsmen. Most newcomers wouldn't even think to look there, let alone know it existed, which gave Williams the perfect reason to go.

He had gone rogue. The question was — why? Had he been infected, or did Williams now feel differently about their research? He knew Williams and Will had gone head to head a few times during the past few years, most notably following what happened last summer. Whatever the case, the doctor was the most likely suspect in the escape of the infected. Ed prayed he hadn't gone after Will Bishop.

If Will was dead then everyone else on the island was doomed. Though Will had been getting increasingly more unstable since October, he was the only one on the island who was able to understand — and predict — some of the things that were happening.

Ed cut the lights before he parked the truck, deciding to go the rest of the way on foot. He grabbed an AR-15 from the back of the truck, along with five clips, which he slid into his tactical vest. He then made sure the sphere was safely tucked in his pocket before setting off into the woods, using the light clipped onto the rifle to guide him.

He was about 40 yards from the old, brick two-story structure — overgrown with trails of vegetation creeping up and along its moss-covered walls, but otherwise still standing after more than a century spent mostly abandoned. The wooden front door had been replaced a few years earlier as part of a restoration project.

It was now open.

Ed slowly approached, his gun and light aimed at the threshold. He was about 20 feet from the doorway when he spotted movement to his right. He almost jumped, nearly squeezing the trigger as he raised his rifle. Somehow, he managed to remain steady and keep himself from sending a bullet into what turned out to be only a white cloth strip either stuck to — or tied — to a branch.

Surrender?

Ed glanced at the open door again, searching for a sign of either Williams or Will Bishop.

Seeing nothing, Ed stepped through the doorway and into the darkness, ears perked, careful to move silently.

Moonlight spilled in from the open windows and into the main room, painting four large squares dimly across the floor's center. Dust floated along motes of light, suspended in space and barely moving. Everything else was dark.

Ed swung the rifle's light around the room. It had been awhile since he'd been to the monastery, but the layout was easy enough to remember. One main chamber, leading to a pair of doors and a stairway on the left. Both doors were open.

Ed made his way through the room, stepping over debris along the ancient stone floor. Apparently, renovations had only extended to the building's outside.

He stayed on the room's far right, sweeping his light over doors as he passed. He looked out the two large windows on the rear wall and saw the moon peering through the forest about 50 yards away.

Ed stepped toward the second of the two rooms with its door half ajar, where any of the people he was searching for could easily be hiding. As he approached, his boot cracked something on the ground — a pane of dusty glass, crunching with an echo across the old building with its high ceilings.

He paused, waiting to see if the sound would draw someone from hiding, but was greeted with nothing but silence.

Ed pushed the door the rest of the way open, wondering if someone had set the glass there as an alarm. Given the layer of dust on the glass, and lack of clean spots outside of his boot print, it seemed unlikely.

He opened the door to a sudden voice.

"Don't shoot."

Ed's light found Will, sitting perfectly still in the darkness on an old, wooden chair as if he were waiting to see a doctor.

"Sir, what are you doing here?" Ed said, moving his light from Will's face to the floor.

"Waiting," he said, his voice eerily calm as if he were talking in his sleep and responding to someone Ed couldn't see.

Ed brought the light up again, just enough to see Will's dark, open, and oversized pupils.

"Waiting for who?" Ed asked, thinking he probably shouldn't bother. The old man had been growing progressively worse since the previous fall. Some said he was senile, but Ed didn't think that was it. Well, not completely, anyway. He was more likely mourning all that he had lost, and what had happened on Oct. 15.

"For Luca and Boricio. They're coming back."

Ed closed his eyes, feeling a cool blade of sadness cut through him. He didn't have the heart to correct Will. "Come on, sir; it's not safe here," he said. "There's been a breach. Two of the infected have escaped, and Dr. Williams is nowhere to be found."

Something snapped Will from his daze. He cocked his head and looked at Ed quizzically. "Escaped? How?"

"We believe Dr. Williams had something to do with it, though we're not sure why."

"Oh my." Will said. "That's not good. Not good at all."

"How long have you been here, Mr. Bishop? Have you seen anyone else?"

"All day. Waiting," Will said, starting to get that glassy look in his eyes again.

"Did you see anybody else?"

"No," Will said, meeting Ed's eyes. "Nobody else."

"Come on, let me bring you back to the Facility so I can get back out and find them."

Will rattled his head as if trying to shake himself from a fugue, then stood. His bones creaked, and Ed wondered how long the man had been sitting in the chair.

"Did Dr. Williams tell you to meet him here?"

"No," Will said. "Why do you ask?"

"Just curious why you came out here of all places."

"The dreams told me to come here tonight. What time is it?"

"Oh-two hundred," Ed said, glancing at his watch.

"Oh, they're gonna be here soon!"

"What?"

"Yes, they're coming at 2:15."

Ed stared at Will, staring absentmindedly back, smiling

like the senile man many thought he'd become. It was obvious to Ed that Will was confused. Even if he had dreamed of 2:15, it wasn't psychic phenomena. Yes, the man was gifted, but this was more likely a blend of dream and memory, twisting itself into rambling prophecy.

The smile on Will's face said it all: The fragile old man needed his dream to come true. And it would break his heart when it didn't. What could Ed do, though? No way would he get the old man to go with him until he saw that his dream was just a dream and nothing more.

"I can't wait to see them," Will said, turning from Ed and returning to his chair.

Ed was going to resist, but decided it wasn't worth it. What was five more minutes? "At least let's wait out there," Ed said as he picked up Will's chair and brought it out into the main room.

"Thank you," Will said, sitting down and folding his hands on his lap like he was waiting on a train rather than an impossibility.

Ed shook his head, "Have you gone upstairs at all?"

"No," Will shook his head, his eyes on the floor where the squares of light illuminated the concrete.

"Wait right here, okay? I'm gonna check up there."

"Don't go," Will said, his voice almost sad. "You'll miss them."

"Just call me if . . . er, *when* they show up. Okay?"

"Okay," Will said, smiling.

Ed shook his head and left Will to wait for nothing. His flashlight probed the darkness of the stairway as he ascended the concrete steps. He didn't want to leave Will alone for long, so he didn't bother with stealth. He quickly bounded the steps and checked out the second floor — a tiny bathroom and seven bedrooms with small beds. Without anyone in them, the vacant rooms with their crumbling beds made Ed think of a haunted orphanage. And he felt like the eyes of the dead were on him.

Once Ed was certain no one was on the second floor, he raced back downstairs and saw Will sitting in the same position he'd left him, and wearing the same stupid grin.

Ed glanced at his watch: 2:17 a.m. with no sign of anyone. The building was silent as a crypt, and he felt a chill in the air. Ed wanted to get out of the creepy building and on the road.

"I don't think they're coming," Ed said, showing Will the watch. It's 2:17."

Will looked at the watch, and the hope in his eyes died like the smile on his face. The shift in mood was immediate; sudden enough to surprise Ed.

Will stood, his face void of emotion. "Let's go."

Will stepped past Ed. As Ed was about to turn and follow Ed, he caught movement in the corner of his eye. He looked up and saw someone outside walk past the window — a man in what looked like a black uniform — though he was past the window before Ed could be certain.

"Oh!" Ed shouted, surprised, his heart racing.

"What is it?" Will asked, looking around.

Ed ran to the window, rifle ready, but saw no one outside.

"What is it?" Will repeated, immediately beside him.

"I think I saw someone out there," Ed said, then turned back to the open door on the far side of the room. "Quick. Let's go."

The door slammed shut when they were three feet away.

Will jumped back, and Ed raised his rifle. A shadow tore across the floor, racing from the window behind him. Ed spun around, and this time saw the man in black standing in the window, his back turned to them. It looked like a Guardsman in uniform. He was without a helmet or mask, which confused Ed, like the man's thick and unkempt mop of dark hair.

What the hell?

Ed approached the window for a closer look. Just as he

was five feet away, the Guardsman turned and revealed a face without any mouth, eyes, nose, or *anything*. His face was smooth and pale as if someone erased his features, with something, or *some things*, moving beneath the flesh, pushing at the skin like bones trying to find their way to right.

Ed raised the rifle.

Behind him, the door flew open, and Will let out a startled yell.

Ed turned back to the front door and saw Dr. Williams standing there, completely nude, his saggy skin caked in dirt, mud, or something else. He wasn't wearing his glasses, and his eyes were as wide and demented as his hair was wild and crazy.

On either side of Dr. Williams were two of the infected — now fully devolved, barely resembling the humans they once were — a woman and child found recently in the city.

"Give us the vials," Williams said, his voice sounding not like one person, but several, almost like he were speaking while gargling.

"There are no more vials," Will said, his voice surprisingly strong and defiant.

"Lie!" Williams said, pointing an accusatory finger at Will. "I know what you did! I know what you did! You have them!"

The window crashed behind them, reminding Ed of the man without a face who'd been behind them.

It was too late to do anything. Ed spun to fire, but the man raised an arm and swung it hard, knocking Ed to the ground. His rifle fell, and the thing leapt on top of his body before Ed could calculate a response.

The thing gripped Ed's neck tight, choking him and shoving his head back hard into the dusty ground. Ed struggled to pull the man-thing's hands away, mesmerized by its face, shifting beneath the skin until it started to tear along the center like a bloody seam, followed by the sickening wet sound of ripping.

From that seam flowed something dark and fibrous, as blood and black goo gushed from the wound and spilled down onto Ed's chin.

He cringed, turning away and clenching his mouth closed so as not to ingest the putrid-smelling shit. It started to spatter Ed's cheek as he struggled and twisted, swinging his legs enough to try and kick the creature from his body.

The liquid began to dribble up and toward Ed's eye.

If it gets in me, I'm infected.

Ed clenched his eyes shut as the thing's grip grew stronger around his neck, choking breath from his body as pain shot through him. Ed felt like his was seconds from being ripped from his body.

A gunshot thundered in the otherwise empty room, followed by a high-pitched whine, as the body on top of him froze and a fresh batch of hot liquid spilled onto his chest and face.

Ed rolled over, quickly wiping his face off with the side of his jacket, and spinning around to see Will holding his rifle and taking aiming at Williams.

Will fired, hitting the infected woman in the head and sending her deformed blackened body to the ground in spasms. Will fired again as the child ran toward them, but missed.

The wee monstrosity was fast. It screeched from some part that was still a child, wailing that Will had shot its mother.

Five feet from Will, it sprang to its feet, swinging its clawed hands at the old man, knocking the rifle to the ground and hitting him hard in the chest as he flew backwards to the ground. The thing tumbled onto the floor as Will rolled over, gasping for air and clutching his chest.

The creature got up, ready to finish Will for good.

Ed's hand found his Glock on his holster and was blasting before the creature made it an inch farther. He fired twice, tearing its small head to nuggets of flesh, bone, and goo. Ed looked up, searching for a Dr. Williams who was already gone.

"Damn it!" he screamed, ignoring Will and running out the front door and into the night, looking for Williams.

There was no Williams, just six Guardsmen, all of them staring with pitch-black eyes and faces beginning to congeal, standing between Ed and the woods where his truck waited. They began walking toward him.

Ed raced back inside and slammed the door shut, locking it, then turned to a staring Will.

"What is it?" Will asked.

"There's six more Guardsmen out there," Ed said. "They've been infected, and at a rapid acceleration."

"It's impossible to become infected and to change so quickly," Will said, "unless . . . "

Ed finished Will's hypothesis. "They've been infected all along, and it's been dormant? If that's the case, then . . . Oh God." He shook his head and tried to close his mouth. "It might have infiltrated the Facility already."

~

THIRTY-ONE

Boricio Bishop

Boricio waited until he knew Will was gone, then crossed the street and opened the door to his old house without knocking.

Sarah looked up in surprise. "Will's not here," she said. "He won't be back until the end of the day."

"That's fine," Boricio said. "I'm here to see my main man, Mr. Luca Bishop!"

Luca tore into the front room yelling, "Boricio!"

He smiled; even after two long years of Luca doing it, Boricio couldn't believe anyone could ever be so consistently happy to see him.

"How come you're here?" Luca asked.

"I came to visit you, Little Man. That's all."

Luca eyed Boricio with suspicion. Boricio nodded at Sarah. She took the hint and left the room. Boricio led Luca to the couch and sat. Before he could say anything, Luca said, "You're here to talk about Dad?"

Boricio nodded.

"Why is he mad?"

Boricio sat in silence before wrapping his arm around Luca and pulling him into a relaxed lean against the back of the couch — much like he imagined they'd be leaning in another 10 years or so, each of them holding a beer — then said, "Dad just has a lot on his mind right now. It's crazy how occupied the old man gets." Then, for a sprinkle of truth, he added, "And there's a lot happening at work that he didn't expect. Nothing for you to worry about, but definitely stuff that's keeping him busy, and not quite here even when he is, if you know what I mean."

"I know what you mean," Luca nodded.

Boricio smiled.

Luca said. "But that's not all the story, or even a lot of it."

"It's all the stuff that matters," Boricio said.

Luca shook his head. "No, it isn't. And now I feel sad because you're lying to me."

"Aww, Little Man," Boricio said. "It's not like that." He squeezed his little brother tighter. "There's just some stuff I don't think you need to know. Not because I don't care if you do, but because I don't think you need to worry about stuff you don't need to be worried about, you know?" He didn't wait for Luca to answer. "A kid should have the chance to be a kid."

"I see it all anyway." Luca said pointing to his head. "If you don't lie to me, then you can help me understand it."

"Oh," Boricio said, "I forget." He paused, then added, "How much can you see?"

Luca said, "I see the *what* in what you're thinking, but can't see the why."

Boricio scooted from Luca and pulled his arm back to his side. "Is this about you digging into other people's minds?"

Luca nodded, then said. "I can see inside everyone now." He swallowed. "And there's more."

Boricio could feel it, a special sort of bullshit that wasn't really bullshit at all. Maybe he was only catching rebounds from Luca's brain, but it felt to Boricio like they were sitting just seconds away from everything changing. He swallowed.

"There's another Earth, mostly just like ours. And I know how to get there."

Boricio laughed. "Hahaha, at least that's funnier than that *Charlie Bit My Finger* thing you made me watch on YouTube."

Luca's face was cool marble, desperately wanting to warm.

Boricio swallowed again and asked, "What do you mean there's *another* Earth?"

He repeated, "There's another Earth, and I can go there." Then probably because Luca knew what Boricio would say next, he added, "I've gone there before, and I'll go there again. I can even bring stuff back with me."

"No way!" Boricio yelled, loud enough to pull Sarah to the doorway. He turned to Sarah, shook his head, and gestured for her that everything was kosher. Sarah left with a shrug, and Boricio turned to Luca.

"That's not possible!" he said, even though he could clearly see in Luca's eyes that it was.

There was nothing but silence and faster breathing from Boricio, until Luca finally spoke. "You want to believe me, Boricio, but you can't," he said. Then after another second, he said, "Dad already saw it. So I can show you, too."

"Wait," Boricio said. "Will has seen this?"

"Yes," Luca nodded. "And call him Dad."

"When did *Dad* see this?"

"I dunno, a few weeks ago," Luca said. "But he didn't go with me, even though I think I might even be able to take people. He didn't want to come. Do you want to come with me?"

"That sounds like six pounds of vanilla ice cream, covered in fudge, kid soldier. Just tell me what to do and you'll be halfway to having it done."

"You don't have to do anything," Luca said. "You can close your eyes, but you probably won't have to. I like to close mine." Luca closed his eyes as he finished his sentence.

Boricio had no idea whether he would have had to close

his eyes or not, since the millisecond he did he was already somewhere else.

He opened his eyes to a chain link fence, a few feet away from where the two of them were standing beneath a stop sign, with patches of grass growing through the cracks in the sidewalk around it.

"Where are we?" Boricio said.

Luca pointed to the chain link. "That's my old school."

"Wait ... what?" Boricio turned to Luca in disbelief, and then up the puffy, white clouds in the perfect California summer sky. "This is Las Orillas?"

Luca nodded again, then turned around and curled his fingers into the chain link, except for his pointer, which was aimed straight at another Luca, who was on a playground pretending like he was Indiana Jones, swinging from a plastic slider, then onto the rubber mat while loudly humming the theme song. The other Luca sprang up from the mat, then ran to the back of the line of kids, laughing.

Boricio shook his head. "It's not possible." He pointed to his chest. "Can he see us?"

Luca nodded. "If he looked over, he could. But I think he's too busy playing. But I talked with my dad . . . or his dad, anyway. He thought I was the other Luca, so I didn't get caught."

Luca looked like he might cry, and then said, "But Luca hasn't seen me. I'm afraid of what will happen if he does. That's why we have to go now. I just wanted to show you so you could believe me like you wanted to."

By the time Luca finished his sentence they were standing in his bedroom, even though they'd been sitting on the couch when they teleported away.

Boricio said, "Can you control where you come back?"

There was a light knock on the door. Sarah said, "Are you guys in there?"

"Yup!" Boricio said.

"I could've sworn you were downstairs."

"We were," Boricio said, "but then we came upstairs."

He waited a second, then said, "Sorry we didn't ask first."

There was light laughter, followed by a long pause, then "Okay," before Boricio heard Sarah's slowly fading footsteps.

"How specific can you get with where you come back?" Boricio asked again. "We were downstairs, and now we're upstairs. How much can you control that?"

"Not sure," Luca shrugged. "I've never really tried. Hold on."

Luca disappeared. Five seconds later, Boricio heard a pebble slap the window. Boricio ran to the glass, and stared down smiling in disbelief. Luca was downstairs by the tree, standing by it and grinning ear to ear.

A big, beautiful idea bloomed inside Boricio's brain as Luca vanished and then appeared back in the room in front of him.

Dr. Williams wouldn't help him. But what if Boricio went to Williams with a vial? Boricio was pretty damned sure he could convince the man to take a chance on Rose then.

But how the hell do I ask Luca to break into Level 7 and steal the vials?

Boricio didn't even need to ask, though.

The boy was staring at him.

Luca smiled and said, "Yes, Boricio, I'll get the vials for you."

TO BE CONTINUED ...

Episode 16

(FOURTH EPISODE OF SEASON THREE)

"The Variable"

THIRTY-TWO

Boricio Bishop

Black Island Research Facility
Level 7
September 2011
Morning
ONE MONTH BEFORE THE EVENT …

WHILE MOST PEOPLE could be swayed by logic or an emotional appeal, Boricio was starting to think that the only way to open Dr. Williams' mind was with a crowbar.

He'd gotten the doctor alone in his office and asked him to work his magic again — to *please* use the vials to create another serum. It had worked with Luca. It would work with Rose.

But Dr. Williams was afraid of incurring the wrath of Boricio's father, Will.

"He's not your boss, he's a consultant," Boricio had said.

"You know as well as I that if he doesn't green-light a project, it goes nowhere. I'm lucky to even have a job after what happened with Luca — and that was a success! Imagine if we fail."

But Boricio couldn't imagine a world where that would happen.

"I'm losing her," Boricio said, his voice cracking as he played up his sadness a bit to try and work on Williams' sympathy. "She's in constant pain, she's paralyzed, and her memory is only getting worse."

"These things take time," Dr. Williams said. "You have to be patient. This isn't nearly as pressing as Luca's situation had been. She is stable and just needs time to heal."

"Do you know what it's like to have the woman you love look at you like you're a stranger?" Boricio asked.

Of course, Dr. Williams didn't have a response to that, either in words or emotion. His face was nearly blank, in fact. He simply said, "I'm sorry, Boricio."

Boricio waited him out a moment, allowing the silence to push the Doc into saying more.

"I understand," Dr. Williams said. "And I want to help you, Boricio. But even if I believed the procedure was safe, which I'm not sure that I do any more, Will Bishop will never allow it. We've done so much with the Remedy Project — *I've* done so much with the project — and I can't risk its future on another of your whims."

Boricio ignored the slight, though it was hard not to blast back. Instead, he tried a reasoned approach, and played one of two cards he had.

"Healing Rose *is* in the best interests of the Remedy Project." Boricio paused, then revealed his second-strongest card. "What if I told you I could get my hands on a vial?"

A sudden streak of red flushed the doctor's face. Williams said. "We're not having this conversation." He cleared his throat, clearly agitated.

Boricio realized he wasn't just crossing the line; he was dragging his ass like a dog on carpet and smearing a trail of shit along the way.

William's said, "This is borderline treason, Boricio. I have to ask you to leave now, and to never bring this up again. I hope things change soon, and that we can figure out what's happening with Luca, and get Rose the help she needs. But in the meantime, I'm growing increasingly uncomfortable with this topic. You promised no more than five minutes, and we're now into our 20th."

Boricio's second-best card hadn't worked, so he played one better — and his last.

"I know about the Goliath Project," he said. "And I know how badly you'd love for Will to sign off on it." Boricio leaned across the desk. "But he won't, will he, Doc? Will's just not much of a team player these days, is he?"

The doctor said nothing.

Boricio leaned back in his seat and continued, "Well, it's a good thing I am. I know how I can get Will to John Hancock all over the Goliath Project, and I'm confident enough to give you a guarantee that I'll make it happen. What do you say, Doc?"

Williams shook his head, his eyes as wide as his face was red. Boricio couldn't tell if he was surprised or angry that Boricio knew about Goliath. Or perhaps he picked up on the subtext — if Williams didn't help him, he'd make it damned difficult to get Goliath passed through.

"I'm saying the same thing I've been saying all along, Boricio — I'd love to help you, but I can't. Not even with a promise of getting me a vial, or a green light on Goliath. Will has his reasons for refusing your requests, and even if I don't agree with all of his reasons, it's my job and responsibility to listen."

"But it's not!" Boricio could feel the growl growing inside his voice. "That's only true if Will genuinely knows better. But he doesn't. Not this time. He's not a scientist, right? At least not like *you*." Boricio waited for the flicker of agreement he knew was inside Williams to flash across his face. "And because Will isn't a scientist, he is impeding the project's progress by withholding the vials from you and your team, right?"

Williams cleared his throat and repeated the party line. "He has his reasons."

"What if you could have absolute, unhindered access to the vials?"

Williams shook his head. "No one has that kind of access."

Boricio pulled one final ace from the inside of his coat, then gently set the vial on the doctor's desk, the glass cylinder of bright-blue liquid packed in clear plastic to protect it.

Williams stared at the vial, his eyes nearly as wide as his open mouth.

His hand dropped to the desk, hovering an inch above the vial before he quickly snatched back his fingers as if they were centimeters from the fangs of a snake.

Williams stroked his chin, then scratched his head and tugged at his ears, wrestling with something inside him for a long while before finally turning to Boricio and saying, "How . . . how did you get that?"

Boricio laughed, though the laugh was closer to a cackle.

"There are two sorts of secrets, Doc — the kind you want to keep inside because they mean a helluva lot more if they're never so much as whispered, and the other sort where you wouldn't dare utter a whisper, even if you wanted to. This one," he nodded toward the vial, "is both."

Williams turned his back to the vial, then got up from his desk and began to pace as if his chair had grown too hot to sit in.

Boricio said, "Take it or leave it, Doc. The choice is yours."

Williams stared at Boricio without saying a word, almost like he was practicing the same sort of in and out, in and out slow breathing Boricio had begun to master over the past few weeks. He finally turned back to his desk and ran his fingers over the vial, his fingers grazing the length of the plastic casing from top to bottom.

"We can't do this," he shook his head and whispered. *"Can we?"*

Boricio had him.

"We can, Doc. That's why I'm here."

TWO DAYS LATER …

BORICIO AND DR. WILLIAMS had been in Rose's room for nearly 15 minutes. Warm anticipation was burning up and down Boricio's back as he made small circles on the linoleum behind the doctor. He'd managed to avoid Will during the past two days, and Will was scheduled for his weekly meeting with Sullivan, which usually ran longer than it was supposed to.

The stage was set, but doubt began to sow seeds in Boricio's head. He tried not to allow it to show, however. If he let his uncertainty show, Rose would get spooked.

It wasn't doubt so much that the serum would work. He had faith that it would, even if it had some slight side effects as it had with Luca.

But, he wondered, was it fair to inflict those side effects on Rose? What if she teleported to another world like Luca had? She'd be terrified. Or worse, what if she teleported into the middle of a highway at rush hour or something? While Luca had seemed somewhat excited about his new ability, Rose might not see it as a gift, but rather a curse.

So, Boricio was forced to consider if the risk was worth the reward.

Was her life truly so miserable now that it wouldn't get better in time?

Am I doing this to help her, or am I doing it out of selfishness to have my old Rose back?

The sting of the question caused Boricio to look down at the floor before meeting her eyes again.

Rose's eyes seemed tiny, silent, and slightly sad, even though they appeared to be missing any true recognition of the men.

She stared at both Boricio and Williams, though mostly Williams, as he took her vitals and ran through every necessary precaution to ensure that her fragile body was aptly prepped to accept the serum he had spent the last 32 hours preparing.

"Are you ready?" Williams turned to Boricio.

Boricio nodded. "Sure thing, Doc. Can I just have a few minutes alone with her before we get started?"

Williams nodded, said, "Of course," then slipped from her room.

Boricio turned back to Rose. "Hi there," he said.

She half smiled, then said, "Hi."

She didn't sound nearly as uncertain of him as she had been on other days. Something was quiet, but undeniably warmer inside her simple greeting. Perhaps she was remembering more. Or maybe just getting better at faking the responses people expected so she wouldn't disappoint them.

"What's happening?" she asked.

Boricio smiled, thrilled to hear Rose stringing two words together into a simple question, especially with the genuine curiosity behind it, minutes before she was about to receive the first drops of her certain cure.

"We're going to make you better now," Boricio promised.

"What's wrong with me?"

Like every other time Rose had asked that question, Boricio felt something horribly blunt punching a hole through the center of his heart. He wasn't sure how many times Rose had asked him already, but he hated the something inside her that wasn't allowing her to remember his answer. He said, "Nothing's wrong with you, Sweet Rose. You're just having a hard time remembering a few things." He paused, then added, "Like you and me, for example."

"I remember you," she said.

His heart dropped so suddenly, Boricio felt as though he was stomping on its beat. Rose hadn't said anything like that since the accident, not at least without him having spent hours reminding her who he was and getting only snippets back.

"You do?" he asked, unable to hide his excitement.

She added, "At least, I sorta do."

"What do you remember?"

"Water, um . . . boats . . . um, pasta . . . and you." She paused for 30 seconds or so, though each one felt like more than its share of forever, while she tried to turn a second thought into another full sentence, but couldn't get the words to tumble from her mouth in any sort of logical order.

Boricio stared at her hard-working face, twisting in concentration as she tried to pull something from her memory's depths. Her eyes said she found something, but its weight must have been too heavy, because her lips seemed to lose it a second before her eyes returned to their usual vacancy.

Boricio pulled Rose's hand into the sandwich of his palms, wanting to weep when she didn't pull it away like had been doing recently. She held his hand like she held his eyes, and for the first time seemed perfectly unafraid.

Boricio didn't care that he was bald and scarred and ugly as an angry action figure. Fuck the world and all the haters in it. A flawless face was pocked with its own sort of flaws, anyway. The only reason Boricio dripped a drop of care about how he looked was that he couldn't stand looking nothing like the man who used to hear Rose whisper, "I can't wait to wake up with you tomorrow," each night before the cool of his pillow sent him to sleep.

"Dr. Williams will be back in a minute," Boricio said. "And

he has something that will make you better. Do you *want* to be all better Rose?"

She nodded, still holding his gaze, as her eyes filled with something Boricio dared to call hope. "Yes, I want to remember." Rose surprised Boricio further by adding, "And I want to walk again."

"You will," he promised.

Tell her about the risks. Tell her maybe you should both wait. Give it a bit more time.

Tell her!

Before he could give voice to the warnings or ask her again, the door opened and Williams entered the room.

"Are we ready?" he said.

Boricio nodded, as did Rose one second behind him.

Tell him no. You need more time to think about it!

But Boricio couldn't open his mouth. He'd forced Williams into this position. If Boricio pulled out now, Williams might tell him to fuck off and just run to Will with everything, and they'd lose what might be Rose's only chance at a normal life. It was now or never, and Boricio couldn't let fear make the choice.

Williams opened a small, black case, then withdrew a syringe filled with an oddly colored lavender liquid, almost beautiful behind the clear glass. He ejected the last bit of air into a second glass vial, not allowing any of the serum to spill out.

Williams rubbed a swab of alcohol across Rose's arm, then said, "You're going to feel a slight prick, but it shouldn't hurt for more than a second. Is that okay?"

Rose nodded, and Williams pressed the syringe to her arm, slowly pushing the plunger until every drop of lavender had disappeared.

Rose squeezed Boricio's hand during the long minutes of silence that followed, as Dr. Williams paced back and forth in front of the room, waiting for some instant reaction. Boricio wasn't sure what would happen to signify that the serum had worked. Would she suddenly feel her legs? Would she burst into tears remembering every memory that had been sealed away? Or would the change be more subtle? If so, the Doc might be pacing a while.

Boricio wondered how much longer silence would choke the room, and was surprised when it was Rose — the light in her eyes making a return – who finally broke it.

"Am I supposed to be feeling something?"

Dr. Williams said, "Just give it a few minutes, Rose. The serum has to work through your body."

Boricio was thrilled at the light in her eyes, the first indication since the accident that someone was home.

"Can I turn on the TV?" she asked.

"Sorry, Rose," Williams shook his head, "but I want to keep our full attention on this right now. Do you understand why?"

She nodded, but glanced over toward the remote sitting four feet from her fingers on the bedside table. Boricio said, "What does it matter if she's watching something while we're waiting to see what happens?"

Before Williams could answer, a smile spread across Rose's face.

"My legs," she said. "They feel tingly."

Boricio tore the sheet from her and let it drape off the bed. Her legs were still bandaged, both of them in casts from her knees to her feet, with only her toes showing. Rose began to wiggle her toes and laughed hysterically.

Williams said, "What does it feel like, Rose? What's happening right now?"

She couldn't stop smiling. Her face was pink and soft and starting to glow. "It feels warm everywhere inside my body, almost hot. But not quite painful. Like an itching burn."

"But good, right?" Boricio asked, thrilled with how much vitality Rose was speaking.

"Oh, God, Baby, yes!" she said, her voice stronger. "I already feel a million times better!"

Boricio's voice was a cracked whisper of disbelief. "Baby?" he said. "Can you remember me?"

"Yes," she said, crying and nodding, "You were planning a special day for me, weren't you?" With a playful smile Boricio couldn't believe he was seeing, Rose said, "Was *this* what you had in mind?"

Boricio erupted into laughter, then dropped her hand and pulled her into an embrace before he showered her with kisses. He smothered Rose's right cheek, then turned from her to Williams and threw his arms around the doctor.

"I love you, man," he said. "And I'll never forget this. I know you didn't have to … "

Boricio's thank you was severed by a sudden scream from Rose.

The two men turned to see her entire body shaking violently as if having a seizure of some kind.

"What's happening, Doc?!" Boricio screamed.

"I don't know," Williams cried, rushing toward the computer, which was monitoring her vitals. Lines were racing up and down in zigzags when Boricio glanced over, before turning back to Rose and trying to calm her while holding her down so she didn't launch off the bed.

She continued to shake until she fell suddenly still, and her eyes closed as if she might never open them again.

"Someone get the fuck in here and help!" Boricio screamed, slamming his palm on the red ALERT button on the side of her bed. "We need help in here, NOW!"

A trio of doctors rushed inside Rose's room and pushed Boricio aside, where he stood helplessly, watching as the doctors tried to revive her.

As he stared, frozen in fear, he found himself praying to God to please, please save his soul mate.

Boricio couldn't watch, so he turned away, and didn't turn

back until he heard the blood-bleaching scream that erupted from her.

Boricio ran back to her bedside, thrusting himself between the doctors surrounding her, trying to keep them from hurting her any more than they already were. Rose was sitting straight up, her eyes wide open and ebony, as an inky blackness spread across her face and then down her entire body. She opened her mouth, but nothing poured forth for a long half minute until her silence suddenly screamed into a howl; an unholy, *inhuman* shriek.

Something started to slither beneath her flesh all at once like a million snakes moving beneath her skin.

Boricio screamed, trying to move toward her, though he had no idea what he'd do once he'd reach her. If he could just reach her, however, he thought somehow he could help. But the three doctors began to drag him back, trying to get him out of the room. Boricio knocked one to the floor, then ran back to Rose's bed, just in time to see her beautiful hair turn as black as her slippery skin, then fall from her scalp in clumps on the sheet as she thrashed in the bed. Dr. Williams shoved Boricio aside and shoved her down, screaming for security.

Boricio started to move toward the bed, but a hand slapped him from behind, and spun him around. It was Will, his eyes wide and terrified.

"My Lord, Boricio, what have you done?!"

~

THIRTY-THREE

Ed Keenan

Black Mountain, Georgia
  March 2012
  FIVE MONTHS AFTER THE EVENT ...

THE VAN HAD LEFT the morning light, trading it for the dark tunnel leading into Black Mountain.

Ed couldn't see what was happening, lying in the back of the van and pretending to be asleep, and was too banged up to care too much at the moment, anyway. Though Lisa had removed the handcuffs from both him and Brent, Ed had no illusions of freedom — and wouldn't until he finally had the chance to speak to someone in charge.

Ed was confident that given the state of the world, he'd be able to work something out with whoever it was who sat behind the biggest desk at Black Mountain. He was a commodity the higher-ups wouldn't easily dismiss, so long as he showed them he was open to a deal. Which, of course, he was.

Ed wasn't interested in sides — Black Island or Black

Mountain. Nor did he care whatever the hell they happened to be at odds over. His only concern was ensuring the safety of his daughter, Jade, along with Teagan and her child, assuming that she had safely delivered her child.

Black Island had taken his people hostage in order to get him to work for them. If Black Mountain could make the same offer of safety for Jade and Teagan, he'd switch sides in a second. Ed learned long ago that allegiance to flags was meaningless because the players behind the flags were an ever-changing merry-go-round, each with their own agendas, which had more to do with self-preservation than ideals.

But any thoughts of switching sides were a bit premature.

Ed still didn't know what in the hell he was dealing with. So far, his impressions of Black Mountain were based solely on Lisa and her crew, which included a child and a team who had been blasted to memory out in the field. It was easy enough for Ed's confidence in the Black Mountain operation to crumble under the weight of what he'd witnessed, but he didn't have all the information, and knew underestimating an organization based on a first impression could be a mistake.

If Black Island was concerned about Black Mountain, they had to have a decent reason. It was certainly possible that the rest of the organization was professional, and that Lisa and her crew were merely the most recent recruits. It wasn't as if either Black Island or Black Mountain had a trained army ready to go when Oct. 15 went down: they were forced to make do with the groups they could gather together. In many ways, Ed was surprised Black Island had found so many capable people to fill the role of Guardsmen. There were, after all, only six island natives left over from The Event. Yet, Black Island managed to put together a decent group of Guardsmen. He wondered if Black Mountain had been similarly fortunate.

Maybe, Ed figured, Black Mountain was made up of more

people from this alternate Earth. If Black Mountain had managed to shelter more of its natives from the Oct. 15 disaster, then perhaps their institutional memory was stronger. And if that were all true, they were likely more organized and stronger than Black Island operations.

Ed opened his eyes, just a slit thin enough to see through. The tunnel was dimly lit, enough so he could see Lisa driving the van, her eyes as straight as the tunnel. The Prophet sat beside her, his eyes on the same nothing ahead of them.

Ed was surprised they'd made it through the storm with only Rojas as a casualty, though it seemed like Brent was almost trying to die, lying on the ground, about to take a nap while the tornado was seconds from scooping him up and twisting his breathing to a finish. Ed was too far away to help. Brent would've died if Lisa hadn't yanked him to safety beneath the overpass.

Lisa was tough, sure, but she didn't seem homegrown Guardsmen. Ed wondered what she'd done before being brought over. While she wasn't Guardsmen material, she definitely wasn't civilian. No way. She was too comfortable with both guns and orders. Maybe she was military, with a few tours in Afghanistan or Iraq. She seemed like someone used to dealing with assholes, and could handle herself just fine, even though Ed didn't like her attitude.

Brent spotted the open slit in Ed's eyes and started to say something to him, but Ed shook his head just enough for Brent to see, then closed his eyes and continued playing Rip van Winkle.

The van had eaten quite a bit of road before it came to a sharp, and seemingly unexpected, stop.

"What the hell?" Lisa said.

Ed opened his eyes, waiting to see what would happen next.

Lisa was staring ahead, though Ed couldn't see what she

was looking at. Moments later, there was a voice outside their window.

"Pull over into the bay, and stay in the van," a man instructed sharply.

"Yes, sir," Lisa said, turning the van to the right and merging slowly into another area branching off from the main tunnel. Ed couldn't tell if Lisa had been expecting these instructions, but judging from her initial "what the hell," he figured the routine had been changed since her last homecoming.

They were probably getting checked for signs of infection, like at the Island where it was standard operating procedure any time the Guardsmen returned from the field.

Lisa stopped the van and killed the engine.

"How many?" a man Ed couldn't see asked from outside.

"Five, including four civilians."

Four? So Billy was a recent addition to the group. Perhaps the kid hadn't been lying when he said he'd been living with a man who was killed and he'd been left on his own.

"You step out first, and tell your people to stay put," the man's voice said outside the van.

Lisa turned and met Ed's eyes.

"I heard," he said.

"What's happening?" The Prophet asked.

She hopped from the van and said, "Nothing to worry about. I'll be right back."

Lisa disappeared and left them to wait.

Ed sat up.

"What do you think is going on?" The Prophet repeated.

Ed said, "They're probably gonna scan us all, one by one, to make sure we're not infected."

"Infected? With what?" the old man looked scared.

"The alien shit that's goin' around," Ed said.

Is this guy really not putting one and one together?

"Alien stuff? You mean the demons?"

"Aliens, demons — whatever. They need to make sure none of us are infected and gonna turn into one of those damned things."

The Prophet said nothing, but for the second time since he'd met the man, Ed got a weird feeling. Something in his eyes — something buried. The man called himself The Prophet, which meant he probably had all sorts of guilt — real or imagined — running through his narrow mind.

What are you hiding, old man?

"Were any of you bit?" Brent asked.

"No," Ed said. "I don't think so. Lisa got cut, but I'm not sure if it spreads by touch."

"Shit," Brent said, adjusting his position to look in the mirror on The Prophet's side of the van.

"I can't see anything."

The van lacked rear windows, and he couldn't hear anything, so Ed could only guess at what was happening outside. He figured he'd hear something soon enough if Lisa tested positive.

Instead, they heard a knock on one of the van's back doors.

A man said, "Come out — *slowly!*"

Brent opened the door from inside. They stepped out and into a large, gray bay separated from the tunnel they'd been driving in, likely hundreds of feet beneath the mountain.

Three Guardsmen in black stood with their rifles; no sign of Lisa. Ed wondered if she'd been infected or if she was simply being debriefed. She was the only surviving member of her squad, so no doubt someone wanted to talk to her ASAP.

"One at a time," said a young man with a buzz cut, pale skin, and a face marred by severe acne. "Step toward us and remove your shirts."

The Prophet looked at Ed nervously, as if asking, *is this customary?*

No, Ed would have said, *usually you get naked.* Ed nodded as he peeled off his shirt. Brent followed immediately. The Prophet took seven days to remove his button-down white shirt.

They were instructed, one at a time, to step forward to a second Guardsman, a thin, Hispanic kid with a light wand, who couldn't have been more than 16. The test, as Ed understood it, picked up on a specific light frequency emitted only by aliens and the infected.

Ed was tested first. He passed and was then ordered to wait beside a door at the end of the room. Brent followed, breathing a bottomless sounding sigh of relief when he was told to join Ed. The Prophet went next, sweating profusely as he approached the kid.

The light immediately glowed bright-blue and started to beep. The kid was so startled he nearly fell on his ass. The two other Guardsmen raised their rifles at The Prophet, who shook his head and started to stutter, "There's g . . . got to be a m . . . m . . . mistake."

The kid ran the light over The Prophet a second time, the light shaking in his hand. The light beeped again. "He's infected!"

"Infected?" The Prophet said. "No, I'm not. I swear!"

"Come with us," the Guardsmen said, approaching The Prophet with their guns aimed at him.

His eyes widened and for a moment, Ed thought the old man was going to try and run. But a second later his shoulders slumped in resignation.

"Please," he said, turning to Ed and Brent. "Tell them I'm with you. I'm not infected."

"I'm sorry," Ed said. "Just go with them. They'll take care of you."

"What are you going to do?" the old man asked.

"We're just going to quarantine you, sir. It's a precautionary thing while we do some secondary tests. You may be just fine, at which time we'll release you to be with your friends." The Guardsmen were far more polite than Ed had seen at Black Island, especially with how they treated their infected.

Ed knew it was a lie. The light test was never wrong. They were just placating him to get him to quietly follow — a necessary lie, and a kind one they didn't need to offer. They could've just shot him right there on the spot.

The Guardsmen led The Prophet through the closer set of doors, leaving Ed and Brent alone with the kid, who was staring at his boots.

"So, what now?" Ed said.

"We'll wait for them to come back, then you'll be brought into Black Mountain for a full medical. And then someone will likely want to talk to you."

The far door opened, and Lisa appeared with a tall, blond-haired man who reminded Ed of an '80s-era Dolph Lundgren, and looked about as pleasant as when he played Ivan Drago in *Rocky IV*. Judging from the way she followed behind like an eager-to-please puppy, and the master sergeant's stripes on the side of his uniform, Dolph was clearly her superior. Ed wondered if those stripes were earned before or after Oct. 15. Was he a real soldier or no different than the kid with the blue light?

Ed thought it funny how quickly people fell into line and deferred to someone with higher rank, even after the world vanished.

The world's gone, but someone will always salute.

Ed used to find comfort in that brand of order. Hell, it helped him lead a group of Guardsmen on Black Island — soldiers who he saw earn their stripes on some harrowing missions into the center of the city's slippery, black heart. But now that Ed was away from a leadership role, he found himself thinking back on the past few years, and how power created two things above all else: corruption and sheep.

Dolph stopped in front of Ed and Brent. He looked them up and down with cold, blue eyes. His badge read, *Jung*.

"Is this them?" he turned to Lisa, his voice edged with Swiss.

"Yes, sir."

He turned his back and said, "Come with me."

Ed and Brent followed with Lisa behind.

They were led through a set of double doors, down a long, rock-walled hall, then into a large cargo elevator.

The doors closed, and the elevator began its descent.

Jung stared at the elevator doors, confident enough to keep his back to the pair of variables, Ed and Brent. Ed wondered if he was really that confident, or if it was Lisa beside him that set the strength in his shoulders?

The elevator felt like it descended forever, the temperature growing noticeably cooler as they dipped deeper into the mountain.

The elevator finally came to a stop, then opened to a wide, white — and brightly lit — sterile-looking hallway that looked like a cross between Black Island's underground facility and a hospital.

Several gray doors lined either side of the hallway, though none had windows. Each had a single blue square with a number written in the middle.

Ed and Brent were led to a room halfway down the hall. As Jung stepped in front of the door it automatically slid open, revealing a large office with an impressive mahogany desk and a bookcase loaded with several volumes. Despite its fineries, the walls were an ignored shade of white.

A tall, red leather chair was behind the desk, facing the back of the room. Two smaller brown leather chairs sat in front of the desk. As Ed entered, the chair spun around and a bald man in black greeted them, smiling. Other than his lack of hair, long scar, and the black patch covering his left eye, he was a spitting image of the man Ed had been sent south to find: Boricio.

Boricio's eye widened, as if he recognized one of the two, if not the both of them. But the moment passed almost immediately, and he instructed everyone to leave his office except for Ed and Brent, whom he invited to take the seats in front of him.

"So, I hear that you're looking for me?" Boricio said, presenting the photo Ed was surprised to see Lisa still had.

"Well," Ed said, "that depends. Are you from here or there?"

"*There?*" Boricio asked, though Ed saw in his eyes that he understood the reference.

"I'm looking for the Boricio from my Earth," Ed said.

"Ah, so you're not from here?" Boricio asked.

"No," Ed said.

"That would explain why you don't remember me."

"Remember you?"

"Well, if you're here from Black Island, I'm guessing you've met your twin, right?"

"Yes," Ed said.

"And he sent you to find the Boricio from *your world?*"

"Yes," Ed nodded.

"Interesting. Did he tell you why?"

"No, sir," Ed shook his head. "But I got the feeling that they said he had something to do with Oct. 15."

Boricio smiled weirdly, then swallowed, "You sure they didn't mean me?"

"They said he was from my world," Ed said. "Why? Were you responsible for this?"

"Not directly, no," Boricio said, answering the question as though the taste was new to his tongue.

Ed wondered why Boricio was telling them the truth, assuming he was.

Ed asked, "What does that mean, *not directly?*"

"It means I don't feel like talking about it," Boricio said with a sudden glare. "Common denominators are that all of us are looking to find this other Boricio, but I'm curious, Mr. Keenan, did your Wonder Twin tell you anything about me? About Oct. 15? Anything at all?"

"Like I said, I didn't even know about you. I was told to find the Boricio from my world. I was, and am, on a need-to-know basis, and either they didn't know what happened, or didn't feel I needed to know. All they told me was that we, most of the people at Black Island, were from my world. We all got sucked over. And most of the people on this world either vanished or were killed. That's the sum of what I know."

"What about you?" Boricio turned to Brent.

"I only know what Ed told me," Brent said.

"Tell me, how many others are on the island?" Boricio asked.

"A few hundred," Ed answered, being purposefully vague. "Led by a civilian President, Andre Pembrook, a figurehead put in place to help keep the people in line. I'm not sure who's really pulling the strings, if it's my double, or someone above him I've not yet met."

"And how many of those are native to this world?"

"Six that I know of," Ed said.

"Do you know their names?"

"Well, there's Keenan, and a man named Sullivan was one of them. Not sure if that's his first or last name."

"It's both, actually," Boricio asked. "His parents had an odd sense of humor. A sense of humor that skipped at least one goddamned generation," he looked at Ed, "in case he was putting on a nice show for you while you were there."

"No," Ed shook his head. "He didn't strike me as a good-time Charlie."

"Anyone else?" Boricio asked.

"Introductions were sparse," Ed said. "Anyone in particular you're wondering about?"

"Do you know if a man named Will survived?"

"Will Bishop?" Ed said.

Boricio's face lit up. "Yes. He's there?"

"He's one of the scientists, or a consultant to the scientists, whatever, but I've not met him."

Boricio whispered to himself, "Oh God, he's alive," but Ed wasn't sure if he was relieved or saddened by the news.

"What about a boy? Luca?"

"Doesn't ring a bell," Ed said. "I think the others were all scientists. They were in a room or something, which somehow spared them."

Boricio's eye grazed the top of his desk.

Ed wondered what in the hell had happened, how Boricio knew these people — he must've been from there — and most of all, why in the hell Black Island was looking for Boricio's twin rather than the man from their own world.

Ed asked, "Why are *you* looking for the other Boricio?"

"To try and right some wrongs," he said. "You two interested in helping?"

"That depends," Ed held Boricio's gaze. "Can you help me get my daughter from Black Island? They're holding her, kind of forcing me to find Boricio in exchange for her return."

"Wow, they're taking this shit seriously," Boricio said. "Guess I can't blame them. Though I'm curious how they know he's here, and why they think *he* can help them."

Ed asked, "So, can you help me get my daughter, her friend, and possibly her friend's baby to safety?"

"Well, if you can help get me on Black Island, I can help you once we're there."

"Sounds like a deal," Ed said.

"Yes, but first we have to get the other Boricio."

"You know where he is?" Ed asked.

"No, but I have two people here that do."

"Why do you think they sent me to look for him rather than you?" Ed asked.

"I'm not sure," Boricio shook his head. "But I think it has something to do with Luca."

Ed wanted to ask Boricio more, but knew he wouldn't answer. Ed had known too many men who lived with an army of skeletons hiding miles of secrets. The man on the other side of the desk looked like he could've been their general.

~

THIRTY-FOUR

Luca Harding

Dunn, Georgia
Boricio's Compound
March 2012
FIVE MONTHS AFTER THE EVENT ...

IN HIS DREAM, Luca was a child again.

He was back home, it was the middle of the night, and he was pushing the door to his parent's bedroom open, peeking into the darkness. They were still sleeping. He crept into the room, then stumbled on something in the middle of the floor.

He expected to hear his mom or dad yell, "Luca!" since that's what always happened when he woke them up by being loud. Nothing but silence greeted him, however.

Just as Luca regained his balance, he tripped on something else, sending his body into an awkward ballet. He twisted toward the foot of the bed, and smashed his side hard against the wood frame.

Luca heard the loud thrump-bdddd-rumps as whatever he kicked — his dad was always leaving his shoes in the middle of the room — rolled across the floor before coming to a stop.

Luca cried out, holding his side from the bed's assault, but fortunately, they had slept through his whine.

Luca climbed onto the bed, then crept up toward the front, squeezing his body in between his mother and father.

As he nudged his way toward the top, he noticed that he was lying in something cold and sticky.

"Mom . . . Dad . . . ?" Luca swallowed.

"Mom . . . Dad . . . ?" His right hand found his mom's stomach, then inched up and along her side, over her shoulders and up to her neck, until Luca was screaming at the jagged meat zigzagging across the sawed-off flesh.

Luca leapt from the bed, landed hard onto the floor, then rose from the wood and raced toward the wall. He flipped on the light then turned back toward the bed, screaming louder as he saw the part of his dad he'd kicked into the corner, and the part of his mom whose face was frozen, staring at him from the floor between the wall and the bed.

The lights flickered, then went daylight bright.

He was in the middle of a big city. Not Las Orillas. It had to be New York since Luca was looking at the same buildings from his vacation two summers before. Except now he was alone, in the middle of a city, surrounded by towering mountains of bent yellow steel, all of them flowing from the top with fountains of blood.

LUCA'S THROAT was too old and caked with age for him to scream, so he woke with the terrible howl caught inside his cracking gullet.

Luca blinked his eyes and trembled beneath the sheets.

Despite the horror of his dream, a part of Luca enjoyed its reality. Even if it was a nightmare, it wasn't real. So, the bad stuff couldn't really happen, but he still got to feel like he was 8, instead of the old man he'd become. It was a miracle his grandpa had been able to laugh as much as he had before he died, since he had to feel about as old as Luca's body felt now. Even when Luca wanted to laugh, just thinking about it was almost more pain than Luca could stand.

He took a full minute to climb from bed, then another getting to the bathroom. Luca constantly had to pee, even though it seemed like he never ever had to poop. And even when he could poop, it took forever and sometimes hurt.

Luca leapt from the toilet seat, startled, as a crack of thunder roared from a pistol outside, followed almost instantly by another. Then silence.

Luca was already dressed from the day before, since he hated changing into pajamas and Mary said he didn't have to. He slipped on his shoes, then went outside, pushed open the fence to the backyard, and then joined to watch the target practice.

Though you couldn't tell who pulled the trigger from the sound of the bullet, Luca felt positive Paola's shot was what he'd heard from the bathroom, so he wasn't the least bit surprised to see her holding the gun and taking fresh aim at a row of bottles on the fence.

Paola pulled the trigger. The bullet blasted from her gun, and whistled into the forest.

Boricio said, "Try again, and stop thinking."

Paola took a few seconds, steadied her arm and closed her eye, then squeezed the trigger and missed again.

Boricio walked up to Paola, held out his palm, curled his fingers around the butt the second it was set inside it, then raised the pistol and blasted two shots from its barrel like he was finishing a sentence.

Twin bottles exploded in unison; glass shattered like the roar of applause.

Boricio handed the gun back to Paola.

"Look, Hannah Montana," he said. "Thinking is A+ when you're sucking face for a grade, but it'll get you a big, fat

F in Staying Alive. If a thought takes you longer than two seconds when you're slipping around the sweaty insides of a *what-in-the-hell-am-I-gonna-do*-sorta moment, then you've gotta know good judgment at the speed of a blink. Now, ole Boricio may say a lot of things that make you wonder whether he's the messiah of mathematical truth, since it's such a high percentage of what I say, but there ain't nothing I've said to you yet, and nothing I'm ever gonna say, that's truer than that. You've gotta trust your gut — everything else is just a lie you've learned to believe."

Paola nodded.

Boricio nodded back. "Look where you're shooting, then pull the trigger. If you have to aim, then learn to do it faster."

He took a step back behind Paola, then turned and winked at Luca. Luca smiled back, though he wasn't really feeling it.

Paola drew a deep breath, aimed the gun — but only for a second — then squeezed the trigger twice, missing both times.

She lowered her arm, yelled at the top of her lungs for what felt like maybe a full minute, though that might've only been because Luca had to pee, then raised it and pulled the trigger twice more.

Both bullets found their mark and the bottles shattered.

Paola's eyes widened and she jumped up and down, squealing. Boricio was whooping and hollering and congratulating Paola, while still managing to keep the morning PG-rated, which was probably why Mary, standing behind them both, was smiling at Boricio, for maybe the first time ever.

Boricio finished reloading the gun — Luca always forgot what their different numbers were called, though he thought it might have been a .45 — when he handed it back to Paola then spun to find the source of the sudden growl he heard behind him.

Before Luca managed to turn his head, Boricio said, "Who left the gate open?"

But Boricio didn't ask like he was mad. It was a soft question, said in a soft voice. Mary and Paola said, "Not me" together.

"I did," Luca said, turning to see what the other three already had: the biggest dog Luca, or maybe anyone in the whole world, had ever seen. It was larger than Paola and almost bigger than Boricio.

It looked like a wolf, but larger than any wolf Luca had ever seen on TV or in a movie. It was dark-gray — having a coat so filthy it was almost black — with teeth that looked like knives. The dogs lips were curled high enough to see the black skin meeting between them.

The dog's heavy snarl rumbled through the backyard, and nobody dared move for fear of alarming the beast.

Boricio stepped to the front of the group as Luca stared, slowly stepping back toward Paola.

Mary looked over at Boricio. "What are you thinking?" she whispered, looking Boricio up and down as if she were trying to figure him out.

Boricio said, "I'm thinking that I've not seen more than a half dozen dogs that I can think of in one half of a beer-battered bullshit of a year, and that right now I'm staring at one that's bigger than three of King Kong's big, swinging cock sacks put together." Still speaking softly, Boricio added, "And my agreement to keep shit PG is null and fucking void when Paul Bunyan's Cujo is in our yard."

The dog remained still, but its growl grew louder.

"You're gonna have to shoot the dog, okay, honey?" Boricio said, cocking his head slightly toward Paola, who was maybe 15 feet away from Boricio, and therefore unable to simply hand him the gun.

Luca could only stare at the back of Paola's lightly swaying head as she whimpered three feet in front of him. "I can't," she squeaked.

"You can," Boricio said calmly, "because you have to, okay?"

Luca couldn't believe it, but Boricio's voice was almost soothing. Adding to the disbelief, he said, "You can do it, sweetheart," then kept speaking in that same soothing voice, his eyes on the unmoving dog while he made all his words for Paola.

"Look at how he's standing, agitated, high on all fours, head straight like he was pledging allegiance to Lassie, back raised like it's a second from launch." Boricio's head barely twitched, like he wanted to gesture more but knew he couldn't. "And see how his tail's sticking straight out? If dogs are as scared of us as we are of them — like stupid people say — then their tails are tucked between their legs. But that tail right there is about as straight as a pecker on prom night."

Paola whimpered again. "I can't . . . " she shook her head. "I just can't do it."

Boricio drew a deep breath, kept his eye on the beast, then said. "Look at his eyes, Paola. See how they're centered on us, especially me? I break contact, and that great, big bear of a dog is gonna be on me like flies on a morning pile. So, I need you to pull the trigger, sweetie, and I need you to do it right fucking now.

"I can't."

Boricio snarled, and for a second Luca was sure he was gonna turn around and yank the gun from Paola. But then the dog snarled back, and Boricio must've figured she was standing too far away to get the gun before the dog was on top of him.

Mary said, "Paola, honey, it's okay. Just pull the trigger."

The gun still at her side, Paola said, "What if I miss? He'll kill us all."

Boricio said, "Then just don't miss."

Mary said, "We're dead for sure if you don't try."

The gun shook at her side. She tried to raise it but whimpered instead.

The giant dog snarled, then roared. Boricio held his gaze, but the dog leapt at him anyway. Paola's fingers stayed as frozen as her eyes were wide.

With no clue what he was doing, Luca suddenly found himself inside Paola's head, then deeper into her mind's twisting tunnels, and finally centered inside the specific memory that allowed him to raise her hand, and the pistol with it, then fire while thinking in less than a blink, landing the first bullet from the freshly loaded gun into the creature's head.

The beast may have been a dog when the first bullet tore through its skull, but that first bullet gave birth to the unholy monstrosity that had been inside the dog all along. It came snarling from the dog's falling skin, stretching its face like putty.

Paola was still aiming without using the trigger, so Luca kept firing from inside her mind, again and again. Each shot seemed to anger the rabid dog further, but was doing nothing to slow it down. But at least it was off of Boricio, rearing back on its hind legs and thrashing wildly through the air, like it was at war with itself, shrieking something that sounded like a dog's bark and a human's scream bleeding together.

The dog's fur came off in chunks, revealing dark-black skin beneath it that reminded Luca of the monsters. It looked soaking wet, and was getting wetter as the massive dog's bones seemed to shove themselves against its skin, pushing against it until it started to tear. The dog lifted his nose to the sun and roared, its mouth twisting, knocking teeth from its maw to the ground to make room for more giant teeth, which erupted from its jaws like jagged swords.

Luca continued to empty Paola's gun, until something inside her shattered and sobbed. Mary and Boricio ran to grab guns of their own from a bench 50 feet away, where

Boricio had been spending each morning showing them how to clean and care for their weapons.

Mary picked up a pistol, Boricio grabbed two, then they emptied all three of them into the creature until it finally stopped twitching.

Like the half demon, half dog that it was, the creature bled in a medley of color, though mostly black and green and red, pouring from multiple holes and pooling into a single brew of dark and shiny purple mess.

Boricio, Mary, and Paola stood around the beast in stunned silence, before they caught one another's expression and started to cheer.

"Fuck yeah! That's what I'm talkin' about!" Boricio said high-fiving Paola.

Luca had returned to his own head, and felt significantly weaker, but he hid the weakness behind a smile. He didn't want Mary, Paola, and Boricio to worry about him.

Luca began to wonder just how much longer he'd be with them.

~

Other Ed Keenan

Black Island, New York
April 2012
SIX MONTHS AFTER THE EVENT ...

ED AND WILL were perched on the monastery's roof, staring down into the darkness. The infected Guardsmen stood in a line in front of the building, but made no attempt to storm inside.

Holding the line, keeping us here.

Ed called Sullivan on the radio, updating him on the situation — the infection may have been incubating in people, and could have infiltrated the Facility.

"Test everyone," Ed instructed. "Test them and quarantine the uninfected on Level 8. If we can't get the situation under control we'll need to activate a Hard Reset Protocol. Get someone out to the ferry and prepare for an evacuation of everyone up top. No one gets on without being tested. Any infected are to be shot on sight and their bodies burned. Understand?"

"Yes. On sight?"

"Yes," Ed said. "We can't take any chances."

Ed brought him current on everything that had happened, as well as with his theory, that Dr. Williams was somehow communicating with the infected and that the infected were acting on his behalf. Ed ended the call on his radio and turned to Will Bishop, who was still looking down at the Guardsmen on the ground.

"They're trying to keep us here," Ed said.

"Yes, they appear to be working in concert with Williams," Bishop said, echoing what Will had just told Sullivan.

"How long do you think Williams has been infected?" Ed asked.

"I dunno. You all should've fired him the second you knew he helped Boricio. But screw consequences, right? Anything for the sake of science!"

"It wasn't my call; you know that," Ed said, annoyed.

He was just as pissed as Will that Overseer Washington hadn't thrown shutters on the project sooner. But arguing about it now, particularly when the Overseer was dead, was pointless. There was a heap of shit they *should've* done differently. But they didn't pay Ed for his opinions. He was paid to manage scientists and make sure they didn't blow up the world or worse. Yet, when they actually tinkered with something as dangerous as the vials, Ed was told to sit down and shut up while the *real scientists* did their thing.

And we all know how that went.

"Let's just stick to what we're gonna do next," he said to Will, who seemed at least a little more present than in recent memory, maybe awakened by the danger. "By the way, what did Williams mean when he said he'd known what you did?"

Will looked confused. "I believe he thinks I have the vials."

"*Are there* any left?" Ed asked.

"No, you know that. All we have left is what was in the serum that our guys are trying to use to find a cure."

"I had to ask," Ed said. "He seemed so certain."

"The crazy ones usually are."

"How do you think he was infected?" Ed asked. "It had to have happened recently, right? We've never seen it lay dormant for longer than 48 hours."

"It had to be recent, yes" Will agreed. "Was he working with the infected patients he helped escape?"

"Yes," Ed said. "Almost daily."

"Perhaps they played his sympathies, and he left himself open to their influence. They must've done it telepathically. We all know that I was changed by mere proximity. Luca more so having been injected with the serum."

"We've never seen them do anything like that," Ed said. "We've never seen an infected with that kind of cognitive function, have we?"

"Once," Bishop said, but then trailed off when Ed's radio rang again.

It was Sullivan saying that Teagan wanted to talk to him.

"Ed, I'm scared. What's happening?"

"Everything will be okay," he said. "Sullivan is going to move you to Level 8. Go with him; do whatever he says. OK? Is Jade with you?"

"Yes," she said, weeping.

Ed couldn't afford the distraction, or the tears that came with it. "I don't have time to talk now, Baby. Sullivan will take care of you. OK? I have to go. Now."

A pause, then Teagan said, "Bye."

Ed hung up without saying another word. The tune of her fear had already compromised his ability to think clearly. He had to figure out a way to get from the monastery to the Facility without running into any of the infected.

Ed looked down at the Guardsman who were no longer Guardsman, six total. He couldn't make out any of their identities, since their mutation was nearly complete and their faces had shifted to monstrosities.

Ed turned to Will with a sudden idea. "If Williams is infected, why hasn't he mutated like these things? His temporal lobe is functioning just fine, unlike the other infected. Could the species be finding a new way to integrate with us? More of an invisible parasite, controlling functions without showing symptoms elsewhere or going full-blown mutation?"

"I wouldn't rule it out at the moment, and that does make the most sense. But we'd need to get a look inside his brain to know for certain."

"Well, first, we need to take care of these down here and then get back to the Facility."

"Okay," Bishop said.

Ed loaded a fresh clip into his Glock, then aimed at the mutant in the center of the line of them and fired, hitting it square in the forehead. It dropped to the ground, screeching as it fell. Ed was't sure if the screech was pain or a warning because the moment it started, the others followed, all opening their mouths and releasing unholy wails, piercing to his ears even from 30 yards away.

Ed fired down into the group and hit another, drowning its fallen comrade's cry with a wail of its own. The other four scattered into the shadows as the first one finished dying from Ed's near-perfect headshot.

"Come on," Ed ordered. "Follow me."

They made their way down to the monastery entrance, then across the courtyard and into the woods.

"The truck is just this way," Ed said, surprised that Will was keeping decent pace.

They made it halfway to the truck when suddenly, movement erupted around them, dark on dark moving fast.

And then they were surrounded by the four infected Guardsman.

Ed stepped in front of Will, shielding him from the closest of the infected. For some reason, however, the infected weren't moving any closer — as if they were frozen in place awaiting instructions.

"They won't fight back," Will suddenly said, sounding far more certain than Ed's hunch.

"I was thinking the same thing."

Ed raised his gun and shot each of the four infected in the head, taking them down by order of proximity. Once on the ground and writhing, Ed emptied his gun, finishing them off in the same order he shot them before.

"Let's go." Ed opened the driver's side and climbed inside, though he didn't have to say anything to Will, who was already sitting in the passenger seat, waiting.

Ed gunned the engine, floored the pedal, and said, "It's almost worse that they didn't put up a fight."

Will said, "That's because it's easier to see the people inside them."

~

THIRTY-SIX

Boricio Bishop

Black Island Research Facility
   September 2011
   ONE MONTH BEFORE THE EVENT …

BORICIO SAT CROSS-LEGGED ON A MATTRESS, alone in the glass quarantine cell, one of 12 cells in the room where he had seen Will oversee so many tests before. However, it was usually animals in the cells. Now, there was he and three doctors, awaiting tests, and a large, old ape named Brian. And then, of course, there was Rose.

The Guardsman threw Boricio inside the cell, leaving him alone and afraid, sitting on the floor with a front-row-center view of Rose — the fresh monstrosity in the cell across from him — mutated, grotesque, and mercifully asleep, lying momentarily still as death on a mattress.

Will's question, as he'd yanked Boricio from Rose's room, played on repeat over and over in Boricio's head, the sole lyrics of a guilty song:

What have you done?

The longer he waited, the longer he had to stew in the pain of that question.

What have I done?

Why?

She said she remembered me. Maybe her memory would've come back.

The pain would've gone away. I could've waited.

I should have stopped it.

Boricio had no idea how long it was from when the Guardsman had first thrown him into the cell to when he finally heard the pressured release of the door lock and his adopted father stepped inside his cell.

"Hey, Boricio," Will said. He was missing the hazmat suit worn by every other Guardsman. "So?" he stood over Boricio's mattress, arms in an X across his chest.

Boricio said nothing.

Will finally said, "Seriously, Son, what were you thinking?" It sounded like he was using everything inside him to keep his voice low and emotions steady.

"You know exactly what I was thinking," Boricio said, "So, don't show up to the barbecue and act surprised to see meat on the grill."

Will didn't respond so Boricio added, "What happened to Rose?"

Will shook his head and said, "Sorry, Boricio," but followed his apology with silence.

Boricio said, "What does *sorry* mean?"

Will drew a breath, then said, "Rose has mutated. We've never seen anything like this. We've got our best people analyzing the serum that Dr. Williams concocted along with her blood and tissue samples. Dr. Williams will be facing punishment for his actions. And I'm sorry to say, you will, too."

"Fine," Boricio said, "I look great in orange."

"I need you to take this seriously," Will said. "You could be court-martialed . . . or *worse*."

Boricio felt a flutter of fear, and he must've showed it on his face because Will stepped into his confidence. "It's possible I could prevent it," he said. "I don't know for certain. But even if you're not court-martialed, they'll want to excommunicate you from the island. Probably forever."

They sat in silence for several minutes, probably since Boricio had warned Will not to ask him the same question he already knew the answer to. Finally, likely because he couldn't help it, Will asked, "Why did you do it, Boricio?"

Boricio didn't answer, just stayed quiet until Will finally lost his temper. "I've never been angrier with you in my entire life!" he screamed. "I don't know what in the hell is the matter with you, Son, that you would ever think it would be okay to jeopardize our jobs, futures, and friendships, not to mention the very fabric of our family, just so you could sneak in here and play scientist. Your behavior was selfish, Boricio. Sure, you can claim it was all for love, or that it was you and Rose against the world. But that's bullshit, Boricio. You put *your* needs above everyone else's, including Rose's, and you've done it for the last time."

Will kept on going, throwing words at Boricio like they were kicks to a beaten dog's belly. Boricio took every syllable, mostly because he knew he deserved them, but finally a month's worth of torment cracked through his facade. His shoulders started shaking, then sagged.

His entire body shuddered, and Boricio finally broke down.

Once his tears started to fall, Will lowered himself to the mattress beside him, wrapping his arms around Boricio's shoulders and softly whispered his apologies.

Boricio gathered his composure and nudged his breathing into the same, steady rhythm he'd been practicing for weeks. Finally, once he felt like he could finish a full sentence without his voice cracking in half, he said, "I don't get it. You all have used the serum on animals and nothing like this has ever happened, right?"

Will nodded.

"And with the first human subject, Luca, it cured him. No bad side effects. Dr. Williams said he'd used the same formulation. There is nothing different about the serum. Nothing! Why did it do . . . *that*, to her?"

"Well, first of all, Luca has been having side effects. I tried to warn you that we didn't know what we're dealing with, but . . ."

"No, he didn't turn into a fucking monster! Why did Rose?"

Will folded his hands in front of him, "I don't know. There're so many variables in play, and our team is looking them over, trying to figure out what happened. Obviously, this is a huge setback in the program, even if Rose wasn't a part of it — she's become a part of it, now."

Boricio swallowed. *One more slice of the guilt pie.*

Boricio swallowed hard, trying to put words to a thought that had been forming in his mind since he'd been thrown into the cell.

"What is it?" Will said, knowing his son like a book he could read without turning a page.

Boricio said. "What if *I'm* the variable?"

"What do you mean?"

"The serum was the same, and Dr. Williams performed both procedures. The biggest variable is me — this time I handled the vial."

"Did you open the vial?" Will asked.

"No, but maybe I didn't need to. Or maybe the seal wasn't as tight as I thought it was."

"That seems unlikely," Will said.

"I know, but ever since I got the vial I've been having these weird dreams. The vial has been all I could think about. It was like an obsession, clouding my thoughts. Like I was suddenly so damned certain that I needed it in order to help Rose. More certain than I'd been with Luca."

"What do you mean?"

"I don't know, but what if I somehow infected the vial? What if I'm the variable? That means maybe the Doc could make a new serum. Get a new vial and just start over without my interference? Maybe it will reverse the effects?"

Will looked at the floor. "I'm not doing that," he said.

Boricio flared with anger, but didn't have the strength to fuel it. He started to sob, again. Then finally, from behind his broken pieces, a cracked voice said, "Please, Will. You're her only hope. That makes you *my* only hope, too."

Will said, "Why don't you first tell me where to find one of the other two vials you took? That might be a good place to start."

His tears vanished. Boricio wiped his eyes and turned to Will.

"What? Are you saying there are *three* vials missing?" He shook his head. I only had two, not three."

Will ignored the discrepancy in the math and said, "How did you get them?"

Boricio should have expected that Will would infiltrate his mind, but sitting beside him sobbing had reduced his guard to rumor. Now that he wanted to keep Will out of his head, it was already too late.

There was one second when Boricio felt especially full, followed by a flash where he felt nothing but empty, then a slight prick inside his brain that felt a bit like a needle slipping into his skin.

"No," Will shook his head. Sudden horror widened his eyes. He stuttered, "You didn't ask *him*. What the hell, Boricio?"

Boricio wondered if Will was saying "him" instead of "Luca" because of the closed-circuit cameras.

"Do you realize the danger you've put us in?" Will seethed. "And I mean all of us?!"

"I'm so sorry," Boricio said. "I had no idea."

Will turned to leave the cell.

"Where are you going?" Boricio called.

Will turned back and hissed, "To fix your mess."

~

THIRTY-SEVEN

Callie Thompson

Black Mountain, Georgia
  March 2012
  FIVE MONTHS AFTER THE EVENT …

CALLIE WONDERED if they'd ever return Charlie to his cell.

So, when she woke in the morning to find the lights on and two guards wheeling someone in on a gurney, she got excited that he was finally coming back. But the guards stopped two cells away, opened the door, then deposited an old, heavyset nude man onto the mattress.

The old man lay motionless, likely sedated as she had been. They closed the door to his cell, then left the hallway.

A while later, the same guards came back with breakfast — Cheerios in a bowl, two bottles of water, and fruit. Before the guards left her, Callie asked, "Where's Charlie?"

But the guards said nothing.

Callie considered yelling, but decided to keep her mouth shut, at least for now. Charlie had gone willingly, or so it seemed. That meant she would have to be patient. She ate the Cheerios with her fingers. At least it was Honey Nut Cheerios, and not plain. She was surprised that even without milk, the Cheerios tasted pretty good.

After a while, the old man began to move on his mattress. He sat, immediately meeting Callie's eyes. Something about his gaze sent a chill down her spine. It was almost as if he'd never been sleeping at all. He simply woke, sat up, then turned his eyes on Callie with a creepy stare that settled somewhere between Willy Wonka and Hannibal Lecter.

He smiled, and Callie looked away.

A bit later, a guard in a yellow hazmat suit appeared, looking at the old man. Callie recognized him immediately as the one whom Charlie had been speaking with earlier as she pretended to sleep. He looked a bit like Boricio, but bald and with an eye patch. He looked a lot like him, in fact, though she couldn't be certain without a closer look or hearing him. If it *was* Boricio, she wondered why was he going through the ruse of holding them?

Most of all, what did Charlie know that she didn't? Why was he out of his cell? Where had they taken him? And why hadn't they taken her?

The man who looked like Boricio started to yell at the old man, though Callie couldn't hear him. But she could still see him, waving his arms and pointing his fingers almost accusingly, it seemed to her.

Callie wondered why.

After five minutes or so, the man who looked like Boricio turned from the cell and left. The old man smiled, staring after Boricio as he went down the hall.

Well, that's just weird.

Then the old man turned his attention to Callie, staring directly at her.

Even weirder.

~

THIRTY-EIGHT

Mary Olson

Dunn, Georgia
  Boricio's Compound
  March 2012
  FIVE MONTHS AFTER THE EVENT ...

THE COOL, spring night did nothing to chill the warm feeling Mary felt as she tossed the empty "bottle of piss" from the wooden picnic table into the large, metal bucket across the yard, where it crashed loudly against the metal, then rained glass into a pile.

Bottles of Piss was what Boricio had called the alcohol-free near beers that she kicked back like they were the real thing. She'd never much liked alcohol-free beer, but she was pregnant, and Boricio had managed to get the generator to run a refrigerator on the back porch, making the drink ice cold, which did a lot to make up for the fact that it wasn't getting her buzzed.

"Shhhh ... you're gonna wake them!" Boricio said, mimicking Mary's earlier warnings she'd been using since Luca and Paola went to bed about two hours before. At least that was the warning that Mary was using before she started throwing bottles herself a half hour ago.

Mary laughed, feeling goofy enough to wonder if Boricio hadn't switched labels on the beer bottles.

"You didn't give me real beer, did you?" she asked.

"I might be an asshole, but I'm not gonna give a pregnant chick beer," Boricio said. "I don't wanna see you giving birth to some short-bus kid."

Mary laughed again, despite the awfulness of his comment.

Mary was on her fourth bottle of piss, or perhaps it might have been her fifth. She was usually good at keeping track, but throwing her empties into the bucket had begun to confuse her. Or maybe it was sitting on the bench beside her new friend Boricio the Killer that had done it.

Mary didn't believe she could ever get used to living in close proximity to Boricio, and nearly everything about him still horrified her. But after several days in his company, and what seemed like a hundred thousand hours or so of his endless mouth, Mary had a vague, but fascinated, under-standing of what it was that made him tick.

Boricio was a genuine killer; that wasn't for show. He was the real deal, and had been long before the end of the world, she figured.

Only after Mary opened her third bottle of piss, the one that might have been her fourth, did she finally get the courage to ask Boricio what she'd been wanting to ask for a while, and even managed to do so without flinching. "What was it like the first time you killed someone?"

Boricio was mid-swig when Mary asked.

He took an extra-long swallow, then smiled like a wolf, returned his lips to the bottle and stole its final swallow, then turned from the table, and the bucket behind it, and tossed his bottle like a dart into the forest.

"That's a helluva good story," he said. "You sure you wanna hear it?"

Mary nodded. "Yes," she said.

Boricio howled. "Well, alrighty then. But I'm not telling you a PG-13 bullshit version of the story. It's a spicy dish, and I'm not holding the pepper."

Mary said, "Has there been anything from your mouth in the last two hours that's been anywhere PG?"

Boricio howled again. "Nope," he shook his head. "But that's because there isn't a point. You censor the words, and you're just giving a dirty mind more to work with."

Mary said, "Well, good thing Paola doesn't have a dirty mind."

Mary waited for Boricio to challenge the thought, perhaps say something vulgar about her daughter. But he didn't. Just opened another bottle, took a long swig, then wiped his mouth and said, "Looking back, Boricio should've waited a while longer before doing what he did when he did it. But I was green as a jalapeño, and so I ended up making a 32-gallon trash can's worth of mess that first night. I remember watching the news the following day, shaking my head, shocked at how much they did and didn't say about all the things I knew I did. But the fucker who had to quit his breathing earlier than he expected to, and quite by force, sure as a new necklace after a titty-fuck deserved it. He was a regular at the restaurant where I'd been cooking for two months at the time of the 'accident' — this shit bar called, The Office."

Boricio took another swig, and Mary felt herself uncomfortably fascinated by his tale, just as she had been for every one in the two hours before it.

"So, this same fucker would come in every night, drunk before he even got there it seemed, then order something fried from the menu and bitch about it five minutes after Jeremy set it on the counter." Boricio looked at Mary. "Every. Fucking. Time. You dig?"

Mary swallowed, then said, "I dig, but does that mean you killed him just because he sent his food back?"

Boricio laughed. "No, I would never do that, at least not unless I felt like it. This fucker didn't earn a grown-up abortion because he sent his food back; he got gutted on account of the gift wrap he gave the complaint. Every time the assfuck sent his food back, he attached an insult that made him deserve to die a little more, so really, the fucker was lucky I let him keep breathing as long as I did. Truth of the matter, Mary Mary Quite Contrary, is that I couldn't understand why Jeremy Pile, the old fucker who owned The Office, was bending over for the shit eater each night. I probably should've figured what the hell and let the shit-covered dick continue to live since making slop on repeat wasn't much different than making slop in the first place. I still punched out at the same goddamned time." Boricio shook his head and took another long swig. "The fucker had said plenty of shit before, but when he said my nachos tasted like I'd put a tiara on a pile of rancid taco meat, and that the only creatures capable of enjoying the meal were the flies at his table, only thing I could see besides the red was the camel crying and the broken straw on its furry fucking back."

Boricio cackled.

"When Jeremy came back in and told me what the fucker had said, I asked him why he didn't throw his ass the fuck out. Pile said it was because the dude drank like a fish so who gave a shit if the place took a bath on 90 cents worth of nachos. Well, I did. So," Boricio shrugged, "I figured I'd give the fucker a bath myself."

Mary swallowed hard again. "What did you do?"

Boricio smiled. "I'm glad you asked, and thank you for playing, *What Would Boricio Do?* I got patient, that's what. Waited three more weeks until the fucker was dumb enough to stay until the bar closed. I met him in the back of the alley, then surprised the fuck out of his holy spirit. Shit dick was always talking about his apartment, 'just two blocks away,' so I made him take me there. He wasn't too drunk to realize he didn't have much of a choice. Once we got inside, I spent the next few hours emptying the fucker's fridge and making him meal after meal of shit that made those nachos taste like sweet ambrosia. He kept crying like a bitch with every bite, but swallowed every mouthful like a good boy, anyway. When the fridge was empty and his belly was full of all sorts of shit you ain't ever supposed to put in your mouth, I made him some new meals with some fresh meat. When he was finished with that, I silenced the fucker forever."

Mary could barely speak, but still managed to half whisper, "Then what did you do?"

"Got the fuck out of Dodge. Left town early the next day, right after I saw the news, in fact. No Bob's Big Boy of a deal; I was ready to leave, anyway."

"And that was the first person you ever killed?" Mary also wanted to ask Boricio how many people he had killed since, but didn't want to know an answer that might keep her from sleeping at night.

Boricio barked a broken hiccup of a laugh. "No, I guess if we're talking Honest Injun, then no, I suppose it wasn't. First was my dear ole fucking stepdad, but that ain't a story I wanna tell right now, ya dig?" He smiled. "But it was the first fucker who ever got his shit premeditated, and no doubt the biggest goddamned mess I ever made."

Boricio looked at Mary, his bottle hovering in the air a few inches from his lips. "You know what the kitchen looks like around Thanksgiving with all the pots and pans and bullshit before you get to setting the table, right? Well, this looked like that, but with about six or seven gallons of blood."

Mary felt like she was about to vomit, and wondered if

she'd be half as patient with Boricio's macabre recital if she wasn't so thoroughly drunk.

"How can you be so honest about everything?" she asked. "Don't you ever feel bad, at all?"

Boricio sucked on the nozzle of his bottle for a while, and Mary wondered if he had any intention of answering the question. She couldn't quite decipher the something on his face, though if she had to give it a name, she'd call it "almost thoughtful." Mary had no idea how long Boricio took to open his mouth again, just that she had time to open one final near beer, just like her last two, and nurse it to a third empty.

"Before a few days ago, no, never," Boricio said. "Not even for a fucking minute. But ever since Luca broke me, I've been seeing shit upside down, and yeah, that's had me wrestling with some of the shit I've done."

"Does that mean you regret it?"

"I don't know if it's *that* exactly," he said. "I don't think I'd be here talking to you today if I weren't that Boricio, you know?" He took a final swig then threw the bottle into the woods, chasing the handfuls he'd already thrown.

Mary didn't agree, but wasn't brave enough to challenge Boricio out loud. But she did ask, "How can you talk so openly about it?"

Boricio shrugged. "Because what happened, happened. Life's too short for regrets. Shit is what it is; you may as well be honest and give it an NC-17 instead of drowning it in lies and dressing it in a PG-13." He winked.

Mary wasn't sure if it was the placebo buzz of the near beer or the frank conversation with Boricio that gave her the confidence, but she said, "How do I know you won't ever hurt me, or Paola?"

"Because you're safe with me," he said, without pause. "Now I'm not saying it's the sort of safe where you're never gonna hear the boogeyman howling outside your window, because here at the end of the world, I think that's the special of the day. But you can feel safe knowing that Boricio isn't the big, bad wolf, huffing and puffing and waiting to get in. He's the one who'll protect you three little piggies and blow all the other houses down."

Mary wanted to say more, but didn't want to push it, or him. So, she went back to her earlier question. "So, there's nothing you regret?"

Boricio shook his head and looked like he was about to say no, then paused and said, "Yeah, I've got regrets."

He went silent after that, so Mary said, "Like?"

"I had this one lady named Sissy, tried taking care of me back when I was a kid. Was one of the only women who ever reached out to me, almost like she actually cared. But I shit on her like I shit on everyone." Boricio looked suddenly hollow. It was another several seconds before he finished with, "Though I'm not sure I've ever given it a lick of thought until today."

He shook his head and muttered, "Fucking Rip van Creepy broke me," then opened another bottle. "How about you, Miss Contrary, any regrets?"

Mary was just fake buzzed enough to bore Boricio with the story of her and Ryan, and how she caught him with Natalie Farmer.

Boricio said, "Well, that's not all that surprising. Men are a helluva lot more likely than women to cheat anyhow, and it sounds like you were giving your man all sorts of reasons."

Mary blinked her eyes, shocked. "Excuse me," she said. "And how's that?"

"Didn't you say you were making like a billion dollars a year with your To Be or Not to Be greeting card shit?"

"Not quite," Mary said. "But yes."

"Well hells bells and cum-filled wells, Miss Mary, that will get a fucker wanting to test the Big Bang theory with a bitch he don't have to hear snoring. Now don't get me wrong, you're a mighty fine-looking piece of ass, but with your little lamb being around for so long, you probably started boring your boy in the bedroom. And us guys like our shit fresh. We don't get it, and it's easy to justify the cheating. Add to that the fact that you're wearing the pants — bringing in the bacon *and* cooking it for dinner, well that's a formula for fucking outside of the house."

It was almost funny. Mary could hear Boricio discuss murder like he was talking about the size of his tomatoes, and it was almost easy to take. A little like watching *Dexter*. But the second he started talking about Ryan's cheating, and making excuses for her ex, she wanted to punch him in the face.

Mary knew that if she didn't change the subject, they'd end up walking into a mess of trouble. "So, how do you think the training's going?" she said.

Boricio smiled wide, said, "Well, lookie lookie, crunchy cookie; looks like Miss Mary doesn't want to see the truth inside her separation." For a few seconds it looked like he was going to twist the knife, but then he followed Mary's lead and changed the subject.

"Training is good," he said, his tone going from playful to thoughtful. "I think another day's worth of shooting at shit would be good, though I don't really know if that's the problem. Seemed like it was nothing more than fear keeping the gun at your baby girl's side today."

"It wasn't that," Mary said. "At least not that simply. The monsters are scary, but Paola wouldn't have frozen like that if it was one of the bleakers that had come through the gate. It was because she was staring at something she'd never seen before. That dog was bigger than you; it would've been scary on Oct. 15, before it was half zombie. Any new thoughts on what giant mutant dogs might mean? Think there's more of 'em out there?"

Boricio shook his head. "Not since the 47th time you asked me, 'round about a half hour ago," he said. "But if the monsters are now coming in all manner of man and beast, I'm thinking we want to mosey up to New York, double time."

"When do you want to go?"

Boricio said, "Tomorrow, day after that at the latest. I make sure Luca's ready for the trip. He didn't look so good today. And since I'm the captain of Team Boricio, I've gotta decide how we'll fight the battle before it begins. That means knowing what everybody is and isn't capable of doing. I don't wanna get on the road and find we need to find a wheelchair or some shit. One more day," he promised. "Two max, okay, Miss Mary?"

Mary nodded, astonished at how much her *knowing* was trusting the monster on the other side of the table.

"Another beer? Just say the word and I'll go grab some," he said.

"You mean near beer, right?" she said, suddenly nervous that he *had* gotten her drunk.

"Yes," Boricio said, smiling, "One more bottle of piss for the lady."

THIRTY-NINE

"The Prophet"

Black Mountain, Georgia
March 2012
FIVE MONTHS AFTER THE EVENT ...

IT LAY on the mattress with Its eyes closed, feigning a sleep *It* did not need.

It used the time to allow the husk to refresh Itself while *It* connected with the parts of Itself outside, roaming the world and among Its beings, slowly absorbing everything into *It*.

This shell, of this fat man calling itself The Prophet was so limiting.

Old. Obese. Used.

It was a wonder that anything could go through life in such worn form, indulging on its very self-destruction.

It needed to change Its shell soon, trade it for something younger, stronger, and with more energy. *Its* purpose was revealing itself in new ways every day. As *It* grew, *It* remembered more of Its life before this.

A life where *It* thrived in another world.

But something had happened — what, *It* could not yet

recall. Something that had changed everything, then brought *It* here to this world.

Where *It* was not alone.

Another *Something* was out there. *Something* that was its opposite, trying to undo *Its* work.

Something *It* sensed on the highway when the *storm* came. That storm wasn't any ordinary storm. The *storm* was the enemy. Fortunately, *It* was able to hide itself inside the old man's husk.

But for how long?

A war raged outside, a war for survival that none of these ignorant humans could either comprehend or possibly see.

It had lost before.

It would never lose again.

First *It* must kill the child. The One, Luca, *It* knew was different. Luca wasn't just *different*. The enemy was hiding inside the child. Why it had chosen a child for a vessel made little sense to *It*, but perhaps brilliance was behind the move.

As a child, it could go undetected and gather strength.

Fortunately for *It*, the child's husk had recently changed, at least that's what *Its* others had reported.

The child had gone from young to old. From strong to weak. Now was the time to strike before the enemy could change hosts and gather strength.

Strike now, take the rest of this world and bring it unto *Itself.*

It would spread.

That was what *It* was meant to do.

All would grow dark. And nothing would stop *It* once it was.

~

FORTY

Charlie Wilkens

Black Mountain, Georgia
  March 2012
  FIVE MONTHS AFTER THE EVENT …

CHARLIE SAT AT A SQUARE, wooden table alone in a 20 by 20 white, sterile room, drinking an ice-cold can of Coca-Cola.

He'd not had a cold drink since forever; ice cold soda was only a memory.

Damn, I almost forgot how good these are!

They'd also given him clothes. A black T-shirt and matching sweats. He requested that Callie get the same thing to wear — his one condition, other than her safety, for helping them. Charlie considered pushing for everyone on the block to get clothes, but stopped short since he had no idea how strong his hand actually was. The last thing he wanted was for the Guardsmen to resent him and take that resentment out on Callie.

In front of Charlie was a paper plate piled surprisingly high with pretzels and chocolate chip cookies, both remarkably fresh given that they were at least a half year old. A

Guardsman named Darren told him to eat as many of the pretzels and cookies as he wanted — the first thing said to him as he was led into the small room after Dr. Rudolph drew his blood in hopes of creating some sort of serum that might cure Ryan.

Charlie didn't understand the science behind the serum, or anything the doctor said, really, but the process seemed painless enough, at least on his end. He hoped they found a cure soon. While Charlie had somehow resisted the full mutation, unlike every other infected body Black Mountain had found, that didn't mean he'd never fully mutate.

The alien thing, whatever it was, was inside Charlie. He was infected. And his life was a ticking time bomb, now more than ever. The after-procedure snack was a nice bonus, though he felt guilty not being able to share it with Callie. He wondered if they'd let him bring her a drink and a cookie.

The door to his room slid open, and Bald Boricio stepped inside, now wearing an all-black outfit similar to the Guardsmen, with a holstered pistol and the same glass mask worn by the other guards. He took a seat across from Charlie and spoke, his voice sounding like a radio, crackly through the mask's speaker, "How are you feeling?"

"Okay," Charlie said. "Any word?"

"No," Boricio said. "Still waiting. I wanted to discuss something else with you, though."

"What is it?" Charlie said, suddenly concerned he was about to hear something bad, maybe terrible.

"What's he like?"

"Who?" Charlie asked.

"The other Boricio. The one from your world. What is he like?"

Charlie laughed as Imaginary Boricio suddenly appeared on his left, sitting beside him at the table, propping his elbows on the table and cradling his face in his hands as he turned to

Charlie batting his eyelashes dramatically. "Yes, Chuck E. CheeseDick, what *am* I like, please tell?"

"He's a stone-cold killer," Charlie said without the slightest pause. "Imagine Dirty Harry, but younger. And faster. Now imagine someone who made Dirty Harry look like a Cub Scout. That someone would still need a *Kill Bill's* worth of bad ass to come close to the Boricio I know."

Imaginary Boricio blinked, pretending to wipe tears from his eyes, "Aw, Chuck, you shouldn't have. You're the biggest pecan in my super-sized sweetie pie."

But the real Boricio just stared for a minute before saying, "You say he's a killer. What sort of killer? You mean he kills bad people and aliens?"

"I don't know what he was like before Oct. 15, but I'm gonna guess he didn't give a fuck then, either. He kills anyone who gets in his way — good, bad, and indifferent. But, weird as it might be, he saved me and my friends, even took us in. He never did anything to us, so I guess he's not *all* bad."

"I'm a regular Mr. Rogers," Imaginary Boricio said. "So, won't you be my fucking neighbor?"

"Why do you ask?" Charlie asked the real Boricio.

"Because I've been having these dreams about him. Almost every time I fall asleep."

Imaginary Boricio laughed, then said in an effeminate lisp, "Oh, *do* go on."

"What sort of dreams?"

"That he's with my brother, and they're together at some big house out in the middle of nowhere. There's a woman and a little girl with them as well."

"You have a brother?" Charlie asked, then, "What's the house look like?"

Boricio explained that he had an 8-year-old adopted brother, though in the dream, he's not a kid. The descriptions of the 100-year-old boy were weird, and definitely like the stuff out of dreams, but then he described the compound exactly like Charlie remembered it, down to the crooked pile of bricks by the back door.

"That's it," Charlie said. "You definitely have the right place. How in the hell did you dream about it?" Charlie asked.

"I dunno, but . . . it all feels threaded together," Boricio said. "And the thing is — I thought my brother, Luca, was gone. If he's really still here, then maybe I can still somehow fix all of this."

"What do you mean fix it all?"

"I dunno," Boricio said, looking off in the distance as if excavating memory. "Cure the infected. Maybe send you back to your world. I'm not sure what's possible, but I can think of more reasons to find him than not."

"What does Luca have to do with what happened in October? With us being here?"

Boricio looked at Charlie for a long moment and then, ignoring his question, asked, "Can your girlfriend lead us to the other Boricio?"

"I don't know if she knows the way there, but she might have a general idea. I could for sure."

"I can't bring you. You're infected, and I can't risk the infection spreading before we get you cured, not when we're so close."

"So, Callie's not infected?"

"No. She's cleared to leave her cell."

Charlie felt an immediate flush of relief knowing she was safe, but a deep and sudden ache knowing she would be leaving the cell beside his.

"Can I go back to my cell tonight?" Charlie said. "I'd like to spend time next to her before you let her go."

"Yeah," Boricio said. "But tomorrow morning, I'm heading out. But you have nothing to worry about, Charlie. I promise to keep an eye on her."

Imaginary Boricio piped in, "Yeah, I bet you will, you sly fuck." He turned to Charlie. "I bet the only eye he'll have on Callie is the one spitting cock juice all over her face!"

The real Boricio stood. "Thank you, Charlie. I'm gonna check on Ryan. If nothing's changed, then I'll have someone return you to your cell. You're not gonna do anything stupid while I'm gone, are you? Please tell me I can trust you. I'd rather not threaten Callie's safety. I don't care for drama."

"Nothing stupid," Charlie said. "You guys are the good guys, right?"

"Yeah, something like that," Boricio said, turning toward the exit.

"One more thing?" Charlie said.

"Yes?" Boricio said, turning back to him.

"Can you give Callie and me some pens and paper, so we can *talk*?"

Boricio chewed on the request, then said, "Nothing stupid?"

"No," Charlie shook his head. "But I can't promise nothing sappy."

Boricio surprised Charlie with a wide smile, something he had never seen *his* Boricio do, at least not without something crude coming before or after it.

"Yeah," Boricio said.

As Boricio left and the door slid closed behind him, Charlie took another sip of his Coca-Cola then closed his eyes, savoring the sweetness in his mouth. It reminded him of being young, back when his dad was still alive. Charlie hadn't been allowed to drink soda like most of the other kids he knew — except on special occasions. One such occasion happened every Friday night when they all went out to dinner at The Burger Palace, and Charlie got to pig out on turkey burgers, fries, and a tall glass of Coca-Cola with chipped ice. Sometimes, the waiter or waitress, dressed in '50s diner style, would pour some cherry syrup into the Coke, amplifying the awesome. Long after he was done with the

Coke, Charlie would suck the puddles of sweetness from the chipped ice.

Charlie closed his eyes, trying not to let thoughts of his father lower the rising summit of his mood.

Tonight would be sad enough, and possibly the last time he'd see Callie for a while.

He finished his Coke and stared at the can, wondering if they'd really be able to go home. And more than that, Charlie wondered if Callie would still be friends with him if they were suddenly able to return to the world they once knew.

If that world was still there, maybe his mother was, too. And that fucker, Bob. A version of Bob whom Charlie didn't murder.

If he could go back, Charlie wouldn't kill that Bob. That Bob hadn't raped Callie. That Bob wasn't the same monster. Or at least hadn't been given enough opportunity to become one yet. So no, Charlie didn't think he'd kill that Bob.

But he *would* kick the living shit out of him.

~

THAT NIGHT …

CHARLIE AND CALLIE sat on their mattresses on opposite sides of a glass wall.

Though all the other cells were dark, theirs were dimly lit, which would have given the cells an almost romantic glow, if calling glass prison cells with video cameras and flame-spouting holes romantic didn't seem like so much of a stretch.

Charlie also felt like their cells being lit, while everyone else's were swallowed in darkness, set them on display and in an unflattering light. That made him feel weird. He didn't want everyone staring, especially after all of the special treat-ment, from fresh clothes to the pens and paper delivered an hour before, right after dinner. Charlie imagined the other six residents of the cell block were pissed.

However, this was Charlie's first chance to communicate with Callie in what seemed like forever, so he didn't care who was watching or what they thought.

They'd been *talking* (via pens and paper) ever since — catch-up stuff mostly, like updates on what had happened to each of them, how there were two Boricios, and two worlds, both facts blowing Callie's mind, and then, of course, that they might be able to find a way home.

Charlie told Callie that the new Boricio was going to ask her to show him the way to the old Boricio's compound. She said okay, and then worked out the directions together as best they could.

Connecting with Callie again felt great. It reminded him of how much he loved her, even if she didn't feel the same. Hell, maybe she did, now. Who knew?

"What's the first thing you'll do if we go home?" Callie wrote.

"Drink a Coke. You?"

"One word: Starbucks."

Charlie laughed. "Then what?"

"I dunno. What do YOU want to do?"

"Whatever you want to do," he wrote.

"Whatever?" she wrote, smiling.

Is she flirting with me? No way.

"Anything," he wrote, smiling, though unsure if his smile matched hers, which still seemed flirty.

She set her pad of paper on the mattress, scribbled something, then held it up for him to see.

"Will you fuck me?" she wrote.

Charlie's eyes widened, and his cock went instantly stiff in his sweats.

Callie laughed hysterically, probably at the look on his face.

Charlie frowned.

"You're messing with me, aren't you?" he wrote.

"Maybe," she wrote. "Maybe not."

Callie put the pad down, then licked her lips.

Charlie's cock went from stiff to a near-bursting pipe.

Callie circled a finger over her nipples. Charlie watched them harden beneath the thin fabric of her shirt.

Oh God.

He picked up his pen and wrote, "What are you doing?"

Callie shook her head, then slowly lifted her shirt. Even though Charlie knew some asshole was likely watching them from the other side of a security camera, he didn't care about anything outside of the moment.

Though Callie had been naked up until about two hours earlier, and he'd not found her nudity arousing in their situation, something had changed. Callie had been given clothes, and was now choosing to reveal herself to Charlie. Slowly. Teasing him.

Callie exposed the bottoms of her breasts, then lifted the shirt to expose just one nipple, which she pinched.

Oh fuck.

Charlie reached down and squeezed the thick of his flesh through the thin of his pants.

Her eyes, big and beautiful, lowered to stare.

Charlie felt odd. He'd touched himself thousands of times, but never in front of someone else. He kept stroking his cock through his sweats, then watched as Callie reached down the front of hers and began to rub herself.

She arched her head back, and though Charlie couldn't hear it, he was sure she moaned.

Callie looked down and mouthed the words, "Show me."

Charlie did as instructed, lowering his sweats just enough to pull out his cock. He started stroking it as he watched her. While Charlie had always felt like his penis was average at best, it felt like a beast between his legs in the nest of his loose fist.

Callie pulled her pants down a bit, then slipped her fingers past the waistband.

Charlie started stroking himself faster, harder, as Callie's fingers plunged into the depths of her sweats. She rubbed herself between her legs, then lowered her sweats to just above her knees.

Oh fuck, yeah.

He stared at her pussy. And she at his cock. And then, their eyes met. In that moment, Callie opened her mouth and bit her bottom lip. Charlie stroked faster and faster as the intensity of their stare seemed to coalesce into something with a force of its own.

He looked down again to see that she was now sliding her fingers in and out of herself as fast as he was stroking, if not faster. He looked up again, and their eyes locked.

She mouthed the word, "Charlie," just as he exploded and splattered the glass. As he emptied the rest of himself onto his hand, Callie's eyes rolled into the back of her head and then she closed them, as her lower body shuddered.

When her eyes met his again, she giggled, almost embarrassed. Charlie looked around for something to wipe up his mess, from both his body and the glass, then stripped his T-shirt off and used it to wipe up the evidence of his embarrassment.

After a long, awkward moment where they were unable to meet one another's eyes, Callie grabbed her pen and paper and wrote, "That was nice. Thank you."

Charlie wrote, "Thank ME?! No, thank YOU! That was SO HOT!!"

Callie smiled.

Charlie wanted to write something else — that he loved her. But that seemed so stupid, immature, and probably weird, that he couldn't bring himself to write it.

So, instead, he wrote, "I'm going to miss you so much tomorrow."

She wrote, for what seemed a long time, and then held it up to the window, "Do you remember when you told me you liked me? I'm not gonna say I'm sorry that I rejected you then. I'm not. Well, I am, and I'm not. I'm not because I'd never lie to you. But I am, because it made you leave. If you hadn't left, none of this would've happened. Maybe we'd have found a way to get along without Bob. And eventually, I would've discovered that you are so much more than I thought."

As Charlie read the page Callie was holding up, she one-handedly scribbled on another, then held it to the glass for Charlie.

It read, "I've never really let people get too close to me. And I didn't want to let you in, either. Yet, you found a way inside my heart. I guess, what I'm trying to say is that I love you, too."

He finished the page and met her eyes. They were tearing.

He cried, too, as he set his hand against the glass, wishing like hell he could touch her and hold her. He was almost willing to break glass again, and get shot to death by Guardsmen, if only to hold her for one more minute.

"I love you," he said, mouthing the words, feeling as if the weight of the world had slipped from his shoulders and his soul. A giddiness took its place.

They lay down, side by side, separated only by glass. Charlie felt himself drifting into a post-orgasm slumber, a stupid grin still lighting his face.

Suddenly, Callie tapped on the window three times in sharp succession. Charlie jumped, startled.

Her eyes were large and frightened. Charlie looked around, but couldn't see what she was afraid of. Callie grabbed her pen and paper and started scribbling, then held up the paper.

"Boricio knows the old man next to you! They were yelling at each other earlier."

"So, what does that mean?" Charlie wrote, shrugging.

"I dunno," she wrote. "But be careful."

"You, too."

They each returned to their mattresses, but Charlie couldn't sleep with his mind circling any of the many reasons Callie might have been spooked by the old, fat man in the cell next to him.

Though he was facing Callie, both their hands touching the glass, Charlie couldn't help but feel like the old man was lying in the dark, awake and watching them both.

THE NEXT MORNING, Charlie woke to the sound of knocking.

Callie was standing at the doorway with a Guardsman in black, waving goodbye.

Charlie jumped from his mattress and went to the door, then set his hand against the glass to meet hers. He mouthed, "I love you. Be careful."

"I love you, too," she said. Their eyes locked in a final lingering moment before the Guardsman gently pulled her away.

Charlie watched them walk down the hall and then to the doors. As Callie slipped from view, Charlie returned to his mattress and lay down. He turned his head to the glass and stared over at Callie's mattress, and the piles of their correspondence from the night before lying scattered across her sheets. Sitting on her pillow was a paper he hadn't seen before — a drawing of a heart, and inside the heart, an almost perfectly rendered drawing of Charlie.

He stared at it, thinking back to the drawing he'd made of her. She'd never said she was as good an artist as he was.

Yet, Charlie was staring at proof.

He looked at the drawing for what felt like forever, feeling like his heart was breaking into pieces too small to stitch, hoping like hell that Black Mountain would cure him so that he could be with Callie again.

As he dared to hope, the lights went black as though they were mocking his ambition.

CHARLIE WOKE to a row of bright lights flickering on in the cells, and a lone Guardsman making his way down the line with a cart full of breakfast trays.

Breakfast was a bowl of cereal without milk, two bottles of water, and a peach, which he figured must have been grown in a garden somewhere on the mountain. His stomach grumbled as Charlie stared down the line, waiting for the Guard to arrive. Suddenly, Charlie realized that the old man in the cell beside him was looking at him.

Not just looking — staring, with all his fat, old, pasty nakedness pressed against Charlie's glass wall.

Charlie nearly jumped back in shock.

What the fuck?!

The man turned away when he noticed Charlie looking back, but it was too late. He'd already spooked Charlie.

The old man went to his door as the Guardsman approached, moving his pasty flesh flat against the entrance.

"What the fuck is his deal?" Imaginary Boricio asked, appearing out of the blue, wearing a black T-shirt and sweats just like Charlie had been given, and jerking his thumb toward the old man's cell.

"I dunno," Charlie said out loud, not even bothering to mask his dialogue back to Boricio in thoughts. He'd put mayo on his knuckle sandwich while the cameras were rolling; he didn't think he could get more embarrassed than that.

"Nice performance last night, by the way," Boricio said clapping his hands. "Ole Chucky finally scored him some Callie! Even if it was a solo performance."

"You were there?" Charlie asked.

"I'm always here, lil' buddy," Boricio tapped his temple. "I'm in your head."

"Well, I'm just glad you didn't pop up last night. That would've been a mood killer for sure."

"Who ya kidding, you would've both loved it if I whipped out my slim reaper and put on a show for the both of ya!"

"Not now," Charlie said, "I don't wanna lose my appetite before breakfast."

Charlie glanced back up to see if the Guardsman was done giving the old man his food, and was shocked to see the old man standing entirely still, his mouth stretched impossibly wide as black, smoke-like liquid rose from his throat, then spilled out of his mouth and floated down toward the slot at the bottom of the door.

"What the fuck is that shit?!" Imaginary Boricio said.

The Guardsman stared, seemingly unable to move away, as the black thing floated through the slot and then up until it was standing in front of him. The darkness started to swirl within itself, gathering mass, then suddenly thrust itself through the man's glass mask and into the Guardsman's helmet as he swiped helplessly with his hands at his headgear, falling to the ground.

"What the fuck?!" Imaginary Boricio screamed, running to Charlie's cell door. "What the fuck is that shit?"

The black thing forced itself into the man's mouth until it had completely disappeared inside him, leaving the Guardsman lying like an empty pile on the ground.

Charlie looked over in the cell beside his just as the old man fell to the floor, so hard the fall must've shattered the back of his skull. His eyes were open, staring at the ceiling as a sea of blood pooled from under his head.

Charlie looked around the cell block, and saw that everyone else was doing exactly as he was — staring in wide-eyed shock at the pair of fallen bodies.

Then one of the bodies stood — the Guardsman.

Charlie stared, wondering what had happened to the man. His helmet's glass mask was shattered, and his eyes were vacant as if he'd suffered a concussion.

Where did the dark thing go?

"I thought it went inside him!" Boricio said. "What the fuck?"

The Guardsman turned to Charlie's cell, removed his glove from his hand, then put it on the pad next to Charlie's cell.

"Is he letting us out?" Imaginary Boricio asked.

The Guardsman's eyes went black. Charlie's heart started beating at triple its usual speed.

"Fuck, it's in him! And now it's coming in here!" Boricio yelled.

The glass door slid open, and Charlie fell three steps back, unsure of what in the hell he was dealing with, preparing for anything. He had to get past the Guardsman and alert someone.

The Guardsman went from slowly shambling toward Charlie to suddenly jumping at him. The man, impossibly strong, lifted Charlie from the floor, then shoved him hard against the glass wall behind him.

"Fuck!" Charlie screamed, trying to kick out, or summon whatever the hell it was inside him that had turned him into Super Charlie when he took the guards out his first day on the block.

The Guardsman, seemingly possessed, clutched Charlie's neck, his fingers squeezing tighter into him as he moved in closer, opening his mouth impossibly wide.

Oh God, no!

A dark bulb, like a rotten fetus, pushed itself from the

Guardsman's mouth, a solid-looking form at first until it went flimsy and began inching toward Charlie's open mouth, which the Guardsman's fingers had roughly plied wide.

Charlie tried to bite down, to chomp off the man's fingers, but it was too late — the darkness was forcing its way into his mouth, with the taste of bitter chemicals and promised death.

Charlie choked, spitting the chunks of black and bile that felt like they were boiling his throat. When he stopped spitting, he had to gasp for air. That's when the blackness infiltrated the rest of him, pouring into his body all at once.

Charlie felt *It* inside him immediately.

He was merely a passenger in his own flesh.

It had taken over.

And *It* was going to break out of Black Mountain.

FORTY-ONE

Boricio Bishop

Black Island Research Facility
  September 2011
  ONE MONTH BEFORE THE EVENT ...

WHEN BORICIO WOKE UP, someone in a yellow hazmat suit was entering Rose's cell. Rose was lying on the mattress, still asleep. At least, Boricio hoped she was only sleeping.

Boricio leapt to his feet and pounded on the glass wall of his cell, seeing a group of three men standing in a semicircle outside of Rose's cell. The group included Will, Ed Keenan, and Sullivan — they were keeping this experiment on the down-low, apparently.

Will turned to Boricio and walked over, and touched a panel beside the door. A radio crackled to life in the cell, "Yes, son?"

"What's going on?" he asked. "What are they doing with Rose?"

"Dr. Williams created a new serum, using a different vial. To see if we can cure her."

Boricio gasped, tears flooding his eyes, surprised that Will had agreed to do what he said he wouldn't.

"Thank you, Dad," Boricio said.

"Don't thank me yet. I have no idea if it will work," Will said before he returned to join the others in front of Rose's cell.

Boricio couldn't see much, since the people were in the way, but he saw the yellow suit bending down, likely injecting Rose with the serum.

Boricio put his hands on the glass, trying to get a better look, hoping like hell the serum would work this time. Dr. Williams, Boricio noted, was not in the room. Perhaps he was on lockdown somewhere, awaiting the results of this experiment.

Boricio swallowed, hoping against hope that they could undo the damage his actions had caused.

Please be okay.

He didn't care if they could cure her paralysis or if she never ever remembered Boricio again, he just wanted her human again. He'd rather her be a stranger than have her live as the monstrosity she'd become.

He didn't even want to think about what would happen if this serum didn't work.

Yet, his mind went there, anyway, wondering if Will would be patient enough to continue experimenting with other serums. They'd have to, he figured. They were scientists, and they'd witnessed a mutation unlike anything ever seen before. Even if Rose was Hitler reincarnated, they'd keep working to cure her. That's what scientists did. And besides, curing her was in line with the Remedy Project's goals.

No way in hell the vials could ever have a human application if they didn't figure out what went wrong and how to fix it. With Rose, they had something years ahead of schedule — a human subject. Without Rose, they had nothing. The project would be set back years, if not permanently. Or — and at this thought, Boricio began to worry — they'd have to experiment on the only other known subject, Luca.

No way in hell Will would allow that.

So, they had to cure Rose.

He hoped.

"It's administered," the man in the hazmat suit said over the speaker.

Keenan said something, but Boricio couldn't hear it above the sudden static of the speakers in his cell.

The man in the hazmat suit was breathing heavy and said, "She's waking up."

Boricio moved to his left, trying to see beyond the men, but couldn't see anything other than the top of the hazmat suit's helmet as the man, who Boricio now recognized by his voice as Anderson, looked down at Rose.

And then came the screaming — a scream so loud and shrill that it crackled the speakers and hurt Boricio's ears. Boricio couldn't tell if the scream was male, female, or even human.

A loud thud crackled over the speakers as the man in the hazmat suit was thrown against the glass wall of Rose's cell, and then he slumped to the ground. Something black moved like lightning in Rose's cell, hopping on top of Anderson. The smash of glass and the sound of wet flesh ripping came through the speakers. The men jumped back, startled, and Boricio was given a clear view inside Rose's cell.

Whatever had been left of the woman he loved was gone — and replaced by a hulking, black monster with a long head, large, black eyes, and a wide mouth filled with rows of jagged teeth. Her body had become as unrecognizable as her face.

Boricio cried out, "Rose!"

The thing that had been Rose looked up at him and for a moment, he thought she recognized him across the room. Then she backed up and ran toward the glass wall of her cell.

Hard. She bounced off the wall, leaving a slimy black and red residue — blood, perhaps.

The men scrambled, Sullivan rushing toward the door panel.

"No!" Will shouted, "It's too late."

What's too late? Saving the man in the hazmat suit?

Boricio then noticed that the man's mask was broken, his face a bloody pulp.

Oh God.

Boricio cried out, "Rose!"

Keenan looked up at Boricio, glaring, accusation in his eyes saying, *This is your fault.*

Rose slammed into the glass again. And again. Cracks began to spread from the points of impact.

"It's going to break through!" Keenan shouted. "Hit the gas."

Sullivan pressed buttons on the door panel, which sent a sleeping gas into Rose's cell.

Rose crashed into the glass again, the gas having no effect on her yet. The glass cracked further, this time sending a chunk to the floor.

Rose saw the hole and started bashing her giant mutant arms into it, sending more chunks of glass to the ground, creating a small hole large enough to stick a hand through. It wouldn't be long before she broke out of the cell.

"It's not working!" Sullivan said.

"Initiate Burn Protocol!" Will yelled.

Sullivan looked at him, and then Keenan, who nodded to confirm the decision.

Boricio's heart sank.

No, they can't.

"No!!" he screamed. "No!!"

"Burn Protocol?" Sullivan asked, seeking a second confirmation.

Boricio slammed his fists on his cell and screamed for Will, "No, Dad, don't!!"

"Yes," Will said. "Do it! Now!"

Rose slammed against the glass again, and then something caught her attention, and she looked up at the ceiling.

Boricio cried out, "No!! Dad!!"

The flames came on.

Rose screamed, her shrieks gurgling in the speakers as her black form was engulfed in flames that filled her entire cell.

Boricio cried out, watching helplessly as Rose writhed in agony.

Will suddenly reached into his pants and retrieved something from his pocket and then thrust it through the hole in the glass into the fiery cell.

"What was that?" Keenan asked sharply.

"The rest of the vials," Will said. "I'm ending this now."

Both Keenan and Sullivan's mouths were agape.

Keenan screamed at Will, "Why?!"

Will got in Keenan's face and screamed, "We should've done this from the start!"

Rose's screams died with the flames a moment later.

In the center of the room, the love of his life, along with the vials, had been reduced to a smoldering pile of ashes.

Boricio fell to the ground, screaming, his world shattered.

He noticed Will approaching his cell.

Boricio looked up at him, barely able to quell the rage simmering inside.

"I'm sorry, Son," Will said.

Boricio slowly stood up and met his father's red eyes.

Whatever love and light that the man had ignited in Boricio's life so many years earlier had been snuffed out and replaced with cold, unending darkness.

~

FORTY-TWO

Boricio Bishop

Somewhere in Alabama
September 2011
ONE MONTH BEFORE THE EVENT ...

FUCK BLACK ISLAND, Boricio thought as he hopped out of the truck that had driven him the last stretch of miles and thanked the man who'd given him a lift.

Boricio had been gone from New York for two weeks, slowly making his way down south to New Orleans, where he planned to get a job as a chef in a restaurant, and hopefully disappear in his work.

He would be thrilled if he never thought of Rose again, or if Will could never find him, and he never had to look at the murdering fuck's face.

Boricio would happily settle for one of the two.

He wandered south for several days, alone and desolate, with nothing but the pack on his back, caretaker of the last vial left, which he'd managed to sneak off the island, thanks to Luca. Boricio was surprised that Luca had helped him, and was certain that Luca would be in huge trouble. When Boricio asked Luca if there had been another vial, as Will suggested another had been taken, Luca pleaded ignorance — which either meant the boy was lying, which Boricio doubted, or someone else had taken a vial. Boricio wondered for a while, but then stopped caring.

Not my problem.

Boricio wasn't sure why he had taken the last vial, other than he felt he had to protect it. Will wanted to destroy them all. And while the vials had turned Rose into a monster, Boricio knew that they were also capable of incredible good.

Someday, Boricio would find a way to start a new project. Perhaps he'd go to Black Mountain, which was run by a more daring group of scientists who often found themselves at odds with the Black Island faction.

But for now, Boricio just wanted to get lost.

Without a car, he hitched his way south until he found himself in Alabama.

He was walking along a road in the middle of nowhere, wondering if he'd even see another car to hitch a ride from, or if he should look for someplace to sleep for the night. He had a decent stash of cash to last him a while, so all he needed was to find a hotel.

Searching the horizon, he looked up and happened to see a sprawling cross standing tall and proud against the bruised purple sky.

Boricio stared up at the cross feeling an odd sort of promise, an oath strong enough to pull him from the road, through an ornate gate opening, where he met a smiling woman in a long, blue dress, and past some houses and through the church's wide open wooden doors on the rear of the sprawling property.

Boricio sat in a pew at the back of the church, listening to the pastor as he paced the pulpit, hands raised in the air as he delivered a sermon.

"Ours is not to question His will. He works in mysterious

ways, as the saying goes. Ways that we mere mortals cannot even hope to understand. Most of human misery comes from us trying to make sense of God's will, to put a human face on divine reason, rather than just accepting His gifts."

The pastor found Boricio's eye, and in that moment, it felt as if the pastor was speaking directly to him, offering a light in the dark nightmare that had become Boricio's life.

The pastor continued, "There will come a time in this Earthly life when The Good Lord will see fit to take someone you love, someone you simply cannot bear to live without. And when that happens, it will feel as though your heart can no longer beat, and your head can no longer think, and the breath inside you feels more like a curse than a gift."

The pastor took a moment to pause, casting his eyes across the room, his soft stare settling again on Boricio's, as his hands continued to hover. He finally dropped both arms to his side, then started to pace the pulpit again.

"I have good news and bad news. The bad news is that you will likely never get over your loss, not all the way, anyhow. It simply hurts too much, and our hearts are too tender and loving. But the good news is that The Good Lord loves you, and if you let Him live forever in your broken heart, you will be mended! You will be enlightened, because you understand that He only asks us to suffer through the sour of this world so that we may fully appreciate the eternal sweet of His King-dom. For even though death leaves a heartache that no one and nothing will ever be able to heal, at least not in this life, The Good Lord offers a salvation and everlasting eternal joy that no one can ever steal."

Boricio was in no way religious, yet he found an odd comfort in the pastor's words, and felt surprisingly at home with his back resting against the freshly polished pew. Boricio didn't move an inch for the remainder of the sermon, or even after it was finished. He sat safely out of sight in the back of the church until the pastor finally stopped shaking hands of the men, women, and children who filed out. The pastor looked up at Boricio and walked over and took a seat next to him.

Normally, that would have been Boricio's cue to leave.

But he stayed.

"It looks like you could use a bit of The Good Lord's light," the pastor said, slapping his hand on the back of Boricio's shoulder. "Welcome to the New Unity Church." The pastor smiled kindly at Boricio, then added, "We're here for you, Son. You can call me The Prophet."

TO BE CONTINUED ...

Episode 17

(FIFTH EPISODE OF SEASON THREE)

"a priori"

FORTY-THREE

Luca Bishop

Our Earth
Las Orillas, California
April 2, 2012
SIX MONTHS AFTER THE EVENT …

LUCA'S LIFE before Oct. 15 was only a shadow.

He could easily ignore the day's shadows. But at night . . . at night, they demanded his attention.

Luca and Anna were lying together on their L-shaped couch watching *The Incredibles*. Neither had picked the movie, since no one seemed to agree on whose turn it was to choose. Luca was certain it was his turn, and he wanted to watch *Return of the Jedi* again. Anna said it was her turn — she wanted to watch *Tangled* for the bajillionth time. Mom had a headache and didn't feel like hearing another argument, so she compromised with *The Incredibles*, which both Luca and Anna loudly complained about, even though they both loved the movie, and it was even one of Luca's three favorite Pixars.

As the movie was ending, and the clock on the cable box was nearing 9 p.m., Luca knew their mom would be in the living room any minute to pick up a few stray kernels of popcorn from the carpet and announce bedtime. Luca glanced over at Anna, lightly snoring above the pool of fresh drool on her pillow. He closed his eyes and pretended to be sleeping, too, hoping their mom might leave them there for the night.

Ever since arriving in the other Luca's world, and claiming his spot in Luca's family, he had grown to hate bedtime. Sometimes, when he and Anna fell asleep together on the couch, their mom would leave them through the night. It was these nights, lying beside his sister, when Luca felt the most safe, comfortable, and, oddly enough, most loved.

When he had to sleep in his bedroom, all alone, he felt like the impostor he was.

"Time for bed," Mom said, spoiling Luca's hope.

Luca rose from the couch, dejected, hoping to win some sympathy and be allowed to maybe sleep in the living room. Anna was already standing, and hugging their mom goodnight, resigned to her fate — and resigning Luca to his.

Luca hugged his mom goodnight, but pushed his face into her harder than usual.

"What's wrong, honey?" she asked.

"Just sad," he said.

"Sad? You can watch *Return of the Jedi* another night, maybe even tomorrow." She patted him on the shoulders.

Luca was going to tell her that it wasn't *The Incredibles* that had made him sad, but decided not to. Because what could he say? That he was sad because he'd taken her *real son's* place? That he left his family behind as monsters tore through his home world?

Luca couldn't even start to explain what he only sort of understood. So, he said the only thing he could.

"Thank you, Mom."

His mom hugged him harder before Luca trudged off to

the bathroom. He brushed his teeth and peed, then headed to his father's office.

His dad was tapping away at a thin aluminum keyboard, his eyes centered on the screen. It took him a moment to notice Luca. Once he did, Luca's dad looked up, without smiling. He seemed more distracted than happy to see him. Luca figured he must be working on something extra special important.

"Goodnight, Buddy," his dad said, hugging him goodnight.

"Goodnight, Dad," Luca said, head down as he shuffled to his bedroom where his mom came inside to tuck him in a few minutes later.

As his mom closed the door, the shadows returned.

Outside his window, through the parted curtains, Luca could see the moon peering through the thousand-fingered trees, its soft glow twisting those fingers into scary shadows on Luca's far wall.

He turned from the window and then turned back, choosing to lie facing the window and its glow instead of the wall and its shadows. Luca closed his eyes and thought about his family — his real family, back on the world he'd abandoned.

Luca had tried to return several times since October so that he could see how they were doing, but was only successful a few times. He hadn't been able to control where he went, however. And each time he'd gone to the other world, he'd wound up with the other Luca. Only that Luca had changed. He was older. And the other Luca couldn't see him. Nobody could see him — as if he were some kind of ghost.

Luca's only success was last month when he saw the other version of his new dad, Will. He was surprised the other Will had been able to see him, and didn't know how long he would be able to do so, so he delivered his message so urgently that he wasn't even sure Will understood what he was saying.

Even if Will *had* understood, he was bleeding so much he looked like he was just minutes from dying. If Will was dead, then he couldn't have given the message to anyone. And if that were the case, then perhaps all hope was lost — for Luca and his world. Perhaps all hope was lost, anyway, though. Because Luca wasn't even sure that the message would help. He was only giving that message because of the dream he'd had — the dream where people were looking for the vial Luca had hidden.

Luca had tried to go back a few times after he saw Will, but nothing was working. Luca wasn't sure why getting to the other world now was so much harder. He'd been able to do it so easily before Oct. 15.

But then something had happened.

Perhaps it had to do with the thing that pulled the others to his world. It wasn't the Darkness that he'd seen taking over his world. It was something else — a brightness that Luca felt more than saw.

He closed his eyes and tried to go back, just as he had tried to do nearly every night since October.

And then he was gone.

LUCA WAS SUDDENLY FLOATING in darkness, salt water splashing his face and into his eyes and mouth as he struggled to keep his nose and mouth above the surface. Luca's arms thrashed in the water as he struggled to see anything. But he couldn't drink his surroundings without also drinking salt.

Luca swallowed a mouthful of sea and went underwater.

He panicked, then somehow managed to come back up, spitting out water as he paddled to stay above the churning waves.

Where am I?

Something splashed loud behind him, hitting the water so

hard it caused a giant wave to plunge him back beneath the surface. He could hear the muffled splashes of more things falling around him. Confused, he opened his eyes underwater, despite the burning, to see what was making so much noise.

Are there other people here?

Luca saw several dozen faint-orange somethings glowing above him.

Pretty.

What are they?

He surfaced for air, wiping water from his eyes as he looked up, peering into the black to see what the orange lights were made of. As he squeezed his eyes in concentration, Luca felt fear, like fingers wrapping tightly around his heart.

Above him, dozens of burning chunks of something were raining from the sky, splashing the water all around him. He couldn't tell what they were, but there were dozens or more orange spots coming at him, some of them huge.

Luca screamed as he desperately paddled, trying to swim free from the falling fire, with no idea where to go.

He swam in blind fear as flaming debris continued to rain around him, smashing tall waves against his body, sometimes hard enough to bury him beneath another choking wave.

Where is this stuff coming from? And what is it?

From what Luca could tell, the something was made from all sorts of stuff: wood, chunks of trees, pieces of cars, clothing, books, and food.

Something splashed beside him, confusing him at first, until he realized it was a person's head, ripped from their body and burned on over half of their face.

Luca screamed, went under, then surfaced again, spitting and gagging on the harsh salt water as he gasped for air.

Keep swimming!

Luca kept going, faster than he'd ever swum in his life, trying to find a way to go back to the other world, where he'd been safe in the other Luca's bed.

But he couldn't get back if he wasn't able to concentrate.

Luca swam for what felt like forever, his entire body in pain and his arms and legs about to turn rubber, unable to float any longer, until he found himself at a safe distance from the falling stuff.

That's when he saw the source of the falling stuff in the distance: two of the largest tornadoes Luca had ever seen. While Luca had only seen tornadoes on TV, he was sure they didn't usually have balls of lightning and fire in the middle, though.

Luca couldn't tell how far away the tornadoes were from one another, but they seemed close, like they were about to collide. He'd never seen two at once, even on TV. It was like the tornados were fighting to see which one could gather then spit the most terrible stuff into the sky as they moved closer to one another.

Luca finally realized that it wasn't just *stuff* they were spitting into the sky. The tornados were spitting what was left of Black Island.

His eyes widened as he screamed.

LUCA WOKE IN HIS BED, soaking wet, and screeching.

No one could hear his scream, however, because someone's hand was covering his mouth.

~

FORTY-FOUR

Brent Foster

Other Earth
  Somewhere in Georgia …
  March 31, 2012
  FIVE MONTHS AFTER THE EVENT …

THE BLACK VAN barreled down the two-lane highway beneath the bright morning sun toward Dunn, Georgia as if on a mission from God.

Boricio was behind the wheel, with Callie in the front seat. Jung, the tall muscular Swiss super-soldier sat behind them, while Ed and Brent took the rear. Ed was resting his eyes, though Brent could never be certain if he were really napping — in which case, the dude was able to sleep anywhere — or if he were just lying low to appear like less of a threat in case he needed to bolt into action.

Brent's mind wandered to their next destination — after they went to the other Boricio's compound — Black Island.

He wondered how Jane and her daughter, Emily, were doing.

It had been a couple of weeks since he'd seen them, but it

felt like months. He was surprised how much he missed them both. He thought of their last dinner, and how Emily had hugged him, filled with sudden sadness when he told her that he had to go on a special trip.

Emily made him promise to return home, safe. Of course he said he would, even though he wasn't sure at the time. Now it looked like he might make good on his promise. Just one more stop, then back to Black Island they'd go, carrying their lingering questions behind them:

Would they be returning with both Boricios? And what had the bald Boricio done that had banished him to Black Mountain? Yes, they might make it back to Black Island in one piece, but Brent wondered what sort of reception would be waiting.

Before the trip, Boricio said Black Island might hold the key to them going home. But he said nothing about how that would happen, and Brent was afraid to ask for specifics, in the same way he'd been afraid to ask Ed for particulars when Ed said they might be able to get home somehow.

Brent was still clinging to the hope that they might get home, and that he would see his wife and son again. He'd not allowed himself more than a few stray thoughts surrounding Ben and Gina during the previous week, particularly when it seemed like they might not make it back to Black Island, let alone home. Now, as they drew closer to Black Island, he found himself daring to hope again.

He thought of Ben and smiled. He couldn't wait to see his son again, to hold him in his arms and hug his tiny buddy. He thought of his son's toy, the Stanley Train that was taken from him by Black Island Guardsmen. He wondered if that toy belonged to the Ben of this world, who was mutated and held in chambers deep in Black Island's bowels, or if he'd somehow brought it from his own world when he was yanked away.

Let me make it back, God, and I swear, I'll quit my job and never neglect my family again. Please. Just let us make it back.

Brent felt hypocritical praying to a God who hadn't earned his faith. If He was real, Brent wondered, did He piss on the prayers of the skeptics, and was he cursing himself by now turning to prayer? As if God somehow would say, "No, you didn't believe in me before now. Fuck off."

Brent wondered what would happen if they actually found a way back to Earth.?

How would they arrive? Would they appear, just like they'd vanished? Would he show up in his bed and scare the hell out of Gina? Or would they be going home through some sort of science-fiction teleportation machine, and wind up on the other Black Island? If so, would that mean they were immediately apprehended by Homeland Security, then held in detention for months on end as suspected terrorists? Or worse, made part of some secret lab experiment, hidden from the rest of the world and kept from their families forever?

Brent swallowed, feeling anxiety thicken his throat.

So close, yet so far. And too many unanswered questions.

Brent hated not knowing, or having control of his own fate.

Brent was pulled from his thoughts as the van suddenly slowed and Boricio said, "What the hell have we got here?"

Boricio stopped the van, but left the engine running.

Brent felt his heartbeat quicken, thinking back to the maze of cars where they'd nearly surrendered their final breaths on their way to Black Mountain. He couldn't stand the thought of going through that particular hell again. Everyone, including Ed — now wide awake and obvious about it — moved to the front of the van and stared out the front window.

The thick lines of trees that had bordered both sides of the highway for nearly every mile of the trip were now gone. In their place, nothing but a half mile or so of dark earth, freshly plowed, as if something, perhaps a super tornado, had stripped the land of everything in sight.

The road was oddly untouched, but only as a canvas for the horror lining it — hundreds, if not thousands of aliens, standing on either side of the highway, perfectly still, like statues paving the way to Dunn.

"What the fuck?" Jung said, the word 'fuck,' sounding unnatural in his accent.

"Oh Jesus!" Callie cried. "What are they doing?"

Boricio joked, "Laying out the welcome mat, maybe?" But the only color on his face was the black on his patch.

"What do we do?" Brent said, his heart beating so loud he felt like it was throwing echoes off the van walls.

"Drive," Ed said, his first words all morning.

"What?" Callie said, shocked he would suggest such a thing.

"Drive," he repeated, meeting Boricio's eye in the mirror.

Jung said, "I'm not sure about that," shifting nervously in his seat.

"He's right," Boricio said. "If they wanted to attack us, they would have already."

Boricio stepped on the gas before anyone else, or more likely his own instincts, could raise debate.

The van rolled down the road, slowly at first, maybe 20 mph, as Jung, Ed, and Brent all held their rifles, aimed at the windows and ready to fire. Brent hoped like hell they wouldn't have occasion to pull the triggers since there was no way they'd be able to take on the wide, churning sea of aliens without eventually joining it.

As they passed, Brent looked out the left-side windows, staring at the aliens in all their many varied forms; repulsed, amazed, and half expecting one or all to leap forward and attack in unison. But they remained still, as if they weren't even aware of the passing van.

Callie sat shotgun in front, aiming a pistol at her window, her hand, and the gun held in it, shaking.

Ed held his rifle trained on his side window, watching the

row fly past as Boricio gathered speed. Brent saw what looked like the end of the aliens' line ahead in the distance.

They were about halfway there when something slammed into the back of the van.

"Fuck!" Callie screamed, then fired her gun, which sounded like a bomb in the enclosed space.

Brent's ears felt shattered, just like Callie's passenger window. He wasn't sure what had slammed into the back of the van, but the aliens' mouths were all suddenly open at once, screaming a shrill screech and gnashing their teeth at the van from all sides.

Between the screaming and the high-pitched ringing in his ears, the pain in Brent's head was unbearable. He dropped his rifle to the floor and covered his ears. Jung, Ed, and Callie were all doing the same, their faces twisted in torment as Boricio struggled to steer them through the dark horde.

The van lurched forward as Brent clutched both sides of his head, trying to dull the terrible shrieking of the aliens. Swarms of the creatures began to move forward into the road, to block their path.

"Fuck!" Boricio screamed as the van tore through the first of them to step in front of the van, their bodies thumping hard against the metal, causing the wheels to wobble against the asphalt, and sending the van steering out of control.

Brent released his ears to grip his seat, as the van flew from the road and onto the freshly turned soil, naked and ugly and stripped of everything but the memory of its once green vegetation.

Brent braced his body, ready for the van to get stuck in the soft soil, giving them unfair seconds before the tires were ensnared in the earth and the aliens surrounded them — seconds before it was finally the end of everything.

The van kept sliding, as if the dirt was hard as pavement, but slick like ice. The van was skidding at a ridiculous speed, and would surely tip if Boricio couldn't steer the wheels into their skid.

Boricio struggled with the steering wheel, screaming a surprising number of obscenities as he fought the van for control as more things started to slap the van's sides and back. Something shattered the rear window. Brent looked down as whatever had shattered the window fell to the carpet, black and squirming.

In the first second, Brent thought it looked like a long, black snake, but then saw its hook and remembered the hook-like things Ed had said they'd shot in the back of the store.

Thicker swarms assaulted the van as it continued its skid across the unfrozen black ice of the forest floor. Brent gripped his seat as Ed held his own with one hand and his rifle with the other, taking aim out the back through the shattered window.

The van came to a jarring, screeching halt, which sent everyone flailing to the left. The engine died as thunder rumbled loudly outside.

Except it wasn't thunder.

As Brent glanced out the window he saw it was a stampede of black, racing toward the van.

"Go! GO!" Ed screamed, sticking his gun out the window and firing.

Boricio pumped the pedal, screaming, "Come on you cock-sucking cunt-fuck!"

Callie and Jung found their guns and took aim, also firing.

The aliens were 100 yards away and closing fast.

Brent fired his rifle blindly out the window, but everything was moving too fast to tell whether he was hitting anything.

Boricio tried turning the ignition again, but the van would only cough and sputter.

"Fuck!" Brent cried out, watching as the army of darkness raced toward them.

This is it! I'm sorry, Gina and Ben! I'm so sorry!

Brent continued firing blindly into the aliens until the engine suddenly turned and Boricio screamed, "Fuck yeah!" flooring the gas pedal.

The van burned rubber and squealed, then started to roll, its sides and back riddled with hundreds of black, hooked flesh, and sounding as though a million rocks were being thrown at the van, all at once.

Jung screamed.

Brent spun around to see a thick, black rope circling around his neck, ripped at one end torn from its host, but still moving, its hook embedded in Jung's right eye.

Boricio screamed victoriously as the van rattled, moving fast and putting distance between themselves and the swarm, unaware of Jung being attacked.

Ed moved toward Jung, trying to pull the black thing from his body, but he was too late. Ed's mouth opened in horror as the black thing snaked its way into Jung's skull.

Brent and Ed stared, both of them frozen in the moment, watching in stunned disbelief as the last of the black thing vanished into Jung's face.

Jung's eyes both went black, then he screamed as he launched himself at Ed.

Jung knocked Ed to the ground, his hands gripping Ed's neck and choking him.

Ed struggled, trying to push and kick Jung away as Brent stared helpless, lost in the moment without any idea of what to do.

"What the fuck is going on back there?" Boricio shouted, turning to look.

Brent's head spun in indecision — was Jung possessed by the aliens? Should he shoot him?

Brent stood, rifle in his hand, paralyzed by uncertainty.

Callie hopped past Brent, raised her pistol to the back of Jung's skull, then pulled the trigger, painting the van's interior with a spray of chunky red.

The gunshot thundered in the cabin as Ed shoved Jung back, then yelled for Brent to open the side door.

Brent moved quickly, hoping to make up for his earlier indecision, and yanked the door open. Ed kicked Jung out of the van, where he bounced off the hardened black earth, fading into the distance as the van kept rolling forward.

Brent exhaled, then yanked the door shut.

Ed, Brent, and Callie all looked at one another, then out the back windows as Boricio put more distance between them and the dark swarm.

They were safe — for now.

FORTY-FIVE

The Prophet

Kingsland, Alabama
September 2011
ONE MONTH BEFORE THE EVENT …

THE PROPHET RECOGNIZED the man in black the moment he first stepped through the doors of his church — the man from his visions; a dream come true sent by The Good Lord to help him usher in the Rapture.

How it would happen, The Prophet did not yet know, and one week after Boricio checked into the rundown Motel 6 up the road, The Prophet had to wonder if God was testing him.

Boricio was the definition of a lost soul — sad, and full as a tick with resentment. He also seemed like a man who was looking to die.

Boricio wasn't just mourning his lost love, whom he'd yet to say two words about, except to mention she was gone; he was boiling over the top of his pot with a furious, bubbling anger. The Prophet invited Boricio to stay at his main house, but the man had foolishly declined. Probably for the best, since The Prophet's family was leery of the stranger.

That didn't stop The Prophet from paying a visit to the man's motel room; no harm in hand-delivering The Good Lord's word.

The first time The Prophet visited Boricio, he could practically smell the drink from the other side of his door. Sure enough, the man was drunk as a Kentucky skunk, and told him to "fuck off" a second after he opened the door.

The Prophet wasn't discouraged.

He returned each day until finally on the seventh, he knocked on a door belonging to a sober Boricio. The man yanked open the door, fast enough to nearly wrest it from its hinges, then said, "What in the hell is it you want from me?"

The Prophet said, "I'd like to take you for a ride."

"A ride?" Boricio was either suspicious of the idea, or didn't like it a lick.

"You've been here, what now, a week? I'm sure you're feeling plenty cooped." The Prophet looked past Boricio, then into a tiny room that had seen its best days maybe three decades before. It was dark, dingy, and plastered with pizza boxes and dozens of oversized bottles of booze, all empty.

Boricio's face was covered in thick, black stubble, though his head was freshly shaved, and shiny enough to show The Prophet his reflection. The man's one eye was bloodshot, but for the first time, his breath wasn't reeking of the Devil's drink.

The Prophet figured the man was beaten and tired, and maybe just worn down enough to allow The Good Lord to reach into his heart and show him His Love. Maybe now The Prophet could finally discover why God had brought the man into his life.

Boricio eyed The Prophet up and down, likely trying to figure his *game*. He was fluent in this reaction; it was the same one The Prophet saw from skeptics all the time.

"So, what? You're gonna give me a guided tour of Bumfuck Egypt?" Boricio said. "You mean to tell me that my Motel 6 isn't Studio Fucking 54?"

The Prophet ignored the man's vulgarity. God had tested him with far worse. Vulgarity was often a defense used by those living in fear. The time for fear was over, though.

"Not a tour," The Prophet shook his head. "More like a particular place I'd like you to see. A place that might just change your life."

Boricio grinned, "You're not gonna take me up to Mount Diddle-Me, are you? 'Cuz while I might be pretty, Boricio don't play for that team."

The Prophet laughed, genuinely, "No, as hard as it may be for you to believe, you're not my type."

"Too old?" Boricio asked.

"Nah, too ugly," The Prophet joked.

Boricio looked at him for a moment, and for that moment The Prophet was afraid he'd mistaken the man's temperament. Then Boricio laughed and said, "Okay, let's go for a ride. Just gimme a minute to wash up."

"I'll be waiting in the truck," The Prophet said, then returned to his F-150, and sat with the engine idling and the A/C on full blast, keeping his eyes at the front of the Motel 6.

Boricio's New York rental was the only car in the lot. In a few hours, once night fell, the place would be hopping with drug abusers and prostitutes like it always was. Some meth addicts were likely shut inside their rooms during the day, seeing as how this motel let a true Devil's den worth of sin to happen behind its aging walls.

The Prophet's face soured at the thought of so many lost souls, so close to salvation and yet still so far away, then wrinkled further at his mind's movie of the motel's owner, an old Russian man, profiting on the misery of so many. While The Prophet felt genuine sympathy for the lost souls, and their fates in the Eternal Fires of Hell, he felt no such sympathy for the man who made his living from the weaknesses of others.

If The Prophet weren't such a holy man, he would have

happily delivered justice to the old Russian with his own hand, taking the life from his beady, soulless eyes.

Justice would come to all soon enough, though.

On Oct. 15, the sinners would pay — each and every one.

And while He might have mercy on the weak, He would have no mercy on the profiteers of evil.

Oh, what a glorious day that will be!

It was what his visions had told him. And as the day crept closer, The Prophet's spirits rose in anticipation.

Boricio emerged from his room carrying a black leather backpack slung over his shoulder, pulling The Prophet from his thoughts.

As Boricio climbed inside the truck, The Prophet said, "Whatchya got in the bag?"

"Just my valuables," Boricio said, "No way I'm leaving my bag in this shit hole."

The Prophet smiled and pulled the F-150 from the motel lot.

~

THEY ARRIVED at Lake Wilton about 10 minutes later, a thickly wooded grove of serenity — home to a glassy beautiful lake, miles of nature trails, several summer camps, and immaculate camping grounds.

They parked near one of the nature trails, then got out of the truck and headed down to a path which offered one of the lake's best views. On the far side of the lake, the sprawling back yards from a few of the richer folks' homes were visible.

"You brought me to a lake?" Boricio said, his backpack still slung over his shoulder. "I told you I'm not making out with you, Father."

"Yes, this is Lake Wilton, one of the most beautiful lakes in all of Alabama. My daddy used to bring me here to fish when I was just a boy. Like his daddy took him before he took me.

Generations of folks from Kingsland, Alabama, call this lake home to some of their most cherished memories. It was such a beautiful place."

"Still is," Boricio said, casting his eyes across the water.

"Yes, it is." The Prophet agreed, nodding as he turned his eyes to Boricio. "But you should've seen it 15 years ago."

"Why's that?" Boricio asked.

"About 15 years back, this company in Georgia started dumping all sorts of pollutants into the lake upstream," The Prophet pointed north. "Pretty soon, fish were dying by the thousands. And of course the birds had to keep their bellies full, so they kept eating the fish even though it was killing them by the barrel. The EPA declared Wilton a toxic dump and demanded it get closed off. Can you imagine?" he turned to Boricio. "Closing off such a beautiful place so people could no longer enjoy it?"

"People suck," Boricio said, like it was fact. "So, what happened? I'm guessing things got better."

"Yes, for a while, though this company was untouchable. It buried its face behind caviar-eating lawyers, lobbyists, and politicians, all crooked as the Mississippi is long. Hell, the company even got to some of the locals here, trying to sway them. But the good people of Kingsland, well they weren't about to sit by and watch as some corporation came in and ruined their lake . . . *our lake*."

"So, what did they do?"

"They banded together, pooled their money, and hired themselves their own high-priced attorney, some fellow on TV, I forget his name, and he stood toe-to-toe with the company. It was David and Goliath, and we all got to watch, smiling from the front row. It was a big win for the good people of Alabama, and we all cheered as our David slung rocks at the wobbling Goliath. It took eight long years, but finally, the fish started coming back, and soon we were able to open the lake back up."

Boricio stared out across the water, quiet for a moment, then said, "That's a ripping yarn, Father. But I don't see how it has anything to do with me."

"You young people, everything has to be about you or it doesn't mean anything," The Prophet said.

"Not what I'm saying, Padre," Boricio said. The man had not yet called him The Prophet, and seemed as though he went out of his way to call him everything but his title. Like most people, he probably found it hard to acknowledge something greater than himself. The idea of God's Eternal Love or visions of the Rapture likely scared the man.

"The point of the story," The Prophet said, turning his eyes from Boricio back to the lake, "is that there was a time, not too long ago, when people would stand together and fight for what they believed. I hate to say it, but I'm sure if some company tried something like that today, the good folks here would just roll right over, and let it happen like it didn't even matter. Too many people have surrendered their rights, handing them gift wrapped to politicians and companies, either too afraid or too apathetic, or hell, just too plain busy to fight back." The Prophet shook his head. "It's a day worth mourning when people turn their eyes from what's right to cast them on what's easy."

Boricio was quiet, still staring at the lake, probably trying to figure where The Prophet was going with his sermon.

"So," The Prophet said, "why did you give up?"

Boricio blinked, then turned to The Prophet and sighed. "Really?" he said. "You're trying to draw a line between what's happening inside my head and a bunch of apathetic losers getting bent over and butt tickled by The Man?" He shook his head. "I expected more from you, Preacher Man, especially after dragging me out of my room so early this morning."

"You think you're any different from these so-called apathetic losers?" The Prophet said. "Sorry, Son, but you

don't seem all that different from most people I see —
drowning in misery, self-delusion, and ultimately, their own
self-destruction. How long are you gonna bury yourself in a
squalid motel drinking yourself into oblivion?"

"Until my bank account runs dry or I'm ready to move on.
I don't see how it's your concern, Padre," Boricio snapped,
anger flashing in his eyes as he turned to face The Prophet.

"I don't believe you," The Prophet said. "I think the real
reason you haven't left is that you're searching for something.
Salvation, perhaps?"

Boricio laughed, turned to the lake and stared, breathing
heavily before he turned back to The Prophet, "Salvation?
You think I'm seeking salvation? I don't know what you *think*
you know about me, but let me just explain one thing to you,
simple so you understand it: *I'm* not seeking salvation. *I'm* not
some wretched sinner like the rest of the white trash losers you
get waltzing into your church every day ending in Y. *I* don't
need the snake oil you're selling or the crutch you're offering."

Boricio stepped forward, inches from The Prophet's face,
eyes narrowed in menace, as he growled through his gritted
teeth, "I don't need you to wave your magic fucking wand and
make all my bad karma go bye-bye. So, save your talk of
salvation for the suckers willing to drop their hard-earned
dough into your collection box, *Prophet*. Or is that *Profit* with
an *F?*"

Boricio turned from The Prophet and began to walk back
up the trail.

The Prophet had clearly erred in his persuasion. "I'm
sorry," he said.

Boricio stopped in his tracks, but didn't turn.

The Prophet said, "I didn't mean to insult you. It's just
that I can see your heavy heart sinking from guilt, and I want
you to understand that God forgives. Everything."

Boricio turned and stared at The Prophet for a moment,
as his eyes filled with water. Finally, he swallowed and spoke.

"I was trying to save her," he said. "I thought I knew the right treatment. I thought I knew what to do to save her, but I only made it worse."

The Prophet wanted to know what Boricio was talking about, and was inches from asking, but he didn't want to make another mistake by interrupting the man in the midst of confession and risk him shutting down.

As Boricio told the story of his girlfriend, Rose, the woman he wanted to marry, and the car accident that had killed their unborn child along with their future together, The Prophet walked to him and found his eyes drifting past the man, settling on the black bag Boricio had yet to let out of his sight.

Something was in the bag — something more valuable than money.

Something that beckoned The Prophet as sure as The Good Lord Himself had been whispering his name since as long as he could remember.

Boricio continued, "My dad wanted us to go with one course of treatment, but I went over his head, reached out to another doctor, and asked him to try an experimental procedure. It was supposed to have worked, but . . . it didn't." His voice was right at the edge of cracking. "Rose died, and I killed her," he said.

"I'm sorry for your loss," The Prophet shook his head. He was going to tell Boricio that Rose was in a better place, as was their unborn baby. But he knew that doing so would lose Boricio for good. Instead, he said, "You did what you thought was right. Correct?"

"Yes," Boricio said.

"And you feel like maybe you were arrogant to go over your father's head, right?"

Boricio met his eyes in a moment of challenge, then looked to the dirt, nodding.

"Let me ask you this, Boricio: Did you act out of love? Did you try to save Rose from a life in pain and endless misery?"

"Yes," Boricio said, trying not to cry.

"Then you did right by her, and by The Lord." The Prophet said. "He knows you did right, and He forgives you. Now, *you* must realize you did the right thing, too. *You* must forgive yourself."

Boricio said nothing. He turned and followed The Prophet back to the truck, but then left him standing by the open driver's side door as he kept walking back down the road they'd taken to the lake.

"Where are you going?" The Prophet asked.

"Back."

"That's a long walk, Son. Do you even know where you're going?"

"I'll find my way," Boricio said as he continued to walk, taking the bag and its mystery away from The Prophet.

～

FORTY-SIX

Ryan Olson

Black Mountain, Georgia
 March 31, 2012
  FIVE MONTHS AFTER THE EVENT …

RYAN'S HEAD ached as he woke, feeling like he'd had way too much to drink, even though he couldn't remember the last time he had.

He vaguely recalled a nightmare — one he didn't want to think about now.

Mary was sleeping in bed beside him. He felt the cool breeze blowing in through the open window and watched as she breathed, her breasts rising and falling along with the soft white comforter that half covered them. He stretched out, feeling the softness of the sheets, happy beneath their comfort and warmth.

I don't ever want to leave this bed.
Every morning should be like this.
Nowhere to go, no rush to wake up.

He reached out and touched Mary's shoulder — soft and

warm — then traced his fingertips along her neck until she opened her eyes and looked at him.

"Hi, Baby," she said.

"Hi."

"What do you wanna do today?" she asked.

"Would it be horribly rude if I said 'you'?"

"Ha, ha. Didn't you get enough last night?"

Somewhere in his brain, a memory stirred from the nightmare — something hideous, chasing him.

No, don't think about the dream. This is reality.

Don't think about what happened.

Mary reached up and ran her palm over Ryan's face, then through his hair as he closed his eyes and luxuriated in the delight of her touch.

"I had the weirdest dream," she said, causing him to open his eyes and look at her.

"*You* had a weird dream? So did I. What was yours about?"

"I woke up and the whole world was gone."

"I had the same dream," he said. "That is so weird." He sat up in bed. "I was looking for you, and . . . "

Another vision from his dream flashed in his memory: a black creature with soaking-wet flesh; bright light beaming beneath its skin and rows of rotting teeth plaguing its misshapen mouth.

Ryan closed his eyes trying to shake the vision from his mind before it took over.

Oh God, I'm dreaming now. No. No. I don't want to wake up.

Stop thinking about the monsters.

I'm here, in bed with Mary. We're in Warson Woods, where everything is perfect.

He opened his eyes, and Mary smiled, "What's wrong?"

"Nothing," he shook his head. "I don't want to talk about dreams. I want to … " he didn't finish his sentence. Instead, he leaned toward her, cupped her soft face in his hands, and took in her scent.

No, this isn't a dream. You don't dream the scent of your wife.

He kissed her neck and she sighed, filling his ear with her warm breath.

He felt his cock stiffen beneath the covers.

"God, I love you," he said, leaning closer and running his open hand under the covers, over her stomach and up to her breasts, cupping the bottom of her left breast and slowly closing his fingers over her nipple which hardened at his touch.

"I love you, too," she said, reaching over and under the sheets to pull him closer.

Their moment was shattered by a scream.

He opened his eyes, startled, as she crawled frantically backward in the bed, trying to get away from him as fast as she could, her eyes wide in horror.

"What?!" was all she could gasp, staring down at him.

What's wrong?

He looked down, figuring maybe she'd seen a giant bug beneath the covers, but then he saw the source of her horror: not a bug, but his lower half, a mutated, twisted, monstrosity, with wet, luminescent black skin, twisted limbs, and something gnarled and malformed where his cock should have been.

"What are you?!" she screamed.

Ryan woke up sobbing, his heart torn by cruel reality yet again.

RYAN HAD BEEN awake for an hour or so when he felt something horribly wrong.

He had sensed something weird the day before, but wasn't sure what it was. The scientists had administered a serum, supposedly with cells from the kid, Charlie, who had somehow managed to resist the same mutation, even with infection.

It seemed like a shot in the dark — the sort of fringe science Ryan didn't understand or particularly have much faith in. But he had nothing to lose. He was all alone, in constant pain, and had been turned into some kind of half-human/half-alien monster. All Ryan had when they found him was the promise that death might end his misery.

Now, perhaps they'd given him a new gift — hope for a normal life. A cure.

Ryan felt nothing following the injections, though he'd been waiting eagerly to feel something — *anything* — different. He longed for some measurable change, for better or worse. Something to let him know for certain that things were shifting inside him.

But Ryan felt nothing, at least not until last night, when the first flush of odd started slowly flooding through his system. It was nothing he could explain, but it was definitely new, and he felt certain it had something to do with the injections.

Either way, Ryan hoped it was a good sign.

That ended this morning, an hour after waking when he suddenly found himself seeing through someone else's eyes and feeling their thoughts.

It was Charlie.

He was standing in his cell watching an old, fat, naked man in the cell next to him. Something about the old man terrified Charlie. Ryan knew because he felt Charlie's fear no differently than if he'd felt it himself.

He saw the dark thing that had once been inside the old man — the Darkness Ryan sensed spreading through the world. It was a part of the creatures that had infected him. He could feel its echoes in his blood. This Darkness was different, though, perhaps even its leader.

The Darkness flowed from the old man, into a guard, and then into Charlie.

Oh God.

Charlie's mind was then a prisoner of the Darkness, walking through the cell, carrying the guard *It* had momentarily possessed to the elevator. *It* pressed the guard's hand to the touch pad, then set *Itself* free.

The Darkness murdered the first guard it met, ripping the head clean from his body. A second guard charged the Darkness, but *It* opened Charlie's mouth and spewed out a part of itself into the air, then onto the Guardsman's face and down his throat, until *It* started to spread inside that man, too.

Ryan felt a horrible cracking inside his mind, a mental fissure from too many perspectives. He cradled his head in his hands, then dropped to his knees, screaming through the pain of his three sudden perspectives: a terrified Charlie witnessing the horror before him, the Darkness inside Charlie, and the stewing Darkness inside the Guardsman.

The Darkness continued to seep through the halls, in search of an exit. *It* wanted to follow Callie and Boricio so *It* could find someone — a child *It* wanted to kill.

As *It* met resistance, *Its* compromised Guardsman trailed beside *It*, shooting anyone trying to stop them. The Darkness and the Guardsman quickly made their way into the civilian sector, where they infected or murdered everyone in sight.

"Oh God," Ryan cried, helplessly watching from the horror in his mind.

He pounded on his cell, screaming for someone to free him so he could help.

"Open the cell! Let me out!"

No one answered.

Ryan fell to the floor, screaming and helpless.

~

FORTY-SEVEN

Boricio Wolfe

Dunn, Georgia
March 31, 2012
FIVE MONTHS AFTER THE EVENT …

BORICIO LEAPT from his bed and threw a wad of covers onto the floor, then bolted to his window, tore a handful of curtains to the side, and peered out and into the empty yard below.

Boricio was certain he'd see something outside, sitting there like danger waiting to hatch. But the yard was empty, unlike Boricio's overburdened mind.

He'd had another beer-battered bullshit of a dream; fucked up beyond all reason, this one with him marching over every end of the impossible. He'd spent his last few hours sleeping, lost in a neverending eternity of demons in hell, and Monopoly games with Rip van Creepy, except van Creepy was a little kid again. And the dreams were weirder for how real they seemed, as if he weren't *just dreaming* — he was seeing something yet to come.

He went into the bathroom, took a shit, then threw on his

shoes and returned to the window, shook off the haze of déjà vu and stared outside at all the empty he wasn't expecting to see.

Boricio wondered why he couldn't shake the weird feeling. Maybe it was a scent in the air that most of his mind was too stupid to understand but some other part of him picked up on and was filtering forward and telling him, "Hey, pay attention, fucker!"

As he'd been telling Paola while trying to show the girl how to shoot straight, some shit you knew faster than you thought. That sorta crazy shit happened in nature all the time. It was people that ignored it. Boricio read about how some botanists at some college infected a group of tobacco plants with a virus. Within days, another group of plants near the infected ones sensed the danger, and produced a chemical in their leaves to protect themselves.

That was crazy shit. And this shit was like that shit, though Boricio didn't quite know how, or what he was sniffing. Because he didn't understand the scent in the air, he didn't know what to do. He took a final look outside before turning from the window.

It was probably just the unease of sleeping without anyone in the house able to stand guard. Boricio hadn't had a decent night's sleep since back when he was bunking with Charlie and the rest of the boys. If he couldn't relax enough to get some decent shut eye, it meant he was either always awake, or haunted by nightmares.

He was majorly on edge, still a bit drunk from his late night shooting the shit with Mary, and just a little fucking exhausted. Ever since he'd healed Luca and aged a decade, he'd yet to feel the same kind of energy he had just a month ago.

But at least he wasn't hungover. Boricio didn't get hangovers. No matter how much he drank, Boricio couldn't remember a single time where he had felt fucked up the following day. Level of consumption made no matter. Boricio could drink himself anywhere from tipsy to totally fuckered, then wake up the next morning with a fanny cleaver fat enough to fuck the remainder of the day.

Frequency of drink didn't mean dick either. Whether Boricio got himself drunk three times a week or three times in one day, inebriation faded equally fast. He would collapse into bed, drunk, then wake eight or so hours later, hungry as fuck. But this morning, Boricio was suffering from a helluva dry mouth, a slight headache that threatened to start pounding, and a flash of irritability at how shit in his head was messier than a murder scene.

Boricio grabbed his knife and gun, then shoved them both into his pants before leaving his bedroom and heading downstairs.

Boricio could smell the pancakes. They had 800 or so giant bags of pancake mix, and an equal amount of syrup that Charlie and the crew had grabbed up a while ago from a Costco, excited as if they'd hit the lottery. Unfortunately, pancakes didn't have the protein Boricio was constantly craving, and preferred first thing in the morning. Judging from the speed at which they were shoving forkfuls into their mouths yesterday, Paola and Luca seemed to be loving them like stupid kids usually did.

But Boricio was starting to worry about the lack of protein, for him and for all of them. They'd need to make a run soon to find some beef jerky, beans, or start hunting some fresh meat. Too many shitty carbs made you fat, slow, and stupid.

And being fat, slow, and stupid was a one-way ticket to the morgue post-Oct. 15.

Boricio stepped into the large dining room, then looked over at Mary tending to a pancake on the portable stove.

"Morning, Miss Mary," he said, looking around the dining room, surprised to see he'd beat both Paola and Luca downstairs, despite the pounding in his head. "Where are the Happy Meals?"

She looked up. "Well, good morning. I'm surprised to see you walking."

Mary smiled, and Boricio was surprised to find himself liking it, and without a dirty thought to chase it.

"Paola's been up for a while," Mary said. "She went upstairs to wake Luca, since he's still sleeping. I'm surprised you guys didn't cross one another in the hall. Want a pancake?" She lifted the pancake with a fork, then set it on a wide plate and held it out for Boricio.

It was the light-brown color of a beautiful woman; Boricio couldn't have cooked it better himself. He raised his eyebrows and nodded. "Thanks," he said, taking the plate and wishing the hammers would stop slamming nails into his skull.

Paola came running downstairs, then spilled into the dining room. "Mom," she cried, her voice slightly high and flying way too fast to not have trouble chasing behind it.

"What is it, Honey?" Mary moved her eyes from the frying batter to Paola.

"It's Luca. He's not waking up. And there's nothing I can do. I keep calling him and shaking him, and I even punched him in the arm once I worked up the courage to do it, but nothing is working."

"Is he breathing?" Mary asked.

"I . . . I think so."

"What do you mean, 'you *think* so'?" Boricio said, his mouth full of pancake. "Fuckers either suck air or don't. There ain't no in-between when it comes to breathing. Is Rip Van Creepy sucking air or not?"

Paola said, "I guess so, but not very much."

Well, FUCK!

Boricio dropped his plate onto the counter, then bolted up the stairs and charged into Luca's room.

The man-kid had to be okay. It wasn't even that Boricio

cared, necessarily; it was that the old fucker was stringing the shit of their world together. He couldn't explain it, even to himself, but Boricio somehow knew that without Luca things would take a sharp detour into Fuckedsville.

"Hey, buddy," Boricio yelled, a foot into his room. "Time to stop dreaming about the *Golden Girls*. Wake up, and I promise we'll find you some granny porn, so you can tug your raisin."

One look at Luca, and Boricio understood why Paola wasn't sure if he was breathing. He looked damned close to dead.

Boricio dropped to a knee and started to shake Luca.

"Is he okay?" Mary asked, suddenly in the room even though Boricio hadn't heard her come in.

Before Boricio could answer, the sound of an engine roared from the front yard, then up into the room, bringing Boricio another sting of déjà vu.

Engines meant enemies and enemies meant fights. Fights likely meant death. Even if that death was dealt to someone other than Boricio, it was an inconvenience to his morning quiet.

Boricio leapt from the bedside and was at the window in a second, peeling the curtains aside. He turned to the girls. "A black van. Looks like it's been beat to hell."

His eyes returned to the window, then Boricio suddenly broke into a grin as the passenger door opened and Callie stepped out. He turned to Mary and said, "Holy fuck yeah, I know her."

Boricio was smiling, though it faded like a hot fog when he saw the ugly mother fucker, bald as an 8-ball, and wearing Bluebeard's eye patch, climb from the driver's side. Something about the way the asshole was walking, gave Boricio the same wretched sense of déjà vu he'd felt when waking that morning, then again a minute before.

This shit isn't right.

Two fresh fuckers — a guy who looked like former military and then a pasty faced soft guy who looked to be in his early thirties — joined the party.

Boricio didn't know who the three fuckers with Callie were. He only knew that he wanted to murder the Jolly Roger before he had the chance to open his big, ugly mouth. Something about the man made Boricio immediately angry. But something else about him made Boricio *almost* want to run and hide, something no man had ever made him want to do before.

Fucking Luca broke me. And now he's gonna die before he can fix me!

It was good to see Callie, but if she was a hostage, and those men meant to harm her, or him, or anyone on Team Boricio, well then they had minutes to live, whether Boricio was frightened or not.

He closed the curtains and turned to Mary.

"I need you to stay upstairs," he said. "You know the drill: Don't come down for dick." He looked from Paola to Mary, all four eyes on his, then over to Luca, who was finally starting to lightly snore — a good sign, even though he still lay there looking mostly dead. "Go to my room and get my shotgun, get Little Lamb her peashooter, then both of you stay in here with Luca. I want all three of you in the same place. Got it?"

"Got it," Mary said. "What are you going to do?"

"I'm gonna take my two friends Peacemaker and Snaggletooth, then go downstairs and see what needs to be seen." Boricio lifted his shirt and showed Mary his pistol and sheathed knife pressed against the tan canvas of his tight abs.

"Okay," Mary said, swallowing. Paola trembled beside her.

Boricio nodded again, left the room, then ran down the hallway to the stairs, leapt them in a trio of strides, and jumped past the bottom four, quickly eclipsing the distance between living room and front door.

Boricio could see the three fuckers and Callie out the window, but mostly as blurs and shapes. His hand was a foot from the knob before he saw the shit that soured his throat and held his breath hostage.

No.

No fucking way.

It isn't possible.

Boricio had seen plenty of beer-battered bullshit, and about a billion pounds of goddamn impossible since he woke up too fucking early on October 15, lucky to wake up at all, wondering if the woman he cut had disappeared like all the rest of the planet's fuck-all.

This was something different.

This changed the meaning of the goddamn word impossible.

Boricio swung the front door and stared into the eye of the bald scarred man; a horrible man with an intelligent stare.

The man who looked exactly like him, but fugly.

Like the man's looks, his voice was Boricio's, even though it wasn't quite.

Boricio tore his eyes from Fugly, then turned them to Callie who seemed shockingly calm, especially since she was standing right beside the impossible, and even tilting her head so she could see it from all sides.

"Good morning, Boricio," said the fugly fucker who couldn't possibly exist. "We've come for Luca."

～

FORTY-EIGHT

Boricio Bishop

Kingsland, Alabama
Oct. 13, 2011
TWO DAYS BEFORE THE EVENT ...

THE DREAMS WERE GETTING WORSE.

Boricio woke with his nose curling at the scent of Jack soaked into his collar. He swung his feet to the floor, rose from bed, then went to the motel window and stared outside at the empty parking lot, and the few beat to hell cars, including an ancient Chevy.

Boricio's dreams, as they had been for the last month, were a special sort of bullshit, and worse for their razored edge of reality.

He went to the bathroom, took a shit, then put on his shoes and collapsed back onto the mattress, wondering if today would be the day he'd finally get the fuck out of Dodge. New Orleans was about seven hours away. If he left this morning he could be there by the end of the day and starting his new life tomorrow.

Boricio was sick of dreaming about Rose, sick of hearing

her final screams screeching every time he closed his eyes, and sick of thinking about the goddamned vials.

He was awake for several minutes before realizing he was still slightly drunk. He'd never had a hangover before, at least nothing beyond a mild headache. He'd never thrown up, at least not from too much alcohol, though the bottle of Jack he'd spilled on himself while falling to sleep the night before made him want to wake with a Technicolor yawn.

Boricio glanced over at the empty bottle, and felt almost happy for the draught. One more reason to shift gears and get the fuck out of town. He was drinking too damned much, even though the too much felt like it was barely enough while he was doing it. Becoming a drunk was too easy, and Boricio had known too many men who were too stupid to live any other way. That was the problem with alcohol: You drank to forget and drank to celebrate. And if you didn't have anything to mourn or memorialize, well hell, you could just drink while waiting.

Boricio wished that so much of his last few months weren't swirled in such a blur. He was having a difficult time separating truth from horror, and the past he was trying to flee. He wasn't sure where the true lines lay between nightmare and reality. Time had turned soupy, and while the calendar clearly said Oct. 13, Boricio could hardly believe so much time had passed since his last time behind the wheel of the Mini-Cooper.

When Boricio fled Black Island, he was searching for the time and space to find himself anywhere else and away from everyone's reach — he longed to find a place beyond the flow of time.

But Boricio had found nothing like that at all. He found The Prophet instead.

It was odd, how much Boricio felt drawn to The New Unity Church, even though he knew religion was bullshit. Even smart theology left you with two choices: Either man was one of God's fuck-ups, or He was one of theirs. Boricio found the second one far easier to believe.

Before walking through the front door of New Unity, Boricio would have claimed, gun to head, that God was definitely not good. Religion was a crutch for the weak, giving you nothing you couldn't get for free, costing plenty you shouldn't have ever had to spend, and ultimately, worth exactly the same squirt of piss it was worth before your ass ever kissed the flat of the pew.

Yet mankind was largely religious, which in Boricio's estimation made people slightly dumber than most animals, since most animals were smart enough to kill for food and protect their young, without being dumb enough to murder another just because their two theories end-to-end failed to make a straight line. It was bullshit, but the truth: Two religions in a valley meant war. Add another dozen and you had enlightenment.

When the old man first started talking about Oct. 15 and the Judgment Day right behind it, Boricio thought he was crazier than a sewer rat. But that was before he said something that momentarily bleached the marrow from Boricio's bones.

The old man had been giving one of his two daily sermons a few nights earlier, about 90 minutes or so before Boricio started emptying his bottle of Jack. He said, "There is no power, short of the gentle hands of The Good Lord Himself, that can pry the secrets from the depths of the human heart."

After he said the word "heart," the old man kept going on and on and on like he always did, except this time Boricio seemed to know every word before it left the old man's mouth. When the old man started talking about standing at the empty well, even describing it down to the pile of bricks beside it, Boricio could see the same well, same as he'd seen in his dreams. Then, when he started talking about the end of it all and the beginning of everything else, Boricio could see it like he did in his dreams, staring down from space at the world, where everything was turning to black like pixels fading from a dying screen.

In that sermon, the old man somehow changed from a smarmy evangelist to something Boricio didn't quite understand, but he was just curious enough to stick around and figure out. The longer Boricio spent around the old man, the more it seemed as though he'd known him, or at least had been dreaming of him, forever. Boricio couldn't tell if that was true, or just part of a larger illusion.

The old man certainly took himself seriously, and carried himself with dignity, but everyone on TV, from news anchors to folks on the street, loudly testified to his lunacy. Of course, Boricio knew one-sided when he saw it. He'd seen plenty of people praising the old man, twice a day for a week, though he never saw the anchors or the interviewers on the news getting *their side* of the story.

The TV talking heads made fun of "The Prophet," crafting jokes and casting him as anything from a raving idiot to a master of deception. Boricio hadn't untangled the second part yet, but knew the first one was downright ridiculous. Anyone who failed to see the intelligence in the old man's eyes a second after staring inside them had to be idiots themselves. And anyone who hadn't looked into his eyes didn't have a right to pound their nails into a rickety bridge of opinion. Assholes were entitled to their own opinions, but not to their own set of facts. Hell, even an 8-year-old knew that.

Boricio suddenly missed Luca with a flare of fierce intensity, as though his little brother could make his world orbit like it did back when everything was better. As if Luca could give him permission to start living, without having to wake in the morning with the scent of Jack on his collar.

Given the time, Luca should be alone, assuming he was

still being home schooled, or maybe with Sarah, but when Boricio called, Will answered on the first ring.

"Hello?"

Boricio was silent.

"Hello?"

Still nothing.

"Is that you, Boricio?"

Will gave Boricio a minute to respond, but Boricio only chewed the air without hanging up.

"I'm sorry, Boricio," Will finally said. "Please, talk to me."

Boricio thought of telling the old man to fuck himself, maybe with something sharp, but silenced the line instead.

He dropped the phone in his pocket, where it buzzed seven or so seconds later. Boricio pulled it back out, looked at the screen to see what he already knew, then opened his nightstand drawer and dropped the phone inside with a thunk before slamming it shut.

He heard a knock at the door, so in time with the slamming drawer that Boricio wondered if it was his imagination.

Three more knocks said it wasn't.

Boricio went to the door and opened it to the round face of the old man, split a third down the middle with the widest smile Boricio had seen before breakfast in months.

"Care to have a talk over drinks?"

Boricio scratched his head. "You kidding, Father? You've any idea how early it is?"

The old man said, "I'm not a Father, just a humble servant of The Good Lord. My cloth gets stained before it gets in the wash, no different from yours." He smiled even wider and patted Boricio on his shoulder. "Besides, I'm not drinking anything but the blood of Christ, and all times of day are great for that. And you," he shook his head, "well, you're not having anything but the hair of the dog that bit you, and I can't see a lick of harm in that."

The Prophet added, "Woe unto them that rise up early in

the morning, that they may follow strong drink," then winked. "Isaiah 5:11."

Boricio said, "Doesn't that verse mean we're *not* supposed to drink?"

"Nope, Son," The Prophet shook his head. "It sounds exactly like permission granted to me." He winked again, then said, "I'll be right back."

The old man nodded at a now smiling Boricio, then disappeared to his F-150, returning a minute later with a full bottle of Jack — replacing the single drop Boricio had left — and a black wine bottle with a large rooster on the label, and a gold twist-top instead of a cork, plus two red plastic cups.

The Prophet set both bottles on the small table in Boricio's room, then turned to Boricio. "What'll it be?"

Boricio said, "Jack, please. I can't trust wine without a cork."

"Corks don't make the wine taste better," The Prophet argued.

"Yeah, but it's how wine's supposed to be finished. Would you listen to a sermon that didn't mention God?"

"That's different."

"Nope," Boricio shook his head. "I don't think it is."

"People want things easy, and don't always have a bottle opener."

Boricio didn't want to argue. He said, "Wine is poetry in a bottle; sunlight, held together by water. The cork is the final verse. I'm not interested in your savior's blood this morning, Padre."

Boricio watched The Prophet, blinking twice as fast while breathing half as slow, trying not to look a quarter flustered as he was, probably trying to figure out how to talk to a man like Boricio — not just the man he was, but the man he was becoming, a man unwilling to wait for the world to tell him who he was.

Boricio wanted to know why the old man was in his room.

If he was drinking this early in the morning, he was likely holding onto a special sort of bullshit he was ready to shovel onto Boricio's plate.

Boricio sipped his Jack beside the old man, more out of curiosity than anything else. Because there was already alcohol in his blood, it was only a half hour or so before he was well on his way to demolished — even though he'd yet to wring his liver from the evening before.

The old man started talking about the coming prophecy again, and Boricio found himself swaying back and forth in half belief. "You know I haven't just been dreaming of this day for years," The Prophet said. "I've been dreaming of *you*."

Boricio felt an icy chill, not just because he was slowly and inexplicably starting to believe, but because he'd been dreaming of the old man too.

The Prophet must have noticed the look on Boricio's face, because he started to question him like a prisoner. "You've dreamed of me, too, haven't you?"

Boricio nodded because anything else would've been a lie screaming inside him.

The old man said, "This isn't a mistake, Boricio." He shook his head back and forth so fast it looked like it had batteries. "God doesn't make mistakes. You and me," he clapped his hand on Boricio's shoulder. "The Good Lord has brought us together, given us a special acquaintance so we could do something as one. Something special." He paused, then, "Something that's never been done on His green Earth before."

Boricio didn't know what to say, so he said nothing. A few minutes faded into five before the old man relieved his bottle of its final drops, then filled Boricio's red cup with another few shots of fuel.

"What can you tell me about the vial, Boricio?"

Boricio suddenly wanted to leap from his chair, and fly toward the old man and start beating his face in.

How the fuck does he know about the vial?

The Prophet was either exactly who he said, or what Boricio feared he might be.

"How do you know about the vial?"

"Same as everything else, Son — when He whispers, I listen."

The old man reached out to Boricio. "Our time is right now," he said.

No, this isn't right.

Boricio stood, then said, "Of all bad men, men of the cloth can be the worst."

The last word was the hardest. His head started to swim, and Boricio wondered how long it had been since he'd felt so drunk.

Except it wasn't drunk, not exactly.

He collapsed to the edge of the bed as the world went dancing in circles.

"What is it, Son?" the old man asked. "Tell me what's in the vial."

Boricio's heart was pounding. He had to reach his bag, make sure the vial was safe.

He rose from the bed again, then swayed but stayed on his feet, swerving back and forth like a pendulum as he tried to keep himself steady.

But he couldn't.

Boricio tried to ask the old man what in the fuck he had done to him, but his words, like his breath, were trapped in his throat.

He collapsed to the floor and fell into a fresh abyss.

~

FORTY-NINE

Ryan Olson

Black Mountain, Georgia
March 31, 2012
FIVE MONTHS AFTER THE EVENT ...

RYAN TRIED to cover his ears from the sound of the braying alarm, buzzing on and off for what seemed an eternity until someone finally appeared outside his cell door.

It was Lisa, one of the Guardsmen who'd found him and brought him to Black Mountain. She was covered in a bucket of blood and sweat, though as far as Ryan could see, none of the blood appeared to be hers.

"Something got in here, or escaped," she said.

"I know," Ryan said, standing. Her shotgun was still in her hand, but she, along with several others, had come to trust him, so it wasn't aimed at him. "I saw. They're doing some sort of experiment, which somehow linked me to the kid, Charlie. Now I can see inside his head."

"Whoa," Lisa said. "That's crazy." Then, "Does that mean you can tell us what in the hell he's doing?"

"He's not the Charlie you know," Ryan said. "He's been

compromised. Something else came in here, in the body of an old fat man they threw in the cell next to Charlie's."

"The Prophet?"

Ryan thought for a moment. He didn't recall the thing thinking of itself as any name, let alone The Prophet, so he shrugged. "I dunno."

He asked, "How many are dead?"

"A lot. Dead, or infected," Lisa said. "And the weirdest thing, most of the infected people are mutating immediately — like you, but without your control. It's happening so fast — I've never seen anything like it."

"Why are you in here?" he asked.

"I need your help. I know what you're capable of," she said. "We've gotta save Billy."

"Who's Billy?"

"This kid I found on our last trip out. He was alone, scared shitless. I told him I'd protect him. He's three levels down, and the thing is making its way toward him right now." She looked in what was left of Ryan's eyes. "Do you need a gun?"

He looked back, then held up his right hand, deformed and ending in a blackened claw, "Can't use one. And don't need one. But I'm glad to see you trust me enough to give me one." He tried to smile but his face hurt too much.

"Don't make me regret it," she said.

THEY STEPPED from the elevator and into a long hallway on a residential level. The alarm continued to buzz, with bright-red lights spaced every 40 feet or so blinking along the ceiling.

The halls were splattered with blood, black liquid, and too many corpses to count. "Jesus Christ," Lisa said, staring at the carnage in horror.

Ryan's elevated senses picked up on two heartbeats nearby,

at the end of the hallway, in one of the rooms to the left. "I can sense two people here, though one heartbeat is way faster than the other," he said to Lisa, pointing toward the far end of the hall. "But I don't think they're mutants or the aliens. I sense them differently."

"Is one of them Billy?"

"I dunno," he shook his head, slowly making his way down the hall.

Before they reached the door, Ryan sensed someone behind it. He turned to Lisa. "Maybe you should go in first, so I don't scare whoever's inside."

"Good idea," she said, then stepped through the doorway, which slid open at her approach.

The door slid closed behind her, leaving Ryan alone in the hall, standing beneath a blinking red light, listening to the alarm, which was growing increasingly annoying.

Lisa was taking forever inside the room. Ryan wondered if something had happened. Perhaps the person was hiding, or maybe they'd left the room. He considered going inside, but was still worried about scaring whoever was in there, or worse, having them mistake him for a monster and opening fire when he stepped through the door.

After a while, Lisa came out of the room with a 20-something, dark-haired woman, looking 10 months pregnant judging by the way her belly pushed tight against her black dress. Her eyes were two confused saucers.

"She doesn't speak English," Lisa said.

"So, what are we doing now?"

"We're gonna get her out of here," Lisa said. "To somewhere safe."

"I think she's safer here," Ryan said. "I can feel them, too many, out there, roaming the halls on the other floors."

"Yeah, but if we leave her here, she's defenseless. Once they get to this level she's done."

Ryan looked at the woman, and sensed the two heartbeats,

hers, along with the child inside her, both beats thrumming like drums in his head.

He wondered if the Darkness, the aliens, or the other mutants could sense people as well, or maybe even better than him. If so, it was only a matter of time before humanity was picked like every cherry from a tree, or transformed into Darkness.

"Come," Lisa said, waving them back toward a connecting hallway. "Can you sense anyone else? Can you sense Charlie?"

Ryan stopped and closed his eyes, searching for Charlie's signal, like trying to tune his mind to a distant radio station.

In his head, he could hear hundreds of echoes from dozens of different sounds — clicking, shrieking, and even random grabs of thought in garbled clicks and beeps. Whatever the sounds were, they likely made sense when passed among the aliens and mutants, but Ryan couldn't untangle the noise, despite his condition.

Most of him was grateful.

He could also see some of the same images the creatures saw as they scoured hallways searching for humans to either murder or draw into their collective Darkness. Each time a fresh body was absorbed Ryan felt a small surge in power. He wondered if the other monsters felt it, too, then swallowed with a sickening certainty, knowing that they did.

We're their food.

As he tuned his senses through the endless assault of sound and image, Ryan found Charlie and the Guardsman — outside the mountain, roaring down the road in a van.

"They're in a van, heading toward wherever Boricio went," he said.

"Shit!" Lisa yelled. "Then we've gotta get to the tunnel and get the fuck outta here now!"

"Why? Are we going after them?"

"We have to," she said. "We've gotta warn Boricio and the

others. They have no idea that something is coming after them."

"You have a radio, don't you?" Ryan said. "Can't you call?"

"I tried, but I'm not getting through. Had problems with reception out there before, too."

Ryan looked around, trying to think of what they should do next. Upstairs, one of the mutants seized on someone, sinking its razored teeth into their neck. It was a young boy. Billy. Ryan felt a refreshing surge of energy rush through his body, could taste the blood in his mouth, and feel the beautiful agony of the boy being bitten.

He closed his eyes, trying to shake the images — and the feelings — from his head.

"What's wrong?" Lisa asked.

"I can feel it . . . "

"Feel what?"

"All of it — all the suffering, all the energy. All of it."

"Energy?"

As his pain started receding, Ryan explained how he could taste the blood, and feel the same energy the creatures felt when they entered someone's body. Each shell absorbed became part of the collective, adding to their power — magnifying the volume in his head, and moving it from intense to nearly unbearable.

"I think they got Billy," he said.

"Are you sure?" Lisa asked, her face going pale.

"Yes, I see glimpses of his memories. I see you with him."

"Fuck!" she cried out.

For a moment he thought she might break down right there. He had to get them moving before it became impossible to do so.

"Let's go," he said, taking the lead, and following Charlie's memory toward the tunnel. They turned down another hall and were close to the tunnel, when Ryan sensed five mutants in the hallway before he could hear them.

"Wait here," he said, turning to Lisa and the terrified pregnant woman.

Ryan went through the door, and immediately sensed how the mutants saw him.

He was just another one of them — a relieving yet horrifying thought.

How much longer until I'm exactly like them?

The group of mutants was made up of two Guardsmen and three civilians, all male. All but one were hybrid mutants like him, slightly more human than alien, though no less deadly. The last one was nearly mutated in full, its skin all black and slippery wet, both hands already twisted to claws, with a wide mouth rowed high and low with razor sharp teeth.

Ryan sensed something new: They'd picked up on the women outside the hallway. They felt a hunger, an immediate craving, which Ryan felt building inside him as well — like sympathy hunger pains. They started toward him, on their way to the door, moving slowly, as if not quite sure how to regard or navigate past him.

Ryan had to protect the women.

He took a swing at the first mutant, his claw slicing through the man's neck, as a gallon of dark-red and almost-black blood seemed to pour from him at once.

One down.

The other mutants turned on him, shrieking and clawing and charging forward with rage. One of their hands caught his ribs and sliced into his slippery skin.

Ryan screamed, then twisted from its grip before the clawed blade could do any more damage. He brought his own clawed hand up and through the fucker's neck, then thrust up and sideways, killing him instantly.

Each time Ryan killed one of the mutants he felt sharp pains where he had inflicted the injuries. The pain was so intense it was nearly blinding. It took Ryan a full minute to shake the feeling, though the pain lingered as he allowed the mutant to slip through his still human hand.

Two down.

Ryan had no time to celebrate his win. The mutant behind him, fully transformed, with the razored teeth to prove it, roared toward him, snapping its jaw on the way to his shoulder.

Ryan dropped to the ground and pumped his legs, thrusting them both up, sending the mutant flying into the wall behind them. Ryan leapt on top of its body, savagely swinging his gnarled claw, tearing into the mutant's guts, driven by a blend of human rage and alien instincts.

Three down.

Wait, where are the others?

He heard the shotgun and felt an intensity of pain, no different from if he himself had been shot. Ryan could see through the dying mutant's eyes — it was still standing, swaying over where it had just knocked Lisa to the ground.

Ryan saw through the other mutant's vision as well, as it attacked the pregnant woman.

The mutant knocked her to the floor, ripped the dress from her body, then opened its maw, sinking its teeth into her full stomach.

Ryan wanted to rush to the door, but was overwhelmed by a sudden flood of disgust as the creature tore the woman open, then pulled the fetus from inside her and started to feast.

He fell back against the wall, then turned and vomited. He looked up as he heard a second shotgun blast, killing the mutant attacking Lisa.

Ryan rushed through the doors, blinded by pain and disgust, but at the same time, relishing the surge of power coming from the mutant feasting on the dying woman's baby.

He launched himself into the air, and landed on top of the remaining mutant as the half-eaten bloody baby fell to the ground in a sickening wet thud. The pregnant woman screamed, one hand on her open guts, the second reaching for her dead baby, both eyes wide in horror.

Ryan unleashed his rage, screaming as he sliced the mutant's throat to an open vent, then plunged his claw into the mutant's burning eyes, gouging them one at a time.

Ryan collapsed to the ground, shaking, crying, and screaming all at once as he stared at the pregnant woman, dead and cradling what was left of her baby in her frozen hands, eyes open to the heavens as if to beg for an answer to "Why?"

Lisa stared at the woman, eyes tearing, unable to move.

Ryan, now on his knees and shaking, stared up at Lisa, "I'm so sorry," he said. "They got past me."

She stared back, and Ryan felt the rage bleeding from her. Maybe it wasn't meant for him, but Ryan couldn't tell the difference. She marched toward him, gritted her teeth, then raised her shotgun to his head.

Her hands started shaking as Ryan met her eyes and begged her.

"Please, kill me. Kill me now."

~

FIFTY

Boricio Bishop

Kingsland, Alabama
Oct. 15, 2011
THE DAY OF THE EVENT ...

BORICIO WAS CHAINED TO A WALL, in reality and in dream.

The last few minutes, which felt like hours of Boricio's fear-battered dream, was spent chained to a dungeon wall as a long line of grotesque demons whipped his body, lashing his back as they screamed through his life's atrocities line by line, starting with the earliest — stabbing Cricket Branson with a Bic pen when he was four — and ending with his last few month's worth of personal terrible before finding the end and starting over again.

The violation the demons kept wanting Boricio to repeat over and over and over again was the one where he murdered Rose from behind the wheel of her Mini Cooper, before leading his own father to finish her forever.

The shackles followed him into the waking world. He was in an underground room with shackles on the walls to either side of him. On the wall to his right was a stairway, all of it lit by a low bulb hanging from a chain in the center of the room.

The whole thing seemed like something out of some old pervert's makeshift sex dungeon.

Where the fuck did The Prophet go?

What did he do with the vial?

He screamed, his bellow fueled by rage and filled with fury. It was also fueled by self-loathing for having been duped by a so-called man of God.

As if on cue, The Prophet descended down the stairs less than a minute later. He removed his hat, set it on a wooden table in the middle of the room, then turned to Boricio.

"I'm so sorry," he said, shaking his head like he was mourning tragedy instead of making it with his own two hands.

Boricio wanted to murder the old man, and probably would have if his wrists weren't keeping him prisoner. He imagined his free hands digging all eight digits and a set of thumbs into the pasty white of the fat fucker's turkey neck.

Boricio yanked against his chains, growling.

"Truly I am," The Prophet continued. "I didn't want it to be this way, Boricio. And so I prayed to The Good Lord that it wouldn't be. But," he shook his head, "His way is the only way."

The old man sighed, taking a moment before he continued. "I had truly hoped for the two of us, you and me together as The Good Lord intended to usher in the Rapture. Yet, because The Good Lord is good enough to give us free will, He also knows I can only lead you to the water." He shook his head. "I can't make you sip from the chalice any more than I can keep you from chewing on the apple. And if I'm to pick one of two dreams, either the one where The Good Lord gives us all Salvation, or the one where He gives us Salvation *and* you're smart enough to make yourself a part of it, well, I imagine you can see how my choice is clear as a proper Alabama sky. I chose you, Son. But that doesn't mean I'll let Satan whisper in my ear long enough to let the other one go."

Boricio was still growling, but the old man stepped into it, patting him on the shoulder.

Boricio wished the man had been fool enough to get within biting range.

"So, I really am truly sorry, but I'd be negligent if I didn't give my gratitude, both to you and to The Good Lord for sending you to me. Now I know exactly what I need to do, and I'm eternally thankful to you for that, Boricio. While He will recognize my good works, I am sure He will reward you for your part."

The Prophet wasn't just crazy, he was insane. And the joker's smile on his face was proof.

It was the same kind of insanity that had moved Boricio from thinking of himself as a stain on the planet to the possible caretaker of its safety. Boricio didn't know what the vial would do, but knew it could do something terrible, and he could tell by The Prophet's dancing eyes that he was ready to find out exactly what that meant.

Boricio breathed his way to calm. "Please," he said. "Don't do anything with the vial. You don't know what you're dealing with."

"Well, that may be true, Son. But that's why I asked you to tell me," the old man said. "I tried to make you a part of this, Boricio. Truly, I did." His voice dropped an octave. "There's nothing I wanted more. But I could tell 'round about your third cup of Jack that it was time to prepare a different sort of sermon between us."

"You can't do this," Boricio thrashed against his chains. "I'll tell you whatever you want to know; I'll help you with your church." Boricio pleaded. "Whatever you want, as long as I can have that vial back."

Boricio flashed back to what the serum had done to Rose.

The serum he felt he had somehow tainted. What might it do if The Prophet opened it? Would it turn him into a beast, also? Or would it give him abilities as it had done to Luca?

Boricio wasn't willing to sit back and see what might happen. He had to talk sense into The Prophet.

But how the fuck do you talk sense into the insane?

"The vial is dangerous," Boricio said. "It killed my girlfriend!"

The Prophet smiled and said, "Did you know that the vial thinks?" the old man said. "I mean truly *thinking*, no different from you or me? Well," he smiled. "It's actually quite different from you and me. All I mean to say is that it knows it's alive, like we do, and it wants to be more alive, and live longer, just like us. I suppose any one of us breathing can relate to that. Well, I'll tell you, Boricio, I was happy to hear its voice, especially speaking to me so clear the way it did. The way He does. It helped me sort through quite a few of my more pressing mysteries, and now I feel like I'm ready for The Good Lord, which I must confess," he laughed, "is quite a relief on a day like today."

The Prophet patted Boricio on the shoulder again, then turned and started toward the stairs.

"Tonight is the night," he said as he reached the bottom step, "that has been foretold, and there is nothing I can, or would, do to change it. But as I said, Boricio, I believe you were meant for much greater things." He pulled a set of keys from the hook by the stairway then dangled them in the air. "If you can prove you have a place for Jesus in your heart, I'd be happy to make your wishes come true the next time I'm down here."

Boricio motioned for the old man to come closer. The Prophet smiled and started walking toward the wall. When he was just a few feet away, Boricio shot a giant ball of saliva right into the old man's face.

The Prophet lost his smile, then pulled a handkerchief

from his pocket and wiped his face. He said, "Such a shame," then shook his head like he'd just seen a puppy shot. "We could've done something special together."

The old man returned the keys to the hook, then creaked his way up the stairs and out of the dungeon.

Boricio was already thinking about Luca before the old man left, but the second he heard the door close above, Boricio closed his eyes and tried to pull his brother to his mind.

Luca.

Nothing.

Luca!

Nothing.

I need you, Luca, please. If you can hear me, we all need you. Now.

Nothing.

Boricio remembered Luca's horrible dreams after he began getting his abilities, back when Will was battering his little brother with test after test. Luca would wake in the middle of the night, sometimes alert, and often screaming about the Terrible Scary.

I'm in the Terrible Scary right now, Luca. I need you to help me.

Boricio was starting to feel a state or two past stupid for trying to *speak* to his brother when he was a thousand miles away.

But Boricio had seen the kid manage the impossible before.

Luca!

Suddenly, Luca answered.

"Boricio?" His voice didn't sound like it was in his head. Luca sounded like he was three feet away.

Yes, it's me. I need your help.

"Where are you?" Luca asked.

I'm in Alabama.

"Alabama! Why are you in Alabama?"

Long story, but I promise I'll tell it to you. Right now, I need your help.

"What can I do?"

I need you to come get me. Come to where I am. Can you do that?

"I don't know," Luca said. "Alabama is far away."

Not as far as Las Orillas.

"But I know Las Orillas. I used to live there."

Just think about me. It will work.

Boricio didn't know if it really would, but was likely dead if it didn't. And God only knew how many more might die if The Prophet opened up the vial and unleashed a mutant plague on the world.

There was a long silence, and Boricio thought his brother may have disappeared. Just as he was about to call for Luca again, Luca spoke.

"Okay," he said. This time he sounded even closer.

Boricio opened his eyes and saw Luca standing in front of him, wearing his blue flannel pajamas.

Despite the danger, Boricio couldn't help but smile. "I missed you," he said, tears in his eyes.

His brother looked angry. "Is that why you called me?" After a second, Luca added, "I'm using sarcasm."

"I'm sorry," Boricio shook his head. "I should've called before now, and I'm sorry I didn't."

"You did call, the other day," Luca said. "Then you hung up on Dad."

"I'm sorry," Boricio said to the floor. "Really I am, Luca. But can we talk about it later? I need you to help me right now."

"What do you want me to do?"

Boricio nodded toward the keys on the wall. "I need you to get those keys and unlock these shackles." He nudged his nose toward his left wrist, then to his right.

Luca pulled the keys from the hook and unlocked his shackles.

Boricio's arms fell free. He gently grabbed his brother by the shoulders, lightly spun him around, then looked him in the eyes and said, "I need you to go home, Luca. Okay?"

Luca shook his head. "Not without you."

"You have to," Boricio said. "I promise I'll come home after this is over, but I have to take care of some stuff first, and I need you to leave before I do. Right now, Luca, for your own good. Okay?"

Luca stared at Boricio, his nostrils flaring and mouth pursed into a tiny O.

He shook his head. "You have to come home now. Dad misses you. So do I."

Boricio felt like time was moving at triple speed.

Luca shook his head no.

"Please, buddy. Do this for me. Just trust me. I promise — on you and Will and Rose and everything I've ever loved or will ever love again. I'm on my way home right now, and you can even tell Will I said so. I just have to take care of one thing and then I'll leave, okay?"

Luca slowly nodded, but didn't say goodbye. He was simply there, and then he wasn't.

Boricio ran from the basement, then outside into the night, frantically searching for the old man and finding him nowhere. The lights in the church were on. Inside, he could see that church was in session, and realized with a sudden, horrible certainty, that the preacher was probably giving a sermon, with the vial as the star.

He ran toward the church, and could hear the old man on the other side of the door. "Then let us open the doors to Heaven and welcome Him back into our world, Amen!"

The chorus of pews sang in reply: "Amen!"

Boricio charged through the doors as the old man opened the vial. He screamed, "No!" as Boricio charged him.

The vial's liquid boiled from the top, spilling out and onto the old man's hand, searing his flesh with an audible sizzle.

The Prophet screamed, but his voice was drowned by thunder crashing outside, followed by several strobing flashes of light, so bright it seemed like lightning was coming from within the church.

Boricio screamed as the world started to shimmer around him.

He fled the church and nearly ran head first into Luca on the other side of the door.

"What are you doing?" Boricio cried.

"I came to get you."

Boricio had never been so happy to see anyone in his life. He threw his arms around his brother as they both began to disappear.

Luca was gone, and so was he, but they weren't gone together.

For Boricio, everything went black, and he opened his eyes completely alone on a mountain, far above a city below.

The lights went out all at once as darkness swallowed it all. A second darkness, festering waves of smoke, clouds, or something unlike anything Boricio had ever seen before, spread across the sky, blotting out the moon.

A pair of gigantic, ink-black tornadoes — as wide as half the city at least — then reached down from the sky, twisting in a tango of anger, tearing the world by its roots as it spun, then slamming its plunder into mountainous piles, which were peppered across the thrashed landscape.

Darkness had come, and there wasn't a damned thing Boricio could do to stop it from consuming the world.

～

FIFTY-ONE

Boricio Wolfe

Dunn, Georgia
March 31, 2012
FIVE MONTHS AFTER THE EVENT …

BORICIO'S bald doppelgänger stood on his porch, calmly
staring as though he wasn't a barrel of Mardi Gras beads
worth of fucking weird. And with the way Callie was just
standing there beside him, it looked like she was agreeing with
his side of the story.

"I'm giving you until the count of pre-cum to tell me what
in the beer-battered bullshit is going on." Boricio turned to
Callie and jerked his thumb toward the bald fucker beside her.

"Captain Copycat can shove the fat of my fuckstick down
his throat and suck on it like it was the sweet inside a Slurpee
until he swallows my dishonorable discharge."

Captain Copycat turned to Callie. "Wow," he said. "You
weren't kidding."

Callie shrugged, then smiled at Boricio.

Boricio moved his eyes from the Captain to Callie. "You
wanna tell me what in the fuck is going on? Or why you

brought a chewed-caramel-looking version of Boricio, who talks slow enough to make me think he ain't learned to swallow fast enough to hurry his sentences, not to mention the two love birds behind you? Because this shit is just weird enough to be one of my fucked-up dreams. And if we're in the middle of one of my fucked-up dreams, well then I'm apt to do all sorts of crazy shit. So tell me, Callie, am I dreaming?"

Callie didn't answer. Instead, she said, "Can we come inside?"

Callie's calm made Boricio step back from the door. He gestured for the group to come inside without quite knowing why, thinking he would've likely killed Callie for the same calm in any one of the sweet minutes before Luca broke him.

Boricio pulled the gun from his belt and waved the pistol, motioning the four of them toward the table.

Captain Copycat turned to the love birds behind him and said, "Leave your guns in the van."

The one who looked like a sissy didn't say shit, but the one who looked like he grew up jacking off to *Die Hard* said, "I don't think that's such a good idea," then nodded toward Boricio like he was solving a mystery.

The Captain shook his head. "That's an order."

"So, you have your own team, too, eh?" Boricio cackled, then plopped into a chair on his side of the table and held his gun on his twin. "My team is named Team Boricio, what's yours? If you don't have a name yet, I'd like to suggest Team Twat Waffles, though of course that's just a suggestion based on a first-blush assessment of your team's overall potential."

Captain Copycat ignored Boricio, lowered himself onto the seat across from him, then looked him in the eyes as if he were no scarier than a scratch.

No one had ever held Boricio's eyes like that before.

"Wanna tell me your name, or should I just keep calling you Captain CumCatcher in my head?"

The fucker then said the unbelievable.

"My name is Boricio, like yours."

Boricio's eyes flew to Callie as his fingers tightened around the butt of his gun. "Wanna explain what this fucker's talking about?" He waved the pistol toward his doppelgänger. "Even if a fucker's smart enough to look like me, minus his chewed caramel fuck face, there ain't but one Boricio, at the end of the world."

Boricio was mostly quiet for the next 15 minutes, perhaps for the first time in as many years, while Callie and the other Boricio brought him up to speed. Die Hard and Wimpy Dick joined the bullshit session, standing at the door while Boricio drifted from disbelief to fascination.

Most of those 15 minutes were spent catching Boricio up on the bare basics rather than the other Boricio's personal history, but it didn't take Boricio long to realize that Captain Copycat had enjoyed many benefits that had been ass-raped from Boricio's life.

Boricio was getting tired of hearing Captain Copycat go on and on, so he interrupted him and asked, "Where the fuck are Charlie and Adam?"

"We were getting to that part," Callie said.

"Well, you weren't getting there fast enough."

Boricio wondered what Mary and the rest of Team Boricio must be thinking upstairs. He wondered how much they could hear, especially since the conversation was fairly muted. He wondered if they knew about, or saw, fugly Boricio.

Even after five minutes, Callie still hadn't said shit worth saying.

"So," Boricio repeated, "once again, where the fuck are Charlie and Adam?"

Callie said, "Adam's dead. He died before we got to Black Mountain. Charlie's at Black Mountain right now."

"Why?" Boricio said. "He didn't want to come to the

happy reunion? Or is this not a happy reunion? Let me know if it ain't, so I can put the ice cream back in the freezer."

"Charlie's infected," she said. "They're holding him in quarantine so the infection doesn't spread. They're trying to help him." She gestured toward the Captain. "Boricio thinks they'll be able to cure him. He thinks Charlie will be fine."

The Captain seemed suddenly impatient. "Where's Luca?" he said, for the fourth time since coming into Boricio's home.

Boricio growled, "Why do you need to see Luca?"

The Captain said, "Because he's my kid brother."

"How's that?" he said. "I don't have a brother. So, you wanna tell me why one Little Boricio gets to go to the market and have roast beef, while the other Little Boricio stays home and has none?"

That's when Boricio remembered what he'd seen when Luca had gone in his head and "fixed him," the other Boricio as a child — a seemingly happy child, adopted by Will.

The Captain said, "In my world, my father, Will, adopted Luca, just like he adopted me."

Boricio said, "But this Luca's from our world, right? The good one. Not your fucked-up under the table other side of the rainbow fuck-all."

The other Boricio apparently had more patience in his pinky than the real one did in his whole body. Because if the Captain was talking to him the way he was talking to the Captain, he'd have already cut the fucker's head from his body, then left the whole lot of them to figure shit out while he found a place to go bowling.

The Captain said, "I'm not sure which world *your* Luca is from. But I must speak with him, regardless. I believe he is the key to all of this."

Goddammit if the fucker wasn't right.

"To all of what?" Boricio asked.

"To everything."

Boricio swallowed, not knowing what the fuck *everything* meant, even though he knew every word was true. "There's something you should know," he said.

The Captain raised his eyebrow. "Yes?"

"Luca's not a kid," he shook his head. "Not anymore. He's nothing like you're probably picturing him."

The Captain still had his eyebrow raised. Boricio wondered if he had just the one, or if the other was hiding under the eye patch. If it was, Boricio wondered whether it was raised as well. "What do you mean?" he asked.

"Just what I said," Boricio said. "Luca's not a kid no more. I can't explain why, but maybe you can, since you've apparently traded handsome for layers of bullshit I'm not stupid enough to peel."

The Captain said, "Where is Luca, and what's wrong with him?"

Boricio grinned, then shrugged. "Like I said, Captain Copycat, I don't know what's wrong with him. He's been healing people, and every time he does it, he gets a little older. He's been doing it a while, so now he looks around eleventy."

Die Hard said, "That's not possible," while Wimpy Dick shook his head.

"Anyone want a ticket to see shit themselves?" Boricio asked.

Without another word, Boricio rose from the table, shoved his gun back into his pants, then said, "Hey you, Wimpy Dick."

The guy standing beside Die Hard turned.

Boricio laughed. "You always turn when you hear those four words together? How about cum-catching cocksucker?" Boricio frowned, then laughed louder and said, "I guess you could probably count them words as three."

Wimpy Dick said, "My name's Brent."

Boricio laughed. "Okay, *Brent.* I want you to walk in front of me while we head up the stairs and I lead you all to my ugly half's ancient little brother. But I don't like the idea of all you guys walking behind me. Seems like I'm leaving myself vulnerable, and not just for a reach around. Take the lead so we can get the party started."

Wimpy Dick looked back at the Captain. He nodded, then Wimpy Dick said, "Where do I go?"

"Over there," Boricio pointed toward the stairs. "We're going up, then down the hallway to the second door on the right."

Brent went up the stairs, then down the hallway to the second door on the right as Boricio followed behind. Callie and Die Hard went next. Fugly Boricio took the rear.

At the top of the stairs Boricio called, "It's okay, Miss Mary, we're about to come into the bedroom, but I swear on my you know what that shit is peachy. But keep your guns ready just in case some shit goes down, eh?"

Wimpy Dick looked back at Boricio, then opened the door when he nodded.

Mary and Paola were sitting protectively on either side of Luca, who was still lying on his bed, barely breathing and looking a million years old while doing it. The Captain approached the bed, then stared at Luca for a long while before shaking his head.

"That's not my brother."

Boricio said, "I told you he wasn't from your world."

"No," he said. "That's not what I mean. I felt him, *my* Luca, here. Here with you. But now I can't feel him at all."

"Is that why you look like you just ate shit pie from the serving spoon?"

The Captain stared at old Luca on the bed and said, "I can't feel my brother anymore, not on that bed or anywhere else. I'm starting to wonder if he's dead."

Boricio had a battery of questions to ask Fugly Boricio about that shit, but he never got a chance since the second he said the word *dead*, Boricio heard the screeching of tires and the death of an engine outside.

"You expecting anyone?" Boricio said to the room.

Die Hard looked bothered, and Wimpy Dick upset. Callie shuffled her feet.

The Captain shook his head as both Boricios went to the window.

Boricio peeled the curtain back and saw a face he never thought he'd see again.

Boricio whooped and hollered and screamed a high-pitched hallelujah, which ended in a whistle when he saw Charlie hopping from the driver's side of another black van.

He turned to Callie. "Looks like your sugar must be extra sweet, seeing as how Charlie came all this way to play the slots." He turned to the Captain. "Don't feel bad. She wouldn't let me taste, neither."

Boricio whooped and hollered again, then left the group, not worrying if anyone was walking behind him, but hearing the whole crowd of them anyway.

He tore through the hallway, then down the stairs and to the front door, swinging it open as Charlie's feet hit the front porch.

"Well, hell's bells, Charlie Cheese Dick," Boricio said. "Welcome the fuck home!"

~

FIFTY-TWO

Ryan Olson

Black Mountain, Georgia
  March 31, 2012
  FIVE MONTHS AFTER THE EVENT …

"PLEASE, KILL ME," Ryan begged Lisa as she aimed the shotgun at his face. "Please. I don't want to be one of them."

The shotgun shook in Lisa's hands, and Ryan could see the emotions spinning like pinwheels in her eyes. She wanted to do it. Wanted to kill him. But a part of her still saw him as human and not one of the monsters that had just butchered the woman and her unborn child.

She pulled the gun away, then sharply spun so she wouldn't have to look at him.

"Kill me!" Ryan repeated, now shouting.

"No!" Lisa said, shaking her head and turning back to face him. "You're not one of them! Boricio said you were different and I believe him. We need to get out of here and save him. And I need your help."

"No," Ryan said. "Go alone." He shook his head. "I can't help you."

He was swirling with too many emotions, mostly rage, along with the endless clicking, beeps, and mutant shrieks swimming across the surface of his mind. Beyond the cacophony was something else — a bottomless hunger nothing would sate.

As Ryan looked at Lisa, he began to imagine how easy it would be to bite into her flesh, and taste whatever it was she had inside her.

He shook his head, closing his eyes, trying to drive the sick thoughts from his head before they drove him to action.

It was happening.

He was turning.

As memories of the mutant feasting on the baby ran through his head, Ryan felt another wave of nausea stewing in his guts.

Then he felt something else . . . a sick delight in the sensation of the unborn flesh in his — and the other mutant's — teeth, ripping the life from its body and gulping it down like milk from a mother's breast.

"We've gotta go," Lisa said, offering Ryan a hand to help him to his feet. "We need to get out of here while we still can."

"I can't go with you," he said.

"You have to!" Lisa cried. "I can't stop them alone."

"I'm . . . changing."

"What?!" Lisa said, taking a step back.

"It's happening. I can feel it."

"No," Lisa said, shaking her head. "No, you're just trying to scare me so I'll shoot you."

Ryan forced himself to look at her, barely able to control his rising urge to bite her. He could sense her fear which further fueled his hunger.

"Fucking kill me or I will eat you just like he ate her and her baby!" Ryan screamed.

He rose to his feet and started to walk toward her, eyes boring into her, glaring. If she wasn't going to shoot him, he'd scare her into it. He had to end this now.

He had nothing left.

He was becoming a monster.

Time to die.

Maybe he'd see Mary and Paola in heaven, assuming heaven wasn't as much of a lie as Earth had turned out to be.

He looked into Lisa's scared eyes and stepped closer, just inches away.

"Do it!" he screamed.

Lisa stepped back and lifted the shotgun, aiming it at him, crying, "Please, don't make me."

"Do it! Do it! Do it!" he goaded her.

"Are you sure?" she cried, shotgun shaking in her hands.

"Please," he begged. "Please."

He closed his eyes, bracing for the bullet. As Ryan waited for death, he drew more thoughts from the mutants, the infected, Charlie, and the Darkness swirling inside him.

He saw that the Darkness was walking up to a house.

Is this where Boricio is?

The door opened.

Ryan saw the other Boricio answering the door, a wide smile of recognition on his face. Beyond Boricio, he saw another familiar face — *Mary!*

And there, beside her . . .

Paola!

They're alive!

They're here and alive!

Ryan couldn't die now.

He had to get to them.

He had to protect them.

He had to say something to stop Lisa before she shot him.

He opened his mouth and cried, "Nooo!"

He was too late.

The gun thundered before the world went silent.

TO BE CONTINUED ...

Episode 18

(SIXTH EPISODE OF SEASON THREE)

"Hard Reset Protocol"

FIFTY-THREE

Luca Harding

Saturday
  Oct. 15, 2011
  Morning
  Las Orillas, California

LUCA'S SKIN WAS BURNING. He opened his eyes and put an end to the dream where Mommy was making eggs on his arms.

The sun was brighter than it should have been. Light poured through the window like buckets splashing against the glass.

Luca turned to look at his *Cars* alarm clock, but it was off.

He didn't like the feeling in his arms, tingly bad and kind of burny. Luca wanted to scratch his skin, but stopped himself because Mommy said that scratching always made things worse.

The itchy burny would probably go away if he ignored it.

Luca pulled off the covers and got out of bed, then went number one in the bathroom. His toothbrush was on the counter when he peed, but was gone by the time he flushed the toilet.

Just like his *Cars* alarm clock when he went back inside his room.

The house was too quiet.

Luca went to the closet, peeled off his Lego pajamas, pulled on his jeans and his favorite *Star Wars* T-shirt — the one that read *"I had friends on that Death Star"* that his dad bought because he thought it was funny.

Luca dropped his Lego pajamas on the floor only a second before, but they were already gone, just like his *Cars* alarm clock and everything else in the room — the bed, the desk, his toys, all of it gone. His room was completely empty, the walls were now white instead of blue, and there was a different carpet on the floor, which smelled new.

He went to the window because he wanted to see the rainbow he thought would be there. But there wasn't a rainbow.

There's supposed to be a rainbow.

This wasn't right.

Nothing was.

Luca couldn't hear his mom or his dad, or his sister, Anna. He felt like he'd been in this feeling before, too. But the house was even emptier than it had been the last time. It felt like his family had moved away in the middle of the night and sold the house.

Luca blinked, and wanted to cry. He hated that everything was different.

He went to his window again and saw a sign in the front yard which read, *FOR SALE*.

Oh my God, they did sell the house?! They moved away without me!

Luca ran to the kitchen, looking for the phone so he could call his mom's cell phone. He had to get a hold of her and tell her to come back. She forgot him. The phone was gone, though. The kitchen was just as empty as every other room. He tensed as something flashed at the corner of his eyes. Luca expected to see his cat, Lucky, but Lucky wasn't there. He saw a dog instead.

And suddenly, memories began to come forth.

"Dog Vader!" Luca cried, happy to see his old friend.

The dog sat on its haunches for several seconds before he opened his slobbery jaw and said, "I never liked that name, you know." Dog Vader made a low rumbling growl to let Luca know he was only joking.

"Do you still want me to call you Kick?"

Dog Vader said, "It doesn't matter what you call me, so long as you listen to what I say." Dog Vader was using his Serious Voice. But Luca didn't want to hear the Serious Voice, at least not inside his too-empty house. "Can we go outside?" Luca asked, then said, "Aren't we supposed to get the bathtub car and follow the rainbow?"

"There are no more rainbows, Luca," Dog Vader shook his snout back and forth. "And there aren't any rainbows like before."

Dog Vader went from his haunches to all fours, then trotted toward the front door where he waited for Luca to open it. They stepped into the bright light outside together. And just as Dog Vader said, there were no rainbows.

"Where did they go?" Luca whispered, realizing that he didn't feel the itchy burny anymore either. "Where's my family?"

"They were never here. On this world, they died two years ago. Everything you saw was a lie," Dog Vader said. "But a necessary lie. A good one." Dog Vader's snout suddenly shortened, and his shoulders started to grow as he lost all his fur. "A lie without cause is a lie without effect." He went from all fours back to his haunches, until he was suddenly standing on two human feet.

Dog Vader was no longer a dog. He was the tall Indian, towering over Luca, with a giant flowing headdress and a long plastic pipe.

"You lied to yourself," the Indian said.

Luca slowly shook his head, trying to understand.

"You have stolen from *you*, Luca. The YOU from the other Earth lost his mother and father, so he decided to steal yours. Then some part of you, maybe some parts of him, made you believe the lie when you arrived here. You saw things as you wanted to see them — as you *needed* to see them — in order to cope. I was here to help you find Will. I made the rainbows, and then led you to him." The Indian looked down, then gently set his palm on the boy's shoulder. "It's okay, Luca" he said. "Don't cry. There are ways to make everything right."

Luca wiped his right cheek, then swiped at the other one. "How?" he asked, looking up at the Indian.

"You must go to Black Island. There is a vial in the moon in the bedroom of the boy who stole your life. In that vial is something which can either be very good or very bad. YOU have to open it, Luca. You do, before anyone else finds it."

"I can't do that," Luca shook his head. "I'm not strong, or brave. I know I look like an old man, but I'm only a boy inside."

"You aren't *only* a boy," the Indian said. "You never were. You are pure, Luca. Even when walking through the mind of another, you've never done so with dirty feet. And yes, you *are* brave, my boy, for it is only the courage to continue that counts, and you've never failed to set one foot firmly in front of the other no matter how scared you were. You are the only one who can balance the world against the Black Pieces."

"The Black Pieces?"

"Yes," the Indian nodded. "The Black Pieces, The Darkness, The Void, The Oblivion, The Wicked Iniquity of Nothing, and The Limbo — it has more names across more universes than there are grains of sand on your beaches or stars in your sky. The Black Pieces," the Indian continued, "are the opposite of me."

"So, what are you?"

"We, the Darkness and Us, started out the same. We are Light. We are Life, Creation, and We are the Infinite Possibility of All. But we can also be tainted and turned into the Darkness. It destroyed one realm we lived in. So our children sent us out in vials, in hopes that we might be found and bring Light back into being."

Luca shuddered. His itchy burny was back, even if it was only in his mind. He was confused. He'd heard people say the monstrous things that had been attacking them were aliens. But the Indian was describing it so differently. Like they were these forces, rather than actual physical alien beings.

"Why can't *you* fight the Black Pieces?"

The Indian shocked Luca with a long fit of laughter before he said, "I *can* fight the Black Pieces, and I *do*." He looked down at Luca, his hand still resting on the boy's shoulder. "I'm fighting The Black Pieces right now by standing here speaking with you. However, I am but a part, a small part against the many. We need to find the vial to become stronger — to multiply as the Darkness has."

The Indian dropped to his knee, then set his pipe on the porch and held Luca's eyes. "You *will do* something about it, Luca. Because you are strong, and because you are brave, even if you do not yet see it. But I am spread too thin to win this war. I am not really here," the Indian waved his hands up and down his body. "At least not like you see me. No more than the rainbows in the sky, which led you to a father from another world. I am but a residual of the Light passed from the Luca of one world to the Luca in another. I am inside you, but I'm not strong enough alone." He pat Luca on the back. "I need, *we need* to get the vial."

"Or what?"

"Or the world will be plunged forever into Darkness. And I, and all the people you know here, will be consumed by, and become part of the Darkness."

Luca had a million more questions that he wanted to ask, but then the Indian said, "Not now. Now is time to wake up."

~

FIFTY-FOUR

Boricio Bishop

Dunn, Georgia
Boricio's Compound
March 31, 2012
FIVE MONTHS AFTER THE EVENT …

BORICIO BISHOP RAN his hands over his bald head as he watched Charlie appear in the doorway.

Every part of Bishop bristled as his doppelgänger, Asshole Boricio, welcomed Charlie like his long-lost brother.

Something's wrong. How the hell did he get out of his cell?

Did he escape?

If so, how many bodies did he leave behind?

Boricio felt a sudden danger he couldn't define, as though it singed his skin with its flames, though he wasn't sure where the fire was. He had to be careful how he handled the Charlie situation. This other Boricio was a loose canon, and while Boricio had been able to handle nearly any situation life threw his way, he wasn't sure he could handle the *him* from another world — the him who seemed all id, no restraint. Asshole Boricio had never been adopted by Will, and had falsely learned that destroying everything around him was the best way to understand himself better.

He wouldn't think twice about getting down and bloody to protect his own.

"Well," the Asshole Boricio said, "get the fuck in here and make yourself at home!"

Charlie smiled, sort of, then stepped inside the house, casting his eyes across the room as though he were taking it all in for the first time, almost with the same look as if he were observing a huddle of strangers he'd never seen before.

He barely glanced at Callie, which struck Boricio as bizarre, especially after what he'd seen passing between the two of them on the cell monitors the night before.

Asshole Boricio led Charlie to the dining room table, then pulled out a chair and gestured for him to sit. "I imagine you couldn't find any open drive-throughs on your way over here, Chucky FuckStick, so you want one of Miss Mary's pancakes to powder your gut?" He nodded toward Mary, standing by the bottom stair, shoulders tensed and arms wrapped around her daughter. "They're not as good as Boricio's World-Famous Flapjacks, which I'm sure you're a lucky enough fucker to remember, but they'll do for short notice, I suppose."

Something about the asshole's pride in his pancakes forced Boricio into the twitch of a grin. He swallowed his smile and said, "What in the hell are you doing here, Charlie? You're infected. And how did you get out of your cell? How did you leave Black Mountain? How did you find us?"

Asshole Boricio didn't even give Charlie a second to answer. He asked, "Infected with what?"

Boricio thought he'd already explained this shit to his asshole counterpart, but for the sake of keeping things calm, he said, "It doesn't have an official name, but some of us at Black Mountain refer to it as 'The Apocalypse Worm.' The monsters aren't monsters; they're aliens. And the aliens aren't friendly. They're parasites that worm their way into your body through physical contact, usually a bite, then slowly — though it seems to be happening faster and faster — take over the body, turning regular people into mutated monstrosities. Charlie is our only subject not to have mutated in outward appearance, though. We have one other subject who is halfway mutated, but everyone else, once they're infected, that's been that. They're lost."

Asshole Boricio then asked, "Is Charlie CheeseDick dangerous? Is he gonna get all slippery when wet on us?"

Callie spoke instead. "We're safe," she said. "I knew Charlie was infected, but wasn't worried. Mr. Bishop said Charlie was fine, and that they'd probably be able to fix him, maybe use his blood to help fix everyone else. Believe me; you've nothing to worry about. He wouldn't hurt a fly, unless it was to protect one of us."

Boricio wanted to believe her, but looking at Charlie, and the odd look in his eyes that he couldn't quite pin, he wasn't so sure. Even if Charlie wouldn't do anything dangerous on purpose, that didn't mean he wasn't a threat.

Bishop considered pushing his position; drawing the line between himself and Charlie and clarifying the threat's severity. If Charlie returned to his world infected, it was only a matter of time until their world went to ash just as this one was.

Charlie still hadn't answered the question, how he'd gotten out. And what the hell kind of mess did he leave behind? Boricio hoped that he didn't break out and kill anyone. If so, he'd personally put a bullet in the kid's head. The first time Charlie went all X-Men, Boricio could forgive. He was scared, his only experience with Black Mountain had been at the hands of assholes who shot the kid he was with. But Boricio had spared the kid, had trusted him. He hoped to God he hadn't made an error.

He considered pressing Charlie for an answer, but decided to go another, more subtle, route.

Brent and Ed, the Black Island Guardsmen who'd proven quite useful, were standing about a foot and a half apart, their bodies tensed and ready; eyes wide and alert, shoulders and jaws set. Ed had one foot forward, ready to spring. He looked pissed, probably because Boricio made him leave his gun in the van. The woman, Mary, looked more upset than frightened, while her daughter looked more frightened than upset.

He had no words to describe the look on Callie.

Boricio didn't have the time or the focus to read all of their thoughts, so he quickly went into their heads, pulling the most dominant thought from every mind in the room.

Charlie: Nothing.

Callie: *He's wrong about Charlie. Real Boricio will make sure everything's okay.*

Ed: *The crazy Boricio's gotta go first. I'll wipe that smug look off his face.*

Brent: *At least she's at the end of the world with her daughter.*

Mary: *If anything happens, we run outside and grab a van ... Sorry, Luca.*

The girl: *Charlie reminds me of John.*

Old Luca was sending nothing but static from upstairs, and that was slightly more than Boricio was pulling from Charlie.

He hated the room's tension, but at least that was something — the emptiness inside Charlie was chilling.

But there was nothing Boricio could do, no way to cleanly win this particular battle.

He'd go with the flow for now, play it cool. But he'd have to keep an eye on Charlie. Then he had to let Ed and Brent know that they needed to do the same. Shoot at the first sign of trouble. Boricio hoped it wouldn't come to that, however. He actually liked Charlie a bit. He was a good kid given a bad deal, and from what Boricio had seen in his head, that had been the story of his life.

Boricio could relate to the abusive step-dad. And he could

see how Asshole Boricio had developed a soft spot for the kid as well. Perhaps he wasn't a complete asshole, after all.

The top stair creaked, and the entire room spun toward the sound. Ed thrust his arm in front of Brent and took a slight step forward as Mary wrapped her arms tighter around her daughter, then fell a step back toward the door.

Another stair squeaked, and Asshole Boricio was suddenly at the bottom of the stairs, looking up toward the top. A smile split his face as he turned to the rest of the room. "Looks like Old Man Luca wanted to come down and meet his brother from another mother."

A second later, Boricio saw Luca's foot, though it took about a half minute for his body to follow. He didn't speak until he reached the bottom stair, and when he did, it sounded as though he was using every last drop of energy to push a few splintered words through his ancient throat.

"We have to go to Black Island. Now." Then, after a few long seconds spent struggling for breath while the rest of the room stood and waited, he whispered, "If we don't go, we're all dead."

～

"Charlie"

Dunn, Georgia
  Boricio's Compound
  March 31, 2012
  FIVE MONTHS AFTER THE EVENT ...

IT WAS HUNGRY.

Starving.

Empty, hollow, deprived.

It smelled the ripened scent of the unfiltered feast *It* longed to consume.

The good one — ancient on the outside, but still gooey in the middle where the child harbored his innocent thoughts — would be bliss to consume.

Soon.

Soon, everything would be finished.

The beginning of the end was already over.

The girl *Its* shell yearned to seed was trying to convince everyone that *Charlie* was safe. He wouldn't hurt any of them.

If only she knew.

The one who held hate where his eye had gone missing

was trying to read the room. But he couldn't — at least not all of it.

Though the man who held hate had a bit of The Enemy within him, which allowed him to read these animals' minds, there was nothing he could do to penetrate *Its* mind.

It waited for the spotlight to fall off of *Charlie*. If *It* was found out, *It* might be killed before *It* could consume *Its* enemy.

It was starving. Deprived. Near hollow.

Ready.

This was taking too long.

The scent from the top of the stairs grew stronger. It felt ripe, beckoning to *It.*

The gooey parts in the middle of the child's thoughts now running like broken yolk.

The end of the beginning was over, but the beginning of the end felt like it was taking forever.

A stair creaked from the top of the stairs — the end, finally on its way.

The aggressive one put his arm before the one who was too thoughtful. The woman *It* met before wrapped her arms around the girl who was too weak for *It* to stay in.

Then the violent one, the one *It* wish *It* had found at The Sanctuary before going into the fat old man, said, "Looks like Old Man Luca wanted to come downstairs and meet his brother from another mother!"

It licked *Its* lips.

Once *It* attacked the child, *It* would be forced to silence every breath in the room.

But it would be worth it.

It would be stronger than ever.

The child in the old man's shell appeared, first his feet, then finally his head.

The child took great labor to speak. "We have to go to Black Island," he said. "Now."

The eternity it took for the child to finish his thought gave *It* plenty of time to see everything the child didn't know he was supposed to be hiding.

It now knew what the child knew.

Its body relaxed, putting aside *Its* hunger now that *It* had seen the far greater meal waiting for *It* at Black Island.

There was plenty of time.

Soon *It* would be full.

Gorged, glutted, satisfied.

It wanted what the child wanted.

But the vial — holding the last of *Its* enemy — would belong to *It*, never the child.

It had all the time in the world, now that *It* knew where *It* needed to go.

The child whispered, "If we don't go, we're all dead."

The beginning of the end was now.

And nothing would stop *It*.

~

FIFTY-SIX

Other Ed Keenan

Black Island
 Black Island Research Facility Level 8
 April 2, 2012
 SIX MONTHS AFTER THE EVENT …

ED STARED at the giant monitor, wondering how long they had before everyone topside was either infected or dead.

More than 100 cameras were on the island, and all three digits' worth were displayed in squares on the large screen in front of himself, Will, and Sullivan in the control room on Level 8; the same room they rushed inside on the early morning of Oct. 15 when Will first told them about his dream: Something bad was about to happen.

That was putting things mildly.

"How many of our own people are left?" Will asked, pacing back and forth, stroking his beard.

"Ten Guardsmen topside, five more on the mainland," Sullivan said, looking at a computer monitor on the table, displaying a map of the island with several red dots detailing each Guardsman's precise position, with a number assigned to each, hovering over the dots. Two dots side by side suddenly went dark.

"Make that eight," Sullivan said.

They glanced at the monitors and saw two Guardsmen ripped into shreds by what could only be called a pack of wild mutants — running and killing together, decimating or infecting every Guardsman in their wake.

They were down to just three Guardsmen in the Facility, protecting 15 civilians. The math was getting uglier by the minute. Ed wasn't sure what Will was trying to calculate, and didn't dare interrupt the man when he was working through a problem. Will was loony, but genius. If anyone could think their way out of this nightmare, it was him. Unfortunately, Will was also harder to deal with since Boricio took off. Boricio had been Will's unofficial translator, the only person who could steer Will through some of his wackier behaviors and get him to focus on the productive stuff. Boricio also provided a much-needed buffer between Will's sometimes gruff obtuseness and the others in the Facility.

Will asked, "How many civilians topside on the island?"

"I'm estimating there are 20 or so, still topside in their homes, with 35 having been brought to the mainland before the aliens crowded the dock, preventing the ferry from its safe return," Sullivan said.

"No sign of Dr. Williams?"

"No," Sullivan shook his head.

Will continued pacing. Finally, Ed said, "Why are you asking about the number of people left?"

"Because we need numbers on our side," Will said, as if the answer was as obvious as daylight.

"Why?" Ed said, glancing at Sullivan, glad to see his eyes as confused as Ed's.

"Because Luca's coming back. And he's going to need allies."

Ed shook his head, *this shit again*, then glanced at Sullivan who also looked as disappointed as Ed felt. "Why do you say that?" he asked. "And don't say because you dreamed it."

Will looked at Ed, then put his fingers over his lips with a zipping gesture.

"You dreamed it?" Ed asked, unable to control his rising temper.

"Your son isn't coming back," Ed said bluntly. "He's gone. They both are. And even if they *did* return, what are they going to do? Unless they bring an army they're as helpless as we are with our dwindling numbers. Why don't you try to come up with something that doesn't rely on dreams or hope, because it's getting late, and our options are running dry."

"They *are* coming back," Will insisted.

Ed sighed.

Their last best hope at defeating the aliens just went full-blown senile.

WILL LEFT the control room and headed down the corridor toward the vending machine.

Sullivan approached, glancing back over his shoulder as if he expected Will to pop back into the room at any moment. "We have to consider the Hard Reset Protocol."

"No," Ed shook his head. "I'm not giving up hope. Not yet. We still have time to make a decision."

"No, sir, we don't. I saw something just before you and Will came in. But I didn't want to say anything until I showed you first."

"What are you talking about?"

Sullivan went to the monitor, then touched one of the squares and tapped out a sequence of four numbers.

A moment later, the box widened, taking up most of the screen, showing Camera 76, which looked out over the west side of the island's shore. The footage was 12 hours old, from when it was still light, and showed several dark shapes dotting the water for as far as the camera could capture — about one quarter mile out.

The shapes were moving.

Toward the island.

"What are those?" Ed asked.

"Aliens."

Ed turned his head and squinted, his eyes straining for a better look.

"Holy shit. They're swimming?"

"Yes," Sullivan nodded.

"There's gotta be hundreds."

"Yes," Sullivan said. "And that's just this morning."

"Are they coming or going?"

"Coming," Sullivan said. "And it looks like they're gearing up for something big."

~

FIFTY-SEVEN

Ryan Olson

Dunn, Georgia
  March 31, 2012
  FIVE MONTHS AFTER THE EVENT …

LISA TURNED TO RYAN, sitting in the passenger seat of the van, and smiled. They were finally a half mile or so from the compound. She had driven the van faster than Ryan thought possible, for which Ryan was thankful, since that meant much less time wanting to consume her.

Ryan had spent the trip wanting to tear into Lisa's flesh, and diving deep inside his mind to monitor and push down the alien urge. He craved the feast of her body, but was even hungrier to get to the compound so he could finally find his wife and daughter.

Lisa had missed shooting his face off, but only by the fraction of a moment. She had moved her hand at the last second, after she said she'd seen something in his face change. She said suddenly he didn't look like a man begging to die, but rather someone with everything to live for.

Though she missed killing him, the gunshot had come

close enough to shatter his eardrums. However, the pain and ringing had lessened in the past 20 minutes, perhaps thanks to his alien side, which seemed to foster fast healing.

Lisa swung the van into the empty driveway of the compound, then looked over at Ryan. "I'm gonna leave the engine running."

"OK," he said.

Lisa climbed from the van and Ryan followed, turning his eyes to look anywhere but her back, hating himself for seeing her as easy prey. She pounded on the door for several minutes, though she didn't have to. Ryan could tell that nobody was inside to answer.

He cursed himself for not having known for sure if they'd left. He'd been so busy resisting the urges to kill Lisa that he'd not been tuned into the Darkness, which had taken control of Charlie. The last he'd seen through the teen's eyes, he was in the room, talking to the group. He could feel the same lust for death in the Darkness as he felt in himself. But the Darkness was also resisting the urge, for reasons Ryan couldn't discern. Nor could he count on the Darkness continuing to resist. Perhaps it was playing the long game, waiting for something.

Ryan tried to reach out and find the Darkness, but was coming up blank.

"I'm kicking it in, cool?" Lisa said, breaking his focus.

"Do your worst," Ryan said. "But I'd check to see if it's locked first."

Lisa said, "Duh," even though Ryan would've bet that her leg was already twitching to go into action.

The door swung open, and Ryan inhaled more of his family's lingering psychic scent. Not a lot was left, but there was just enough. He closed his eyes, imagining them so wholly that he could almost reach out and touch them. But all that was left was their auras, echoes of their souls. He may as well have tried to touch a ghost. His heart crushed beneath the weight of his growing sadness.

Ryan could smell Mary's protective shield wrapped around their daughter's heavy terror. Ryan longed to see more of their memories, maybe something specific, but those memories were now dead — dust drifting into a different wind.

Something stabbed inside Ryan's mind, sending him to his knees in a scream.

"You okay?" Lisa looked down, eager to help.

Ryan swallowed, then said, "Yeah, thanks." He shook his head, then set his claw against it, rocking it for comfort. "I'm fine, just felt something . . . weird."

"You sure?" Lisa's eyes said she wasn't, even if Ryan was.

But he wasn't fine. Not at all. The pain was gone, but it was replaced with an increased hunger. Ryan wanted to tear Lisa limb from limb, he longed to taste her, and wanted to share her flavor with others like him. The others he was growing closer to by the minute.

Ryan wanted to join them.

With so many mutants and aliens around, Ryan could easily find the growing collective. He should just forget about Mary and Paola — it wasn't like he could enjoy any sort of normal life with them — and feast on Lisa.

Then he could join his new family.

No!

Fuck you, I'm still human!

The hive in his mind grew worse for its volume. Ryan had to force himself to stand up or else he might not ever get up . . . not as a human, anyway.

The living room felt emptier than it was. He saw signs of recent life — a bowl of batter and a couple of half-eaten pancakes on the bar — but not a single breath was in the house.

Mary and Paola's scents, physical and psychic, were strongest, at least until Ryan smelled Charlie's.

Except Charlie's trail wasn't a scent; it was more like a broadcast.

Charlie had what he'd come for, but decided he wanted more.

Another sudden flicker — no, a flash — inside Ryan's mind sent him back to his knees. It was something horrible, something crowding his mind. Something from outside. They were coming. The dark horde sensed them and was coming.

"We have to go," Ryan said, trying to stand. "We have to follow them and get to Black Island immediately."

Ryan tried to stand while Lisa stood openmouthed and unsure.

"Are you sure you're okay?"

Ryan nodded. "Yes, but we've gotta go."

Lisa didn't question him, just looked at him while trying not to stare, grazing her eyes up and along his mutated body, while Ryan tried to set his eyes anywhere but on his potential meal.

Lisa swallowed, then said, "Okay," and headed for the front door.

Ryan scrambled to his feet, screamed, "No!" then ran toward Lisa as she was halfway through the threshold. He reached out, his claw grabbing the edge of her shirt and pulling her back toward him. The fabric tore with a loud RIP! as Ryan fell hard to his bottom and Lisa fell on top of him.

She screamed, then quickly crawled away backward and scurried to her feet.

Once standing, Lisa screamed, "What the fuck!" while kicking at Ryan and taking a step to the side, away from the door.

"I'm not trying to hurt you," Ryan said, calmly waving his claw in front of his face to shield himself from Lisa's feet. He stood, then said, "I swear," though the drool dripping from his hungry maw probably made him hard to believe. He added, "I'm trying to help you."

Lisa took another several steps back, then turned toward

the door, closed it, and spun back toward Ryan. "Want to tell me what the fuck is up then?"

Ryan thought it was funny, how he wanted to save Lisa's life, and take it from her at the same time. He wondered which of his two sides would be most likely to win, and how much longer it would be before he found out for certain. But whatever gallows humor he found in his condition ended immediately when he followed the thoughts to their next logical destination — *what happens when I find my family? Can I protect them? Or will I endanger them?*

"What the hell's happening?" Lisa repeated, her voice shaking behind.

Ryan walked to the door and said, "I'll show you. But you have to stay behind me, okay?" Lisa nodded, and he opened the door, slowly stepping through the threshold with Lisa a half-step behind.

On the other side of the door, Lisa gasped.

There were at least 15 mutants and aliens standing between the gate and the house, with four on either side of the van.

"Will we be okay?" she whispered, raising her gun.

"Don't shoot," he said. "Let's just walk real slow."

Lisa wrapped her arm around his waist, as if he could protect her, and like he wasn't thinking the same thing they were.

"Yes," he said. "But we have to get to the van. Once we get to the van, we'll be safe. I promise."

"Should we run?" she asked.

"No," Ryan shook his head and took a tentative step forward. They were about six feet away from the van. Two mutants stood to the right. Two to the left. They'd have to get close to them in order to get in the van. That's when shit would get tricky. He turned to Lisa and said, "Don't make any quick moves unless they attack. Just keep doing what we're doing, we're almost there."

He and Lisa crept toward the van, as the two aliens on either side swayed on their feet, waiting for the one that was sort of like them and the one who was nothing like them at all to make a move. Ryan wasn't sure if they would strike or not. Even they seemed confused as to what to do. Ryan's alienness had taken a simple decision, whether to kill the girl, and made it difficult. They were hive mind and did not fuck with the hive thought.

And Ryan was thinking: *Do not hurt her. She is with me.*

They were almost to the front of the van, with maybe four steps to go on either side doors, when the stabbing pain returned to cripple Ryan. He hunched over, hands clutching his aching skull, crushed by the weight of the hive suddenly inside his mind.

Ryan screamed, trying to drive the clicking and beeping hive thoughts from his head.

Stop it, stop it! GET OUT!!

Ryan couldn't think straight, so Lisa thought for him.

He saw nothing, but heard four shots — two sets separated by a heartbeat's worth of silence, then two thuds followed by a chorus of shrieks. And he felt intense pain in his chest and head, where he figured the gunshots hit the creatures.

Lisa pulled Ryan to his feet, then dragged him the four remaining steps, sliding the van's side door open with one hand, throwing him inside with the other, and climbing in behind him, then locking the door as the first alien pounded its body hard against the metal.

She climbed into the driver's seat, leaving Ryan in a moaning puddle at the back.

"Fuck yeah," she said, then threw the van into reverse and rolled over a pair of rampaging aliens.

"Now!" Ryan screamed. "Get us out of here and out to Black Island before we're overrun."

"You think I'm a fucking idiot?" Lisa screamed back, pulling the van from the compound.

"Well," he said. "You are traveling with me."

Lisa said something else, but Ryan couldn't hear it. His head was swimming — flashes of Mary and Paola, on their way to Black Island with everyone else as the Darkness inside Charlie patiently waited to end them.

The Darkness waited because *It* had a new goal.

"*It* wants the vial," Ryan said, suddenly knowing for certain, and wondering how long it would be before he would finally kill Lisa and join the Darkness.

~

FIFTY-EIGHT

Brent Foster

East Hampton, New York
East Hampton Docks
April 2, 2012
SIX MONTHS AFTER THE EVENT ...

THEIR VANS ARRIVED as the last of the purple twilight surrendered to black, pulling up to the East Hampton Docks that were as dark as the desolate cities.

Lights from the ferry flickered in the distance, a few hundred yards offshore. Further out, Brent could see the barely-there outline of Black Island, a dark smudge you'd miss if you didn't know where to look.

Boricio Bishop, Ed, and Brent took one van, while Boricio Wolfe, Mary, Paola, Luca, Charlie, and Callie followed in the other. Brent was glad to not have been stuck in the van with Wolfe, who may have been the most arrogant person he'd ever had the displeasure of meeting. Bishop was far less crude and maybe 2 percent as terrifying, despite his bald head, scarred face, and pirate's eye patch.

"Is the ferry just sitting out there?" Brent whispered so

that his voice would not carry to whatever might be lurking in the darkness. "Are we gonna have to wait for the morning?"

"A Guardsman should be stationed on shore," Ed said, looking up the dark street and into the driver's-side mirror.

Apart from the houses to the left, and a restaurant along the boardwalk to the right, there wasn't anything or anyone else but them on the dark street.

"And you don't have a radio, do you?" Bishop said.

"No," Ed shook his head.

A salty breeze gusted through the shattered passenger window, and carried the sound of the surf with it. Other than the ocean, and the sound of the van's low purr, they heard nothing but eerie silence.

That silence lasted a moment, then was shattered by the blasting of a horn and flashing of headlights behind them.

"What the fuck?! Is that asshole trying to get us killed?" Bishop shouted as he hopped from the van, pistol in hand.

Ed followed, rifle ready.

Brent stepped out of the van, holding his pistol, hoping he wouldn't need it, and remembering how he'd frozen in the van when an infected Jung attacked.

Bishop raced to the second van as Boricio Wolfe hopped from the passenger side and yelled, "Where the fuck's our welcoming committee, Captain?"

"Shut the hell up, you'll draw the aliens!" Bishop yelled at his revolting twin.

"Let 'em come," Wolfe said, full of machismo and idiot one-liners.

Brent looked at Ed and rolled his eyes.

Suddenly, another voice called out, coming from behind them, "Drop the weapons and down on your knees!"

Brent turned to see two Guardsmen aiming assault rifles and lights at them.

Ed turned to face them, placed his gun on the street, then stepped into their light, and said, "Stand down, I'm Guardsman! Commander Edward Keenan — returning from special assignment."

After a moment's hesitation, the Guardsmen slowly approached the group, getting a closer look before lowering their guns.

"Sorry, Commander," said the one on the right.

Ed nodded, then, "What's happening? Why is the ferry out there?"

"The island is on lockdown. Two infected subjects have broken free from the Facility."

"Hold on," Ed said, waving for Bishop to join them. "This is Boricio Bishop, Will Bishop's son, who I was tasked with bringing back here. Please start from the beginning."

"The island is on lockdown. Two infected subjects broke out of the Facility and have infected, and taken control of, several Guardsmen and civilians. We believe Dr. Williams may be involved in the breakout. We evacuated one group of people to the mainland; they're harbored back in the restaurant, but when we went back for more, several of the infected were waiting, blocking access to the docks. It's like they're working together."

"What's the status of Keenan and Will Bishop?" Ed asked.

"They're secure in the Facility, along with some others."

"What about my brother, Luca?" Bishop said.

"Luca?" the Guardsman said, his face confused. "Oh, the kid. No, no word on him. We've got his picture and have been told to keep a lookout, but no one's reported anything."

Brent started to ask about Jane and Emily, but Ed cut him off, asking the Guardsmen, "You have a radio? I need you to get Keenan on the line."

"Yes, sir," the Guardsman nodded, then handed him the two-way radio.

A gunshot split the moment of silence in the moment that Ed was taking the radio into his hand.

Brent spun around to see the girl, Paola, now out of the

other van, firing her pistol a second time. Fifty yards off, coming out of the very house Brent and Luis had stayed in a lifetime ago — the one with the car through the hole in the wall — an alien fell to the ground.

Another five — aliens and mutants both, though they looked more or less the same the further they were into their mutations — charged toward them, shrieking and clicking.

Wolfe fired next, dropping two aliens in two shots. Callie and Mary stepped forward, both firing. Charlie, looked down at his pistol, clearly confused, then lifted and fired at the aliens as well. Brent wasn't sure whose shots hit and whose missed, but they'd killed the last of the aliens before Charlie even raised his gun. At least that's what Brent thought in the following silence, as their eyes passed in a circle of congratulatory relief.

A sudden shriek from Paola ended the quiet.

More aliens poured into the street from the south and west. At least a hundred appeared, likely more, all moving slowly as though trying to untangle their next move — or waiting for instructions.

"Run!" someone yelled.

"This way!" Ed shouted, pointing toward the Boardwalk Diner & Cafe, where one of the Guardsmen who greeted them was already banging on a corrugated metal sheet covering the entrance. Brent saw that all the windows and doors were shuttered in metal sheets — a shelter they must've set up before they started their evacuation, since he didn't recall seeing it the first time he'd been to the docks.

Paola started shooting at the aliens as if her gun had infinite ammo. But her shots only angered the aliens. They started moving faster and with a bit more clarity, shrieking and clicking. Mary, sensing her daughter's danger, spun around and joined the girl in shooting the aliens.

Wolfe appeared between them, yelling, "Come on! We can't shoot them all!"

They turned, then sprinted toward the restaurant, as Brent and Ed helped assure Luca would make it.

Once they were all inside the restaurant, a Guardsman slammed the door behind them, then locked it by sliding a bar into a metal brace, attached to the inside of the door, wedged against either side of the door frame. The dining hall was dimly lit by several portable lanterns, cloaking most of the 40 or so people in shadows.

Brent expected the aliens to rush the building to try and break in. But only quiet followed, as if they'd decided not to pursue, or perhaps had already tried to breach the barrier before but had no luck. *Maybe,* Brent thought with a sick in his stomach, *they're just waiting us out.*

Brent turned and scoured the room, searching for Jane and Emily. Men, women, and a few kids sat at tables scattered around the restaurant, huddled together in separate groups of two, three, and up to five. Some were eating, but most were simply speaking in whispers, perhaps discussing what might happen next.

Not able to tell who was who among the shadows, Brent broke from his group and began to move through the room to get a closer look, feeling as if every eye was either on him or his companions. He saw a few familiar faces from the island, but no one he really knew.

Brent looked back at his group and saw both Boricios and Ed speaking with a pair of Guardsmen, with Mary and Paola beside them. Mary had her arms around her daughter, but her attention was fixed on the conversation between the Guardsmen, Ed, and the semi-matching set of Boricios.

Brent looked around again, sighing when he didn't see either Jane or Emily.

He hoped they were okay, and wanted more than ever to get back to the island — not just to get home, but because he wanted to see them, and make sure they were safe. Brent was surprised to realize how much he cared.

"Mr. Brent," a young girl's voice called from across the room.

He turned, heart swelling as he saw Emily racing toward him, her pigtails bouncing on top of her head. She was maybe three feet away when she leapt into Brent's arms. He caught her, then pulled her into a giant hug. As he hugged Emily, Brent scanned the room for Jane, but didn't see her anywhere.

"Where's your mommy?" Brent asked.

"Mommy wasn't feeling well," Emily said.

"What do you mean?"

"She was sick, and they wouldn't let her come on the boat."

Brent set Emily on the floor, then met her eyes, "What happened?"

"Some men came to the house and told us to get ready. They said we had to go, then they ran a blue light over us like they did that day we all came over. Mommy's light beeped, and they said she had to go back inside the house, and then they took me."

Brent's heart was at full gallop. He tried to catch his breath and not look like he was a half minute from a freakout.

"Then what?"

"Mommy said not to worry. She was crying, and one of the men stayed with her to help her get better. She said that everything would be okay, I should go with the men, and that she'd see me later."

Oh God, she's dead, and Emily doesn't even know it.

Brent felt sick, seconds from vomit, but he had to keep his composure.

Emily's eyes began to well with tears as she looked up at Brent. "What's wrong?" she said. "Are you okay?"

"Yes, I'm fine. Can you point out the man who brought you here?"

Emily looked around the room, then pointed to an impossibly tall, barrel-chested Guardsman with a red beard and curly, red hair standing next to the front door. Brent remembered seeing him a few times, a tough Irish man named Morris. Brent remembered the name easily since the guy was a redhead, like Morris the Cat from the 9Lives commercials.

"Wait right here, okay, Honey?" Brent said, kissing Emily on the top of her head.

"Okay, Mr. Brent."

Brent stood, swallowed his rising acid, then headed toward Morris.

Morris was peering out a slit in the door, keeping watch.

"Excuse me," Brent said.

Morris turned, and with seemingly no recognition, said, "Yeah?"

"You see that little girl over there who you brought in?" Brent nodded toward Emily. She was staring at them.

"Yeah, poor thing. You know her?"

"Friend of the family. What happened to her mom?"

Morris looked down, then at Emily before looking back at Brent. "She was infected."

"And? What does that mean? Emily said someone went into the house after they left, to 'take care of her.' Was she brought to the Facility?"

Morris shook his head, and met Brent's eyes. He didn't need to say another word.

Brent asked anyway. "Did you kill her?"

"Not me, my partner. The island is on lockdown, and orders from above are to kill infected on sight."

Brent closed his eyes, to hide the tears and squelch his rising tide of anger.

"Why?" Brent asked.

"Excuse me?" Morris asked, clearly annoyed that someone would deign to question the "orders from above."

"Why are they killing people on sight? I thought they, I thought we, were bringing the sick to Level 7."

"Not when there's a lockdown." The Guardsmen shook

his head. "Two of the infected escaped, and infection is spreading fast. It's them or us, and no time or space to set anyone aside now for a maybe cure later."

"That little girl thinks her mom is still alive. That she's gonna see her again!" Brent was unable to control the swell inside his voice. He could feel the eyes multiply on his back as his sudden volume made him the most popular person in the room.

Morris met Brent's eyes, but instead of the ice Brent expected, they glistened with sympathy.

"I'm sorry," he said. "I didn't know how to tell her. I was hoping we'd run into someone she knew, and . . . well, do you want to tell her?"

Brent looked over at Emily, her face filled with anxiety, like she knew they were talking about her and her mother.

"Fuck," Brent said. "Fuck. Fuck. Fuck."

Brent turned from Morris and began walking back toward Emily, not sure what in the hell he should say.

How do you tell a kid her mother is dead, and that she'll never see her again?

Brent approached Emily and met her eyes, preparing to deliver the worst.

∼

FIFTY-NINE

Boricio Wolfe

East Hampton, New York
East Hampton Docks
April 2, 2012
SIX MONTHS AFTER THE EVENT ...

BORICIO STARED as Limp Dick approached the Paul Bunyan-looking motherfucker at the front door, and thought for sure a fight was about to erupt.

He wasn't sure why, but Boricio wanted to see the little guy get knocked the fuck to the floor. It was the sort of irrational hate Boricio had never questioned before, but rather indulged, figuring most people — if you really got to know them — had at least one or 14 things that made hating them easy as fuck.

Boricio kept one eye on Die Hard talking to the Guardsmen and Pirate Boricio about whatever shit was happening on the island and around the restaurant. From what Boricio could tell, the island seemed fuckered, overrun with about a billion of the ugly black monsters, which weren't monsters, but aliens and infected fuckers too stupid or sorry to outrun the aliens — mutants, they were calling 'em.

Boricio didn't care what the fuck they were called — people, aliens, mutants. They all bled, which meant all of them died.

Boricio watched as Limp Dick walked away from Paul Bunyan with his tail between his legs. Boricio smiled.

Fucking pussy. Should've at least taken a shot at the fucker. I might've had a squirt of piss worth of respect for ya then.

Limp Dick was walking toward a little girl. He got down on his knees, met her eyes, then put a hand on her shoulder.

What's goin' on here? I doubt that little girl has a single blade of grass on her patch. Ain't no way she's old enough to play ball.

The girl burst into tears, sobbing, "Mommy!" on repeat.

Limp Dick picked her up, then held her tight.

Boricio looked over to Paul Bunyan, watching the scene with watery eyes.

Boricio walked over to Paul Bunyan, nodded toward Limp Dick and the girl in his arms and said, "What the fuck is up with *General Hospital* over there?"

Paul Bunyan wiped his eyes, then said, "We've got orders to kill infected on sight. The girl's mom was infected and had to be put down. Girl didn't know. That guy, Brent, I think, is a friend of the family. He volunteered to break the news to the girl."

"Put down?" Boricio asked. "Like a dog?"

"We have to kill all infected."

Boricio whistled, then nodded on his way back to his spot near Ed and Pirate Boricio — both of them still speaking to the Guardsman, and now on the radio with home base or some such shit.

Boricio looked back over at Limp Dick, the girl still in his arms.

Boricio saw the pain in the girl's eyes, then felt a sharp and sudden stab, no different from if he were a kid with his own mother shot. Boricio wondered, for the first time ever, how many kids he'd made cry by putting their mommies or daddies into the dirt. Boricio prided himself on never raping or killing a kid — he might've been a monster, but he wasn't sick — but he must've handed pain like candy to at least a few kids over the years.

Boricio surely broke some little girl's heart, like the one still sobbing in Limp Dick's arms.

Limp Dick wiped the tears from the little girl's eyes, and Boricio suddenly felt like a giant asshole for thinking of Brent as a pussy, when the truth was the fucker was brave enough to tell a tater tot that her mother wasn't ever baking potatoes again.

A girl's voice pulled Boricio from the scene, asking, "Are you crying?"

He looked down and saw Little Lamb, with Mary and Luca standing behind her.

"No, I'm not fucking crying, Paola," Boricio said, turning away and wiping his eyes. "It's goddamned dusty in here, and I've got allergies conspiring to fuck my shit up."

Mary burst out laughing, but her laughter collapsed when she saw what had held Boricio's attention — Brent and the little girl.

"What happened?" she said.

"The fucking Gestapo here killed the girl's momma because she was infected. They've got orders, kill on sight, and POW! that's just what they did. Apparently, the girl didn't know because the Brawny Man over there didn't have the balls to do it, so Brent, who knew the girl and her mom, said he'd break the news."

"Jesus," Mary said.

"But I wasn't fucking crying," Boricio said. "And even if I was getting a sniffle, it's only 'cuz Rip van Creepy here broke me!"

Boricio looked over at Luca, who was staring at Brent and the girl, head tilted like he was trying to read the tattoo on a stripper's left tit from the cheap seats at a strip joint.

Luca started walking toward Brent and the child.

"Where the fuck is he going?" Boricio asked Mary.

Luca kept walking, even though he must've heard Boricio.

Luca walked up to Brent and the girl, now sitting beside one another at a table. Brent's arms were wrapped around the child, and her eyes were on the tabletop. Boricio followed, out of curiosity, hoping like hell he wouldn't see any more sad shit that would agitate the dust situation in the room.

Luca stood an inch from the girl and said, "Hi."

Brent looked up at them as if to ask, "Really, now?"

Boricio shrugged, as if to say, "What am I gonna do; the old fucker's senile."

The girl sniffled, then wiped at her eyes, looking curiously at Luca.

"What's your name?" he asked the girl like an ancient Mr. Rogers catering to newly grief-stricken children.

"Emily," she said through her tears.

"My name is Luca," he said. "I heard that your mom died."

Jesus Christ, Luca! Way to be sensitive! Fuck, dude! Good thing you hop, skipped, and jumped right through dating age, with an opening line like that!

Boricio stared at Mary and Paola, both wide-eyed and loudly wearing their shock.

"Would you like to see her again?" Luca asked. "Just to say good-bye?"

"Yes," Emily nodded, crying.

Brent looked up at Luca, and seemed like he might be gearing up to punch the old man-kid square in the jaw.

Boricio shook his head and looked at Mary, prompting her to intervene before Luca said something even more astonishingly stupid than he already had.

Maybe he is getting senile.

Mary said, "I'm sorry," and put a hand on Luca's shoulder. "Let's give her some time. She just found out."

"No," Luca said, shaking his head and shrugging Mary's hand from his shoulder, then turning with a surprising awareness to look the little girl in the eyes. "She wants to see her mommy."

Everyone shifted uncomfortably as Luca sat across from Emily, stretching his hands out, open palmed. He said, "Can you put your hands on mine?"

Brent glared as if Luca was about to pull some phony bullshit psychic reading routine to exploit the child's tragedy. For all Boricio knew, he was. The boy had clearly lost his marbles. Before Mary could gently pull Luca away without making a scene, Emily slipped her hands onto his.

Every eye was turned to the four clasped hands.

Paola looked at Mary and Boricio, then whispered, "He knows what he's doing."

"Shut your eyes," Luca said, closing his own.

Emily did.

As she did, Boricio felt something shifting inside him, some force or energy was the only way to describe it, swelling so much it felt like it might pop from his body. Then he saw the light bleeding from Luca's hands — from his fingers and into the girl's.

"Oh my God," Mary whispered.

The same soft glow was wrapped like a blanket around Mary and Paola — the two other people Luca had brought back from the dead.

"You're glowing," Mary said to Boricio, her eyes wide as she looked at him, then at her daughter, and then herself.

Boricio looked down, but couldn't see the aura around himself like he could see it around Luca and the girls.

Emily said, "Mommy?" then a wide smile spread across her face.

Boricio saw a slight Asian woman in his mind a moment before he heard her voice.

"Emily," she said.

Whoa, what the fuck?

"Mommy, are you alive?"

The woman was suddenly sitting there, right where Luca was, like a ghost superimposed over his body.

"Oh, Baby," she said, reaching out, her spectral hand grazing Emily's cheek. "You're okay."

Judging from the stone on Brent's face, he wasn't seeing dick of what Boricio, Mary, Paola, and Emily were seeing. But he did nothing to interrupt.

"Are you alive?" Emily asked.

"No," the specter shook her head. "That doesn't mean I'm not here, or that I can't see you, though. I'll be watching out for you, Baby."

The woman started to fade as Luca's body began to shake. Sweat plastered his head, and it seemed like he was suffering from the strain of whatever it was he was doing. Boricio was about to shake Luca out of it, but then the woman looked at Brent, and said, "Brent, you made it back! Please take care of my baby girl."

Brent didn't seem to hear her.

Emily said, "Mommy wants you to take care of me, Mr. Brent."

"What?" Brent said, staring at the girl, then up at Mary and Paola, both of them nodding.

"We can see her," they said together, creeping Boricio way the fuck out, especially since he said the same shit at the same time, as if the same voice was speaking through all three of them at once.

What the fuck?

"Please take care of my baby," they said together again, even though Boricio had no knowledge of thinking the words before they fled his mouth.

"I love you, Emily. Please don't be sad. We'll be together again," they said in unison.

Emily reached out to touch the specter, her eyes wide and

filled with tears.

Their hands touched, and a sad smile broke across the little girl's face.

Luca slumped forward, as if someone took the batteries out of him, and the ghost was gone.

Brent reached forward and helped Luca sit up. "You okay?"

Luca shook his head, "Yeah," he said, then looked up at Emily, who smiled up at him, wiping tears from her eyes.

"Thank you," she said.

Boricio turned to Mary and Paola and said, "What kinda *Touched By An Angel* shit was that?"

Before Mary came up with a theory or Luca could respond, Boricio's attention was pulled away by Charlie who approached him, walking beside Callie.

"Is he okay?" Charlie said, looking at Luca about as weird as Luca had been looking at Emily before he went and played Whoopi Goldberg in *Ghost*.

"I think so," Mary said, her hand on Luca's shoulder as Emily told Brent what she'd seen.

"I think we're gonna have a problem getting to the island," Charlie said.

"Why's that?"

"Someone just told Ed that they're not making any trips over until they get things sealed on the island or something. They said it's too dangerous."

"Bullshit," Boricio said, as he marched over to where Ed, Pirate Boricio, and two Guardsmen were standing in a circle with Ed trying to persuade someone to get the ferry in motion.

Boricio slid between them, then grabbed the radio from Ed before he could say dick. "Don't mean to break up the circle jerk," Boricio said to whoever was on the other side of the radio. "But we got something you want."

"Who is this?" a man's voice asked.

"Boricio Fucking Wolfe, who the hell is this?"

"This is Acting Ed Keenan; give the radio back to Captain Keenan,"

"No," Boricio said. "Is there a Will Bishop in your room?"

A moment passed before Keenan said, "Yes. Why?"

"Because Will's lil' Luca paid us a visit with a very special message."

Six seconds passed, then Will Bishop was suddenly on the radio. "What? You saw him? Where is he?"

"I dunno where he went. He came and went like a ghost. But your Luca came to *our Will* just before he died and said we had to get a message to Black Island, that it might get us back home and save the world and all that happy horse shit. Now I don't know about you, but I don't like to take long-ass trips across the country, then get kept waitin' in the middle of Shitsville. So, you better get your bumper boat back here, pronto."

"It's too dangerous," Will said. "There are aliens on the docks, and our manpower is limited."

"Well, lucky for you, Team Boricio just drafted a buncha new soldiers, so you get your ferry over here and let us worry about the E-Fucking-T's."

"Please, just give us the message now," Will said, his voice desperate.

"No, no, I'm not sayin' shit until we're standing on the other side of the goddamned water."

After a long pause, Will said, "We'll send the ferry to you, but you have to give me the message before it docks. I can't guarantee you safe passage once you get off the boat."

"Fine by me," Boricio said, then handed the phone to Ed and walked away.

He returned to Charlie and said, "They'll be sending the Love Boat before the next commercial break."

"Good," Charlie said, smiling a bit too wide for Boricio's liking.

SIXTY

Boricio Bishop

Black Island, New York
April 2, 2012
SIX MONTHS AFTER THE EVENT …

THEY HAD PRACTICALLY FLOWN from Georgia to New York, taking turns behind the wheel and flooring the pedal the entire way. The trip could only be described as eerie, not for what happened, but for everything that didn't.

Even when they had to find alternate routes and take back roads because entire chunks of highway had simply vanished, which easily doubled their trip time, nothing got in their way or attacked them along the way. It was as if every alien, mutant, and bandit had decided to take the day off.

And while Boricio was grateful to fly through the omnipresent danger all the way to Black Island, it felt *wrong*.

When they hit New York, it seemed even worse, the empty seemed somehow emptier, like a red carpet rolled before them. Once Will finally cleared the ferry, and they were standing at the docks ready to cross, Boricio could almost feel the waiting army of eyes behind, watching from the shadows, but not striking for reasons he could only imagine.

Even on the ferry, in the middle of the water and away from any chance of attack, Boricio bristled with unease. The two Guardsmen on the ferry eyed him with suspicion, looking like the men from Black Mountain, though somehow softer. They were definitely new, and didn't recognize him at all.

Before they were allowed off the ferry, Will radioed them and asked what the message was. Luca stepped forward and told them about the vial — the last vial — tucked away in a moon globe. Boricio wasn't sure why his brother had hid the vial away, but hoped like hell the kid knew something that he didn't.

Their walk across the island grounds was as uneventful as their drive into the city, terrifying because of its thousand-pound silence. When they arrived at the Facility gates, Ed stepped to the front of the group, then hit the intercom button and identified himself. There was a long silence, then another try from Ed before they heard a crackling response from Will.

"Let me speak to my son," he said.

Boricio stepped to the front. "I'm here."

Will said, "A.D. Keenan will let you inside, but one wrong move and the Guardsmen have been instructed to shoot. I don't know all of what you've done, Boricio. But I know enough. You have no margin for error. Understand?"

"I understand."

The outer doors parted, and the group stepped into the Facility's reception area — a sprawling lobby with a welcome desk in the front and a high tiled wall behind, more like a posh hotel than a research center, spilling into a long, wide hallway with a bank of eight elevators leading down to the lower levels.

They were halfway to the elevators when Boricio realized that bringing Charlie down to Level 8 would violate every instinct inside him. Charlie was dangerous; Boricio could feel it. Not being able to see inside Charlie's mind fueled his rising worry.

Boricio pulled Ed back toward him, and into a conspiratorial whisper. "I need you to knock Charlie out, now. He isn't safe." Boricio didn't even have to add, "Trust me." Ed winked, then nodded. He may as well have said, "Glad you asked."

Ed brought the flat of his palm against the back of Charlie's skull, sending him into a silent collapse. Ed hit him a second time when he was halfway to the floor, where he lay like an empty bag of skin and bones.

Callie screamed, "What the fuck?!"

Her yell was louder, but Asshole Boricio's was meaner.

"What the fuck you trying to do?" Asshole Boricio screamed, getting in Boricio's face, pistol out and aimed at him. Ed and Brent immediately responded, guns trained on Asshole Boricio.

His asshole twin laughed as he looked around at the Mexican standoff and seemed to almost relish the situation.

"You wanna take us out one by one, and your adopted daddy taught you to hit people on the back of the head like a yellow-bellied candy ass? I knew you were a tiny-pricked fucker without a ball in his sack, but this is some goddamned bullshit!"

Boricio ignored the asshole's anger and calmly said, "Ed, Brent, put your guns down. You all need to understand that we can't take Charlie where we're going. He's infected, and if we bring an infected person into Level 8 right now, we will be jeopardizing everything. I never would have allowed that at Black Mountain, and I'm certainly not going to do it here. Besides, we head down there with an infected, and we'll all get shot the minute those elevator doors open."

Asshole Boricio kept his gun on Boricio. Ed and Brent looked at Boricio for instruction, but he simply kept his eyes on the asshole in front of him.

Boricio added, "We'll leave him in this elevator bay, then

lock it down. He'll be safe until we get everything settled. Okay?"

Boricio stared down Asshole Boricio's gun, figuring the chances of the asshole firing were about 50/50. Clearly, the other Boricio wasn't a guy who really thought through things like consequences of his actions. At the moment, Boricio almost didn't care whether he lived or died. He did his job — he delivered the message. Let his father and the others save the world. He was tired.

Asshole Boricio must've seen the resignation in his eyes and lowered his gun, saying, "Fine," then turned from Boricio as though he couldn't be bothered to finish his sentence.

Boricio looked down at Charlie and then nodded at Ed and Brent, who dragged Charlie's body to an open elevator and then closed the door. Brent placed his hand on the panel beside the door and said, "Lockdown Elevator Bay Three."

"Confirmed lockdown," a computerized woman's voice said.

Boricio was glad that his security was reinstated enough to lock the elevator down. If Charlie woke up and got loose, things could get ugly. Things could get ugly anyway, however, given how Charlie had broken at least one containment cell, perhaps more if he'd broken out of Black Mountain. Fortunately, the elevators were also equipped with sleeping gas, which could be administered if Charlie woke and started causing a scene.

Boricio then opened the elevator two down from Charlie's, and the group stepped inside. As the doors closed and the elevator began its descent, Boricio's stomach followed suit, imagining his reunion with Will. He wondered if Will believed him responsible for releasing the vial. Did he think him capable of such an act? He also wondered what Will would think about the old Luca and the other Boricio.

The elevator whirred, along with the subtle drop in his

stomach, then chimed and settled as the doors opened to Will waiting on the other side.

Boricio expected Will to be angry, but thought that he'd at least hear a hello before the growling, "What in the hell have you done, Boricio?" slapping him in the face before the elevator doors were halfway open.

Boricio fell into immediate apology.

"I'm so sorry, Dad. I never meant for any of this to happen. I met a man, and I was foolish enough to let him steal the vial from me." He shook his head, staring at the glossy white floor, trying not to let his guilty torment and undiluted rage push the welling tears from inside him. "I'm so, so sorry," he kept shaking his head. "It's all my fault. I wish I could take it all back."

Boricio felt every eye burning his back with the many questions that no one dared ask. Of all the eyes, Boricio only cared about Will's.

As angry as Will was, something about Boricio's sorrow softened the old man. His eyes were nearly as wet as Boricio's when he said, "It's okay, Son. Everything will turn out okay."

It was Will's nature to say it, but Boricio knew the truth: Nothing was okay. He had helped The Prophet murder their world, whether the old fucker had meant to or not. So no, it wasn't okay, and would never be again. At least now Boricio had a chance to do whatever he could to right the wrongs he'd invited into the world.

Boricio raised his gaze from the floor, then tried to index the thousand expressions etched into his father's face. Will broke his son's stare, then moved his eyes across the rest of the group. Most of Will's reaction seemed stuck between horror and fascination when his eyes settled on the other Boricio.

Then he saw the other, significantly older, Luca.

Will gasped, struggling to stay standing. His eyes flashed to Boricio, before flying back to Luca where they held their study for another several seconds.

"This is Luca," Boricio said, patting the old boy on the shoulder, then nudging him a step forward toward the old man.

The skin on Luca's face was so brittle; his smile looked like it came with a deep ravine of pain. Will probably didn't mean to shake his head slowly back and forth any more than he meant to retreat the three small steps that he did.

Luca said, "Your Luca is in my world, with my family. When I got pulled over here, he took my place."

Will's palm was suddenly over his mouth. "Oh my God," he whispered. "That's horrible." He shook his head. "I'm so, so sorry."

"It's okay," Luca said, his voice hoarse. "I understand. I probably would have done the same thing. He didn't bring me here. The Light did. It told me. It brought us all here."

"What are you talking about?" Will asked.

Luca met his eyes. "I'll tell you on the way, but first we have to get to your house and get the vial." He choked and coughed, then caught his breath before he said, "By the way, thank you for taking care of me."

Will's eyes were blank. "What do you mean?"

"When the other Luca's parents died," he said, "you took care of him. And when *I* was lost, the other you took care of me here. You and the other Will were always there for us, and I never really had a chance to fully say thank you."

Will blushed. "Of course," he said, then put his hand on old Luca's shoulder.

"Now," Luca said. "You have to bring me to the vial. I am the only one who can open it. If anyone else opens it, bad things will happen."

"How do you know?" Will asked.

"Dog Vader, the Indian, the Light," Luca said. Then, he pointed to his head and said, "It's okay, you can come inside. See for yourself."

Will looked baffled, but then Boricio watched his father's face flicker with the same vacancy it always did when he entered another's mind. A second later, Will's face went white. "Oh my … "

~

SIXTY-ONE

Ed Keenan

Black Island, New York
  April 2012
  SIX MONTHS AFTER THE EVENT …

"THEY'D BETTER BE OKAY," Ed said to Sullivan as they crossed the long hallway. "I did my job and brought Boricio back. You all had better of kept them safe."

"Yes, and as I think you will now see, we're not the bad guys. We held our word."

Sullivan waved his hand on a panel outside the final door on the right, then stood back as it slid open to a small, dorm-like room, similar to the one where he'd stayed before heading south to find Boricio, except this one had two beds. Jade was sitting on one, with Teagan beside her, holding a baby girl.

Ed stepped inside, then Sullivan nodded and left them alone.

Ed's heart swelled the moment he saw them — not just Jade, but Teagan and her baby as well. It felt like an eternity since he last saw either one smile. Jade's eyes widened in shock as she leapt from her bed, squealing with more enthusiasm than he'd seen from her in years.

She hugged him tight while crying, "Dad! Oh God, I never thought I'd see you again!"

As Ed lost himself in his daughter's embrace, he felt the thousand pounds of the past six months slide from his shoulders.

"Are you okay?" he asked, holding her tight, closing his eyes, and not wanting to let go. "Did they hurt you?"

"No, I'm fine. We're both fine. They took good care of us."

Ed opened his eyes to see Teagan, now standing and holding her baby girl up for Ed to see.

"This is Becca," Teagan said, beaming.

"She's beautiful," Ed said, hugging Teagan and looking down at the baby.

Seeing a fresh-faced innocent infant after seeing so much death and desolation in the world felt like a balm — a balm that promised that the world wasn't thoroughly lost just yet. There was hope. There were babies to be born, and so long as he breathed, someone willing to protect them and their mothers.

Jade and Ed sat on one bed, while Teagan sat on the other, holding Becca, catching one another up on the last several months. Ed toned down some of what he'd seen so as not to terrify the girls any more than he had to, particularly Teagan who was so young and had grown up so sheltered.

Ed was happy to find their events relatively mundane. They spoke through many minutes of all the things the girls weren't saying — all the things he could feel them wanting to say, but for some reason couldn't. Once the awkward glances and silences grew too frequent to ignore, Ed had to chew on his bottom lip to keep himself from demanding answers. Whatever news they were hiding, he wouldn't like it a bit.

Did something happen to Jade?

Did someone here knock her up?

What aren't they saying?

Ed couldn't take it any longer. He finally blurted, "What is it you girls aren't telling me?"

Teagan and Jade traded a glance.

"Tell him," Jade said.

"I can't," Teagan shook her head.

"Someone better tell me something," Ed said.

"I met someone," Teagan said, her face flushed, bright-red like a schoolgirl admitting her first crush. And other than the guy who put the bun in her oven, this might *have* been her first crush.

"Ohhhhkay," Ed said, shifting on the bed, waiting for the other shoe to hit the floor. "And?"

"This is so weird," she said, looking toward the door instead of Ed's eyes.

"Yeah, super weird," Jade agreed, raising her eyebrows.

"Stop it," Teagan said.

"I'm sorry, it's just . . . well, you know," she said.

Ed was getting frustrated with all the coded young-girl chatter, "Will someone just say it?!"

Teagan turned to him, then blurted, "I'm seeing Ed Keenan. The other Ed Keenan," then quickly looked away again.

Ed stood, feeling a flush of anger as if he were the girl's father. "What?!" he tried not to roar, and mostly failed.

"I know, I know, I didn't expect it to happen. *Believe me,*" she said in a way that made Ed feel as though he were the last old codger in the world a girl like her would find attractive.

"Yeah, right?" Jade said, smiling.

"But," Teagan continued. "He took care of me and Becca, and he was so nice."

"I'll bet he did," Ed said, about to storm from the room and go beat the shit out of the pervert who was old enough to be the girl's father.

"No, Dad!" Jade cried, jumping from the bed and

inserting herself between him and the door with her hands out. "It isn't like that."

"It's not," Teagan pleaded. "He is so sweet. He never even tried anything. It was just friendship for a long time."

"He held you prisoner," Ed said. "He kept you, both of you, hidden from me while he forced me to work for the Black Island Guard, to put my life on the line for them! I don't know what you *think* you know about him, but he's *not* a decent man. No decent man would take advantage of a gullible teenage girl like that."

Teagan rested Becca on the bed, then stood, her face red and twisted with fury. "What? Do you think I'm some stupid hillbilly girl who got suckered by the first man she met? Maybe you think I have daddy issues or something, making me a ripe target for a pervy old guy? Is that it?"

Ed was exasperated, as he'd felt so many times with Jade. "It's not an insult to say you're young and inexperienced, is it? It's the truth. It doesn't reflect badly on *you* that an old guy took advantage of you. It's on him. He should know better. I only know a little bit of what you told me about your dad, and I hate to use a cliché, but yes, you *do* have daddy issues. Hell, most people have daddy issues. Find someone whose father wasn't an asshole, or busy, or somehow messed them up just a little, and I'll show you the face of a certified liar. I'm sure I screwed Jade up, too. Fathers do dumb shit because, most times, they were too damned young or too damned stupid to know any better. And it messes up their kids — boys and girls both. It's just when it comes to girls, it manifests in a way that makes them needy, and … "

"Just stop it, Dad," Jade said. "She doesn't need a lesson in family dynamics from you, of all people. It's her life, and Ed, despite being another version of you, is a surprisingly sweet man. And, he's emotionally available."

Ed ignored the slight. He didn't feel like arguing with the girls, particularly after just reconciling with his daughter.

He looked at Teagan, meeting her wounded eyes. He'd offended her, and as he took a moment to calm down, felt bad. He wasn't wrong. Even if the other Ed was a perfectly nice guy, he was still too damned old for her. When it came down to it, who was he to question her choices, to say her love wasn't real just because it may have been born of circumstance?

"I'm sorry," he said. "I'm not sure I'm wrong about this, but I am sorry I shot my mouth off before waiting to see for myself. It's just that I … " He stopped himself before he went on to say that he was all too familiar with how guys like this operate, because that would only reinforce all the things he'd already said. And he was trying to make things right — for a bit anyway, until he grabbed a hold of the other Ed and got a feel for his take on the relationship.

Ed continued, "It's just that I kind of got attached to you . . . even though you were a massive pain in my ass."

He grinned, and Teagan smiled back through her watery eyes.

"You're like a daughter to me, Teagan, and I just want to make sure you're okay. If you say he treats you right, and he's helped you, that's all that matters right now. Things could've been so much worse. I thought I might never see either of you again. But here we are, and for a moment anyway, let's just be happy with that."

He held his arms out, inviting them both to hug him.

He felt weird and uncharacteristically affectionate, and a bit like a phony, but he forced himself to do it anyway, because he knew it was the right thing to do. It's what a loving, happy father — *surely, there must be some in the world* — would do.

They embraced, and to Ed's surprise, the hug felt right.

~

THE DOOR SLID OPEN, with the other Keenan and Sullivan on the other side, standing beside Boricio Bishop.

Ed looked at Other Keenan, giving him a glare to let him know he knew. Other Keenan met his gaze without defense, offering only a subtle nod. He said, "We're rounding up a few people to go and get the vial. I don't know if it's gonna do anything, but Will, Luca, and Boricio seem to think it's our only hope of defeating the aliens."

"How?" Ed asked.

"I'm not going to pretend to know," Keenan said, "but I think we've all seen enough weird stuff that it's justifiable to go on faith here, and trust in something beyond what we know. Will, the other Luca and Boricio all say that if Luca can get the vial, it could counteract the spreading infection and possibly return you all to your homes."

Ed wasn't sure if their faith was good enough, but it wasn't like they could make the situation much worse if their attempt failed.

"What about you all?" Ed asked. "If it returns us to our world, what will it do to you, the few natives?"

"I have no idea," Other Keenan said. "But there's so few of us, versus so many people from your world, that I must act in the interest of the greater good."

Ed looked back at Teagan, uncertain if she were doing the same mental math as he — and figuring that if they were returned home, she and her new guy could be split up. If so, she wasn't reacting yet.

"OK," Ed said. "Let me get to the armory and I'll ... "

"No," Other Keenan shook his head and put a hand to Ed's chest. "I need you to stay."

"Like hell," Ed took a step back, shrugging Other Keenan's hand from his body. "I'm not sitting here hiding away while you all go out there. It's too dangerous."

"That's exactly why I want you here," Other Keenan said, calmly. "If something happens to us, or, God forbid, the vial turns us into more of these mutants, then I need someone here who can defend the Facility. Who can help rebuild things."

"What do you mean, *rebuild*?"

Sullivan stepped forward and held up a glass sphere with an orange, swirling light inside.

"What the hell is that?" Ed asked.

Sullivan answered, "This is our Hard Reset Protocol. The island is built on top of a machine which emits a powerful blast of energy that will disrupt the life of any living thing on the island. Plants, animals, people, aliens, all of it wiped out within seconds of activating the sphere."

"A Doomsday device?" Ed's eyes were wide, his voice almost hoarse. "What about everyone in here?"

Sullivan continued, "The Facility's seventh and eighth levels are lined with lead and a counter energy field, which starts up once the Hard Reset Protocol is initiated. Everyone inside will be safe."

"What about you?" Teagan said, looking at her lover.

"If we use this, then that means we were already lost," Other Keenan said.

Teagan cried out, "You're not going out there, are you?"

Other Keenan nodded. "I have to," he said. "It's my island. My duty."

Ed shook his head. "Let me go in your place," he said.

"No, Daddy," Jade now argued. "You just got back. You said you almost died. Do you really want to be away from me so much that you're gonna run out again and throw yourself into yet more danger?"

Ed shook his head, "I'm doing this for all of us."

"No," Other Keenan said. "You're not doing it at all. You're far more equipped to deal with rebuilding. I've seen what you're capable of. While we might look the same, and have more than a few similarities, you're obviously more suited to the tasks that must be done than I am. Trust me."

Ed looked at Jade, who stared at him as if waiting for him to disappoint her again. Waiting for him to run off to fight again. It was all he'd ever done, after all. Live to serve.

But whose interests was I serving all those years? Certainly not my family's.

Something told him to stay put.

It's time to stop running away. Stay and fight to rebuild the life with Jade. Stay and make sure Teagan and Becca are okay. Stop fucking running.

Ed wasn't sure if it was his instincts, which had never led him astray, fear, or perhaps the emotion of seeing the girls again after such a long time.

Whatever it was, Ed decided to listen to his gut. "OK," he said. "I'll stay, but only under one condition."

"What's that?" Other Keenan said.

"Brent Foster and the little girl he's with stay here, too."

"No problem," Other Keenan said.

Teagan threw her arms around Other Keenan, tears streaming down her face, "Please, don't go."

He shook his head, "I'm sorry. But believe me, if something goes bad, you and Becca are better off with this man."

She cried, hugging him tighter.

Other Keenan kissed Teagan on the cheek, gently pushed her from his body, then picked Becca up from the bed, kissed her on the head, and said, "I'll be back soon, Baby Doll."

Ed watched how Other Keenan was so gentle and caring with Teagan and the baby while saying his goodbyes, and figured that he was probably wrong after all. Maybe Other Keenan was a good guy, better than he was, and possibly one of the rare men who would actually be a decent father.

Then again, maybe Ed was getting his second chance right now.

～

SIXTY-TWO

Boricio Wolfe

Black Island, New York
   April 2012
   SIX MONTHS AFTER THE EVENT…

IT WAS like a Very Special Episode of *The Brady Bunch* or some goddamned shit, how the entire fucking short bus was hitting the road, headed for Will's house to pull some magical fucking vial out of a globe.

Except in this case, instead of a short bus, they were riding in two small, black trucks.

The Brady Bunch in this very special episode was himself — the Original Gangsta Boricio; his fugly body double, Pirate Boricio; Nerdy Die Hard; Mary and her Little Lamb; and Will's less crazy-looking double, who apparently let Pirate Boricio sit on his lap through puberty. Of course, there was also Grandpa Luca, some cunt hair named Sullivan, and Chuckie CheeseDick's cock warmer, Callie, all of them whistling while they worked like the Seven Fucking Dwarves on their way to get the vial.

There was quite the melee at the Ponderosa. However,

before they hit the trail Nerdy Die Hard and Keenan suggested that Mary and her Little Lamb stay behind at the ranch. That was just fine with Miss Mary, but Luca wouldn't hear it. He said they both had to come because "Paola and Mary increased the power inside him."

Luca didn't say shit past that, though everyone wanted to know what in the fuck it meant. Apparently, having a raisin cock gave you the juice to call the shots.

Shit was a mile and a half past nucking futs, but at least Boricio figured the end was near enough to hit when he spit. Whatever was about to happen, it was going to happen goddamned soon. If Old Man Luca was right, then they could be home soon, which meant Boricio could finally quit playing babysitter and get back to what it was he did best: hunting solo — even though he wasn't sure if Luca had "fixed him" too well to go after the same types of targets.

Boricio wondered how long he'd actually think about shit like people's feelings before he took what he wanted. He thought again of the little girl, Emily — *Why the fuck do I remember her name?* — and the guilt he felt for being an orphan factory.

Fuck you, Luca, for stripping the fun from this shit!

Boricio wasn't too worried, though. Because even though the man-child had broken him, he'd left his taste for murder intact. Perhaps Boricio would make his murder premium. It would be like that four months when he gave up beef because some bitch bet he couldn't. He didn't give up meat, entirely, though. Just because he couldn't have a burger didn't mean he couldn't eat the fuck outta some hot wings. Same rules, different coat of paint.

Boricio's nose was bothering him, his inner wolf insisting something was following behind. He wished he knew what it was, especially since he couldn't shake the feeling, but predator's guess said it was something even worse than one of them aliens or mutants.

A few minutes before they reached Will's house, they started seeing all sorts of holy shit, aliens and mutants running past them in the woods, like they were tailing them, and confirming Boricio's suspicions that they were being followed. But that holy shit was only a teaser for the main attraction waiting on the street they needed to pass through to get to the one that led to Will's house by the shore. There were around 40 of the alien and mutated fuckers, maybe more. Boricio gripped his pistol, itching to fight, and hoping for one of the first times in his life that he wasn't outgunned — or outclawed, as the case may be.

The aliens gathered, blocking both the road ahead and the road back — trapping them. The woods on either side of the road bubbled in darkness, though it was tough to tell what was shadows and what was aliens and mutants. Whatever the case, they were fucked.

"OK, Team Boricio," he said to both groups as they got out of their trucks, and got their guns ready for a firefight, "Let's kill some fuckers. And remember, we've gotta protect Luca!"

The creatures were clawing, gnashing, and screaming into the air as the Brady Bunch tensed in a half circle between the two trucks, creating a barrier to protect Luca.

Boricio smiled, looking around at his team, everyone with guns drawn and ready. His smile went especially wide when he saw Paola, remembering how he taught her to shoot a fucker dead before she took a second to think.

With the creatures closing in around them, Boricio was surprised at his pride. He winked at Paola, and she smiled back. "Y'all ready for shit to get steamy?" he asked.

No one answered, though Nerdy Die Hard looked like he was about to bark an order. He never got a chance, just fired his gun as the first creature reared its head, eye slits to the sky and screeching, then charged toward the group at a full gallop, fast enough for Boricio to hear its slippery slosh.

Boricio stepped forward, taking lead, and opened fire, joining the chorus around him. Laughing, he pulled the trigger on repeat, dropping fuckers one by one without blinking, surprising himself again as he slowly took aim around the Brady Bunch, guarding the circle, and knocking anything down which came even close to Team Boricio.

Too soon his gun went empty.

And at that exact moment, several of the aliens broke through, racing toward them, scattering the group in all directions from the protection of the two trucks.

Fuck, fuck!

No time for a fresh clip, Boricio dropped the gun, then dropped to his knees as a giant claw whistled through the air above his head. He swept the creature's feet from its body then rolled out of the way as it crashed to the ground with a squishy thud. Boricio sprang to his feet, then slammed his heel into the back of the alien's head.

The creature's body was the softest Boricio'd yet seen, and his heel went straight through its flesh, like it was made of nothing but rotten fruit. An eruption of black goo bubbled out.

Another creature shrieked, so close it was like a lion roaring in his ear. Boricio pivoted, expecting to see the creature barreling toward him, but it flew by on its way toward Paola, whose gun had jammed and was now cowering behind Boricio, near the front of one of the trucks.

Boricio screamed, suddenly furious. Wasn't no creature on this planet gonna hurt Mary's Little Lamb. Fuck that shit — they'd have to go through him first.

Boricio roared, causing the mutant to turn and look at him, though its body was still moving toward Paola. Boricio grabbed his blade from his waistband and unsheathed it, brought it up and through the mutant's face, tearing its head into two as he wrestled it down to the ground.

Paola jumped back as the mutant died just inches from her, and she met Boricio's eyes.

Boricio smiled at her and winked as he wiped the gore off his blade, sheathed it, then found his gun on the ground. "Get in the truck," he said, because he sure as shit didn't have time to fix her gun. "Stay down."

She got into the truck and Boricio was about to load a fresh clip into it when another mutant rushed him, a fast, black blur that sent him to the ground, gasping for air.

Fuck!

Boricio scrambled to his feet, searching for the mutant, grabbing his blade again, but didn't see the beast until it knocked him to the ground again and landed on top of him, pinning his arms beneath its tree-sized legs. It stared down into Boricio's eyes with its cold, black eyes full of nothing, and Boricio felt a chill that momentarily paralyzed him.

The mutant raised its bladed hand high and shrieked something akin to a battle cry. The scream reached into some part of Boricio and hurt his insides.

Boricio stared up, still paralyzed — not by fear, but by something he couldn't quite comprehend. It was something that he'd never have time to figure out before the blade ended his life.

The mutant's death blow was cut short by two shots, however, sending it to the ground, shrieking.

Boricio looked up to see Mary standing over him, offering him a hand up.

"Thanks," he said, smiling as she hoisted him up.

It looked like she wanted to say something, but instead she spun around and started emptying her gun into another charging creature instead.

Boricio grabbed his gun again and loaded a clip as Mary kept him covered. Callie ran toward them, and crouched as she reloaded her pistol.

"Stay here and protect the kids in the truck, can you?" Boricio asked.

Callie looked inside, saw Old Man Luca and Paola, and nodded.

Mary yelled, "I think someone needs to go get Luca." He followed her gaze to Luca, cowering behind Nerdy Die Hard, who was holding his own while protecting the man-kid, tearing through creatures with an M-16, probably faster than anyone else. However, he was so focused on pulling the trigger at the approaching horde that he was leaving Luca in danger from a growing mass coming from the other side.

Boricio said, "I'm on it," then ran to Luca and dragged him back toward the relative safety of the truck where Paola was hiding. As he got Luca settled inside the truck and told Paola to keep an eye on him and scream if she needed anything, the creatures began to recede. Boricio looked up, slowly shaking his head and trying to understand.

This isn't right.

He looked around at the crowd of creatures, and sure as shit, every one of them fuckers was falling back into the shadows. The aliens had never seemed smart enough to retreat simply because they were being decimated, at least they'd never shown those sorts of smarts before. Predator's guess was back — this time saying the creatures were getting called like puppies to the mama bitch.

Boricio looked down at Luca, who looked like he wanted to say something, though he seemed too tired, or maybe too old or too RipvanWhateverTheFUCKed to do anything other than lay splayed across the back seat like a half-dead body.

Boricio moved his eyes from Luca to the Brady Bunch and, crap on a cracker, saw Charlie strolling toward them, his eyes straight ahead and a stride that said he owned half the goddamned island, along with Park Place, Boardwalk, and all four of the fucking railroads.

"Be right back, kids," Boricio said to Luca and Paola and

shut the door of the truck and jogged over to the group to see what the hell was going on.

Charlie stopped walking, his eyes on Boricio and waiting.

Pirate Boricio asked, "How the hell did you get out?"

Charlie's face suddenly feigned distress. "There was a disaster at the Facility. The aliens got in and went on a full rampage. I barely managed to escape the elevator shaft. Everyone is dead."

Charlie was an emotional kid, but there wasn't a drop of feeling in his story. He said that shit like he was ordering off a menu, without seeing nothing he liked.

"Wait," Nerdy Die Hard said, "Everyone is dead? Everyone?"

He reached for his two-way radio and tried to reach someone.

The radio only offered silence and static, however.

"How?" Nerdy Die Hard asked, staring at Charlie. "How?!"

"I dunno," Charlie said, backing up, hands out defensively. "They tried to kill me, too."

"You motherfucker!" Nerdy Die Hard said, enraged, aiming his M-16 at Charlie's face.

"Whoa, wait a second," Boricio said, stepping between them. "He said he didn't do it!"

Nerdy Die Hard put the gun down, collapsing to the ground in tears. "Oh God, Teagan. Becca."

Boricio swallowed, looking back at Charlie, trying to suss out what he didn't like about his story.

Nerdy Die Hard stood up, glaring at Charlie, "No. There's no way they breached the bottom levels. No way. You're lying."

Charlie practically laughed, "Don't believe me, I don't care. Go check for yourself."

Boricio stared at Charlie then looked at Nerdy Die Hard

as he was clearly trying to decide whether or not to go back and check.

Sullivan grabbed the man's shoulder, "We can go back when we're done. You're not going back alone."

"Don't listen to him," a man's voice called out from the darkness behind them.

"What the fuck?" Boricio said, suddenly falling a step back and into a defensive position as a half-creature half-man suddenly surfaced into view, walking side by side with some tough-looking chick Boricio had never seen, dressed like one of the black-clad Guardsmen.

Boricio saw the recognition all around him — the guns that weren't being aimed, and the general lack of worry despite the slippery Frankenfucker-looking mutant that looked like someone had sewn half an alien to half a man, almost right down the middle. This was the first mutant Boricio had seen that still had human qualities, save for Charlie, if what they'd said about him was true.

Nerdy Die Hard looked plenty worried, but Pirate Boricio shot him a look that said shit was cool.

"I take it you know Girl and Monster here?" Boricio asked, looking at the creature again, with its twisted torso of terror; two claws jutting from a set of charred-looking limbs, slick and dangling from its side.

Pirate Boricio nodded, his eyes narrowed like he was trying to get the colors the same on the side of the Rubik's Cube.

Boricio looked at Charlie. He knew nervous when he saw it, and sure as shit that was exactly what Charlie was, shifting on his feet and taking a light step back as he pulled the group's attention away from Girl and Monster.

"Did you escape Black Mountain?" Charlie said to the Frankenfucker.

Frankenfucker didn't answer Charlie, turning to the group

instead, and aiming his eyes at Pirate Boricio. "He's lying," Frankenfucker said. "There was no accident at the Facility, and no alien attack. *He* is the monster." Then, probably because he saw the same whatthefuck on all the faces as the one being worn by Pirate Boricio, added, "The Darkness is inside him."

Boricio tensed. Sure, Charlie might have been infected, but he wasn't some evil monster, or *Darkness*, or whatever the fuck Frankenfucker wanted to call it. Boricio wasn't about to stand by and let anyone say shit about Charles in Charge, not when he'd been as loyal as he had. Sure, he probably wanted to catch up with Callie so he could get to the center of her Tootsie Roll Tootsie Pop, but Boricio was sure Charlie's return had something to do with his allegiance to Boricio, too.

"What fucking *Darkness?*" Boricio said, taking a step toward Frankenfucker, as though he didn't have dangerous black claws that could tear Boricio's flesh like meat from a lobster's shell. "You're the one who looks like Alien raped Predator!"

Mary was suddenly in front of Boricio, her mouth hanging open, standing a short half step in front of her little lamb, whose mouth was hanging even lower than her mother's.

"Ryan," Mary said, stepping forward and reaching her hand out toward Frankenfucker's face, which still looked mostly normal, except for the giant, black goiter bubbling on his neck, and an ashen pallor like a shadow spilled on his face.

"You know him?" Boricio asked, even though it was as obvious as day.

Miss Mary didn't need to answer. Her little lamb said, "Daddy?"

Holy fucking shit!

They were one John Williams score away from a goddamned melodrama.

Pirate Boricio looked as confused as the rest of The Brady Bunch, but he stepped to the front of the crowd, then turned and said, "Everyone stay calm. Everything is okay. He turned to Girl and Monster. "What's going on, Lisa?"

Charlie used the happy reunion and Pirate Boricio's confusion to drift closer to Callie, pulling her hand into his. She seemed more uncertain than Boricio would've expected, but finally softened, then rested her head against Charlie's body.

Frankenfucker said, "I'll take it, Lisa," then turned to Mary and his daughter. "Yes, it's me." Boricio thought the half alien might've been crying, but with the shadows all over his face, it was impossible to tell. "I've been searching for you since October." He looked down. "I'm sorry it took me so long."

Mary choked, then sobbed and said, "It's okay," through a harsh curtain of tears as her baby girl shuddered beside her. Neither of them had gone close enough to hug him, however.

Something inside Boricio felt like it was cracking.

Ryan turned to the Brady Bunch. "I was being held in Black Mountain, like Charlie. I saw some sort of Darkness — the same Darkness that's controlling all the creatures," he looked down, "including me, sorta."

Ryan shook his head, then turned back to stare the Bunch in the eyes. "I saw the Darkness go inside Charlie, and then he just started killing people on his way out of the Mountain. It's the same Darkness that had been inside The Prophet and John before that."

"Wait a second, how do you know them?" Mary asked.

"I've seen what *It* sees. *It* wants to kill you all, starting with Luca. And then *It* wants the vial."

Before Nerdy Die Hard and the rest of Team Boricio could turn their guns on Charlie, the boy with the monster inside him suddenly wrestled Callie's gun from her hand, pushed her three feet from him, then trained his gun on the back of her head. "No one come near me," he said, his voice somehow . . . different. "I don't want to hurt her, but I will if you continue to force my hand."

Scary Charlie half smiled at Callie. Boricio almost winced when he did.

Charlie turned to the Bunch, his voice growing soft, then said, "You're not gonna actually *believe* this fucking freak are you? Look at him, he's obviously sick!" Charlie swallowed, then turned to Callie. "You believe me, right, Callie? You know I love you. You're the only reason my heart keeps beating."

That shit sounded as phony as the flavors at Applebee's. Callie must've thought so, too. She looked Charlie in the eyes, held his gaze for a second, but then stumbled back a step, then two. Scary Charlie suddenly growled, then lurched forward and reached out a hand, smacking Callie so hard across the face that she flew back and fell onto the road.

She screamed, and Charlie roared — a horrible, screeching bellow of rage.

Maybe a tantrum; definitely a summons.

The area all around them erupted with swarms of monstrosities, all charging toward them in an elegant explosion of perfect chaos.

"Well, fuck a duck, son," Boricio said, "looks like you just screwed the pooch." He raised his gun to clear Scary Charlie's head from his body, but Scary Charlie was faster, ducking beneath Boricio's aim and flying toward him, taking him down at the waist.

Boricio growled like a wolf as the gun flew from his hand and skidded across the dirt road.

Boricio punched, clawed, kicked, and tumbled in battle with Scary Charlie as the end of everything erupted all around them.

~

SIXTY-THREE

Ryan Olson

Black Island, New York
   April 2012
   SIX MONTHS AFTER THE EVENT ...

THE CRAZY VERSION of Boricio was exactly that — a crazed ball of raging insanity as he wrestled the Darkness-infected Charlie to the ground.

The Darkness *should have* easily finished Crazy Boricio off, but the crazy bastard managed to get *It* to retreat into the shadows instead, where It crouched and cried with a horrible series of terrible screams, calling for alien reinforcements with an urgency that Ryan could clearly feel in his head and body.

KILL HIM!! the Darkness screamed.

Charlie was only off of Crazy Boricio for a few seconds before an especially large mutant took his place. The mutant that should have shredded Crazy Boricio to nothing ended up as a pile of nothing itself after a minute spent at the hands of the man's rage and blade.

Ryan turned to Mary and Paola. So much to say and no

time to say it. "Stay safe so we can get through this. I promise I'll explain everything." He pointed toward the relative safety of the trucks.

"No," Mary shook her head. "We're fighting, too." She lifted her pistol for Ryan to see, then Paola did the same.

"We're trained," Paola said. "And I fixed my jammed gun all by myself!"

Ryan could tell by their eyes. NO wasn't an option, and he hadn't earned the right to insist. He wasn't sure how many of the mutants were already surrounding them, or how many more were approaching, and while he tried to see the answer in his mind, the truth was as blurry as the island's gnarled shadows.

"Okay," Ryan said, as though permission mattered. His girls were already firing into the dark, bullets slamming into their targets with a horrible squishing.

Ryan roared, then charged forward toward a cluster coming at them, shredding aliens with a crazed blend of alien intensity, human cunning, and a father's need to protect his wife and child.

Ryan continued to drop creature upon creature, as the dark hordes continued to close in around them. Both Boricios were out of bullets and fighting beside one another, Bald Boricio using a machete and Crazy Boricio using a knife. Ed still had plenty of rounds, and was taking aliens down one carefully placed burst of gunfire at a time. Mary and Paola stood back to back, firing only at the creatures actually coming toward them, though they were hitting their marks and dropping every one, with Ryan shocked by the accuracy of their aim. Sullivan rotated in small circles, firing into the sound of the gnashing aliens.

The girl who was threatened by Charlie showed no fear on her face, though it was twisted with rage as she stared into the shadows, probably searching for Charlie, likely wanting to see him dead as much as Ryan wanted to see his family safe. She finally growled, then ran into the shadows of the forest.

Ryan was surrounded by a trio of aliens, quickly closing in around him. He raised his claw and hand as the largest of the three creatures brought him hard to the ground. Ryan gnashed and raged and screamed and bucked his body hard against the ground, thrashing about as he tried to throw the mounting aliens from his slippery body.

Ryan's world was quickly fading to dark as another pair of aliens joined the trio.

He was as good as dead.

Ryan squeezed his eyes and twisted his head, swaying his body as he tried to grab a final glimpse of his girls.

The first of the five aliens fell, quickly followed by a second.

Crazy Boricio screamed, "Come and get me, you slippery soul-eating fucks!"

The alien swiped at Crazy Boricio, its claw connecting with Boricio's arm and spraying a jet of crimson, which rained across the sky and splattered Ryan's still mostly human face.

Bald Boricio joined him, screaming just as loud, though nowhere near as crazy, while waving some sort of giant stick.

Ryan slipped from the bottom of the huddle and saw Mary with an alien charging toward her. She raised her gun, but the alien slapped the pistol from her hand. Paola raised her gun and pulled the trigger but the gun only mocked her with an empty clicking.

Ryan charged forward, closing the distance in less than two seconds, thrusting his claw deep into the alien's torso, then twisted the blade inside the creature's body, pulling the alien's still-beating ebony heart from its body, then throwing it into the darkness with a wailing bellow.

Mary screamed, terrified, then swallowed her fear and ran toward Ryan. "Thank you," she cried out, hugging him.

He looked around. Aliens were everywhere, circling them at a bit of a distance instead of attacking, as if they seemed to be moving with less urgency. The hive buzzed with discord in his mind, and there was nothing Ryan could do to filter through the countless lines of chaos.

The aliens seemed suddenly confused, and Ryan could feel something interfering with their commands from the Darkness. He looked around, but couldn't discern the source.

Charlie was gone, and his minions had stopped attacking, but at the same time, they weren't leaving. The aliens numbered in the hundreds, surrounding them on all sides.

Ryan looked around at Mary's companions. They were still alive, but not for much longer. Ryan had heard enough empty clicking, and had seen enough discarded guns, to know they were out of bullets. Everyone was covered in blood, and the bright crimson with only shadows of black said most of the blood was human. They gathered between the trucks with two old men in the back seat of one of the trucks. Ryan recognized one of the men from Charlie's vision as Luca — their last true hope.

Ryan didn't think the old man looked like much of a hope, however.

A man with glasses cried out, "Keenan!" running toward one of the fallen men, 30 yards away from the others.

Keenan was lying in a pool of quickly spreading blood beneath him, "Go, Sullivan," he said, his voice frail. "Get Luca to the house. And take this."

Ed pulled a glowing orange ball from his tactical jacket, then handed the ball to Sullivan as the two Boricios ran over to join them.

"If you can't get Luca to the house, or if that monster makes it there first, use it."

Sullivan, his face lit from below by the orange light, swallowed as Ed sputtered through his final breaths.

Ryan asked, "What is that?" nodding toward the orange ball.

Sullivan said, "The end of this island."

Ed coughed up blood, then stopped moving, eyes staring at the darkness above.

Sullivan closed his eyes, seeming to whisper a prayer.

Ryan didn't think anyone was gonna answer, though.

~

SIXTY-FOUR

Callie Thompson

Black Island, New York
   April 2012
   SIX MONTHS AFTER THE EVENT ...

CALLIE STOOD up as the madness broke out all around them.

She couldn't believe Charlie had smacked her. She was pissed, but more than that, she was afraid. She knew that Charlie would never do that to her. There was something inside him. And that something was after the same thing they'd come to the island for — the vial.

She looked around, surveying the scene. She saw him slipping into the darkness of the woods on the way to Will's house. He must've taken off while everyone was distracted. She could stay and help the others fight, but she didn't think she'd make that much of a difference.

But if nobody had even noticed Charlie was gone, then that meant nobody else could stop him— which meant she had to.

Callie scooped up her gun and chased Charlie. He was

about 80 yards or so ahead of her, barely a blip of pale flesh in the black forest, but he was walking, not running, so she thought she might be able to catch him — so long as no aliens got in her way.

Charlie reached the backyard of a two-story home, set in the woods, its front facing the ocean beyond, which she could hear even from this distance and above the gunfire behind her. Charlie bashed in a sliding glass door and stepped inside the house.

Shit! Shit!

Callie ran faster, certain that as she drew closer to the backyard, an alien would surface from nowhere and kill her progress. Even if she were able to shoot the alien, or aliens, there was a damned good chance the gunshot would alert Charlie to her proximity, which would definitely speed him up.

I can't let him get the vial.

Callie breathed a sigh of relief as she reached the back yard. She peered into the dark house, unable to see anything. She hesitated before stepping into the house. Since it was so dark, Charlie, or the evil inside him, was at an obvious advantage.

Callie closed her eyes as she stepped inside, to better balance the difference between the moonlit night and the pitch black house. She opened her eyes, and in the moonlight spilling through the open windows, was able to make out the rough shapes of furniture and a stairway.

No sign of Charlie.

Callie inched forward, gun held in front of her.

She wasn't sure if she should hold the gun straight out, like she was, or more at a downward angle like she'd seen on *The Shield*. She wondered if holding the gun straight out was an open invitation for Charlie to knock it from her hand.

Callie heard a loud bang from upstairs. Then another; the sound of furniture being tossed around.

Is he looking for it? Is it not in the moon?

What if it's not here?

Would that be good or bad?

She headed to the stairway hoping like hell Boricio and the others could find her, and would show up soon. Now that she was close to catching Charlie, she had no idea what she would do.

I'm not gonna shoot him, am I? It's Charlie!

But what am I gonna do? TALK HIM into handing the vial over?

What the hell am I thinking?

Do not go up the stairs.

Just wait.

Boricio and everyone will show up.

Just.

Wait.

Callie waited, looking out the rear window, but she saw nothing but black.

Damn it.

Callie started climbing the stairs.

Slowly — One.

Step.

At.

A.

Time.

Another loud crash of furniture made Callie jump, and she nearly fired her gun. She grabbed the railing, breathing relief for not pulling the trigger.

The movement upstairs suddenly stopped.

Shit, It heard me!

Silence stretched as Callie kept herself frozen, gun aimed up the stairs, waiting, and praying that Charlie wouldn't show his face.

"I hear your heartbeat," Charlie said in a voice that was only his because it came from his throat. The music of his speech was horrible; void of emotion.

"Leave now or I will kill you," he said.

Callie swallowed, her heart threatening to burst from her chest.

Should I say something?

Maybe he doesn't know I'm here. Maybe he's just testing.

"Leave. Now, Callie."

She opened her mouth, and at first, could barely speak. Finally, she found her voice, cracked and frightened. "No! You leave! Whatever you are, leave Charlie!"

"No. I rather like this body. The best I've had so far."

Callie could almost feel the Evil's sneer.

She cried out as she heard footsteps above her, approaching the stairway.

"This is your final chance not to die," Charlie said.

"I'll shoot you!" she cried.

"Shoot me, and I'll go inside you. No problem. I haven't been inside a woman yet. But you won't stop me from finding it. Ah . . . what's this?"

Callie looked up, certain that he was above her, poised to attack. But he wasn't. Instead, she heard the sound of something unscrewing. A bright light suddenly illuminated the upper floor and spread to the stairs.

Oh God, he found it!

Callie ran up the stairs, forcing herself to ignore every pore in her body, saturated with fear and certainty that she was knee deep in a terrible mistake. She reached the top floor and saw Charlie standing in Luca's bedroom in front of an open moon globe sitting on his desk.

The white was blinding, Vegas in one bulb, throwing shadows on the wall behind Charlie, who stood over the globe looking down like Gollum ready to seize his "precious."

Callie raised her gun, shouted "Get back!"

She fired a warning shot out the window behind him.

Charlie ignored it.

As he moved toward the globe, the light began to dim.

He smiled.

"Ah, you know I'm here, don't you? You're ready to become one with *Us*."

Charlie reached down, his hands inches from the vial.

Callie fired another shot, missing intentionally for the second time.

Charlie looked up. This time she had his attention. Her eyes met his — dark and blacker than miles of nothingness.

"Please," she cried. "Don't make me shoot you. Please. Just wait for Luca. He can heal you with the vial. He can save you."

Callie wasn't sure he could, but she had nothing else to try and lure whatever part of Charlie might still be awake inside the monster.

Charlie stepped toward her. His head lashed violently to the left, then to the right, whipping back and forth so fast, it looked as if he was somehow moving in fast forward.

Charlie fell to his knees, then buried his now-still head in his hands.

He started to sob, sounding like a scared child.

Did he get control?

"Charlie?" she whispered.

"Callie?" he asked, his voice cracked with fear as he looked up. He sounded more like Charlie than before. The white went back in his eyes as he met her stare, looking up from the floor like a helpless, wounded child.

"Please, Callie, don't kill me," he cried, looking up at her. "I think *It's* gone."

"Where did *It* go?" she asked, looking around the room, afraid it might make good on *Its* threat to go into her.

"I don't know," Charlie said, shaking his head. "But I can't move."

"What's wrong?" Callie stepped slowly toward him, careful to keep her gun on him, in case he was trying to trick her.

"I don't know," he cried. "I can't move. And I'm so . . . so cold."

His teeth started to chatter as he trembled. The house was cool, not cold. Something must have been happening inside him. Charlie buried his head in his hands, his entire body shaking. He cried, "Please, help me! Help, Callie!"

She moved forward, not knowing what to do.

Every alarm in her head was screaming, *It's a trap! It's a trap.*

But Callie couldn't ignore the pain in his voice, or his pleading for help. It was Charlie. *He* was inside with the Evil. She couldn't ignore that part of him that was fighting to be free.

"I love you," he cried, face still buried in his hands. "Please, just hold me."

Callie was inches away when something struck her as odd. Something in the tone of his voice.

"Say it again."

"What?" he cried, still shaking.

"Say you love me."

"I love you," he said.

Something was wrong.

Callie fell back a step.

He sensed her retreat and leapt to his feet in an instant, wildly swinging his arm and narrowly missing her face.

Callie screamed, firing two shots in a row, hitting Charlie right in his face.

He fell to the ground, his face reduced to red and black gore. Callie stepped back, screaming and crying at once, the gun shaking in her hand.

"Oh God! Oh God!"

She couldn't believe she killed Charlie. The boy she'd come to love. The boy who had risked his life to save her. The sad, but sweet boy whom she passed notes with just one night before. Now he was dead, his body motionless, lying on the floor.

Callie jumped as a deafening hum belched from the globe.

She looked up and saw the light's brightness grow even more intense, surging from dim to bright to blinding white, as if it were somehow aware of her. The hum grew louder, beckoning her toward the globe.

"Come. Open it," a voice whispered in her mind. Not her internal thoughts, but an external thought, from someone — *something* — else.

Callie looked over.

Did it just talk to me?

"Yes. Come. Open me. I will save you all."

Callie inched toward the globe.

No, no, wait for Boricio and Luca. Wait.

"No, Callie. You. Come. Open me."

Callie stepped closer and looked down at the vial, glowing bright-white, so bright she couldn't see its shape through the light. It was as if someone had just flicked on a million watts in the room. The light was so bright, and so beautiful despite its intensity, Callie nearly missed the darkness gathering form beside her — the Darkness pouring from Charlie and up toward her.

"Let me in," the Darkness whispered in her head.

Callie turned to run, but couldn't. She was rooted to the spot as *It* crept closer. The smoky entrails slithered around her, bringing *Its* icy slaughter.

"Let me in," It repeated, snaking toward her mouth as *It* spread her lips wide.

Callie cried out, but her throat made no sound and her feet refused to move.

Her eyes found Charlie's corpse on the floor and her heart shattered again.

I love you.

The gun trembled in her hand, and she lifted it fast, before she could change her mind. As the Darkness rushed inside her throat, drowning her with its form, it began to sift through her memories, tossing them everywhere in an attempt to keep her from doing what she had to do.

Callie saw her mom.

"Hi, Baby," her mother said. "Don't do that, okay? Put the gun down, Callie."

Tears streamed down Callie's cheeks. She chewed the salt from her lip as she felt the Darkness burrow deeper into her mind.

Callie said, "Sorry, Mommy," then pulled the trigger.

∽

SIXTY-FIVE

Boricio Wolfe

Black Island, New York
  April 2012
  SIX MONTHS AFTER THE EVENT …

THE ALIENS HAD ALL RETREATED, leaving Team Boricio free to make their final trek to Will's house. They were 100 feet or so from the front porch when two gunshots raged, one right after the other.

The team froze, trading glances in the black as icy rain began to fall and the wind began to rattle the trees.

"Callie!" Boricio screamed.

The wind's howl accompanied his anguished cry, or maybe mocked it.

The group slowly approached the house, guns drawn with the last of the ammunition from the trucks. Boricio and Pirate Boricio ran point as Mary, Paola, Will, and Luca followed. Bringing up the rear were Ryan and Sullivan.

Boricio looked up at the house, wondering who shot whom, and waiting for someone, either Charlie or Callie, to step into view in the brightly lit second-story window.

Another gunshot.

Both Boricios ran toward the house as Ryan screamed, "They're coming!"

"Who?" Boricio said, spinning around.

As he turned, he saw a horde of aliens breaking through the tree line — too many to count.

"Jesus, how many more of these motherfuckers are there?" he said as two of the aliens raced ahead of the others, running on all fours as fast as cheetahs, roaring toward Sullivan and Ryan.

Ryan leaned down and raced toward one of the creatures. The two collided in midair, then rolled to the ground in a blur of black and blood. Sullivan fired his M-16 at the second alien as it bore down on him. His shots hit, but didn't stop the alien as it barreled forward.

Boricio leveled his pistol and fired three shots in rapid fire succession, sending the alien into an eternity of quiet.

Mary took aim at Ryan and the alien as they tumbled, clawing and tearing at one another. She couldn't get a clear shot, so she instead fired at the closest aliens. Sullivan fired into the horde again, taking a couple more down before he had to stop and reload a clip.

Boricio looked back toward the house and saw Pirate Boricio standing at the back porch of the house, his gun aimed into the horde. He didn't fire, but yelled, "Come on, Luca!" instead. "We've gotta get to the vial."

Will and Luca stumbled forward with Mary and Paola as Boricio and Sullivan fired, picking off as many of the aliens as they could.

No way in hell we're gonna be able to kill them all. I hope to fuck that Luca's magical potion is there and it works!

Ryan stood, and was immediately pounced upon by a mutated dog, as large and ugly as the mangy fucker Paola had shot the other morning. Ryan flipped the beast, then gripped its hind legs as he spun the dog on its back, tearing the legs from the dog's body as it howled and fell to the ground dying.

"Fuck yeah!" Boricio shouted as he turned and headed into the house.

Boricio raced up the stairs to find Pirate Boricio, Will, Luca, Mary, and Paola, all standing around the glowing globe, staring inside it as if hypnotized. On the floor, he saw Charlie and Callie both dead, shot in the head.

His stomach turned, but they didn't have time for mourning the dead. The aliens were galloping toward the house and nothing short of a miracle would save the day.

"What the fuck y'all waiting for?" Boricio said, stepping toward the others.

As he drew closer to the globe, he was suddenly frozen, like the others, imprisoned by the glowing beauty before him.

"Oh God," he said, using an expression he didn't think he'd ever used in his life. "It's . . . stunning."

Boricio felt the light's warmth spreading through his body like drugs from the rich fucker's house, but with none of the murky, trippy confusion.

The opposite of confusion flooded his mind.

Clarity.

Inside that clarity and impossible light, Boricio could feel the others' thoughts, hundreds of random memories coursing in a current through them all — from Luca petting his cat, to Mary giving birth, to the first time Will danced with a girl — and later, with a man. In those shared memories, Boricio felt something he'd never felt before — love for these strangers — as if they were all bonding through some communal drawing into a well of eternal light.

Until something dark circled the rim.

At first, it was a nebulous haze Boricio saw floating around them as they sat transfixed by the light. He could feel *Its* contempt, *Its* hate, but he was unable to break from the beauty of the light.

It circled them.

It looked down upon them.

It judged.

Then *It* entered Pirate Boricio's mouth.

Boricio couldn't tell if the others could see what was happening, or if it were only him. Suddenly other emotions and memories started seeping into the light, many from Boricio's personal scrapbook of pain — the time his step-dad killed Boricio's 4-week-old kitten, the time his step-dad punched him so hard they had to keep him home from school with "pneumonia" for a week, the times his step-dad made him ...

Boricio looked up, glaring at the light.

Why are you pulling this out of me?

Why are you sharing this?

As memories spilled like red paint onto a freshly varnished floor, the light grew dimmer.

The beautiful light was turning black.

No!

Another dark memory swallowed the light — this one from Pirate Boricio, sitting helplessly in the cell while Will ordered the execution of Rose.

They all saw — and felt Boricio Bishop's pain — as the fire engulfed the cell and destroyed everything.

The vial was turning black.

Soon, the Darkness in Pirate Boricio would fulfill its mission.

Soon, it would corrupt the light.

Boricio wanted to reach out, but they were all still transfixed, now in anguish as the Darkness unleashed a torrent of miseries upon them, hundreds of thousands of murders from the moment *It* was first unleashed, as it murdered the world's men, women, children, and animals, engulfing and ingesting all into Itself.

"Stop it!" Mary cried out.

Will was shaking violently.

Luca sobbed, squeezing his eyes tight, as if he could dim, or unsee, the horrors in his head.

He couldn't.

Boricio wanted to seize the vial, take it, and use it to do whatever would destroy the Darkness across from him, smiling from behind Boricio Bishop's mask.

Only Luca can touch It.

Only Luca is pure enough.

Boricio wasn't sure where the thoughts were coming from, until he realized they were bleeding from both Will and Luca; a shared dream or thought, where Luca was the rightful heir to the vial — the child who smothered the Darkness.

But Luca isn't touching It!

He's frozen like me!

Then, Boricio knew.

He had to go into Luca's head.

~

BORICIO WAS NO LONGER in Other Luca's bedroom.

He had no idea where he was, but it looked like a forest of Tim Burton's nightmares, with crooked trees and giant worms pushing their mottled bodies through rows of bloody soil.

Between the two rows of fat, crooked trunks with long and gnarled roots, and thousand-fingered branches braided above Boricio's head, Luca lay sprawled across the forest floor, crying.

Luca was no longer old.

He was young, so young he seemed almost tiny.

As Boricio ran through the forest toward Luca, branches clawed at him from both sides, trying to pull him back into the black.

"Luca!" Boricio screamed, trying to get the boy's attention.

Luca didn't answer, he only made his crumpled figure smaller, huddled and crying and sobbing in a pile, begging for help.

The darkness from the forest was creeping into Boricio's lungs like a thousand pounds of smoke. Boricio ran faster and harder, pumping his legs until he finally reached Luca, where he dropped to his knees and pulled the boy into his arms.

"You gotta wake up, Kid. It's time."

Luca shook his head, still sobbing. "I can't," he said. "I can't fight when the Terrible Scary is everywhere."

"The Terrible Scary?"

"Yes, The Terrible Scary," Luca nodded. "The Black Pieces. The end of everything." He looked up at Boricio, then fell back on his palms and scooted back, gasping. "The other one of you!"

"No," Boricio shook his head. "That's not me."

Boricio could feel the horror on the other side of reality, ready to end everything as his *friends* stood frozen.

He stood, then held his outstretched hand to Luca. "You can't be scared of the Terrible Scary." He shook his head. "Not now or ever again."

Luca lay on the ground, cowering and unconvinced, as worms began to erupt from the soil, inching their slick, segmented, plump bodies toward him, trying to drive him away.

Boricio snarled another order, at Luca but the boy still lay there.

So, Boricio roared:

"The Terrible Scary is nothing!" he yelled as the black started whistling around them. Boricio could feel the Darkness growing in power, shaking the trees around him in the world in Luca's head, and dimming the light in the real world his body still stood in.

The Darkness would soon swallow them both if Luca wouldn't stand and fight. "Do you remember when you went inside my head back when you were being held in that dungeon? How I huffed and puffed and tried to blow your house down? But you stood up to me. You found the part of me that was broken, and you . . . *fixed me,* Luca. You fixed ME, a monster! Don't be afraid of this. It's nothing, unless you let it be."

Luca nodded, and said, "I'm scared."

"The Terrible Scary tries to hold you down, bury you inside your deepest fears, because it can smell your power, Luca. *It* burns with black, and that makes *It* terrified of your light. If you let *It* win, you will never see your family again. Your daddy, your mommy, your sister, you'll never see them again. Ever. Stay scared, Luca, and you ruin the world. Stand now to save us all."

Boricio held his hand out to Luca, hoping the boy would take it.

He did, then the world around them went white.

The gnarled trees on either side of the Terrible Scary straightened as the road paved itself with a row of freshly laid brick, neatly trimmed with rich green grass. The sky went from oil to azure and the clouds from coal to milk.

Once the Terrible Scary was entirely gone, they found themselves back in Other Luca's room, now flooded with a light so white it was as though no other color existed.

Luca blinked his eyes, though Boricio could barely see him.

Boricio screamed, "You know what to do?" and was sure Luca nodded, even though he couldn't see.

Boricio stepped into the brilliance as Luca's fingers curled around the vial. The man-kid flickered; a skeleton, then a child, then, for the thinnest slice of a second, nothing but light.

The Darkness swallowed Boricio Bishop, as Luca was born from the Light.

The room began to shake, wind howling through the shattered window, as the light dimmed from blinding to bright. In a voice that no longer belonged to Luca, but to eternity itself, Luca thundered:

"Go! Run!"

What was left of Team Boricio bolted out of the bedroom, but the Darkness reached out with a knotted spear of sable, goring Will through the back, then bursting through his chest as he was inches from the door. Will's body was yanked back into the room, then into the vortex of swirling Darkness, as it spun Will's body, sucking his blood and guts into its center, then spewed them across the room.

The poor old fucker couldn't even scream.

The house shook violently around them as the wind raged outside. Luca, now nothing but a brilliant orb of growing light, thundered again, his voice now a hundred souls speaking from the inside of a single scream:

"GO! GO!"

Every window shattered at once as wind, rain, and debris swarmed through the house, as if the foundation were birthing a tornado.

Mary should have been running, but she stood rooted beside Paola, both fixed to the floor in horror, unable to move.

Boricio grabbed two arms, one from each girl, and shoved them both out the door, then down the stairs and through the swirling chaos. They made it outside just as the house collapsed and was siphoned into the two swelling, swirling tornadoes — one as wretchedly black as an infinite night, the other as white as Siberian snow, both of them spitting debris to the sky like the heavens were starving.

Sullivan and Ryan were still battling a couple dozen aliens on the ground. Boricio was shocked to see them still standing.

The white tornado suddenly spit sparks of bright light from the gaping mouth in its center, disintegrating the remaining aliens.

"Holy shit!" Boricio shouted. "Let's get the fuck outta here!"

Mary ran to meet her mutant husband, dragging their daughter behind her. Halfway there, a piece of the black reached out and grabbed Ryan like a twig, then plucked him into the air screaming into its widening vortex.

Mary lost her voice in an anguished bellow as the Darkness turned toward her, swirling its hungry tendrils and grabbed her, too.

"No!" Boricio and Paola both screamed.

The white tornado sent a swirl of bright, crackling light into the heart of Darkness, pulled Mary from its horrible depths, then dropped her gently on the ground next to her daughter. Mary stood up, wet and scratched to hell, and picked Paola up and began to run away.

Boricio heard Luca's voice inside in his head, "Use the orange ball!"

"What?" Boricio screamed at the bright tornado that was once the man-kid Luca, or the vial, maybe both.

"The orange ball," it bellowed. "Tell Sullivan to use it."

Boricio shouted to Sullivan, "He said use the orange ball!"

"Who?!"

"That!" Boricio said, pointing at the Light tornado snaking around the Dark one.

"We'll all die!" Sullivan screamed.

The pair of vortexes started to yank surrounding trees, dirt, rocks, and debris into themselves, gathering mass so fast, that every one of them was sure to be pulled into the swirling chaos in a matter of seconds.

Sullivan held the glowing orange sphere in his palm.

He squeezed the ball hard, and the orange light grew brighter and brighter, until it started screaming red.

Everything vanished in a blaze of impossible light.

~

SIXTY-SIX

Luca Bishop

Black Island, New York
April 2012
SIX MONTHS AFTER THE EVENT …

KEEP SWIMMING!

Luca kept going, faster than he'd ever swum in his life, trying to find a way back to the other world, where he'd been safe and sound in the other Luca's bed.

But he could never return if he was unable to concentrate.

Luca swam for what felt like forever, until his entire body was aching, his limbs turning to rubber. He could float no longer, though he was finally a safe distance from the falling stuff.

He saw the source of the falling stuff in the distance — the two largest tornadoes Luca had ever seen. While Luca had only seen tornadoes on TV, he was sure they didn't usually have balls of lightning and fire swirling from their middle.

Luca couldn't tell how far away the tornadoes were from each other, but they seemed inches from collision. He had also never seen two tornadoes at once, even in movies. It was like they were fighting to see which could gather and spit the most terrible stuff into the sky as they continued to drift closer and closer.

Luca finally realized that it wasn't just *stuff* they were spitting into the sky.

The tornados were spitting what was left of Black Island.

His eyes widened as he screamed.

~

OUR EARTH

Los Orillas, California
April 2, 2012
SIX MONTHS AFTER THE EVENT …

LUCA WOKE IN HIS BED, soaking wet, and screeching.

But no one could hear his scream through the hand on his mouth.

Luca stared in disbelief as the other Luca, the one who belonged here in this world, the one whose life he had stolen. But he was young again, not old. He sat across from him on the bed, his palm pressed hard against Luca's mouth, trapping his scream mostly in his throat.

He's come to take his life back.

He's mad, and he's come to get me!

"Shhh," the other Luca whispered, looking at the closed bedroom door, then back to Luca. "Okay?"

Luca nodded, and Other Luca slowly removed his hand.

"What happened?" Luca said, "How did we get here? How did *you* get here? What happened to the island?"

"It's all gone," Other Luca said, his voice calm, no emotion. "The Darkness won."

"What?"

"The Darkness. It had another name long ago. Now it is just the Darkness. It took over everything."

Luca swallowed, thinking back to what happened on Oct. 15 — how the old preacher man had taken the vial from his brother and opened it. When darkness spilled out and started to swallow everything, Luca had managed to get away, and pulled Boricio away, too, though he wasn't sure where he'd pulled his brother to.

That's when he wound up here. It was the last time he'd seen his brother. Luca had tried to contact Boricio several times, but was never able. Instead, he only saw the Other Boricio, with the Other Luca and Will.

"Was it the vials? Is that what was in the vials Boricio asked me to get?"

"We are the Light, but also can be made into Darkness by intervention from dark souls. We changed you when your brother used us to cure you. And you carried the Light over here to this world and put it in this child. But then you changed us when you found us again. You, your brother, and the others, tainted some of us — turned them into the Darkness. Our only hope was this child, Luca."

"What do you mean *this child?*" Luca whispered. "You're not Luca?"

Other Luca began to softly glow, as an impossibly bright light seeped through the child, then spilled onto the blankets and wall.

"What are you?" Luca asked.

"What are *we*," Other Luca answered, pointing to Luca's stomach, which, to his surprise, was glowing with the same light.

Luca let out a startled yelp, as Other Luca quickly returned his hand to the boy's mouth. When skin met skin, a spark of electricity shot through him, causing him to jump from the bed, in surprise rather than pain.

He stepped back from Other Luca, trying to figure him out.

"No, I'm human. I'm still me," Luca said.

"Yes, you only have a part of us inside you. This child, Luca, opened the final vial. His purity, his kindness, gave us strength to fight. But we could not defeat *It*. Despite all the people I pulled over to fight, we were not enough. Now the war is over, and that world is lost."

"Where is my family?"

"Your father is dead. Your brother has become the Darkness, Chaos, The Void. I could not destroy it. I could not bring him back. I had to leave before he murdered us all."

Luca cried, swallowing tears, along with the urge to wail and wake his — Other Luca's — parents.

Luca suffered through a long silence, where Other Luca stared at him as if observing a rare insect even though he was the one glowing more, until he finally asked, "What happened to everyone? The other people I saw with you? The other Will, the other Boricio? Are they . . . . dead?"

"Will died. Boricio Wolfe, he is alive. Many died. Many are now part of the Darkness. Others, I saved, as I did you, and returned them back to their world before the Darkness could claim them."

Luca fell to the floor, sobbing. "I'm so sorry. I thought I was helping Boricio. I thought he'd save Rose."

"I know your intentions were good," Other Luca said.

"And I didn't mean for *you* to be taken from your family and brought to my world," Luca cried. "I didn't mean to take your family. But I didn't know where else to go, and I was scared. When I came here, you were gone. I didn't know you were gone. Then, when I did see you over there, and tried to switch places back, tried to talk to you, you couldn't see me."

"It's okay," Other Luca said as his light began to burn brighter.

"What's happening to you?" Luca asked.

"I have to go."

"Go? Go where? Don't you want your life back?"

"That's not possible." Other Luca shook his head. "We are now one — Luca, and the Light. We cannot stay here."

"What? Where are you going?"

The glowing child began to fade, barely there and about to vanish.

"No!" Luca cried. "Don't leave me here! I don't belong here. I can't look at your family knowing I took you from them. Please. Come back. Or whoever, or whatever you are, come into me, and give Luca his life back."

"We can't," Other Luca said.

"Why not?"

"You are not pure."

"What am I supposed to do?" Luca cried. "I'm not Luca! They aren't my parents. I feel like a big phony!"

Other Luca's eyes stared from behind the light. "Do you want to forget? Do you want to *be* the other Luca?" Its words were everywhere and nowhere at once.

"What do you mean?"

"We can give you his memories. We can erase yours, except your recent ones, which we can partially remove. You will wake up believing that you are him. With his memories. *Your parents* will never have died. You will never have known Will and Boricio Bishop. You will be Luca as he was before the Darkness."

Luca stared into the light. "You can do that?"

Other Luca nodded.

But can I? Can I forget everything? My family. My real family — my mom, dad, and sister who died? And then my other family, Will and Boricio? Do I want to forget them?

"You must decide now." Other Luca's body was gone already, and now the light was disappearing too. "We must go. But we can take your pain with us."

"And what happens to you, to the Other Luca? Where are you going? Won't you miss your family?"

"We are one, now, you and I, Luca. I feel what you feel. I can be with them through you. Feel their love. Feel them. But I cannot live here in body. I've grown too weak. I've changed too much. But you can forget it all. But you must decide now."

Other Luca's light began to flicker.

It's now or never.

All the pain. All the regrets. Everything can go away.

"Will I still be me?"

"Yes, but you must …"

The light crackled. The Light was almost gone.

No, don't go!

Luca cried out, "Yes! I'll do it!"

Other Luca flared, and the light went so suddenly bright that the room seemed as though it was nothing but pure white.

Then it went dark and back to normal until Other Luca was only a mist.

Am I too late?

Luca couldn't see the hand he felt on top of his head, but he felt it there like the nose on his face or the arm hanging from his shoulder.

Warmth spread through his body.

Luca's eyes fell involuntarily shut as shadows crept around the edge of his memory. He thought of his little sister — his *real* sister. The first time he looked into her crib and made her laugh. And how excited he was.

He had looked at his mom, who he didn't know was watching them.

She had smiled at them in a way that made him feel loved from the inside out.

Wait. No, I don't want to forget.

I want to be me.

Then, the memory was gone, and he fell into his bed,

trying to remember what it was he'd forgotten. And why he was wet, smelling of saltwater.

And why he was going to bed soaking.

Luca was too tired to try and make sense of messy thoughts that didn't want to be cleaned. He curled into bed, pulled the covers up to just under his chin, then closed his eyes. For a moment, he thought he saw a light floating over his bed, but then figured his mind was playing tricks.

Maybe it was a dream.

Sleep swallowed Luca with a smile.

~

SIXTY-SEVEN

Ed Keenan

Our Earth
Palm Coves, Florida
Ed's safehouse
July 2012
NINE MONTHS AFTER THE EVENT ...

ED PATTED Becca's back and glanced at the TV's clock for the hundredth time, still waiting for the 15-minute mark to pass.

He wished he'd eaten *before* trying to put Becca down for her noontime nap, because this was the third time he'd tried, and they'd been sitting on the couch for nearly an hour.

Fifteen minutes seemed to be the minimum it took for Teagan's baby to fall into a deep enough sleep for a trip to the crib without her waking. If Ed rose from the couch too soon, Becca would start crying. He'd have to start the whole process over, starting with the rocking. If he waited too long, same thing.

Ed had been held hostage at gunpoint a half dozen times in his career, but he was now held hostage by something that remained years away from being able to clean itself, and he was held hostage nearly every damn day.

Ed decided next time, *he'd* do the grocery shopping instead of surrendering to Jade and Teagan. It was if they were so excited to get out of the house, especially together, that they took FOREVER to do what he could have easily done in 20 minutes. He imagined the two of them sitting in the grocery store cafe, sipping on the chai lattes they both liked so much — though for the life of him he couldn't see why — and eating overpriced scones, while his lunch schedule was dictated by the tiny tyrant in his arms.

He looked down at Becca, and most of his annoyance faded like daylight at dusk and he found a smile pulling at the corners of his mouth.

It seemed like forever since Jade was this age. Ed could hardly remember her so small, nor being so hard to get down for a nap. Though, it wasn't like he'd really been around much during those early years. These were probably the kinds of things he'd missed out on. This was normal life for normal fathers. Well, as normal as life could be at the moment, living in hiding under assumed identities, following the hell and fury of the past half year that started on Oct. 15.

As the clock finally ticked past the 15-minute mark, again, Ed stood, slowly, careful not to stir Becca, displaying a dexterity he'd not used since escaping from an underground cage in the Ukraine six years ago.

He navigated across the toy-littered floor with the same grace, making it to the other side of the house to Becca and Teagan's bedroom.

As he reached for the knob, his doorbell rang.

Shit!

These damned solicitors always come at nap time!
Can't they read the NO SOLICITORS sign on the door?

He looked down, terrified that Becca would open her eyes and start screaming.

But her eyes remained still, fluttering under her lids as he rushed her into the room, then carefully set her beneath the Pooh Bear mobile in her crib. As Ed eased away from the crib, the doorbell rang again. Ed cringed, certain Becca would wake up and he'd have to hurt — maybe kill — whoever was on the other side of the door, threatening his lunch.

Ed raced from one end of the house to the other, and froze when he looked at the security monitor in the kitchen, which should have displayed feed from above the front door, but instead, showed only static.

His heart raced as he reached into the top of the pantry, retrieved his shotgun, and started toward the front door.

He approached slowly, quietly.

The doorbell rang again, twice in a row.

You fucker! You just WANT to wake her up, don't you?

Or, is the Agency finally here to take me out?

Ed peered through the peephole to see a face he never thought he'd see again — Sullivan, the man from Black Island — a man he'd not seen since they all vanished in a flash of white before somehow getting returned to their Earth.

What the hell? What's he doing on this Earth? What's he doing at MY door?

"What do you want?" Ed asked through the door, keeping his aim steady.

"You're a hard man to find, Mr. Keenan," Sullivan said. "We need to talk."

Ed growled, "I'm hard to find because I don't feel like talking."

"May I please come in?"

"What's this about?" Ed asked.

"Please," Sullivan said, moving his face closer to the peephole. "I'm not here to cause trouble or interfere in your lives. But we need to talk."

Ed closed his eyes, sighing. He didn't have any reason to distrust Sullivan, but he found it odd that the man had been

"Or maybe you all should move to the island," Boricio said. "It's beautiful."

"I know," her mom said. "But I don't think I want to be anywhere near Black Island. Or any island."

Paola's mom trailed off, but Paola knew what she meant. It had been three months since her father died on Black Island, and while Boricio wasn't living on Black Island, and it wasn't even the same Black Island they were attacked on, being anywhere near any large rock in the middle of water was enough to bring back too many painful memories. It had been hard enough coming back, starting over after they'd been declared missing by state officials. Fortunately, Sullivan had somehow managed to pull enough strings to straighten things out and help them get another home, far enough from the other bad memories that would eternally surround Warson Woods.

"Did you all start without me?" The pleasant voice came from the top of the stairs.

"I thought I'd let you sleep in until breakfast was ready," Boricio said, setting a plate on the table, then walking over to the girl with a pixie cut and kissing her on the cheek.

Paola couldn't help but laugh, seeing Boricio, Mr. Tough Guy himself, as soft and cuddly as a bear when with his girlfriend, Rose, a super-nice woman he'd met a month after returning to Earth.

Boricio caught Paola laughing, and pointed a finger at her, "You watch it young lady, or I'll stuff spinach in your pancakes."

"Ew," Paola said.

The woman took a seat beside Boricio and smiled, then picked up her fork as they all dug into their breakfast together.

It had been a long time since Paola had shared a meal with anything close to a family. This was nice, even if only temporary.

able to find him. Ed had gone through great pains to set this house up long before he was declared an enemy by the Agency. Nobody could trace the house to him. He was a ghost, so far as the world was concerned. If Sullivan, someone without any resources on this planet, was able to pinpoint Ed's location, who else could?

Ed opened the door, keeping his gun on Sullivan, then ushered the youthful-looking, neatly dressed man inside. Sullivan looked like he was going door-to-door peddling religion.

"Keep it quiet, Becca's sleeping."

Sullivan smiled. "I'm glad to see that you're taking care of Teagan and Becca. Keenan, the other Keenan, would be happy to know that. You know, if he'd made it."

Ed wanted to say that he didn't really give a shit what the other Keenan would've thought, but the look in Sullivan's eyes, his sincerity and friendliness, kept Ed's tongue from flapping. Besides, Ed had seen on one of the video feeds on Black Island how the other Keenan had died, bravely fighting a fight that Ed should've been there for. Hell, perhaps Ed would've died instead of his doppelgänger.

Ed looked Sullivan up and down, "Are you carrying?"

"Always." Sullivan reached into his pocket and pulled out a pistol, an HK USP .45, and handed it to Ed, butt first.

Ed patted him down, searching for more weapons, but found none. He led Sullivan toward his study, where a bank of monitors showed every room of the six-bedroom house, as well as all the areas outside. Ed glanced at the screen showing Becca still sleeping, then offered Sullivan a seat opposite him, at his planning table.

"How did you find me?" Ed said, cutting to the chase.

"I'm a resourceful person."

"Bullshit," Ed countered. "Tell me now. Who else knows I'm here?"

"Don't worry, you're safe. I found you because Will and

She looked up to see Boricio smile at Rose, then giggled again.

Luca weren't the only ones granted abilities by the vials. I'm not nearly as gifted as either of them, but I'm gifted enough to find the four of you." He shook his head. "But you don't need to worry about whoever else is trying to find you."

Ed wasn't sure if he believed Sullivan, but Sullivan was always an honest broker, and Ed sensed nothing fishy, so he was inches from buying the guy's story.

"So," Ed said, "what *do* I have to worry about? I assume you're not just here to say hello."

Sullivan swallowed, adjusting himself in his seat.

"Luca brought most of us back home," he said, then cleared his throat. "But we're not alone. Something else came back with us."

SIXTY-EIGHT

Paola Olson

Our Earth
Harrison, North Carolina
July 2012
NINE MONTHS AFTER THE EVENT …

PAOLA DIPPED her fork into the quiche, her hand practically trembling. The bite was inches from her mouth when she suddenly stopped, inspecting the chunk of egg, ham, cheese, and the specks of green spinach bulging from the white as though taunting her, and ruining a perfectly good breakfast.

Spinach was the devil's vegetable.

"Just try it," Boricio said coming from the kitchen to the dining room and setting a basket of muffins in the center of the table. "Breakfast doesn't always have to be pancakes."

"But pancakes are yummy!"

"So is this. Have I ever bullshitted you, Kid? And besides, didn't you have enough pancakes during the Apocalypse? Hell, a short stack would practically have to bulge with blueberries and the promise of a half billion dollars to get me to chew 'em again."

Boricio laughed, and Paola's mom laughed with him. She took a seat beside her daughter and said, "Come on, you're gonna hurt Boricio's feelings. Just try it."

"Yeah, please don't make me cry." Boricio rubbed his fists into his eyes and loudly boo-hooed. "Besides, you know how much most people would pay for a breakfast like this? I worked at this joint called Au Poivre in Georgia where people who liked to have the best stuff in their mouths, and had wallets fat enough to pay for it, spent north of 25 greenbacks for a slice of my quiche!"

"I'd pay 25 dollars *not* to eat it," Paola laughed.

"OK," Boricio said, pretending to be upset, "Get out! Oh wait, this is your place. Well, you're lucky I'm a guest, or you'd see me throw a real shit fit."

Paola nudged the food into her mouth, then quickly swallowed, gagging as it went down. She grabbed her glass of milk and took a long swig, though it did little to disguise the gross aftertaste of spinach.

"There! Tried it. Don't like it!" Paola said. "No offense."

Her mom laughed.

"Damn, kids these days have no appreciation for good food!" Boricio said, playfully throwing his apron on the granite island countertop. He went back into the kitchen, then returned a moment later with a plate-sized pancake, covered in freshly sliced fruit and lightly dusted with powdered sugar.

"Luckily, I made pancakes, too," he said with a wink.

"Yeah, I knew you did," Paola smiled. "I smelled them when I woke up."

"Man, I can't pull anything over on you, Little Lamb."

Paola poured syrup on the pancake as Boricio brought her mom a plate with a large slice of quiche, then set a platter of bagels in the center of the table.

"I should have you all over more often," her mom said. "Breakfast around here is usually a smoothie, at best. And a bowl of Fruity Pebbles at worst."

SIXTY-NINE

Brent Foster

Our Earth
  New York City
  April 3, 2012
  Predawn

ONE MINUTE, Brent had been sitting in the Facility with the others. The next, he was back home, standing in the dark of his apartment.

"Oh God, they did it. I'm home," he whispered, looking around, hardly able to believe his eyes. "Oh God."

He swallowed hard, wondering where Emily was.

He started to panic, then remembered when he'd first met her and her mother, Jane, near the ferry. Jane said her husband had vanished. At the time, of course, Jane didn't know the truth — that it was *they* who had vanished to the other Earth, which meant her husband was probably still home, wondering where his wife and daughter went. And if Brent was returned to his home, it stood to reason Emily was returned to hers — he hoped.

Brent looked around the apartment long enough to figure

out that it was still his family living there, and that they hadn't moved out in the six months since he left. Gina's purse was sitting on the kitchen counter, keys and glasses next to it — always well prepared for the next day.

Brent raced down the hall.

The door on the right led to his bedroom, where Gina was probably sleeping.

He longed to see her, but that would mean explaining a lot, if not everything. At the moment, Brent wanted nothing more than to see his son, Ben, though.

He passed his bedroom and went into his son's room, freezing at the sight of the drawing taped to the front of the door — a heart with two crudely drawn circle figures in it. Beneath the heart, Gina had written in crayon, "Ben and Daddy."

He wasn't sure how he would explain his absence to his wife. But even less so how he would explain to his son. He could only imagine the abandonment that Ben felt — that Daddy left because he didn't love him.

The pain sliced through Brent's heart and he began to cry as he reached to open the door.

The room was dark, except for the soft, blue hue of the nightlight.

Brent's eyes adjusted as he stepped toward the bed, barely making out the shape of his son beneath the covers.

He couldn't see his son's face in the darkness, and as Brent stepped toward the bed, his heart swelled in anticipation of seeing it. It had been so long.

Oh God, Ben, I missed you so much.

As he inched closer, Brent's shoe slipped on something, and he nearly stumbled. He caught his balance, then bent to see what he'd stepped on, hoping he hadn't broken it.

Stanley Train smiled at him, unbroken.

Brent grinned, clutching the train whose duplicate was

taken by the Guardsmen at the docks; the train which he'd cried over losing several times since then.

Stanley is here.

Ben is here.

I am here.

Tears flowed down Brent's cheeks as he looked down at his son's face, so angelic and peaceful in his cozy bed. The stuffed dog that Brent had given Ben last Christmas was tucked under the boy's arm.

He crawled into bed beside his son, wrapping his arm around him, drawing from his warmth, and never wanting to let go.

Ben turned over and his eyes began to open. "Daddy?" he said, groggy.

"Yes, buddy," Brent said. "I'm back."

"Where were you?" Ben's voice asked, still in the grips of sleep. Otherwise, he would have certainly leapt up excited to see his daddy.

"Far away, but I'm home now, Buddy. And I'm never leaving again."

"Promise?" Ben said, eyes closed and lips barely parting.

"I promise," Brent said, hugging his son tighter.

"I love you, Daddy," Ben said.

"I love you, too."

~

Epilogue

Our Earth

Aug. 4, 2012

Ten Months After The Event …

THE DARKNESS STARED into the mirror, examining *Its* face.

It could heal the scar and the eye. But there was something about the patch that disarmed humans.

It liked that feeling.

It also liked that the echoes of the human, Boricio Bishop, hated the scar and the patch. Boricio was stronger than the other shells *It* had used. The more *It* could do to break what was left of his will, the better.

It lifted the patch, looking at the hole where an eye had once been, now nothing more than a core of mottled skin.

It smiled into the mirror.

It set *Its* hands in the sink and allowed the cool water to sooth *Its* burning body before splashing *Its* face.

Someone knocked on the door. Again.

It opened the door to a fat bearded man, stupidly glaring.

The man didn't dare speak his displeasure. *Its* husk was too intimidating.

And that was good.

It made *Its* way back to *Its* seat in the third row of first class, then sat and stretched *Its* legs, thankful not to have another stinking human in the seat beside *It*. There were three others in first class — a tall black man in a gray suit, leaning back and sleeping in the front row; an older woman in the row behind the man, her head buried in a Kindle; and a tall, muscular man in the row in front of *It*. The man was watching a movie on his iPad.

It could feel the man's rage burning inside, could see his primitive thoughts playing themselves out in his stupid brain. He was angry at his ex-wife. So angry he could hardly pay attention to his insipid film.

He thought only of violence; all the things he wanted to do to the "lying, fucking bitch."

Yes, he will make an excellent acquisition.

It looked over to the old woman again. She wouldn't notice if *It* removed *Its* clothing and proceeded to shit in the aisle's center.

Humans were so easily placated.

It opened its mouth, allowing part of *Itself* — just a wisp, so small she might not have noticed even if she had been paying attention — to float out and then over the seat in front of *It*.

The Darkness crept into the man's mouth so subtly he hardly noticed.

Then, in seconds, *It* infiltrated the man, burrowing deep inside. Infecting him.

The man was just one of 300 so far.

But it wouldn't be long before *It* had an army at *Its* disposal.

Then, *It* would find Luca.

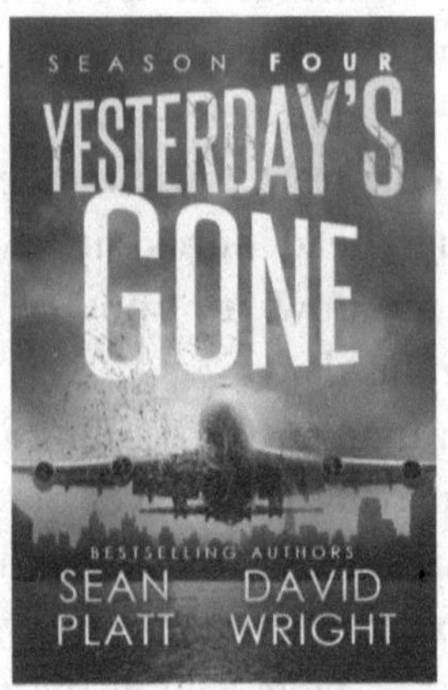

How do you live a normal life when you've been through hell?

More than a year has passed since The Event, and the survivors who returned home are trying to stitch their lives back together. They think they are safe. But that is a lie.

GET YESTERDAY'S GONE: SEASON FOUR

A Note from the Authors

Thanks for reading *Yesterday's Gone: Season 3*

If you enjoyed this book please write a review on your favorite bookselling site so other readers can enjoy it too. Just a couple of sentences would mean a lot to us.

Thank you!

Sean & Dave

About the Authors

Sean Platt is an entrepreneur and founder of Sterling & Stone, where he makes stories with his partners, Johnny B. Truant, and David W. Wright, and a family of storytellers.

Sean is the bestselling author of over 10 million words' worth of books, including the Yesterday's Gone and Invasion series. Sean is also co-author of the indie publishing cornerstone, Write. Publish. Repeat. and co-host of the Story Studio Podcast.

Originally from Long Beach, California, Sean now lives in Austin, Texas with his wife and two children. He has more than his share of nose.

~

David W. Wright is the co-author of edge-of-your seat thrillers including the best-selling post-apocalyptic series *Yesterday's Gone*, the paranoid sci-fi *WhiteSpace* series, and the vigilante series, *No Justice*, as well as standalone thrillers *12*, and *Crash* which was recently optioned for a movie.

David is an accomplished, though intermittent, cartoonist who lives in [LOCATION REDACTED] with his wife and son [NAMES REDACTED.]

He is not at all paranoid.

He is "the grumpy one" on the *The Story Studio Podcast* with fellow Sterling and Stone founders, Sean Platt and Johnny B. Truant.

David writes about books, TV shows, movies, and video games he enjoys; his struggles with anxiety and OCD; writing; and posts the occasional drawing at his personal blog at davidwwright.com

You can email him at david@sterlingandstone.net

We swear, he almost never bites. Unless you feed him after midnight.

For a full list of his most recent books visit sterlingand-stone.net.

Also By Sean Platt

The Dead World Series

Dead Zero

Dead City

Dead Nation

Dead Planet

Empty Nest

The Beam Series

The Beam Season One

The Beam Season Two

The Beam Season Three

Robot Proletariat Series

En3my

Robot Proletariat

The Infinite Loop

The Hard Reset

Cascade Failure

Reboot

The Tomorrow Gene Series

Null Identity

The Tomorrow Gene

The Tomorrow Clone

The Eden Experiment

Karma Police Series

Jumper

Karma Police

The Collectors

Deviant

The Fall

Homecoming

Yesterday's Gone

October's Gone

Yesterday's Gone Season One

Yesterday's Gone Season Two

Yesterday's Gone Season Three

Yesterday's Gone Season Four

Yesterday's Gone Season Five

Yesterday's Gone Season Six

Tomorrow's Gone

Tomorrow's Gone Season One

Tomorrow's Gone Season Two

Tomorrow's Gone Season Three

Available Darkness

Darkness Itself

Available Darkness Book One

Available Darkness Book Two

Available Darkness Book Three

WhiteSpace

WhiteSpace Season One

WhiteSpace Season Two

WhiteSpace Season Three

Stand Alone Novels

Burnout

The Island

Crash

Emily's List

Pattern Black

Devil May Care

The Secret Within

Yesterday's Gone

October's Gone

Yesterday's Gone Season One

Yesterday's Gone Season Two

Yesterday's Gone Season Three

Yesterday's Gone Season Four

Yesterday's Gone Season Five

Yesterday's Gone Season Six

Tomorrow's Gone

Tomorrow's Gone Season One

Tomorrow's Gone Season Two

Tomorrow's Gone Season Three

Available Darkness

Darkness Itself

Available Darkness Book One

Available Darkness Book Two

Available Darkness Book Three

WhiteSpace

WhiteSpace Season One

WhiteSpace Season Two

WhiteSpace Season Three

Stand Alone Novels

12

Crash

Emily's List

Threshold
The Secret Within